KA DOYLE

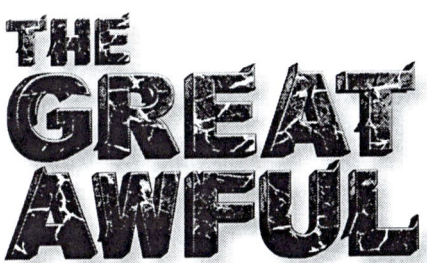

THE GREAT AWFUL

Reivers' Incursion Trilogy

*To Debbie,
All best to a super
friend*
Kaylan Doyle

~ CHRONICLES PUBLISHING ~

Published by CHRONICLES PUBLISHING LLC
PO Box 8459, Kirkland, WA 98034
© Copyright 2014 by Kaylan Doyle
ALL RIGHTS RESERVED

This is a work of fiction. All of the characters, organizations and events portrayed in this book are fictional, and any resemblance to real people or incidents is purely coincidental.

www.MoreThanPublicity.com
Book Cover Design by © MoreThanPublicity
Book Cover Artist © Lora Lee
Book Cover Interior Pages Illustration by © MoreThanPublicity

Publishing History
Chronicles Publishing/Paperback edition/April 2014
Chronicles Publishing/eBook edition/April 2014

ISBN-13: 978-0-9910123-0-5
ISBN-10: 0991012305

Published & Released in the United States of America
10   9   8   7   6   5   4   3   2   1

MORE BOOKS BY KAYLAN DOYLE

Science Fiction Space Opera
SURVIVORS' DREAMS
The Kra'aken Dynasty Chronicles
"A breathless rushing for the bus read."

Urban Fantasy
BIJOUX MAJIK

DEDICATION

To Bill
"It's the little things"

ACKNOWLEDGEMENTS

I would need an additional novel to thank everyone who helped me bring this story to publication. You know who you are, and you also know how much you are appreciated.

For those of you familiar with the Treasure Valley, I've taken some liberties with locations, landmark placements and distances in order to make the story flow more smoothly. Thanks for your understanding. This is a work of fiction and any and all errors are completely mine.

Special appreciation to the following people:

For technical advice on subjects ranging from geology through weaponry – Bill Cole, Steve Johnson, Ken O'Keefe, Bill Windham.

For Linda Lamb, Linda Kovik-Skow, Joyce O'Keefe, Susan Schreyer, Lisa Stowe – who plodded through the rough draft, then again through the revisions – heartfelt thanks! A deep genuflection to MaryAnn Hightower for her sharp proofreading eyes.

Many, many thanks to Lora Lee for my awesome cover art.

To Lyn Thornton – for hours contributed to wading through various drafts, and listening to me read aloud. Thank you, Lynnie!

To my husband, Bill … who cooked, and cleaned, and kept the household going while providing unwavering support and belief in me.

Last, but in no way least – huge thanks to Shannon Aviles – without you and your expertise, there would be no book. You are the best!

THE GREAT AWFUL

PROLOGUE

Annelise huddled on the stained vinyl floor in the corner of the room. The smell of Mommy's blood on her clothing made her sick; the screams from her mother in the next room froze her mind in terror. Sobs shook her body, tears flooded her eyes, ran down her face. Why would anyone hurt Mommy? A shriek swelled inside her throat.

"Be still, don't make a sound," whispered the voice in her mind.

She obeyed, pressing tight as possible against the wall, head down, long hair hanging over her face. She peeked at the man with the huge gun.

He leaned against the far wall. Watching her. Big, bigger than Daddy. She shuddered when his eyes locked on hers.

"Yes," he nodded. "You're next. What are you – six? Just the age I like. Za was right. You two are the best bait in the world." His low chuckle brought the fine hairs upright all over her body.

"No," Annelise whispered. "Please, no."

"Shhhh," said the mindvoice. "Don't answer."

"Don't you want to know why you're going to die? Are you too little to understand?" The man shoved away from the wall; crossed the room in three strides. One large hand twisted in her hair, dragged her head up. "Your fucking father killed my brothers. Now we kill what is most precious to him."

He jerked her to her tiptoes by her hair.

Warmth ran down the side of her head, trickled behind one ear.

Annelise pressed her lips together, made no sound.

His eyes wandered, assessed, roamed again.

Her insides froze. Primal instinct told her she was in deep, deep trouble. She held her breath to keep from whimpering, begging, pleading.

"Be still, Annelise. Do not show fear." The voice in her head spoke again. "It will make him worse."

Behind the closed door, in the adjoining room, her mother's screams muted to a gutteral moan. The sound wiped fear from Annelise's mind, replaced it with burgeoning fire – fury burning hotter and hotter – her *mad*.

No one knew about *it* – except the voice in her mind. *If only my* mad *could kill this bad man.*

He leaned his gun against the wall. With a flash of stained teeth and a leer that pierced her heart like a spike of ice, he gripped the front of her pants and yanked them down.

She tried to cover her nakedness with both hands.

He slapped her.

Annelise's head bounced off the wall. Her ears rang and black fuzzy clouds filled her sight. Then his hand slid between her legs from her knees to her – *nonononono* – most private place.

A blast rocked the room; blew apart the front of the old house. A muffled bang followed and red rain splashed Annelise's clothes, her face and hands.

The bad man no longer held her. The bad man didn't have a head. A scarlet fountain geysered from his neck. His body turned, crumpled and thumped to the floor.

Annelise's heart jumped. *Happyhappyhappy.*

Two men came low and fast through the exploded opening and crossed the room. One stood pressed against the side wall beside the closed door, the other crouched in front of her.

From the adjoining room, a high piercing scream ripped the air.

The man squatting before Annelise snarled, the veins in his temples swelled and pulsed.

She flinched and scooted away, dragging up her pants.

"You're safe, Leesie. Did he hurt you anywhere?"

With the green and black and brown paint streaking his face; the guns and knives sticking out all over him, Annelise didn't recognize this stranger. But his voice was Daddy's.

"No-o-o. S-s-scared me," she got out just before she started to shake.

"Can you lie on the floor? Hide behind him?" Her father pointed at the dead bad man. "Just for a minute?"

"Mommy's …."

"I know, Leesie. I'm going to get Mommy right now. Do this for me baby, please."

"Mind your father," ordered the voice inside. "It will help him."

She got back down in the blood and other awful sticky stuff on the floor behind the dead man's body. She shuddered, her heart thudded, and tears streamed from her eyes. She tried to be quiet, but she couldn't control her sobs. *I'm safe.* The body of the bad man faced her now but it was okay.

Daddy fixed him – he's dead with no head.

"Snake," Daddy's friend motioned with his gun.

"The door opens in. Our advantage …." The bedroom door flew open, bullets strafed the opposite wall, pocking it at man height.

Is Daddy okay? Annelise couldn't get her breath. She wiggled sideways behind the corpse until she could see. *Both fine.*

Daddy's friend held up two fingers pointing at his eyes. Then, indicating inside the room, he added two more, followed by a swift gesture.

Daddy nodded, crouched against the wall next to the door.

Four fingers, Annelise figured. *Four more men?*

Two figures firing guns charged from the bedroom.

Annelise's father held a huge knife in his hand. Fast, smooth, like a cobra she saw on TV, he buried the blade between the first shooter's legs. Twisting the steel, he sliced up and out.

A howl escalated into a high shriek.

On the other side of the door, mirroring Daddy's movements, his friend cut the second man. A screech of agony morphed into a thin ululating scream.

Guns bounced on the floor, dropped by men now trying to hold in body parts. *Yes!* Daddy hurt the man who hurt Mommy. And his friend hurt the other one. *Goodgoodgood.* Blood and pink and gray stuff splattered everywhere and Annelise forgot her tears and cheered. But Daddy wasn't done.

The gutted men held before them like shields, her father and his friend rushed into the bedroom. Annelise heard a bunch of pop-pop-pop sounds. She scrambled to her knees, heart clogging her throat. *Pleasepleaseplease let Daddy be okay.*

"Get down. Stay hidden." The voice in her head snapped at her, like Mommy when she disobeyed. Annelise dropped back into the mess on the floor.

The gunfire stopped, silence descended. Annelise heard her father cursing, low, steady. Heard him say, "Don't you dare leave me, Sharon."

Annelise spotted a black handle sticking up from a holder-thing on the dead man's belt. *A knife – a big one, like Daddy's.* She obeyed, stayed low and hidden while she worked the blade free. The *mad* surged again, roared in her head. Because she couldn't take his pants down like he did hers, she focused on the place the evil man touched her and stabbed and stabbed and stabbed.

"Leesie," said her Daddy from the bedroom door. He held Mommy cradled in his arms.

Her *mad* faded to mist; her father's face swam into focus.

"It's safe," Daddy said. "Let Cipher carry you. Let's go far away."

She stood, knife gripped in her hand, heard a splot-splot-splot on the floor. Daddy flinched.

Annelise stared at the painted face of her father's friend, with its hard planes and set jaw. She saw kind eyes. "Okay," she said, stood and lifted her arms. "I keep my knife, Daddy."

Cipher's eyes were on the dripping blade. "Snake?"

"Snap it in the sheath, then let her take it. I think she needs it."

Safe in the arms of Daddy's friend, they ran from the house. Cipher strapped her into the front seat of the big black truck, then helped Daddy lift and settle Mommy on the flat back section behind. Annelise's heart thumped at her mother's moans and whimpers. She gripped the sheath in her right hand, the handle of the knife in her left. Gripped them hard. Ready.

"Cipher, I'll start the IV's while you blow the place. Then drive."

"On it."

Annelise watched Cipher grab a black duffle and run for the house. She tracked him, almost missed when he glided into the garage. *Like the ghosts on TV.* She lost him until he tossed the bag into the truck; slid into the driver's seat. He fired the engine, shifted into first, drove the big SUV away from the house.

An explosion buffeted the truck. Annelise clutched her knife and wondered at the tiny twitch in the corner of Cipher's mouth. A smile?

"Another great job my friend?"

"Adequate," Cipher said. And shoved the gas pedal down hard.

This time Annelise saw it for sure. Daddy's friend smiled.

Mommy was quiet now. Tears stung her eyelids; she tried to stop them. Tried to see Mommy but the seats stuck up too high so she peeked between.

"Fuck." Daddy yelled. "Fuck, fuck, fuck. Sharon, no. Don't do this. Cipher. Need you here. Now."

Daddy's friend stomped on the brakes. The nose of the truck dived toward the pavement and slammed to a stop. Just like before, Cipher went out the driver's door and into the back faster than Annelise's eyes could track. *How does he do that?*

"Oh Jesus, Snake. Okay. Back up man – give me room."

4

Annelise saw Daddy's caterpillar eyebrows bunch in a frown.

"Cipher?"

"Got it, Snake. Got it. Doing okay."

When Daddy folded against the side of the truck and took a huge breath, something inside Annelise released. She sat gripping the knife in both hands like it was the single thing keeping her heart beating.

"Cipher, can I give Leesie Rohypnol?"

"She's too little. I don't know how much …." Daddy's friend's voice quavered. "Jesus, Snake. Yeah, we should induce amnesia. But dammit, we could kill her."

"I think I have to," her father said.

Annelise saw him glance at her knife, reach a hand toward it. She shook her head. "Mine. Keep it."

"Look at her. She's not good. Guess the dose, Cipher. I'll administer it."

"This is my fault, Snake." Daddy's friend buried his face in his hands. "Getting involved with Za."

"We all believed her story. How could anyone know we killed her husband and two of her brothers on that mission?"

"I should never have introduced her to the group – to our wives."

"Let it go, Cipher. She, her two brothers and the rest of the bunch are secure in that Idaho military facility. They'll die there."

"We should have killed them all, right then."

"Yes," her father growled. "But there were too many witnesses. Measure out the med. Please."

Cipher shook his head, blew out a long breath. Things rustled and rattled – then he laid something in Daddy's open hand.

Her father crawled from the back of the truck, opened her door.

"No medicine," Annelise pressed her lips together.

"No problem, sweetie." Her father actually smiled, a small grim thing. Slipping a finger between her lips, he pushed one cheek out to the side, making a pouch. Sliding the little syringe inside, he depressed the plunger.

"Ooooo," Annelise said. "Nice." She laughed, floated warm and happy and relaxed.

"Is she out?" Cipher said.

"Fighting it. Another second and she will be," her father said. "Let's roll."

Chapter One

Ten years later
June
High Country Desert SW of the Owyhee Dam
Nyssa, Oregon

I opened my eyes, heard my parents downstairs, smelled coffee and breakfast. A side-ways slide out of bed kept me from braining myself on the sloping dormer ceiling of my bedroom. *No more.* I grabbed the old iron bedstead and dragged it two feet further into the center of the room.

I'd grown tall – leaving my short, slender mother behind. At six foot three, Dad still stood five inches above me, but, as he said, "You're sixteen. Who knows – you could catch me yet."

I headed for the bathroom. From the doorway, my wolf Lupine, protector and friend, watched me splash my face with water, brush my teeth and braid my dark hair. When I pulled on my new red tank and khaki shorts, socks and hiking boots, she surged to her feet. I bounded down the stairs, Lu at my side, to join Mom and Dad.

Mom was pretty in a sleeveless aqua blouse and jean capris, laughing at something my father said. Dad wore a plain white tee and green canvas shorts, his exposed skin crisscrossed with the traceries of long-healed wounds.

I assessed the morning mood, found it good, and greeted my folks.

"Katie," Mom said. "I knew that red top would be stunning on you. What do you think?"

"Like it lots, Mom," I said and gave her a big hug. Then I wrapped an arm around Dad's thick neck and squeezed. Grabbing a cup of coffee, and the full plate my mother handed me, I slid into a chair at the kitchen table.

Lupine inhaled her dog chow, then sat on the rug next to our guard dog Terror, Dad's big black *Bouvier*.

The conversation flowed through breakfast. Dad finished first, shoved back his chair. I swallowed my last bite, finished my coffee and carried our plates to the sink.

"Need anything from town, Sharon? Got a grocery list?"

"Yes." Mom slanted him a sideways glance. "What do you want for dinner tonight? Besides wine?"

The love between them, so honest and open, made my throat swell, made me avert my eyes. They have each other, and me. *I've never had a friend. Except Terror and Lu.* I waited what I thought to be an appropriate time, then asked, "Hey, I did all my chores yesterday. Can I go rock hunting?"

Mom's full lips pinched to a pair of flat bloodless lines.

"I need to, Dad," I said. "I sold my last Thunder Egg two days ago."

Round brown ugly rocks, filled with breathtaking multicolored crystals, were plentiful in our area of Oregon. Native American legend provided their name and the tiny pioneer town of Nyssa held the title of Thunder Egg Capital of the World. People came from everywhere to comb our Treasure Valley lands for the ancient mudballs from the volcanic-age.

I found mine scattered in the hills around the Owyhee Dam, within a day's hike of our house. The rocks sometimes disappointed – but sometimes, sawing the geodes in half revealed either amazing, unique crystal, or agate formations. When I posted the good ones on the internet, collectors snapped them up. My college fund grew and grew.

I watched Mom from the corner of my eye, my *mad* crawling warm, lighting up the tops of my ears. I wanted to argue, anticipating her automatic no, but instead I waited for Dad's decision. He held final say.

"Get a grip on your temper," whispered the voice in my mind. "Losing it won't help one bit."

Across the room, my mother squared her shoulders, shook her head. Her pale brown curls became a shifting nimbus, a gold-touched crown. Mom pulled a breath, prepared to try and stop me. Again.

Old resentments surged, hot in my chest. *I need to get out of here.* For ten years, since the day we moved in, Mom and I never left this place. We'd moved from a town where something bad happened. But my memory went fuzzy, details just wouldn't come. Neither of my parents would say why Mom and I couldn't go shopping, or go to town. Mom didn't even want me to hike. *The internet just isn't enough. I want more. I want freedom.*

"No hiking, Katie," she snapped, right on cue. "Especially if your father's gone. You stay here with me."

I tried to stop the half-lift of my upper lip. I didn't manage it. Her pretty face twisted, I'd hurt her feelings. Guilt stabbed my heart like a sharp blade.

I gave her my little-girl grin – the one she couldn't resist. "Mom," I wheedled. "You know I save the best ones for your collection."

"Don," she turned to my father. "She can't be off in the hills alone." Her smooth forehead creased into three horizontal lines; she segued into prevent-defense mode. "Something might happen."

"Sharon, something might happen anywhere. She's got a pistol – and a rifle if she wants it. Between Terror and Lu, she has three hundred sixty pounds of combined canine protection. She packs a mini-aid kit. What worries you?"

"Rattlesnakes, scorpions, black widows. Strangers, other hikers. She might slip, fall, be killed. Hit her head, drown." Mom's face suffused with blood, then went the color of chalk. "Or be kidnapped."

The last word hung in the air, so charged with fear I felt static electricity spark. But why? It meant something key, something terrible. This wasn't the first time she'd mentioned it. Why so paranoid about this one thing? My mouth went dry and my pulse pounded double-time.

"Sharon." Dad's heavy sigh said it all. He'd argued this with her over and over and over. "She's sixteen. You can't keep her cooped up in the house like a bird in a cage."

Mom sucked a deep breath, opened her mouth to argue.

Dad raised one big hand. "Stop it, Sharon. It's not healthy – for her or for you." His heavy black brows pulled together. "Katie, you can go. You know the rules."

"Be safe, be home before dusk," I chanted and forced my triumphant grin back into hiding.

My mother snatched the red and white towel from her rising bread dough, slammed the ball onto a floured surface, and punched it. Hard. *God! Does she wish it was me?*

The heady smell of yeast flooded the kitchen, made my mouth water.

Mom smacked the dough again. Harder.

I fled.

"I promise, Dad. Thanks!" I tore up the stairs to my room, checked my Beretta for full load, belted on my holster and secured my gun inside. I hooked a collapsible basket to a clip on my fanny pack. Added my skinning knife to my belt. Smeared sunscreen on all my exposed skin, rolled and tied a handkerchief around my head to catch the sweat and donned my sunglasses. *Ready.*

I eyeballed the bannister for a fast descent. *Nah. Don't need worse trouble.*

Down the stairs, two at a time, on a hard stride for the kitchen.

"Lupine? Where are you girl?" She met me at the back door, trailed by Terror. "Wanna go hiking?"

Lu's long silver plume of a tail flayed the air, creating a breeze. T-dog's stubby one did helicopter rotors. Oh yes, they sure did.

"Let me fill my canteen, guys. Then we're outta here."

Dad stepped out on the porch. Inside, Mom still nattered her objections to my solitary walk.

"I sold every rock, Dad. I did. The one you mailed for me yesterday was my last."

"I know, Katie. It's okay. She gets over it. Plus I'll go to town for a bit." Dad grinned, and the sight of his slightly overlapped bottom teeth made me laugh. "How's your savings account? Just in case you don't get accepted into West Point?"

"Growing – but I expect you to pull strings." I studied him from beneath my eyelids, hoping to catch him unguarded. I'd stopped asking about his job a long time ago, but ever so often, I sneaked in a comment. "Someday you have to tell me who owes you that big a favor and what you did to earn it."

"You'll earn acceptance, Katie, or you won't get in." He wasn't kidding. "But I do have the signatures lined up if you pass the testing."

"Aha," I pounced. "So you do have friends in high places."

Dad swallowed a laugh, passed a big hand across his face smoothing away any hint of a smile. Because he gave nothing away, he provided my biggest confirmation yet.

His face so close, eyes so serious, my father studied me like he'd never seen me before. Sometimes, for no reason, he just did it. *What is he searching for?* Something I did, or should have done? Something I should remember – or he wondered if I did? Lots of times I'd almost asked, but something held me back.

"Which way you planning to hike today, Katie? Succor Creek?" he asked. "Or all the way to your 'secret' cave?"

"No cave today. Just to the creek where I found Mom's favorite egg." I slanted him a glance. "You remember?"

Dad nodded.

"My last trip I found more rocks than I could carry. I buried them by the big patch of Blackcap briars and I want to get them. If I find berries, I'll pick."

"Bring enough for a pie and it will placate your mother."

Such deep sorrow, such heaviness, laced his words. My eyes shimmered and burned. I wondered, for about the thousandth time, what secrets he carried. *Wish I knew why she ... but then, maybe I don't.*

"I'll hunt extra hard," I said. "Maybe get lucky and beat the deer to them."

"And the birds, and the chipmunks, and the ...." Dad rolled his eyes.

I snorted, and he laughed too.

"See you in ..."

I checked my watch against the sun overhead in the clear blue sky.

"Three hours or so?"

"Sounds good. Don't make me come find you." He gave me his lazy grin and my heart swelled. I loved my Mom, but my Dad ... well, Dad's special. Except for keeping me locked up here with my mother. *One of these days I'll ....*

Then, with no warning, Dad's smile morphed into his deadly serious face. "Watch for strangers. Your mother's right about that.... If you see anyone, hide. When it's clear, run for home."

"Why are we so ...?" My voice trailed away at the empty pain in his coal dark eyes. *I'm not a kid anymore – I can take care of myself. We have to talk about it soon. Just not today.* "Never mind, Dad, I promise. See you soon."

I stepped off the porch onto the lawn; saw Mom come out of the house. A moment later, I felt her shoulder against my side, sensed more than heard her soft sobs.

My guts twisted – my fault she cried. I wrapped an arm around her, gave her a quick, hard hug and moved away.

She opened her mouth.

"It's fine, Mom. Honest." *Don't start with the orders.* I needed to get gone before I said something hurtful. Spinning on one heel, I half-jogged for the forest. Heard her quick steps behind me; knew when they slowed. My mother followed to the treeline and no further. Almost like she couldn't. Why?

I kept moving. My burning lungs told me I held my breath; I gulped air. *Will I ever get answers?*

The dogs and I headed out through the trees. Butted up against the blue juniper forest, a twenty-foot-thick planted barrier of poplars, elms, birch and weeping willows encircled our house. The trees made us almost impossible to see. No one 'just happened' on the Davis place.

Why couldn't we live in town? Why did I have to be home schooled? I didn't want to wait for West Point, I wanted friends now. Frustration simmered, reached my typical slow boil. The tops of my ears flamed, my *mad* wanting out. *One of these days, I'll go see for myself.*

The worst thing of all – when Dad left – he put me in charge of Mom. But he didn't tell her so.

"Things would be much easier without her," whispered the voice in my head.

"Shut up," I snapped. "It's Dad too, with the rules. You know it is. Go away."

"I only say what you really think, deep down inside. I'm the honest part of you, Katie Davis."

"You're not honest, you're bad. Dark and mean." My easy stride shortened, went choppy. I gasped as angst wrapped my chest in an iron band. "Leave. Me. Alone."

I refused to let the darkness in my mind spoil the perfect day. A breeze gusted, enough to cool the sun on my skin. My furry protectors lolled long pink tongues.

The sloping trail I took followed an easy grade down a narrow ravine. It wound through the basalt and lava rocks peppering the landscape. Dried tumbleweeds rolled and bounced in the sporadic breeze. Bushes, trees and wildflowers bloomed profusely by the creek. I spotted the Blackcap briars marking the spot of my hidden geodes. A huge bunch of apricot-colored globemallow flowers flanked the bushes.

T-dog and Lupine ranged, noses down, following trails only they understood.

I dropped to one knee, scooped the thin layer of dirt off my cache. There they were, all four. My breathing slowed as I loaded my fanny pack with rocks. Without my binocs, I couldn't see how much fruit waited on the bushes across the stream. The tiny berries were a pain in the butt to gather but so good. The sparse fruit on this side would be quick picking. I lifted the glasses, found the Blackcap bushes on the far side of the creek were loaded. Well worth wet feet. I unfolded the basket, found a cold nose thrust into my hand. Another joined it.

"Oh no." I hardened my resolve against two pair of pleading eyes. "You guys know how to pick for yourselves." In ten minutes, I'd worked my way from one end of the brambles to the other. "Lu? Terror? Let's go."

The first step into the stream bed soaked my hiking boot, sent a row of goose bumps up my leg. The second wasn't such a shock, but both my legs and arms still pimpled. The loud burbling water rose knee high in the center of the stream.

The dogs didn't care, they splashed, romped, mashed my legs and soaked me to the skin. On the far side, they shook.

"Ack, you two. All these water spots, I look like an Appaloosa." Lu and Terror laughed at me, I swear they did. "You silly guys," I said. "You have no clue what an Appaloosa is. Do you?"

"Woof," said Lu and leaned against my leg.

A glance at all the fruit made me grin. "This will get me off Mom's shit-list."

I crouched, wedged my basket between my knees and used both hands. On either side, T-dog and Lu lipped the sweet berries off the vines.

Then two dog heads snapped up, ears lifted, twitched. Two big heads rotated, staring behind me.

Lupine's black lips wreathed away from sharp wolf fangs. Terror's growl came from the depth of his deep barrel chest. They snarled, eyes fixed on a point up the hill behind me.

My body turned to ice. Dropping the basket, I spun. Before my brain could send the order, my Beretta sat in my hand, safety off, the slide racked. *Thank you, Dad.*

Chapter Two

"Whoa, whoa, whoa," a nasal male voice yelled. "I'm harmless. Don't shoot. Please."

I stared up the hill. About twenty feet away, stood a tall guy with long blond hair and emerald eyes. His tanned face belonged in a magazine. My heart thumped, excitement fizzed through my body. Strange warm sensations flooded my chest, made it hard to breathe.

"Can I come down?"

I nodded, because my voice wouldn't work, then watched him take the dozen steps around the rocks and boulders to stand in front of me. I studied him, realized every muscle in my body tensed. *I should be running.* A guilty reaction to my disobedience, broken promises?

Or something more?

"Could you point that thing somewhere else?" He flashed a dimpled smile, showing very white teeth. "I'm Todd Wills." He stuck out a large manicured hand, waited a long second while eyeballing my gun.

I didn't put the Beretta away, I only lowered the muzzle.

He stared at his hand like he'd never seen it before, then shrugged and shoved it in his pocket.

"Okay, then."

"Who are you?" My voice cracked, a strangled sounding thing. "What are you doing out here?"

"I was scanning the countryside through the Forest Service telescope. My folks are manning the lookout tower for the summer – I'm visiting. I saw this great looking girl in a red tank top, hiking by the creek. Figured I'd come down and meet you." His eyes widened, one corner of his mouth twisted.

I watched muscles play under his tight tee shirt and my throat closed. Tan, with a swimmer's build, he smelled of soap and a spicy aftershave, all amplified by the summer heat. I swallowed so I wouldn't drool.

"Shit, I never imagined you'd pull a gun," his green eyes were wide. "What did you do that for, anyway?"

"Automatic reflex when the dogs alerted me. I carry because there are dangers out here – wild animals and things. Why don't you have some protection?"

"I go to school at the University of Oregon, born and raised in the city. Didn't even think about danger."

"You need to be careful," I said. "Really." I slid the Beretta back in its holster, let my eyes devour him. Liked what I saw – a lot. But the dogs didn't. *Why?* At my command, they sat but their stares never wavered.

"Do you live around here?" Todd asked, his eyes still glued on my gun.

I opened my mouth.

The voice in my head shouted, "Shut up, Katie. Right now."

"I … ah …. no. I just come hiking and hunting Thunder Eggs." My throat went dry and hot, then closed. Air whistled trying to exhale. *Great.* Now I'd just broken another rule. First, I talked to a stranger, then I lied.

One sun bleached eyebrow lifted, unconvinced. His full lips twisted. Then Todd's other brow shot up, joining its twin. "Did you say Thunder Egg?" He frowned. "What the hell is a Thunder Egg?"

"They're geodes. Thunder Eggs start out as ugly brown rocks," I blurted. "Compressed mudballs shoved up to the surface by lava flow. I find them around here." My hands waved, sketched outlines of round shapes. I searched the ground around the berry bushes, picked up a tangerine-sized rock. "See, here. This might be one, it's little, but the shape is right."

"Doesn't look like … much," skepticism threaded Todd's voice.

"Well, I just said they were ugly, didn't I?" I cringed at my snotty tone, tried for nice. "When you cut them open, they can be full of different colored crystals."

Todd's slow nod made his long blonde hair swing.

"I bet it's what I saw on the table in the lookout. There's a big half rock with blue crystals inside – Mom said it looks like a three-masted schooner."

"Sure," I said. "I bet you're right." Winced, hearing too much enthusiasm in my voice. "This is a good spot to find them."

"So you're here a lot?"

"No. Just … when I can. My Mom collects the geodes."

Beside me, Lu growled, deep and unfriendly.

Todd flinched.

"So tell me," I said, trying to act like I did this every day. "What's the U like? I'm still trying to make up my mind where to go after I graduate."

"You're still in high school?" His green eyes widened. "I figured you for older."

14

"Well, I'm almost out," I said. "Got my applications in a few places but you could tell me better than any visit, right?"

"Yeah, I guess. Sure." His chest puffed a little, the big college man. "It's cool, great campus. I got a swim scholarship, plus my parents are profs. Good a place as any other."

"Maybe I'll give them another look, then."

"Since I'm there?" His voice teased, but something told me he really did believe it.

"Maybe," I added just a touch of sarcasm. Evidently, I touched a nerve.

"Your grades good enough?" His words had an edge.

"Of course," I heard acid try to come through mine, squelched it fast. "I got acceptance letters from four schools. Just need to decide." *Let him figure out if I just lied.*

Todd's eyes wandered over me, hesitated on my gun, slid across to the knife on my belt. "You majoring in weapons?" He laughed, then sobered. "You hike prepared, I'll give you that. I didn't even think. I hurried to make sure I met you."

And those words cut right through my defenses. Heat slid up my neck headed for my face, my ears. *Please don't blush*, I begged my body. But of course I did.

Todd didn't act like he saw, he dipped his head in my direction, gave me the sly grin of a conspirator. "How's about my next visit, we go hiking? You can be my protector?"

"O-okay," I managed. "It'll be fun." My lungs slid into my throat, made taking a full breath out of the question. I fought for control. All I managed were tiny sips of air.

My protectors sensed my emotions. Terror rumbled deep in his huge chest, and Lupine echoed him.

I shot them a quelling glance, saw Todd flinch and back up a step. "They're fine," I said. "Just ignore them."

Todd flashed me a quick smile that threw my heart into arrythmia. He took another step closer.

Lupine moved to sit between us, her haunches pressed against my leg. She fixed lantern yellow eyes on Todd. She didn't growl, she didn't blink.

When he gave me a slow sexy grin, a pulse thumped low in my abdomen. *God! He's so good looking.*

"What's your name?" He stood, head tilted toward me. Waited.

My mouth went bone-guy dry and I croaked, "I'm Katie Davis."

"Oh, well done," said my mindvoice. "Stupid twit. Told him your real name? Your Dad will be furious."

Todd eyeballed Lu, stepped close to the bushes, lifted a branch and pointed at the berries. "Which ones are ripe?"

I moved from Lupine's side, stood next to him. "These are …."

Todd laid one arm across my shoulders, his palm resting soft and warm against my bicep.

So different from my rough and callused guy-hands. *It never mattered … before.* Blood pounded in my temples.

"You shouldn't be talking to a stranger," snarled the voice in my head. "Shouldn't have allowed him anywhere near you."

I knew it. I moved from beneath his arm to another berry bush, and stripped the fruit with both hands, eyes glued on my task. My head fought with my emotions, made my insides roil. But this nice, handsome guy personified every thing I ever dreamed of in a boyfriend. Hair, face, smile, eyes. *I can't do this – it's forbidden. Yet, I can't NOT do this.*

Lupine shoved between Todd and me. I wanted to smack her – but …. I couldn't ignore the fact Terror sat on Todd's other side with his eyes locked on. He didn't move, he just breathed. Heavy, disapproving.

I worked through two more bushes, making small talk. "What's your major, Todd?"

"I'm thinking law or business. But it doesn't matter right now – I've got to get the basics out of the way."

I swallowed hard, tried to think of something to say. Came up blank.

"How about you, Katie?" Those lazy green eyes caught mine; tried to hold them.

I broke the connection. I'd been avoiding his gaze for the past ten minutes, just because I didn't want to and knew I should. "I'm not sure," I said. "I have another year to make up my mind." *Why do I think if I mention West Point he'll think less of me?*

Lupine shadowed me from bush to bush. Terror moved just enough to keep both unblinking cocoa eyes on the young man who tried to follow me.

"What's with your dogs?" Todd asked, and put his arm around me again.

"I don't know. They never act like this." I slid from beneath Todd's arm, turned to Lu and said, "Down." She went belly on the ground, but stayed between us.

Crouching, I gathered the fruit from the bottom of the bushes. Keeping distance between us, I concentrated on picking berries and gasping for air.

"What are they for?" He stepped close, peeked in my basket.

Lupine pushed in, separated us again and a tiny vertical line appeared between Todd's eyebrows.

I played like I didn't see and answered his question.

"Mom bakes pies." Keeping my eyes fixed on the berry bushes helped control the dragonflies swooping in my belly. I so hoped he wouldn't notice my trembling hands.

"Where do you live?"

"Oh, about an hour from here. That way." I pointed in the distance toward Boise.

"Funny," Todd said. "When I looked through the tower telescope, I thought I saw a roof. Over there." He pointed in the direction of our house. "Real close to where I first saw you. Know who lives in it?"

"No clue," I said, and my hands coated with sweat. "I never knew there was anything over there. Somebody maybe lives there, but I sure don't."

Todd's eyes widened, both brows headed for his hairline and a tiny smile pulled at the corner of his mouth.

He didn't believe me. Hell, such a terrible lie, even I didn't believe me. *Now what do I do?*

"Whuff," said Lu and glared at me.

"Okay, I know," I said. I wanted to kiss her for the interruption. "It's time to go."

"What? The dog tells time too?" Todd slid me another slow smile, moved close and rested his hands on my shoulders.

My lungs seized and my underarms went sweaty. I gripped my basket with both hands.

From my books, from the internet, from watching movies – Todd should be about to kiss me. *Please, oh please, let it him do that.*

He did. The first one explored – gentle, respectful and sweet. The strange press of soft lips. The faint taste of mint. The second kiss, well … my heart thumped so hard I bet Todd saw it through my thin cotton tank.

Lu rumbled soft from her spot on the ground. *What in hell is wrong with my wolf?*

"I'm coming back here next weekend." Emerald eyes searched mine. "Will you meet me again? Same time but Sunday instead?"

My lips were … not bruised, exactly. They just felt … fuller, swollen. Kinda tingly.

"Yes," I said. *Miss a chance for a date? More kissing?* "Sure. I'll be here."

"Can you leave her somewhere else?" His blonde head tilted toward Lu.

"I'll see," I said.

He flashed those white even teeth, waved goodbye and turned to go.

I gazed at my wolf. Guilt's stiletto skewered me for even pretending to consider it.

"No, Todd," I whispered, but I made sure he didn't hear. "I won't ever leave her behind."

He picked his way through the rocks, heading up the hillside toward the lookout. I filled my basket and admired his fine backside while I waited and watched him climb. I tracked Todd until I saw him pass into the big stand of trees down the ravine. From there, he'd be unable to see where I went.

I signaled T-dog and Lu, slipped behind a bunch of boulders and hiked up the creek. Crossing the quick-running water, I headed for home. If we hurried, we'd be there and hidden inside long before Todd reached the tower.

I grinned, patting my lips, remembering his – so soft, the faint taste of mint.

"I know you're glad he's gone, Lupine," I whispered. "But I just fell in love. I know for sure – I want to spend my life with him. And I want him to kiss me more." *In eight days, he'll be back to do just that.* My emotions did a slow joyous turnover. I'd be here to meet him, no matter what Mom said. Or Dad either.

"You can't do this, Katie," said the voice in my head. "You don't know him, you don't know what you might screw up."

"I know I'm not supposed to let anyone see me, not supposed to talk to strangers. But this is different. Those rules apply to creepy people – not to a nice, cute guy like Todd. Mom and Dad will like him – they will."

"The dogs don't like him. Your parents will hate him," snapped the voice. "And you know it."

"What – now you're my conscience too?"

"No, Katie. I'm your darkness," said the voice and its words carried a hard edge.

"I don't care," I said. "I'm doing it."

Chapter Three

Dad's pickup sat in the driveway when I got back.

Oh shit. I have to act normal. How will I manage that? I squared my shoulders, sucked a deep breath and plastered a smile on my face. I led the dogs up the steps, said a silent thanks they couldn't talk, went across the porch and into the kitchen.

My parents sat at the table, drinking lemonade.

"Hey, you guys. See what I got."

"Oh, Katie," Mom grabbed the berry basket. "How wonderful! I've got time to put a pie together for supper. Great job." She leaped to her feet, pulling open cupboard doors. In seconds, bowls clattered and flour flew.

And she didn't want me to go. But since I'm safe, all is forgotten. I grinned at Dad and unbuckled my fanny pack. "Got my rocks," I said. "Can we cut them later?"

"Sure, girl. Good hike?" He sat easy, one elbow resting on the tabletop, one hand on a muscular leg. Powerful, in-control man enjoying his solitude and his family.

Dinner over, pie with ice cream consumed, I needed to get away. I wanted to relive those two kisses in private.

"I'm going up to my room," I said. "Think I'll go to bed early."

"You feeling okay, baby?" Mom's forehead creased. "Not sick?"

"No, Mom. I'm fine. It was a little hot out there today, that's all."

"Told you not to go," she said but the sparkle in her eyes took the sting from the words.

I didn't sleep one minute all night.

The warm June morning made me dial the shower to lukewarm. I heard Mom and Dad downstairs, smelled coffee brewing. *I'll make this a short one.* I stepped in. My intentions were good, but I always did my best thinking under warm running water. Today proved no exception. When I shut the shower off, toweled dry and dressed in a tan tank and cargo shorts, I found my thoughts on my father and my Todd dilemma.

How could I get them to meet him, never mind accept him spending time with me? What would Dad do? He was scary, no question. And he didn't want anyone to know where we were. Dad wouldn't harm Todd. Would he?

There is an Air Force Base in Mountain Home, Idaho. It's about a hundred miles, as the crow flies, from our house. Dad says he's a Game Warden, works for the Forest Service. I haven't believed that for a long time.

Mom swears he's a "hunting guide." *Riiight.*

"He's taking a group of businessmen on a big game safari to Africa," she said during his last long trip away. *Double Riiight.*

I've read lots of spy novels and military fiction so when Mom said Dad hunted for big game, I agreed. *I just don't think he hunts animals.*

All my life, my father has come home injured, bandaged or stitched together – additions to the old burn, slash and bullet-hole size scars. They couldn't be from lion or tiger claws. Or crocodile bites. I'm sure they're the reason he rarely takes off his shirt.

When I was ten, I decided my father was some kind of secret soldier. The special phone in his office rang and I answered. I don't know about Dad, but I got in serious trouble because I'd been told to leave it alone. Whenever the phone rang, my father talked, then almost always went away. For a day, a week or a month.

Dad used to drive our old International, but for the past year, a camo-painted Hummer, driven by a dark-haired young man, picked him up.

My father issued standing orders for Mom and me to hide if anyone came. I'm sure the driver was under some kind of privacy orders too, because he always stopped the vehicle just beyond the ring of trees concealing our house.

The soldier tried to see. I know, because when I peeked, we locked gazes. I smiled and I think he did too.

Twice lately, after those phone calls, a big chopper landed high on the plateau up on the bluff behind our farmhouse. Dad climbed the trail, and the pilot flew him out. The other rule seemed to be Dad only used a helicopter after dark. If you researched 'isolated' in Webster's Dictionary, the definition should be 'Davis family'.

I want freedom. When I asked why I couldn't leave, Mom got hysterical.

Dad chewed my ass out for upsetting her. He refused to give me an answer. *There's no one else to ask.*

I remembered the time years ago when I asked about my grandparents. Mom's lips trembled and her eyes got wet. Dad said I didn't have any, but his voice sounded weird. *Is our name even Davis?*

A hard little spot of resentment stirred in my heart.

God. I can't mention Todd. Dad will kill me.

Lu at my side, I headed downstairs. Breakfast aromas loaded the kitchen. Fresh baked cinnamon rolls, brewing coffee, cooking bacon. Saliva flooded my mouth, and I pressed my lips together. My stomach growled so loud I slapped my hand over it, shot a peek at my parents.

They both wore smirks, they didn't even try to hide them.

T-dog and Lupine hovered, noses wet and dripping, held just below table level. I swallowed my grin, caught Mom's eye.

She winked, tilted her head at Terror. She knew what I'd been thinking. When Dad wasn't home, the dogs rested their chins on the tabletop. And drooled.

I grabbed her in a hug, smacked a sloppy kiss on the side of her face and made her squeal. I squeezed Dad's shoulder with one hand, took the plate she handed me with the other, sat down at the table and dug in.

"More coffee, Don?"

"Great breakfast, Mom." I handed off two chunks of bacon, one in each hand, to the big furry guys sitting, waiting, on either side of me. I popped the last bite of hot roll into my mouth, saliva pooled as the still-warm glaze melted on my tongue. A warm rush of well-being flooded my body. Things weren't so bad, really.

The special phone rang.

Oh shit! Breakfast soured in my gut.

"Dammit," my father snarled and shoved back his chair.

"Don …" remonstrated my mother, finely arched brows pulling together above wide blue eyes.

Since eavesdropping is forbidden, I waited until I heard my dad bark, "Hello."

"Powder room, Mom," I said, and rolled my eyes at her.

She grinned, waved her spatula, nodded.

I sneaked down the hall, slid into the little jog in the wall where Mom couldn't see me from the kitchen.

Dad never talked about his job so I gathered information where I could.

Mom said my father had ears like a bat – I think I inherited those too, because even when he almost whispered, I heard lots more than I should.

"Yes," he growled. "I'll come – tomorrow?" The pitch of his words changed. If a man could salute over the phone, Dad did. "Now? But it's day." Then I heard his response, formal and angry, "Yes sir."

Skeletal fingers gripped my lungs. A premonition – a bad one – stopped my breath in my throat. I braced a hand against the wall. *Oh, no. No.*

Years ago, Mom hung a full-length mirror at the end of our hall. At the same time, I found that if I situated mid-point on the left side of the hallway, in my little niche, and if Dad's office door stood ajar, I could glimpse his reflection. His body language always told me more than his words.

Heavy brows pulled together, a flush suffused his face, turned it dark. *He's beyond pissed.* When he spoke, I shivered – his voice cold enough to freeze gasoline.

"No," he said. "Those were, and are, my conditions. You agreed, years ago." A long pause stretched and I watched Dad clench and release one big hand. "They stay hidden. There will be no changes," he growled. "No. They are no part of this." He grabbed a deep breath. "Against my better judgment, I'll agree to daylight pickup. Nothing else."

I couldn't hear the words from the caller, muffled and garbled by distance. I did hear my father's abrupt, "No."

I hurried back down the hallway toward the kitchen. *God. He'd be like this about Todd. What am I going to do?* I stayed out of line of sight, but still close. Bad news. Dad's wrath made the hair crawl on the top of my head. I'd never seen him in such a rage. Not the day to get busted eavesdropping on his classified business.

"They are safer right here," he snapped. "You want my help, respect our contract."

My heart went into overdrive, hammered against my breastbone. Somebody wanted to take Mom and me out of this place? *Yes! Please!*

"Wait, Katie," whispered the mindvoice. "What does "we're safer here" mean?"

My mind went sideways. The adviser in my head could be right. What might be waiting out there for us?

My father hung up the phone. It wasn't gentle. In fact, I heard something crash and snap, then pieces sounding like chunks of plastic ricocheted and bounced.

Dad's footsteps, or lack of them, leaving his office and ascending the stairs always amazed me – so incredibly silent for such a large man.

In the distance, I heard the whop-whop-whop of chopper blades. *Whoever gives the orders already sent the bird for Dad.* Different procedure, different protocol. The caller didn't ask my father to come – he commanded him. A glance out the window showed me the dark shape of a menacing murder machine dropping from the blue sky. It settled on top of the bluff, concealed by clouds of billowing dust. A noise from the stairs pulled me around.

My stomach jammed my throat. For just a second, face to face in the hallway, I didn't know this dangerous stranger, dressed in camo, bristling with weapons.

God! For the first time, he went fully armed, instead of his usual single sidearm. The fury glittering from him made me flinch. I locked eyes with Dad – saw only sheer black wrath. My recoil drained his anger like air escaping a balloon. Sadness and regret took its place.

"Apologies, Katie – I didn't mean to scare you. You're not the reason I'm pissed."

"It's okay, Dad." My heart skidded in my chest, then settled.

Locking his midnight dark eyes with mine – *like staring in a mirror* – he said, "You take care, Katie." His accent on the first word made the intent clear; he moved down the hall toward the front door.

Cold sweat puddled in my armpits, soaked my tee, slid down my sides. His hidden meaning – I must keep my mother safe. He expected me to make it work. I'd be okay with it, I would, except, trouble was, she didn't know. She knew he'd been teaching me to shoot and track for years. *She has no idea I'm lethal.*

"It makes you mad," said the voice in my head. "You don't think it's fair. You're right. It's not."

"Dad," I blurted, rushed the words. "You don't know how bad it is when you go. You have to tell her to do what I say."

His black eyes bored into mine. "Can't, Katie. Won't."

"Then I'm not responsible. I'm not doing it. She can't be managed, sometimes. You have to make her understand. She has to mind me."

He jerked, his face went all hard angry planes and I braced for his reaction. He'd never struck me, but the desire loomed dark. "No. You'll do what you're told and say nothing to her."

"I won't. I'm gonna tell her ...." I shut up.

Mom came down the hall.

I turned, headed into the kitchen, stopping at the table where I could still see them.

Dad hugged and kissed her and then came to me. Tried for a side-to-side shoulder hug.

I dodged, moved away. Saw Mom's eyes go too wide.

Dad strode into the great room; I heard dog claws on the pine plank flooring as they leaped to their feet. Heard a pat on each big canine head, heard an admonition to be good and protect his girls.

"Katie," he turned to me again. "A hug?"

I shrugged, shook my head no. "Not until …."

Something sad and a little lost ghosted across his face.

"You sure?" asked the voice in my head. "You better. What if he never comes back?"

I wanted to, but pride and resentment won. I bit my lip, crossed my arms and shook my head again.

I heard his sigh, then watched him turn, step through the door, and jump off our porch.

On the plateau above, the helicopter's heavy blades spun at slow speed, noisy and obvious. Dad glared overhead, his lips pressed together so hard they disappeared.

"I'd best go quickly," he said. "Be safe." I watched him disappear up the trail.

Resentment stirred. *He refused to help me.* I felt the *mad* heat my neck, slide up and over my face. It sizzled in the tops of my ears.

It's not fair, I'm not the parent. But some days Mom barely took care of herself, never mind me. Dad taught me to shoot at ten, and afterward, when he traveled, he depended on me. I knew, and likely he did too, no matter what I said, I would watch out for Mom.

I can. I have to. I will.

Standing next to her on the porch, I evaluated us like an onlooker might. Me, tall and muscular; my mother, short and slender. The assumption: I'd be the one in charge. Wrapping an arm around her shoulders, I hugged her hard.

Seconds later, engines spooled up, rotors whirred, lights strobed bright. The chopper lifted off, its huge weapons silhouetted against the azure sky.

He's gone.

Mom brushed one hand across her eyes; turned and went in the house.

The conversation with Dad's boss, commanding officer, whatever … replayed in my mind. Okay, it confirmed my suspicions. Sorta. Obviously, our seclusion here by the Owyhee Dam had to do with Dad, Dad's past, and Dad's work.

"Are you sure, Katie?" whispered the voice in my head. "Perhaps it isn't about your father. Perhaps it's about your mother? Or you?"

Skeletal fingers crawled my spine, chill and frightening. Somewhere, in the back of my mind a door cracked, ever so slightly. My body froze as a bit of memory skittered through. A room full of terror, a room splashed with scarlet. Did I hear screaming?

"Holy Shit," I whispered. "There's something I can't remember." I shook myself, placed my hand on Lupine's head.

Whatever the memory, I truly did not want to know.

Chapter Four

The next day

I managed a short shower, slid into khaki shorts and a blue tank and headed for the kitchen. Secure in my appearance, I lost no time mocking my mother's screaming purple, orange and green floral printed apron.

"That's hideous, Mom. Where did you find it?"

"On sale, in a kitchen catalogue. Didn't look so bad in the picture." She laughed. "I agree. It's terrible."

She cooked us a huge breakfast – but then she always did. When distressed, anxious, or angry, Mom cooked. But she seemed in a good mood and I relaxed just a little.

"Something wrong between you and your father?"

Dammit. I hoped she'd missed that. "No, Mom. It's nothing."

"You didn't hug him goodbye. No kiss either."

"I'm getting a little big for such things, don't you think?"

"No, I don't. I think you hurt his feelings."

Fine. "Okay, Mom. I'll straighten it out when he gets back."

"Good," she said and went back to her cooking.

My Belgian waffle attracted the unwavering attention of our two furry protectors. I slid them a few bites, finished my coffee and headed out to do morning chores.

The chickens came running. *It's hard to stay grumpy when they are so funny.* I snorted and wrote the headline in my mind: Attack of the Killer Chickens – Girl Pecked to Death in Barnyard.

Well, no. They were all nice birds, but seeing the big scoop of feed in my hand when I left the barn always brought them on the half-fly. And clucking. And pecking.

I scattered their grain; spread it so everyone got their share. If I didn't, Gordita, our biggest hen, crowded out the smaller chickens. While my hands were busy, my brain worked and worked and worked.

Since my hiking encounter with Todd, two thoughts refused to go away, both guaranteed to get me in trouble. I refused to think what Dad would do if he knew I'd talked to a stranger. *I couldn't help it – would have been rude not to.* Dad would explode if he knew I'd kissed him, and planned to do it again.

"Your father will find out," snarked the voice in my head. "And he will absolutely kill you."

"I hoped you'd finally gone away," I snapped. "Would you, if I say please?"

"You've screwed up big time, Katie. And you're planning to make it worse? Put everyone in danger. Your mother most of all." Then the voice delivered the killer blow. "Your father trusts you."

Now there's the part that bites. Letting Dad down.

"Fine," I snarled at my mindvoice. "I'll do the right thing. I won't go."

"Ha," it answered. "You'll go." It chuckled, a dark, evil thing. "If you don't, any bets Todd might show up here? Sure, you lied – but he didn't buy it."

Oh shit. Still, in spite of my fear, every time I remembered the kisses, my heart pounded, threatened to burst.

Last night, when I couldn't sleep, a thought arrived. Now, it tormented, refused to be banished. The more I tried to ignore it, the more it chewed at me.

Every night Mom took her medications, every night Mom took a sleeping pill. And every night Mom slept eight hours, straight through, without waking.

I could take the pickup, drive into Nyssa and see ... a town. Hell, talk to ... kids. No one would know.

Before Todd, I'd never have thought of it. I'd been content to wait for West Point. *Why is going there next year okay, when nowhere else is right now? I want more. I have to go. I love Todd, I do. But I want to taste other boys' kisses too.*

"You are so stupid," sniped the voice in my head. "How would you know what love is?"

"Well, I do," I snarled. "I'm sixteen, I'm not naïve. I've read books, magazines. Watched movies, use the internet. I love everything about Todd."

"Yeah, sure?" The voice layered heavy with sarcasm. "If you've found real, true love, why are you thinking about other boys?"

"Shut up," I punched my pillow. "You just leave me alone." *Could the voice be right? I mean, the only man I've ever talked to is Dad. I know I'm right. My heart tells me – it's love. It is.*

When I woke this morning, the bad idea remained. I shoved it aside, did my chores. Helped Mom in the garden. But the lure of freedom refused to be banished.

We worked all day, cleaning house, keeping busy. Mom took more breaks than usual, went to the front porch to stare down the hill.

I climbed to the attic four times – for the very same reason. *Where is Dad?*

We weren't hungry, so we ate fried egg sandwiches for dinner. Mom and I sat in the porch swing, chewing and watching the road.

Lu and Terror didn't sniff their food until they'd helped us finish ours.

I picked up Mom's plate, added it to mine and took them to the kitchen. Then I stuck my head back into the great room.

"Mom, I'm taking the dogs and going out just to look around. Be right back."

Her mouth opened, her pretty brows pulled together. "But Katie, it's dark."

"It's just getting dusk. I'm doing what Dad wants, Mom. It's safe enough." *I'm not afraid of the dark – just of small enclosed places.*

Miracle of miracles, she didn't argue.

I palmed the truck keys and walked to the barn – just stood and stared at my freedom. I fought the urge, turned away, closed and locked the barn door.

"Good choice," whispered the voice.

"Are you my soul?"

"You are your mother's keeper, Katie Davis."

"You bastard." I gritted my teeth. "What about me?"

"Did you stop to think your father could come home any minute. Catch you gone?"

Nausea surged, cold and sour. My anticipation and excitement evaporated before the truth, like morning mist fades beneath the rising sun.

"Oh shit," I whispered. "I never even thought about that." *Going to town is a wonderful, scary, exciting but terrible idea. And dreaming, maybe plotting is fun. I just won't go tonight.*

I walked the yard. Not a sound emerged from the chicken coop. With each step, my unease grew. I couldn't put my finger on it. Was it a hind-brain thing, the lizard survival part of our original DNA? *The one keeping us alive?*

Chill bony fingers squeezed my lungs. The wintry sweat of a premonition coated my body. I knew something far larger and more dangerous than anything this world had ever faced lurked in wait. Something with a timetable all its own.

I moved, dogs tracking me on either side, double-checking our perimeter. *It's too quiet. No night critters moving. Why?*

My mind veered to the one person who made my worries disappear. *Where the hell is Dad? He's been gone longer than this, I never worried about him before. Why now?* I found I didn't want an answer. Not really.

The dogs ranged the yard, noses to the ground, tails down and tucked close to their bodies. They stayed close to me. Their eyes rolled, showing whites; ears pressed tight against their skulls.

What the hell? I searched the darkening sky. *No cause for alarm.* Just the same, I kept snatching rapid glances all around while I crossed the lawn and hurried across the porch.

"Terror? Lu? Come on." I didn't have to ask twice.

They beat me into the kitchen.

I secured the house, closing and locking every door and window. When I passed between the two waist-high geodes in front of the shelves holding Mom's Thunder Eggs, every rock illuminated like someone threw a switch. *The clouds passed across the moon, changed the light, their appearance. That's it.* But I knew I lied. Just for an instant the crystals, clumped, angled in all sizes and formations, glowed in a myriad of colors. Every edge, whether smoothed by sawblades, or angular chunks where geodes were broken by nature, lit like they held tiny light bulbs.

Then as suddenly, in unison, they went dark.

I did not see that. They are rocks. Inanimate objects. I did not feel a harmonic resonance in my body, an electric current kind of buzz. I did not.

Placing my weapons on the side table, I grabbed the edge, leaned against it; fought for breath. *I refuse to panic. I refuse to accept what just happened.*

"Did you see that?" I whispered to the dark voice in my mind. When it didn't answer, I gathered my wits, continued into the family room and sat on the sofa. Waited. Wondered. Worried. My chest felt like Lupine sat on it.

Mom curled up on her end of the couch, absorbed in the satellite dish menu. Humming, fooling with the remote, she hadn't noticed anything different.

Maybe I'm just being weird.

Terror and Lupine lay on the braided navy rug in front of the TV. But they weren't still, or sleeping. I pretended to watch television but instead, I studied the dogs. Heads tilted, ears twitched, eyes searched. *Why are they uneasy?*

Lu rolled eerie yellow eyes, grunted to her feet and came to lean against my bare leg.

T-dog whimpered, laid his massive head on one of Mom's feet.

She reached down, rubbed the top of his head, gently pulled his pointed ears. "What's up, T? Everything's just fine."

What do the dogs sense that we can't?

"What do you want to watch, Katie?" Mom pointed the remote at me like a weapon. "History channel, National Geographic. Or … we have duelling marathons: CSI or Clint Eastwood."

"I know you hate westerns, but I love his old spaghetti's. You pick, Mom."

Lupine's ears went flat against her head. My canine friend who feared nothing shuddered and pressed hard against me. Terror leaped to his feet, shoved his head in Mom's lap, and stood quivering.

"Well for heaven's sake, Terror. What's gotten into you?" Mom hugged his thick neck, patted his back.

God. The cold things writhing in my belly escaped, wrapped and squeezed my spine.

"What's wrong with the dogs, Katie?" Mom turned to peer out the window but the only thing visible was the slice of moon in the black dark overhead and the brights dots of a million stars.

"I don't …." I pushed to my feet to look outside.

Our plank flooring shimmied, rippled beneath my feet. I staggered, grabbed the couch for balance.

"Katie?" Mom's voice slid to a scream. "What's happening?"

"Earthquake, I think." *We don't have them.* I panted, my heart mimicked the floor, did a stutter and dance. The damn shaking went on and on and on.

Shocking flashes of brilliance followed by the distant crump of explosions turned our night sky bright. I leaped from the couch. My sweaty foot slid sideways off my flip-flop, made me stumble. I wound up with my chin smashed against the great room window. The stabbing pain in my tongue brought a salty copper spurt.

Blast after blast tore the peaceful summer quiet. Fourth of July colors rainbowed the dark. *Those aren't fireworks.*

"Don!" My mother shrieked, both demand and plea.

"Dammit!" I snapped. *Dad's gone and she knows it.*

A huge slam, impact and noise, rocked the house. The crash pulled a high thin scream from Mom. The big hutch leaped five inches away from the wall, the furniture slid around the room. I heard the sound of smashing dishes in the kitchen, saw our lamps toppling, knick-knacks falling to the floor, pictures jumping off the walls. The big picture window sounded like a zipper when it cracked from top to bottom.

My terrified brain produced an explanation: a semi-truck drove into our house at a hundred miles an hour. *Impossible. Has to be an earthquake.*

My head went woozy.

"Breathe," snapped the voice in my mind.

The shaking quit, the sudden stillness underfoot seemed surreal. My mother huddled on the floor, arms wrapped around her head, screaming and crying, babbling prayers and nonsense.

Terror and Lupine lay beside her, ears flat and tails tucked under their bodies.

"Come on, Mom. We have to get outside."

Then it started all over again. Dishes rattled and rattled and rattled. Mom's chandelier tinkled, my eyes tracked the dancing fixture. It swung, crashed into the ceiling, rained pieces of ceramic and slivers of crystal all around the room. Our pine flooring zig-zagged and danced beneath my feet.

An aftershock?

Brilliance illuminated the sky, a long thin trace of whited silver streaked through the black-blue night.

Terror and Lu whined, eyes huge and rolling.

"My God, it's a rocket," I blurted. "What in hell?" The words escaped before I thought. "That launched from Mountain Home. Had to. I'm going up on the bluff."

"Katie Davis, don't curse," Mom snapped, her lips pinched thin in disapproval. "There's nothing wrong. You're staying right here."

Did she just say there's nothing wrong? I closed my quivering lips against the next words fighting to be said. *Take a look out the window, Mom. Try again.*

The floor settled back into quiet and solid. I crossed mental fingers. *Please let it stay still.* No way for me to pry my mother out of the house without a stick of dynamite.

"Appropriate, under the circumstances, wouldn't you say?" piped my dark little voice.

"Shut it," I snarled, then flinched, worried Mom heard.

"Katie, my phone doesn't work. I need to call Don."

I fished my cell from my purse. "Mine's out too. I'm going to go up top

to see what's going on. I'll try to call from up there – maybe it will work."
Grabbing an elastic band from the coffee table, I snaked my long dark hair into a tail. "Be back in a bit." I picked up the big Maglite from beside Dad's recliner, snagged the sawed-off shotgun from its place above the door.

"No, Katie. You stay here with me." Her voice rose an octave.

I wish I could. Wish I could be the kid who left the hard stuff to an adult. I turned my face away. She'd misunderstand my bitter smile – it would only upset her.

"Mom, I have to see." *I can't say Dad's orders. I can't say Dad's been teaching me for almost eight years.* "I'll leave T-dog with you. I'll be fast."

"I forbid it …" her voice faded.

The *mad* boiled hot in the tops of my ears, surged through my veins. Red film shimmered across my vision. *Dammit, it's not like I want to go out there.* I pushed back anger; pretended not to hear. I wanted to slap her. *The excusable reason – she's bordering on hysteria.*

"But it's not why, is it?" whispered the mindvoice. "The real reason is because you are scared to death yourself and don't know what to do."

"Okay, yeah, I am. And on top of that, I have to deal with the earthquake and her state of mind, too."

"So what will you do, Katie Davis?" the dark voice asked.

"Shut up, shut up, shut up," I snarled. *I have to think.*

Outside trees crashed, explosions boomed and echoed in the distance.

"Terror, stay with Mom."

I hurried through the kitchen. Lupine belly-crawled after me, growled deep, just once and pushed to her feet. She shoved through the door and I sprinted after. The noise from across the valley traveled and echoed.

Dread coiled deep in my insides.

We headed around the house, across the clearing, threaded through the trees. Loose rocks tumbled and bounced, peppered my calves. I tripped over a branch from a downed tree and scraped the hell out of my knee.

My wolf took the lead, dug in her claws and lunged up the hill. Pebbles and earth scattered and rattled down on us. We made our way up the narrow vertical trail, fit only for mountain goats, and emerged atop the plateau.

The ground rocked and heaved again, shook and groaned. Across the valley I saw glowing yellow-orange spots, the color of molten lava. They appeared, grew in size, then spewed skyward. I watched them run together, a line crossing the deep dark below. But we didn't have volcanos here.

Explosions crept west across the valley – popped like balloons squeezed by inexorable fists. Geysers of destruction lit each factory, each town, each power source. The noise came louder now, outside the house and high on the bluff. I didn't need the flashlight.

Electric lights shot sparks, the twisting, flipping glowing strings had to be downed power lines. Bright areas across the valley did a slow roll, turned dim brown, then faded to black – a lethal progression swallowing the illuminated spots. Wavering on the horizon, the shimmering red glow reminded me of an artist's rendering of hell. Nampa disappeared into darkness, then Caldwell, Ontario, and finally Nyssa and all the small towns in between. The only remaining dots were hot spots where fires raged. And lava surged and spewed.

My legs unhinged, my knees dissolved. I wound up on the ground with a nose full of dust and my arm around Lu's neck for comfort.

"Please, God, don't let Dad be trapped at the Air Force Base."

I watched the destruction spread. Across the valley a jet of yellow and white and red fountained. Blue flame shot skyward. *What burns blue? Dad said ... natural gas. God – did the pipeline just rupture?* A tightly focused white beam streaked above the inferno. Then another and another and another. *Missiles? Why are they firing missles?*

"Lupine," I talked to my wolf because if I didn't, I'd scream. "It's pretty far from here to Mountain Home. How big do those explosions have to be if it's like we're watching them on TV?" I shuddered and swallowed a sob.

Lu whined, nudged my hand.

"You're right. It's huge, girl." My stomach lurched. "If Dad went to the base, odds are he won't be coming home." *No, no, no. That's wrong.* "Dad's good, he's better than good, and he'd know things were going sideways. He'd find a way out." I gripped my temples, squeezed my head. "But, Jesus, what do I tell Mom?"

Huge explosions climbed high into the black night sky, one after another after another. Then I heard heavy exploding blasts thundering in the night. Endless combustions, a myriad of colors followed by sounds. The entire base ammo dump? Weapons? What kind? How old? *Do they store bombs at the air force base? Nuclear bombs?*

"Silly Katie," I whispered, just to hear a voice, even my own. "Of course they do." *Please Dad, don't be dead.* "Are you there?" I asked. "You in my head? I could use some advice."

But the dark little thing kept silent.

Familiar icy needles stabbed my spine, cold washed my body.

"Not again," I begged. This second premonition, so close to the first – I knew, at my most primal level – something awful had just happened. And I knew another something – even worse – waited, poised to pounce.

The last bright spots in the valley below winked out.

A single pair of headlights, far in the distance, moved slowly along a roadway.

"Here we go, girl," I said. Below me, our house plunged into darkness. "Oh, shit. Mom's going to lose it now."

The wind kicked up, and at first I couldn't figure why it felt odd. Then I realized it blew the wrong way, bringing the first smell of smoke, and sulphur. A gritty substance coated my skin like fine powder. The smells of explosives, acrid like gunpowder followed. I sneezed, and so did Lu.

The wind switched direction, blowing east, in its normal pattern. Still the air around me felt thick, full of things that didn't belong.

"Get down there and close up the house," said my darkness. "Before the place is full of it."

I watched the valley, the bright burning spots seared into my retinas. *What if Dad never comes back? What do I do? Stuck here alone with my mother?* My mind veered from the ghastly possibility – it simply dug in its heels and refused to go there.

"Kaaaayteee! Kaaaayteee! Kaaaayteee!" Mom's voice, screaming my name, yanked me into the present. From the sound of it, she stood on the porch and I heard terror mixed with something more.

She needs me. I think she'll stay where she is until I get there. But I better hurry.

Switching the Maglite on again, I followed its shine down the slope by the creek.

Beady little eyes gleamed in the dark. Okay, lots of things lived out here. Raccoons, mice, chipmunks. Night smells floated on the breeze, the moist loam by the creek, damp scent of the grass where I stepped. But some primal change just happened – the familiar odors were different, menacing. *Did the earthquake wake up something old? Maybe timeless. Is it waiting – between me and the house?*

The short hairs stood on the nape of my neck.

Shadows thrown by the flashlight turned our blueberry bushes into menacing monsters. Terrifying creatures with long skinny arms ending in clawed hands. They hid, crouched and lurked for the unwary. *Me? Oh God!*

Chills racked my body, made me shiver. Goosebumps pimpled my arms and legs.

I never outgrew my childhood fears after all. I just ignored them.

Somebody whispered, "Uhhh, uhhh, uhhh."

Sweat coated my body. *Do I run for the house? Turn my back on whatever said that?*

I cocked the shotgun with a one-handed pump, spun in a circle, searching for the source.

It took me a second to realize I'd said the words. It took me all the way back to the house to get a grip on my breathing.

Chapter Five

The next morning

Mom and I sat at the kitchen table to drinking coffee and arguing about going outside. Mom was determined to work in her garden; I was insisting we all stay indoors. I had one of Dad's geological reference books open before me, reading about volcanic eruptions.

Now, I knew how lethal, how much damage the jagged pieces of rock and glass, even the tiny ones, could do.

"Mom, listen to this. The book says volcanic ash particles are hard, abrasive, mildly corrosive, they conduct electricity when wet, and don't dissolve in water. That's what's in the air outside."

"Nonsense, Katie. There's probably been a bit of a fire somewhere." She shook a finger at me. "I've told you before about exaggerating danger."

A yellow-beige haze full of pale gray ash hung outside our windows until a gust of wind blew it away. The smell of burning wood, scorched electrical wires, the bitter bite of chemicals and roasted meat came and went on the breeze. The bright green of our lawn, bushes and trees all were muted, coated in a film of gray ash.

"Mom, I need to tell you what I saw from the bluff. Just look outside."

"It's nothing. Your father will be here soon."

I opened my mouth and she raised a hand, cut me off. "Start the generator and we can do our chores." A pair of vertical lines appeared between her perfect eyebrows. "I'm wearing my last clean outfit."

"Mom, we shouldn't."

I didn't know what was going on outside our tiny little world, but I knew Dad wanted us to be low-profile. The generator was protected in a shed, but how long before the ash burned out the motor? Still, Mom had to be managed.

"Can we make it quick. You know how Dad is about that."

"Okay," she said. "We'll just do the basics. But we need everything done when your Dad gets home."

"Let it go," said my mindvoice. "You better not push her too far."

"Okay," I muttered. *Damn thing is probably right.*

I put on an N95 respirator mask, left Lu in the house and ran to the shed, fired up the generator for electricity and power and raced back inside. We took showers, flushed our toilets, ran the washer. We discussed hanging our clothes on the line outside. Mom decided to run the dryer but wouldn't admit the stuff in the air outside was the reason why.

Mom and I checked the TV, the phones and the radio but didn't hear a thing. Not even white noise, or static hum.

"We finished, Mom?" I pointed outside. "I need to shut the generator off." *It's just too loud.*

"Sure, Katie, we're good."

I huffed a huge sigh and she shot me a hard glance. Mom couldn't know pure relief drove my involuntary breath. I'd feared she'd fight me.

"I'm going up top," I said. "Take a quick look around."

"You stay here," she ordered.

"You won't listen to what I saw last night. Fine. But Dad would want me to go check."

Big tears filled her blue eyes. The ultimate weapon.

"There's nothing wrong, Katie."

"Then there's no reason for me not to go. I'm leaving Terror with you," I said, grabbed my pistol, my rifle, my sunglasses, picked up my face mask. Thought a moment, went to Dad's weapons cache and took the sniper spotter scope. I evaluated Lu and the chances of getting her to wear something over her nose. Decided she wouldn't put up with it. We slipped out the kitchen door.

The quake destroyed our trail to the plateau – it was almost impassable. Downed trees, dislocated boulders, empty pockets in the ground, and new splits in the canyon walls made every step a challenge. We climbed and dodged rocks suddenly toppled by tiny aftershocks. I stepped on a gritty boulder and slipped. The rock rolled forward, disappeared into a big hole behind it. I found myself on all fours, half in and half out of a large depression which hadn't been there yesterday. Blood mixed with dirt coated my palms, and knees.

"Dammit," I snarled.

Lu nudged me with her nose.

"No," I said. "I'm okay, just pissed."

Lupine didn't like it one bit – her ears were flat to her head and she whined, a low unhappy sound. But she stuck with me.

We picked our way around the hazards, stepped over tree trunks. Clung to tree roots, and clawed our way to the top of the plateau.

The valley below was unrecognizable. Before, I'd seen brown and green squares of farms, either cultivated, or growing crops. They'd been outlined by the irrigation canals and ditches. Lovely, orderly farms growing a myriad of crops. Now, the area looked like a demented giant had raked huge hands across the valley, digging trenches, and rearranging the order. Then shook gray powder over the entire thing.

One long chasm yawned far as I could see, black and deep, red-orange simmered in the bottom. The tractor of a semi-truck was down in the hole, its trailer sticking skyward. *My God, he drove right into the crack.* I tried to guess the width of the crevasse. Perhaps 50 feet, perhaps 100. Maybe in places I couldn't see, it was wider still? The black asphalt roads were broken, smashed in random places, thrown to one side, or heaved up by the earth beneath.

I saw a few vehicles moving, only to be stopped by wrecks, huge breaks in the asphalt, by the crack splitting the valley, or by debris from explosions. I watched them turn around and head back the way they came. Cars and trucks sat unmoving. Abandoned?

"My God, Lu," I breathed. "People down there have to be dead or injured. We need to get higher. See more if we can."

A droning pulled my eyes overhead. Three big-bellied military transport planes, painted matte gray, flew past, headed in the direction of Mountain Home Air Force Base. *Bringing in help. Whatever it is, the people down there need it.* For the first time, I smiled.

Lu and I made our way across the top of the plateau, took a trail used by hikers that led up and over higher ground and eventually wound up at a spot above the Owyhee Dam. When we reached the overview, Lupine sat and refused to move.

"What?" I shook my head, then I saw her quiver. My wolf, who feared nothing.

I set up the scope, and looked out. The haze obstructed my view, but when gusts of wind cleared the air, I got glimpses of what lay below. Seen closer, I almost wished I hadn't. I couldn't believe the damage. The road to the dam was covered in rockslides, chunks of blacktop dotted the hillside where it loosened and fell. But something fuzzy, wavering, caught my eye.

I zoomed in, inspecting the huge wall from top to bottom, almost 500 feet high. Such an awesome thing, with the highway running across the top. An unusual charcoal spot in the pale gray concrete drew my attention.

"Oh shit, Lu," I said. "It's wet."

I watched thin steams of water trickle, then spray from the bottom. Water ran from both sides of the dam, down at the bottom where the pressure was most intense.

The earthquake. The dam's leaking!

Beside me, Lu whined, tugged at the leg of my shorts.

"We're fine here, girl," I said. "Mom is fine. Our house is high and it sets back behind two canyons."

I glued my eyes on the wall, and then scanned the water backed up behind it. The lake stretched 57 miles. How much water was there? "Oh shit, Lu," I whispered. "What if?"

I saw a maintenance vehicle racing across Haystack Rock Road. It made it almost to the center of the highway that crossed the top of the dam. I saw men running, yelling, pointing and waving their arms.

The air shook with a grinding, roaring noise. A huge chunk blew out of the center, propelled by a gush of water that carried it airborne, away from the wall. It arced; then slammed into the river bed below, throwing a huge splash. The dam groaned, like a monstrous dying beast, and split in halves, spilling the men and the vehicle into the breach. Rolling, tumbling, chunks of concrete, everything tossed by the rushing, surging tsunami. The sudden release of the huge amount of water, the enormous pressure captured everything in its way – trees, boulders, structures, concrete – and carried it into the canyon below.

I heard ripping, tearing, growling sounds; watched the water frothing, splashing back and up as it slashed down the canyon, flooding, taking every obstruction with it. No way to warn, no way to save. Just a wall of water destroying everything in its path. Pictures of tsunami damage, and waves played through my mind. A cold hand clamped my heart at what I saw, what would happen. And I couldn't do a thing to stop it. I'd never been down there, but I knew from Dad's conversations and from the internet, that a llama ranch, and about 30 family farms sat at around the mouth of the canyon, maybe ten miles down. Houses, kids, likestock, pets. Farm machinery, cars and pickups. *It will reach them, wipe them out.*

"Of course it will," said the darkness. "Without any warning. The water will spread fifty miles beyond, easy."

I stood frozen. Watched in shock, as if in slow motion, each new piece of devastation played out below me. The water boiled until it found the path of least resistance, then followed the rush of gravity out of the canyon.

I grabbed my cell, tried for a signal. Nothing. My knees melted beneath me. I sat in the dirt on the plateau above the ruined dam and shook. People died. I just saw it. Tears ran down my face.

Lupine butted me with her head, and whined.

"Yes," I said. "We need to go home. Terror is probably having fits and Mom hasn't a clue how to help him. Maybe Dad will be back."

I packed the spotter's scope, wiped the moisture from my cheeks, gathered my things and followed Lu back down the trail, headed for our house.

Dad wasn't there.

Mom was physically present, but she wouldn't listen.

"Stop exaggerating, Katie." She gave me a hard look, narrowed her eyes. Shook her finger at me. "You need to stop lying. You perhaps saw something, but you didn't see the dam break. There's no crack across the valley, no volcanic eruptions. Those things just don't happen."

I bit my tongue. Several times. In fact, it probably had marks all over it. But I didn't yell at my mother. I didn't tell her to hike up to higher ground and take a look for herself.

"Wise," said the dark part of my mind. "Make her face something really awful, she might flip out."

I went along with my mother, pretended life was the same. We sewed on a new quilt she intended for my bed. We sat on the front porch, sipped warm lemonade and watched the road up the steep hill to our house, hoping for Dad. I tended the chickens and Mom worked in her garden. We chatted and pretended. Mom laughed; I couldn't. People were dead or dying. Everywhere.

The summer sun hung noon high, blazing yellow-white against a cloudless azure sky. A perfect day – if Dad was home. Mom baked like a maniac on the wood stove. Our ways of coping with fear – she cooked and I ate.

What if he never returns? I'll have to go out there – and do what? Get supplies? Get Mom's meds? I don't even know where he goes. Is Nyssa even there? Or a passable road? Everything is in ruins.

For five days Mom and I hung out. Every night, while we waited for Dad, Mom and I lit two 36-hour survival candles and broke two eight-hour light sticks. She did needlework and I read.

And when she wasn't looking, I paced.

The air cleared, although the powdery ash still coated everything outside. Today, for the first time, I left my mask inside. The dogs and I sat on the front porch.

"Woof," said Lu, at the instant a nasty rumble shook T-dog's massive chest. I realized both big heads were up, eyes tightly focused on a distant point, ears alert. Then I knew why.

What's that? Movement caught my attention. Turning for a better view, my heart hiccupped in my chest.

Tan clouds of dust billowed, fogged the road below our house, obscuring who came. Someone drove up our hill faster than safe on the unpaved surface, pushing around the switchbacks, heading for our hiding place. *Someone who shouldn't be here.*

Panic pawed at the edges of my mind. I remembered Dad's words. I'd always told myself there was no real threat, no need to worry. But deep inside, I knew the truth.

My mind churned, fear turned it to mush. *Ohgodohgodohgod. I'm a kid. What do I do?* Memory of Dad's words cut through my paralysis. *Weapons, Katie. Run.* I leaped like I'd been doused with ice water.

The dogs flanked me, one on either side. Grumbles from two barrel chests let me know they were uneasy. Neither showed distress. Yet.

The binoculars. I spun on one heel and ran. Chest forward, arms pumping, I sprinted across the wide expanse of our front yard, running full-on for the house. I slipped on the ash, caught my balance, took off again. Snatching the glasses from their hook outside the screen door, I raced back to my vantage point.

"Too late, damn it." I flinched at my curse even though I knew Mom couldn't hear me.

The clouds of dust boiled closer. The truck remained hidden from view beneath the drop-off bluff below me. Its wheels broke free, it slid, slinging gravel. I heard the vehicle skid, then slow.

It isn't over the rise yet, but it's still too close.

The engine screamed. I heard spraying rock and the sound of spinning tires. Then came a grabbing noise – *tires catching purchase?* – and the straining motor settled. Again, the vehicle climbed the hill. A series of sharp downshifts told me the driver fought for the most speed.

Fear spiked, my heart hammered. I stared at the rising dirt, heard a wheezing, and realized my breath whistled through a throat almost closed by terror. The porch tilted and rotated around me like a lazy merry-go-round.

I need to be doing … something. My mind bent like poured honey.

Terror and Lupine barked, more concerned for me, than the coming vehicle. "I'm fine." I gave them the quiet, stay, and guard hand signals, and then pounded my fist on my forehead.

"God bless it, Katie," I croaked. "Breathe." The words, in my own voice, came surreal. "Think, damn you. Think." *The rifle. Dad always said the rifle or the pistols. Or both. I need to know who comes.*

"Oh shit. No time." Before I knew if the vehicle brought danger, it would broach the yard. Still, I stood frozen. I didn't – couldn't move. My feet refused to obey my brain.

NOW, Katie! My father's voice cracked in my mind. *MOVE!*

Adrenaline shoved through my veins. I motioned the dogs with me, turned tail, stretched my sprint into a flat-out run for the house. And for the weapons I knew waited.

I grabbed the 30.06 deer rifle with the Bushnell scope.

"No need for that," a voice cackled in my mind. "By the time you see the driver, he'll already be too close." It added in cheerful glee, "By the time you get ready, he'll be through the front door."

What do I do about Mom? As if in answer, I heard her voice in the kitchen, singing an old church hymn. *Good enough. She's protected back there.*

Bursting through the front screen, I dropped to my knees behind the solid porch railing.

When we moved in, the pickets were all lacy openwork that matched the trim on the house. Mom loved it. Then there was a bad argument, and Mom cried. Dad nailed two layers of ¾" plywood behind all the porch gingerbread anyway.

I laid the gun barrel steady on the 2x4 top plate, flicked off the safety and sighted in where the driveway enters the yard. *Easy, Katie. Easy.* I recalled Dad's words. *Just like shooting rabbits on the ditchbank.*

Terror and Lupine read my mood, dropped, crouched, guarded.

The barrel danced and jittered, like my hands did the time I'd grabbed the electric fence. *God, I need to pee.* I sucked air, cleared my mind and tried again. This time, although the rifle trembled, I knew I couldn't miss. *How do I know if I should shoot? How do I recognize a bad person? Dad didn't teach me that.* I rested my finger against the trigger and listened to the engine shoving the truck up the final few feet.

A burst of billowing dirt blew through the treeline followed by a Jeep, painted in desert brown Army camo.

Every muscle in my body tensed – including my trigger finger – before my brain registered who must be driving. I shoved the gun barrel up.

The windshield of the Jeep exploded.

"Oh Christ," I whispered. "Did I just shoot Dad?" I stared through the hole in the passenger side window, saw movement. *I missed.* The instant I knew for sure, my knees jello-ed and I sagged against the porch rail.

Flicking the gun safety on, I laid the rifle on the deck and gulped air – so fast, so hard, violins sang in my head. Shaking it off, I stumbled down the stairs. Found two large furry backs sturdy beneath my hands. So easy, with them bracing me, to hurry and help the driver out of the truck.

"Holy Shit, Katie," Dad said. "You damn near killed me. There's fucking safety glass all over the front seat."

"Are you okay? Are you hit? Are you cut?" I babbled, heard a breathy tone in my voice.

"You didn't shoot me, no. You missed. How the hell could you at this range?"

Was that … laughter in his words?

"I … I pulled the shot at the last second."

My father eased from behind the steering wheel. A dirty burgundy-smeared bandage wrapped his head above a face bruised to almost unrecognizable. He held one arm close against his side.

I skidded to a stop, clutched my throat, tried to swallow. He'd come home before, beat-up, scratched, bloodied, but never like this.

"D-ad?" My voice cracked on the word. "My God, Dad. You okay?" The grim expression on his face made my heart hiccup. "How did you get around the huge crack in the valley floor? How did you get through the water? You look like hell … um … sorry."

"What water? What crack?"

"The dam broke, Dad. Flooded everything. And the earthquake opened up a huge canyon clear across the valley."

"Jesus!" he said. "Those poor people." He squeezed his eyes closed for a moment, then looked at me. "I came west, took the back roads from the base over high country. Give me a hand inside, Katie. I need to tend my wounds, then we'll talk. How is your mother?"

"Fine, she's fine." I said and he nodded.

"I worried," he said. "No, not about you. About everything else."

Dad's a big man, a thick, muscular, tall man. I'm strong like him but it took everything I possessed to get him up the stairs, across the porch and into the house. For the first time in my life, with my father near, fear owned me.

We shuffled, out of synch, over the weatherstripping on the threshold, and staggered into the great room. I moved to stop, hearing his great tearing breaths. Worse yet, something glistened, bubbled a deep scarlet, shining on the side of his shirt.

He stumbled, lurched.

I grabbed him and we stood for a second, braced like lovers, until we caught our balance.

"The couch," I said and made an almost-move.

Dad swayed, fought for balance, his hand an iron shackle around my bicep, unaware he squeezed.

I'll hide the bruises. He'd hate himself, and it isn't his fault.

"Not yet, Katie," he husked. "Get me to the kitchen. I'll make a helluva mess here and your mother will have a coronary."

I sincerely doubted it, I sincerely did. No matter how she felt about dirt, and things being out of place, if Mom saw Dad wounded, she'd lay him down on her prized Persian. *This I know.* But we made our slow, and – I knew by the whistle in his exhales – painful way down the hall and into the warm kitchen smelling of apple pie.

"Katie," Mom's voice floated up from in front of the oven. Bending, checking the doneness of her baking, she asked, "Where've you been?"

How could she miss hearing my shot? I didn't answer – all my concentration centered on levering Dad into a kitchen chair.

He tried to help but his legs collapsed. The thump brought Mom up and around like she'd been goosed with a cattle prod.

"Dooooooon," left her lips, high thin rising hysteria. Huge cornflower blue eyes stretched too wide, Mom opened her mouth again.

"No, Sharon," Dad's voice cracked with an authority I'd never heard him use … with her. *He's used it on me before.* Then, more softly, he said, "Don't scream. I need you to help me. Katie too. Calm yourself."

To my amazement, she did.

At the far end of the kitchen, T-dog and Lu dropped onto their rugs, but they didn't lie down. Just sat, perfectly still, alert and on duty, aware of everything in and around our farmhouse. With those two sentries, we relaxed, secure in the knowledge they'd spot any danger long before we did.

"Don," my mother whispered. "How did this happen? You've had accidents before – but this …." Then, her eyes dropped and she sucked air. "Don Davis, is that a bullet hole in your shirt?"

Dad hurt. He shifted in the hard kitchen chair, then half-grunted, half-inhaled a breath before he answered Mom.

"A graze, Sharon. Only a graze. Hunting accident. Just get the first aid kit, okay? I'll need to patch myself up, and take some antibiotics."

A graze, my ass. I raised an eyebrow but didn't glance at Dad. I didn't want Mom to catch me. *He's hurt, maybe bad, but he won't let her know. Will he tell me?*

My mother's eyes went wide, glassy for just a second. Then she shook herself like one of our chickens dusting off, nodded, and rushed from the room.

"What's happening, Dad? A problem at the base?" I wanted something, anything, before my mother returned. "I had a bad premonition. Actually, two. Then came the earthquake and aftershocks. The explosions …."

The way he shook his head made hair rise on the back of my neck, icy fingers skittered down my spine.

"I got a three-day pass to come check on you." He said this loud enough for Mom to hear. Then he whispered, "Later, Katie-girl. When we're alone."

Then he raised his voice to carry into the other room. "Sharon? Can you help me get this shirt off?"

Mom clucked her way back into the kitchen, fluttered her hands. She used her sewing scissors to cut away his stained shirt. The grim compression of her lips said she hated his wounds and his pain.

I wanted to argue, to know everything right now, but I knew better. Dad always told me what he wanted me to know, in his own time, and never a second before. *But he doesn't have hunting accidents. And the way he drove up the hill …. Bad shit's going down.*

I told my jittering heart to stop it and took a huge breath. The copper odor of blood saturated the kitchen – so heavy it coated the roof of my mouth. A wad of gauze taped to Dad's side glistened with spots of burgundy. My gag reflex kicked in; I swallowed hard.

"We need to change that." My look at his bandage held the question.

"Yes."

I glanced at Mom, watched her panting.

"Can you, Katie?" she asked. "I'm a little queasy."

"Sure," I lied. "No problem." *Honestly, I don't think I can.*

I grabbed another breath and held it. As gently as possible, I peeled the dressing away and made myself inspect the wound.

Two black holes, like eyes, peered back through the red smear above his waist.

I breathed, slow and even, through my nose. *Good so far. I haven't fainted or puked.*

My lessons from Dad had included trauma theory. *And my mind's blank. What in hell am I supposed to be doing?*

"One shot or two?" I heard my voice, low and steady. It didn't quaver like my insides. It didn't give me away.

"One," he said, and his voice cracked on the word. "Yesterday. Soldier nailed me when I stole the Jeep. It felt like a pinch. I think it skipped in, bounced off a rib, and went back out again. I was hiding behind a dumpster. I think the ricochet took the velocity out of the shot. Kept it from going deep."

"Dumpster?" My question pulled a fast warning glance from his coal dark eyes.

"Um ... never mind," I mumbled. "The holes are about an inch apart."

"I think they're topical. Check them. If my abdominal wall is perforated, I'll have to find a doc."

"Urk," Mom said in my ear. I turned; saw the whites of her rolling eyes.

"Sharon ...," Dad said.

A red flush crept up her neck, across her face.

She straightened her shoulders, wiped her palms on the thighs of her shorts. "I'll get the first aid box now," she said. "I forgot, just for a second, what I was doing. Be right back."

"Cool. Thanks." *God, Mom.* My insides rippled like our creek. I couldn't confess I was faking it too – she might come apart.

"What happened, Don?" Mom's hand, wrapped around the first-aid kit, snaked over my shoulder.

I wondered what he'd tell her.

"Should be entertaining," whispered the little dark voice in my mind.

Shut the hell up, I told it.

"Mom? You wanna do this?"

"No, Katie. I'll tend his face, if that's okay with you."

I really, really don't want to. "Sure," I said, took the box, laid it on the kitchen table, and cracked the lid.

"This one?" I asked Dad, my fingertip on a white cap. At his nod, I pulled the dark brown bottle from the kit, unscrewed the top. The strong odor of antiseptic filled the kitchen and made me wrinkle my nose.

"Phew," Mom said.

From her spot on the floor, Lupine sneezed and Terror rubbed his muzzle across the pine planking.

I soaked a gauze sponge with the antiseptic and made a tentative swab at a patch of blood. Evaluated what needed cleaning, or worse. *Oooo.*

"This is gonna hurt."

Coal dark eyes met mine and he grunted a nod. "It's okay. I'm tough." A small grin creased one side of his face.

I held up a green container, with a child-proof cap and lifted a questioning brow.

"A couple, please," he said. "Second thought, you're gonna clean. Make it three."

Chapter Six

Dad shifted in the hard kitchen chair, grunted against the pain. I watched Mom stuff a pillow in the small of his back, and he settled in. He stuck out his cupped palm and I dropped the pills in it, watched him dry-swallow them.

"How can you do that?" It always amazed me – I needed a gallon of water to swallow one tiny pill.

"Just practice, Katie." He laughed, hiccupped, grabbed his side. "Ahhh. I do need hydration. Sharon, would you be a doll and get me some water?"

Mom sprang toward the sink, then stopped.

Yesterday, before I shut the generator down, Mom and I gathered every spare container in the house and filled them with water. Turning from the faucet, she tapped the sun tea crock on the counter.

"Thanks," he said and downed the glassful.

I filled a 60cc plastic syringe with saline solution, cleared my throat. Shot the solution into one open wound and made my first swipe.

Dad held a wad of gauze against the other hole, and I heard him swear, very softly, very vehemently, beneath his breath.

Lupine caught my worry, and whuffed from her rug. Those intelligent lantern-yellow eyes never stopped moving, assessing. I swear I heard gears and wheels turning in her head.

Terror whined his distress.

"Anyway, a week ago, when I was called into the base? We were briefed on the problem." Dad's voice rose on the last syllable.

I hurt him, dammit. "Sorry," I muttered. Heat crawled my neck and face, sharp, hot little prickles stabbed my skin. Intent on cleaning his wounds, I swabbed a little too deep, maybe a little too thorough. Dad sucked a quick half-breath. *Shit. Shit. Shit.*

"Ahhh …," he grunted and choked it off fast. At my hesitation he grinned. "Do it. Just like I taught you."

I cleaned some more.

"You're right, Dad." I swiped the sweat off my forehead with my forearm. "The bullet passed under the skin – through some muscle. Do I have do flush it again before I stitch it?"

"Yesss," he hissed. "But I can't promise I'm going to enjoy it."

I flinched.

A snorted half-chuckle escaped him. "I'm teasing you. Go ahead, Katie."

Lu moved and settled, guarding the kitchen door. Terror whined again and nosed Dad's hand.

He stroked the dog's massive charcoal head. "I'm okay, boy. Honest. Katie's just mean."

"Keep talking, Dad." I tried to laugh at his joke, but it stuck in my powder-coated throat.. "It'll help me focus."

"You remember the big meteor in the ground, close to the military base?"

"Ummhmm," I mumbled, intent on my task. "Beaver … something. Been there about a million years?" *He's beat up, shot, and talking about ancient history? Maybe he's distracting himself too.*

"Beaverhead Crater. Buried about 900 million years. Anyway, the scientists said the earthquake and built-up lava probably shoved it to the surface. They think it might have something to do with the earthquakes and volcanic eruptions."

"Nonsense, Don. We haven't had either one." My mother's voice quivered, but I gave her points, she cleaned the crusty blood from Dad's face with a steady hand.

My father shot me a stealthy look and I gave him an almost imperceptible shake of my head. Mouthed "*denial.*"

His bushy brows drew down above his nose. He pooched his lips, nodded.

"What's a meteor have to do with the stuff I saw?" I asked.

"The scientists told us volcanic flow, moving below the surface, caused shifting of the tectonic plates. The man I heard said this lets the lava surge and form 'hot spots.' That activity created upward pressure – which caused the eruptions, earthquakes and aftershocks we had."

My father's shoulders tensed when I probed. "They're still having small quakes at the base about every hour."

"But the explosions, Dad …?"

"Lava came to the surface under the munitions storage at Mountain Home. Cooked them off."

"At the base?" Mom asked, her voice rising. She moved to one side and began bandaging torn skin on Dad's arm. "Who shot you? Where were you?"

"Coming home."

Not the same answer he gave me. Gooseflesh pimpled my arms, my legs; I tried to hide my shiver. What else did Dad hide?

"It's bad," I said. "But it can all be fixed, right?" *By the time I go to West Point.*

"Selfish girl," snarled my mindvoice. "For shame."

"Ordinarily, yes," my father answered. "FEMA teams would handle the civilian matters, and the military would repair the base. And the Army Corps of Engineers would handle the dam." Dad turned his head so Mom couldn't see and fixed me with his dark no-nonsense stare. "But there are other mitigating factors."

I nodded and went back to stitching his side. *More bad news for later.*

My mother and I worked in silence while we patched Dad back together.

He wouldn't go to bed but he did let us install him in his recliner. He didn't wince or suck air so the pills must have been working.

I parked myself in 'Katie's designated section' of the big leather sofa, keeping an eye on my father. Mom came into the family room, looked Dad over, nodded, and went back to the kitchen.

Lupine grunted, groaned and stretched full length on the rug at my feet.

Terror lay pressed against Dad's chair. Brows twitching, the brown marbles of his eyes followed every move, every noise, his unease written plain for anyone to see. His master hurt and Terror didn't like it one bit. He didn't know how to fix Dad, but while T-dog guarded, nothing else would touch my father.

Mom tore up the kitchen, blunt force noises, pans banged, utensils clanged. Whatever dinner might be, major construction occupied the back of the house.

Dad and I sat, for what seemed about an hour, just listening to her work.

"Cornbread, unless I'm much mistaken." Dad broke our silence.

"Yeah, it's what I smell too. I'd go help her but she'd throw me out."

Dad snorted, then groaned. "Don't make me laugh, Katie. Hurts. But you're right – she doesn't tolerate kitchen interference well."

I laughed, then. He sounded like my in-charge Dad again. He lifted my spirits, made me feel secure.

"Are you going to discuss your argument?" whispered the voice in my mind.

I sincerely hoped Dad wouldn't bring it up. When his breathing went slow and deep, I relaxed and just sat, watching him sleep. An hour or so passed, and I got up, slipped into the kitchen. Mom still cooked.

"Gonna sit in the porch swing for a while," I said. "Dad's asleep."

"Good," she said, slightly breathless. "Maybe I'll join you later."

Lu and I watched the sun lower, the sky streaked with coral and hot pink, then orange and deep blue. When full dark came, we went back inside.

Dad spoke from the depths of his recliner. "My pistol, Katie," he said. "Could you get it from the Jeep? I can't believe I forgot it." He huffed a few shallow pants, then said, "I need you to do a good observation from the top of the trail." He grunted a breath. "Take your gun. And the shotgun. And Lu."

"Sure, Dad."

My heart missed a couple of beats, made me cough. *Is he hurt worse than he said? The Dad I know would never forget his weapon.*

Lu got up, padded at my side, head up, eyes and ears alert.

The remote country around our place stayed quiet. *This dark is so deep I could scoop it with a spoon.* Always before, from the top of the bluff, I saw the barn lights of farms, plus the lighted cityscapes scattered across the horizon. Now, without those familiar glows, the peaceful night turned ominous. Like a serial murderer waiting for an opportunity, or a horrific monster hidden in the dark.

I flicked the flashlight on just long enough to make my way up the trail. Lupine leaped in front, leading the way, her scrabbling claws tossing dirt and pebbles. At the top, I killed my light and scrutinized the valley.

Lights and fires dotted the dark. One pair of headlights shone from a lone vehicle. People were moving, but very few. A small light glowed across the canyon. From the lookout tower? Memory struck.

Oh shit! Todd. My date. What day is this? Saturday. It's tomorrow I'm supposed to meet him. I can't. Can I? Did he get here before everything went to hell? Or is he stuck in college town?

Lupine shoved me with her cold nose. The full moon's light reflected glassy silver in her eyes.

"Okay, okay." I roughed the thick fur on her head, stood it on end, then stroked it smooth. "I'm taking care of business now. Let's go."

In front of the house, I cracked the Jeep door, blinked against the bright unexpected dome light. I found Dad's big Ruger on the passenger seat, picked it up, checked the safety and flipped it on. The stench of dirt and blood inside made my stomach twisty, but I swallowed the upchuck. Made a mental note to clean the truck for Dad. *What the hell did he crawl through to get away? Who was trying to keep him there? Why?*

Lu and I slipped through the front door, down the hall and into the main part of the house. Mom's finger against her lips warned me to silence.

Moonlight slanted through the big window in the family room, casting enough light for me to see Dad's face. I laid his Ruger in its usual place on the table by his chair. Close at hand. Always.

Terror and Lu settled on the braided rug. Without television, or lights, I heard every creak and moan of our old house.

Dad snored gently.

"He needs the rest. I'm going to bed," Mom whispered. "How about you?"

"I'll sit up a little bit. Pleasant dreams."

She'd no more than climbed the stairs, barely closed the bedroom door, when Dad opened his eyes.

"You faker," I said. "Want more water?"

"I would, thanks," he said. "How's it look outside?"

"Quiet and dark. But there are fires scattered across the valley," I told him. "Maybe the worst is over?"

He didn't comment, didn't grunt.

I went cold inside. "I'll get your water," I said and went to the kitchen. I felt for the cookie jar, took out a couple of Mom's fresh baked chocolate chips. A dim light glowed behind me. Dad had turned on the lantern.

The whispered expletives from the family room startled me. Dad didn't know I inherited his hearing. He didn't realize I heard every curse he uttered.

The words didn't shake me to my core – the weary vehemence and defeat in his voice did. *Why is he so upset?*

I filled our glasses, waited until he stopped swearing; made noises on my way back to the family room. I placed his glass on the table by his elbow; handed him a cookie. Sat on my end of the couch.

"Thanks," he said. "When did the dam break?"

"Five days ago. I went up to Pinnacle Point to look around. I saw it happen. It was awful ... I ... I don't have the words ...."

"So sorry you saw it, but I'm glad you're safe. Glad our house sits here." Dad coughed, grabbed his side, and nodded. "There has to be enormous damage, lots of people hurt or killed. Bad for us, because the people wanting to leave the state will be forced up here in our direction."

"Why do they want to leave, Dad? I don't understand."

"They're fleeing the ash, the flooding. It's part of why it took me longer to get home. I had to change the oil and filters, and flush the radiator three times to keep from burning up the motor." He shifted in his chair. "But your mother can't know the other parts."

Oh shit. What could be worse? I nodded understanding.

"First thing: the military prison building blew up. Some very dangerous people escaped. With everything that's happened, there just aren't enough troops to do it all. Some of these criminals have to be tracked down and locked back up – for reasons you don't need to know." Dad breathed, a slow movement favoring his side. His face was as grim as I'd ever seen it. He clenched his teeth. "The lava and the earthquake aren't all, Katie." A muscle jumped in his jaw. "True, they started the explosions, broke the pipelines and cooked off the weapons. Blew the old bombs – mustard gas, other things – then the new ones, like the daisy-cutters and MOAB's went."

"Okay," I said. "I get it. I saw stuff happening everywhere. It wasn't all at the base."

"Right," he agreed. "The destruction expanded, leaped outward. One explosion, or one fire triggered another. The chemical factories torched – spraying death everywhere."

"So now everything has exploded, burned out or burned up, that's the end of it. I mean, sure, we have to clean up and rebuild the valley and the military base. The rest of the US will come help, right? Like the hurricane catastrophes? Won't kill us to be without power or TV for awhile. We can do it." *Please Dad, tell me my future isn't over before it's begun. I have to ask.* "West Point's still there, right?"

I didn't recognize my father's voice. So suddenly hopeless.

"Katie," he said. "I just don't know. But …." He took a hard breath, pushed it out.

I held mine, unable to exhale until he spoke.

"The exploded weapons, the volcanic eruptions, the earthquakes, the destroyed dam – even the escaped criminals – none of those are the real problem," he said.

"What could be worse?" My voice quavered, and shook. Even to me, I sounded a hundred years old.

"People are dying. They're getting sick and dying. In just a few days."

"Radiation poisoning?"

"That's what they say, but the symptoms don't match." Dad shook his head, faraway eyes glued on some horrible memory. "Now the feds are involved. Transport planes, loaded with people, soldiers, supplies and instruments came in."

"I saw three big ones go overhead. Gray with fat-bellies, headed in the direction of Mountain Home. Not five minutes before the dam let go."

"Those are the ones. The feds set up a tent and quarantined the meteor. Scientists came from the government and everywhere – evidently it's a big deal – the once in a lifetime chance to observe and study something so ancient."

"How big is it? I thought those things burned up in the atmosphere."

"They mostly do. This meteor is one of the biggest ones to make it to Earth's surface."

"So how big?"

"Twenty feet by thirty by thirteen.Weighs about sixteen tons. Small, really."

"It's just an old rock." I waited but he didn't answer for the longest time. Then I heard him move, not quite groan, and shift in his chair. "I don't understand the fuss."

The familiar sound of Dad's deadly Ka-Bar knife scraped on his whetstone. Keeping his hands busy while he tried to marshal his thoughts.

"It's not the meteor that's the problem. It's this flu."

"Flu's no fun but people get over it. How bad can it be?"

"The experts don't know what it is. They're studying the birds and animals, but none of them are sick. This strain is so agonizing, so deadly, that those who've caught it are calling it The Great Awful."

Dad's eyes were two bleak dark pools. I looked deep, wished I hadn't. Wished he hadn't turned on the lantern. A stiletto of fear skewered my heart.

"What about antibiotics?"

"Nothing works on this, Katie. If you get sick, you die."

"Everybody?"

"Well, I worked with Lyn Silver, a lady doc at the base. I helped her care for patients for two days, figuring I was dead anyway – I'd been exposed to a bunch of sick people. But I didn't catch it. Neither did Lyn. But few people are immune. Lyn told me, out of all the people in the hospital, only two patients lived through The Great Awful. That's about one in a hundred."

"Why? Why them, and not someone else?" *This doesn't make sense.*

"Her theory is they had an immune parent – made them less vulnerable or gave them enough resistance to survive." My Dad shook his head. "It's the only thing that makes sense."

"How do you know you've got it?" I whispered, and my voice shook.

"The fever comes within a few hours and the sick person is covered with a red rash, like measles. They get disoriented and confused. The incubation period is 24-hours. Then lymph floods under the skin and finally blood seeps through."

I heard leather squeak and Dad's half-breath, watched him shift in his recliner.

"God, Dad." Bile roiled, climbed my esophagus. I swallowed hard against the nausea.

"It's awful, Katie," he whispered. "Worst thing I ever saw. The pain – the organs liquefy. Lyn said when people finally die, their bodies are just puddles."

My breath caught in my throat. "H-how long – to die, I mean?"

"Generally four hard days."

"What do we do?"

"Everybody in my group got sick at the same time. I didn't show a single symptom. They all died within hours of each other. I stayed away from here for extra days, Katie, to make sure I wasn't going to come down with it later. I stole the Jeep from a remote part of the base – hoping no one sick had touched it. I stripped, showered, disinfected three different times on the way home."

"While you were shot? Needing help?"

"I had to make sure. When the warehouse guards died, I went in and took supplies. I found new clothes – still in their plastic bags. Figured they'd be safe. I did everything I could think of."

Dad shook his big head, slumped in his chair like a beaten prizefighter. "Katie, because I am, you could be."

"What?" *Okay, is he delirious? Do I need to worry about him too?* I locked a scream behind my clenched teeth.

"Ah – immune, I mean," Dad said. "I'm not making good sense. But, see, I couldn't take the chance. Not with your mother, either."

Oh, thank God. He's okay. I couldn't stop my sudden heavy exhale.

Three heads turned in the night; three pairs of eyes studied me.

"How does a person get immune?"

"Has to be something already in your body – in your DNA, maybe," my father said. "No one knows."

"What are we going to do? Where is safe?" My voice quavered, terror surged close to the surface, wanting to be freed.

"I'm not going back," Dad said.

"Don't you have to? Won't you be AWOL if you don't?"

"Katie," my father said, his voice flat, emotionless as a machine. "You have no idea what I left behind. The feds have the entire base under lockdown. Lyn's the only doctor still alive – far as I know. Because they tried to save the sick people, the doctors, nurses and paramedics died first. Then the police and firemen. We've got a good chance to survive if we stay here."

"So if your patriot father, of all people, doesn't care if he's AWOL," whispered the dark little kernel in my mind. "What's happening? Something so awful he's not telling you? What is the government doing? What has he been ordered to do? What could be so bad that your father – the cold-blooded assassin – can't? Or won't do? What could be so horrific he would ignore direct orders?"

My mind ran into a solid wall and stopped. The voice in my head made terrifying sense. My heart stuttered. I coughed, and swallowed hard. *I could ask Dad – but he wouldn't answer.* Meanwhile, my father sat, waiting patiently, for my response.

"How long, Dad? Will we have to stay here? For days?"

"Oh, Katie. Could be weeks, could be months, maybe longer."

"I won't. I can't be here forever." My *mad* surged, heating the tips of my ears. I heard the fury and desperation lacing my words. "I've never gone anywhere, done anything. I'm going crazy."

"I know, and I'm sorry," he said. "It was the only way to keep you and your mother alive."

What? Why? My mind bounced on his words, and something I didn't want to know stirred in memory. I changed the subject. "The dam has to be fixed. The roads and the canyon across the valley. Won't the government help? They always do."

"Not this time, Katie. There aren't any people to do the work."

"What do you mean? You just said they flew in people to help." I heard my voice rising, heard the beginnings of panic.

"Let me put it to you this way," Dad whispered. "If new people come in – say a hundred and ninety-eight of them die? Or all of them? No more are coming. We don't have enough resources to do everything. Plus the flu keeps spreading."

I felt my head go light, do a spin. I grabbed hold of the arm of the couch to keep from falling.

"The government has quarantined Oregon, Idaho, Washington, Wyoming and Montana," Dad said. His deep voice sounded like boulders rubbing together. "Roadblocks are manned by military personnel with guns. No one is coming in – no one wants to."

We sat there in the half-dark, and I saw my father take a deep breath. *Oh, God, please. No more bad news.*

Dad cleared his throat, and softly added. "Katie, the government has to keep the rest of the United States safe from our flu. The military cordon has standing orders – anyone attempting to leave will be shot."

Chapter Seven

The next day

I woke early, heard voices downstairs. I washed my face and brushed my teeth with water from the container in my bathroom, pulled on a green tank and denim shorts. Lu matched me step for step as we went to join my parents.

Dad still sat in his recliner and I felt sure he'd been there all night. I heard him groan when he shifted his weight. "Morning, Dad. Do you need a refill on your coffee?"

"No, thanks." He shook his head. I watched him fasten white teeth in his lower lip when he pried his way from his chair to go outside and pee. My body flinched in sympathy. Lu went with him. When he came back and settled in, Mom brought his breakfast on a tray and placed it across his lap.

"Don," she said. "Katie and I are carrying water to flush our toilets and I need to do laundry. Can't we use the generator?"

"Don't want to burn up the motor. Plus, I'm uncomfortable making so much noise, Sharon. Better we keep a low profile until we find what we're up against."

"Well, I just don't see …," she began. Something twisted across Mom's face, stopped her in mid-sentence. Then, eerie in contrast, a smooth doll-like expression took its place.

My heart hammered, fit to explode. Cold sweat coated my palms.

What in the world just happened? I waited for the voice in my head to explain but it didn't say a word.

"Of course," she said. "Never mind." Mom pulled a mixing bowl from the cupboard, dumped in scoops of flour.

"I need to walk the perimeter," Dad said. "I got here fast. Others could do the same."

"Let me," I said. "I'll take both the dogs and two guns."

"No," Mom's voice rang too loud in the morning air. "I forbid it. She will not leave this house."

My *mad* crawled hot up the back of my neck, suffused my ears. *Here she goes again.*

It spoke volumes about how bad Dad hurt, or perhaps how safe he thought we were, because he let me go and then asked me to check outside twice more before lunch.

That scares me … bad.

Mom raised hell with him … every single time. He must have been hurting, or just tired, because the last time, he snapped at her.

Tears squirted from her big blue eyes, and she hurried into the kitchen.

"Ah, hell," he said. Levering from his chair, he went to apologize.

A little before noon, I took the binoculars and climbed the bluff. I searched the countryside, tried to see beneath every leaf, behind every bush. In the distance, accented by bright sunshine, water glimmered where it never had before. I checked the lookout tower a half-dozen times but I couldn't see a thing. No clues whether, even if Todd made the trip, he found a way to his parents. I couldn't tell if anyone was still there. No way I could go anyway – not now. *My first date … and I stand him up.*

Being alone in the hills, with my wolf for company, usually brought me peace and comfort. All around me, everything lay quiet, too still. *I feel trapped.*

When I got back, we cranked the emergency radio and listened. We didn't find a single signal. All day we cranked and listened, searching for information. Any information – even a scrap. Found only silence.

"Katie-girl," my father said. "Get some extra ammunition – a supply for all the guns – from the basement, would you? While it's light enough to see. Don't want you falling over something down there."

"Well," said the voice in my head. "Things have sure changed, haven't they? I mean, you need to consider the consequences of everything. If you hurt yourself, you can't go running off to the doctor anymore. They're all dead."

Shit, the damn thing's right.

Mom cooked a great dinner on the wood stove, but our attempts at high spirits, at pretending we lived our normal lives failed. Miserably.

The brilliant disc of white-yellow sun dropped, headed for the horizon.

"Gonna be dusk soon," I said, putting the lantern on the table. "Should I check the perimeter now? Be back before dark?" I figured Dad might insist on doing this round himself. *He needs to rest, to heal, because we need him. But he's stubborn. I know – I'm just like him.*

59

"No," he said. "I'll go." My father pushed up from the chair. Sucked air, his face chalky beneath his tan. Bracing on the recliner arms, he lowered himself back, slow and easy, into his chair.

My mouth dried just watching.

"Okay, Katie," he said, his lips pressed into a pair of white lines. "You go. But anything, and I mean anything, makes you uneasy, you scat back here. No flashlight. Be home before you need one."

"No, no. No, Don. She can't go. She's just a child."

Dammit, dammit, damn her. Can't she ever just leave it alone?

I glared at my mother, fury crawled hot up my neck. I don't know what showed on my face.

Mom's hands fluttered like a dropped deck of playing cards. "It's not safe. Don, something will happen to her." She reached, grabbed my arms, and held on.

Man, she's strong. I had no idea.

"Sharon, she'll be fine. Let go of her."

"I will not. Don, you're high on pills. You're not thinking clearly."

I exchanged a glance with my father.

"Mom, I'll be just fine," I said, striving for soothing when I really wanted to scream at her to let me go. *Oh God, I'm bad.* Twisting my arms, I gently broke her grip and peeled away her grasping fingers.

"Hurry, before she grabs you again," advised my mindvoice.

"I'm taking my Beretta, Dad. What else? Shotgun or rifle?"

"The shotgun."

"Gotcha."

I snagged the weapons, motioned to Terror and dodged Mom.

Lu moved between my mother and me, already at my side. I wondered how she managed to stay so close and never crowd me. But she never did, not the smallest nudge. The dogs and I sidled toward the kitchen.

Dad ran interference. "Now would be good, Katie," he said and winked. Just that quick, he dispelled my guilt. Raising his voice, he said, "Sharon, I need you to find the …." What he asked for, I missed. But I saw Mom headed up the stairs like her heels were aflame.

I opened the kitchen door, and we slipped outside, made our way across the lawn, and into the edge of the trees. I checked to be sure my weapons safeties were set on Fire.

My heart hammered staccato, blood pounded in my ears. I couldn't hear anything but that. I tried to slow my breathing, but only huffed and puffed more.

"Scared, are we?" snarked my dark little voice.

I didn't answer. After about five minutes, I began to settle, began to think again. *Katie, you idiot. Just watch T-dog and Lupine's body language.*

We surprised three whitetail deer, a lazy rattlesnake, and took a scolding from two chipmunks and a magpie. I wished for my camera. Magpies were unique, striking birds, their glossy solid black feathers accented by a single stripe of white. Shy and solitary, they kept their distance. I didn't see them often.

The dogs flushed a flock of jakes – wild young turkeys – and I swear they laughed. Moving careful, slow and silent, the entire circuit around our place took me more than an hour. Lu and Terror didn't smell the ground and bushes, not like usual. The ash probably irritated their tender nasal membranes. Maybe it prevented scents too? But, tails waving like flags, my guardians were unconcerned.

Okay then, so am I. I concentrated on moving smooth and stealthy – *ha* – through the undergrowth. I looked for things out of the ordinary: disturbed ground, discarded trash. I searched everywhere – then I searched again. I looked hard. I listened with all my being. But I didn't find one damn suspicious thing on our property.

After dark, Dad motioned Mom and me into the walk-in pantry in the kitchen. "Bring the radio, some extra batteries and the lantern, Katie. Thanks. And shut the door."

"Why are we in here, Don?" My mother's voice pitched a little too high.

"We can't show light. Out here, in the dark, it would be a beacon. Could draw people to us – good or bad. We can't be noticed – we don't know what's happening out there." Dad set the Coleman on the floor. "This way, we can check for news at night, too. We might get lucky."

Backlit by the light, I saw his jaw twitch. A muscle bunched where he clenched his teeth.

We got a signal. *Aaanck, aaanck, aaanck.* The nasal donkey bray, the intermittent honking blatt of the Civil Defense alert. So unexpected, we all jumped. But the damnable alert didn't broadcast a single word.

Uh oh. My stomach knotted, slid into my throat, cut off my air.

"Hoolah, loolah," Mom shrieked, waving her hands in the air like she warded off evil spirits.

Dad jumped, like he'd been tasered. Something crossed his face, turned its planes harsh, his eyes flat and dark.

Cold sweat coated my underarms. *She's unraveling. Where in hell did that phrase come from?* My wet hands were freezing. *I've never heard it before ... but Dad has.*

My father's awful expression disappeared, his face smoothed like it never happened. He grabbed her shoulders, then tilted her chin with one big hand. Although he whispered, his voice came hard enough to cut wire.

"Stop it, Sharon. We have to know what's happening; figure out what to do. Your voice carries – you'll be heard. You can't panic. You have to be quiet."

Oh shit. What the hell is this? He's right. What good did screaming do? I loved my sweet, kind Mom. But, long as I remembered, she'd been high strung. No sense getting mad at her, she couldn't help it. *No – wait. That's wrong. She wasn't always ... she only got weird after something awful ....* Panic struck me, a blind breathsucking fear.

A buried memory, a snippet, swam up from the depths. Something scary happened – right before we moved here. *A bunch of bad men took us, Mom and me. Then ... Dad ... and another man ... Sy? No, I can't remember. And ... Dad and ... they killed the bad ones fast as knives could cut and guns could fire. How could I forget?*

My face burned, shame flooded me, guilt twisted my mind.

"Dad ...." I turned to my father, questions tumbling over each other, trying to be the first one asked. His eyes were as arctic and impersonal as I'd ever seen; his face shuttered and closed. *He will not allow it.*

"Best to conserve resources," he said and shut off the Coleman.

I need to know. Rage tinted the edges of my vision scarlet. *I have to know. This concerns me and the why of everything. And I cannot ask because it would upset them.*

"Leave it alone," said the mindvoice.

Mom and I fumbled our separate ways back to the family room. I heard a thump and Mom's sharp intake of breath right before I whacked the doorjamb with my shoulder. I swallowed the bad word I almost said. Dad moved easier now. I decided he must have eyes like a cat because he didn't bump a thing.

I'd never appreciated the bright pool thrown by the big barn light until we didn't have it. Always before, we'd just fired up the generator. Now, the outside, with all its possible dangers, pressed hard against my mind. *If my goal to leave here was granted right now – I wouldn't.*

I tried not to think about what I'd just remembered. Found it was the only thing I could think of. The details were hazy, and I couldn't figure the where or when, only the terribleness of it all. And the fact it really happened.

Dad sat in his recliner while Mom and I curled on each end of our couch. We waited, quietly, in a dark so deep, so heavy my heartbeat thumped in my ears.

Dad broke the silence. "Sharon, I need a promise."

"Sure, Don. Anything."

"If there is ever any shooting outside the house, I need you to get into the clawfoot tub in the upstairs bath. Will you do that for me?"

"Why?"

"It's cast iron, safest place to be."

"Then Katie should be the one in there."

"No, she will have another safe place. Promise me you will."

"Long as Katie is safe, I promise," Mom said.

"Atta girl," he said and blew her a kiss. "Did you take your evening meds?"

"Oh," she said. "I forgot. I'll do it right now."

"Now how does that make you feel?" The dark voice inside asked.

Like shit, okay? I thought back. *Leave me alone.*

Back on her end of the couch, wrapped in a fleece blanket, Mom snored. A little soft sound. With her fast asleep, Dad and I went back to the kitchen. We cranked the radio and listened. Cranked and listened all damn night. Bad things happen at three or four in the morning. People get tired, less alert, their guards come down. Dad told me so, and he told me a lot of other things while Mom slept.

"I'll just have a look outside." Sliding his pistol in the back of his belt, my father grabbed the shotgun from the pegs over the front door. A flip of his hand brought Terror to his feet.

He's moving better, already on the mend.

Lu didn't stir from her rug.

"Back in a bit," Dad said. "Lock the door behind me." He murmured under his breath, "It's too quiet. Something just isn't right."

I know he didn't intend me to hear, but I did.

A fist of ice seized my spine. It seemed the air pressed close on me, heavy with my fear. Clung like sweat on my skin. Sure as sure, I knew something terrible and wrong lurked out there. Coming for us.

I tried, and tried again, but I couldn't pull a full breath. I checked the load in my Beretta, realize my spare ammo was all upstairs in my bedroom. I needed it. I needed reassurance so badly I headed upstairs in the dark.

Lu came with me, a noiseless shadow. I laid my gun on my nightstand next to my flashlight. I didn't even consider turning it on. I liked being hidden in the shadows. Like Dad said, out here, in the almost wilderness, a tiny light shows a good long distance. *Yes, it does.* I remembered the glow from the lookout tower.

Fishing my ammunition box from the drawer, I put a spare clip and half the bullets into my fanny pack and strapped it around my waist. I left the rest in my nightstand drawer.

Back downstairs, Mom still curled in her usual spot. Awake, but quiet, she murmured prayers interspersed with tiny "hoolah, loolahs."

The nonsensical phrase, weird and new, made the hair stand on my arms in hard painful points. The way she kept repeating it gave me the creeps. It related to something terrible – I knew it from my father's face. *I can't stay in here and listen to that.*

Lu and I went out on the front porch and stood watch side-by-side. My wolf easy and relaxed, and me, stiff as a pine board, my heart drumming way too fast.

Nothing stopped the terrors rippling through me until Dad came home.

Chapter Eight

The next morning, 3:30 am

A sharp crack and a bark from Terror, at his post outside my parents' door, yanked me from sleep. Beside my bed, Lupine growled, a low threatening rumble deep in her chest.

My heart went arrhythmic against my ribs.

"Hoolah, loolah." From the master bedroom across the hall.

"Hush," I heard my father say. "Let me dress."

A gunshot? Yes. Another followed fast, from the direction of the lookout, their echoes harsh, slightly muted, in the silence of the countryside. Could I see the tower with the binocs from the attic? It would be a while until dawn.

I leaped from my bed, into yesterday's clothes, and snatched the Beretta from my nightstand. Jerking open my door, I collided with a huge strange man in the hall. I stared down the barrel of his gun and recoiled. "Shit, Dad."

The apparition in the hall wore camo, his face streaked with green and black. The only thing I recognized was his Uzi.

"Sorry, Katie." The gun barrel dropped. The muscles in his face were rigid, set in harsh planes.

"Those were shots …?" I said, but it wasn't a question. Not really. Unmistakable smells of gun oil, metals, leather and paint filled the hall. Other unfamiliar scents drifted from his room. *Scents of war? Or warriors?*

"Don't know what we've got, Katie. Keep Lu with you, I'm taking Terror. Get the shotgun and your rifle. Keep the Beretta close too – better yet, wear it. Protect your mother. Keep your head down, stay away from the windows. And keep her still."

How am I supposed to do that? The *mad* stirred, hot and angry. "Where are you going?"

"To see."

"But you're shot." This uniform had a light brown-gray pattern, baggy pantlegs tucked into unfamiliar tan boots. A bandolier, with a small 's' insignia, crossed his body, his skinning knife sheathed at his belt. The tops of knife handles protruded from half-a-dozen pockets on his weapons rig, his clothing. The Ruger nestled in its holster on his right hip, his Glock sat in another on his left. He cradled his Uzi in a large arm. Dad had a silencer on every gun.

My knees trembled, threatened to drop me on my ass. I stiffened them, hung on to the wall. *This stranger is death on two legs.*

"I'm fine," he said. "This must be done. I'm the one who can." With a deft motion to Terror, he slipped down the stairs silent as the first flakes of snow. The only sound I heard, the click-click-click of dog claws on wood.

Dad's voice drifted up the stairwell, soft as an afterthought. "Don't let the other day bother you. You shoot. And Katie, Lu will tell you if it's not me coming in. Don't hesitate."

With the hinges and locks so well oiled, I almost didn't hear the back door close. I did hear the turns of the keys. Then I heard "Hoolah, loolah."

The *mad* stirred again, prickled the tops of my ears. Heat crawled my neck. I shoved the anger away.

"Dammittohell," I snarled, sucked it up and went to quiet my mother.

Mom waited on her end of the couch; I sat on mine. I got up, prowled the room. Stopped, then sat down again.

"Will he be okay, Katie?"

"Sure, Mom. It's Dad we're talking about."

The sound of muffled firecrackers brought me straight up from my chair. Lu surged to her feet, hackles stiff and hard beneath my palm.

Brrrt. One burst of three. The sound of Dad's Uzi – I know, I've fired it.

A single crack split the air.

Brrrt. Brrrt.

Black dots, or maybe white brilliants on an ebony background, spun behind my eyelids. "God, it's Dad," I blurted. *Breathe, Katie. Dammit.* My dry mouth tasted like chalk.

"Hoolah, loolah," screamed my mother.

"Shut up," I snapped. "I have to listen."

The silence stretched beyond bearing, like salt water taffy pulled at the fair.

Brrrt. Brrrt. The Uzi told me my father still lived. *Unless someone's killed him and stolen his gun. Should I take Lu and go? No … Dad knows what he's doing. And I have my mother to protect.*

I turned to see her eyes stretched wide. Tears ran fast, dripping off her chin. *Ah, shit!* Shame bloomed hot on my face.

"Mom, I'm sorry I yelled. I didn't mean it, I was scared. It just came out."

"It's okay," she said but her voice quivered.

I put Lu at the door to guard, wrapped my mother in my arms and held her for a long time while she cried herself in and out of the shudders. Then I led her to the couch.

"See if you can sleep a bit," I coaxed. I shook a pill from the bottle on Dad's table and handed it to her. "Take this, Mom. Lie down." I covered her with the fleece blanket, kissed her cheek.

I waited in the porch swing, my guns in my hands, Lupine at my feet.

"You should have Lupine watching the back door," came the dark voice.

"Maybe," I said. "But I want her here. She'll let me know if anything is wrong."

Dawn's pale streaks turned the sky purple, slate blue, then silver. Against the horizon, puffs of cirrus clouds glowed, backlit with red-orange, then apricot, then pink.

I brewed coffee on the Coleman stove, sat in the swing, and drank three cups. I checked my watch, checked it again. It seemed to be working but I swear three days passed since dawn instead of three hours. Still no Dad.

I went inside to check on my mother.

Except for the one exchange of gunfire, things stayed quiet. Too quiet, maybe.

Mom snoozed on the couch, the deep sleep of the medicated.

I fretted. *What if the extra pill I gave her was too much on top of her regular meds?* I moved close, watched the rise and fall of her chest. Even, easy. Probably okay. I studied her beautiful face, smooth, and unlined, searching for traces of myself. I didn't find them.

I paced, checked the windows, paced some more. Lupine stretched full length on the floor and took a nap. But I didn't relax until my wolf sat up on her rug, stood and wagged her tail. She moved to peer out the window.

I slipped to her side and saw, first Terror, then Dad, break free of the trees and head to the house. He came in fast, a big man managing to stay low and silent. I caught and held my breath in appreciation of his skill. My stealth father.

"You might want to wait," said my mindvoice when I reached for Mom's shoulder. "Until you talk to your Dad and see how it went."

"They're okay," I said. "I'm waking her up." I wrapped my hand around her shoulder, squeezed gently.

"Dad's back, Mom," I whispered. "I'm going to unlock the door."

"Okay," she whispered. My rational Mom looked out through her eyes.

"Thank you, God," I breathed, racing across the house.

Lupine shadowed me so tight her fur brushed my thigh.

I threw the locks and bolts, pulled the kitchen door open. A gust of wind blew ferrous stench inside, my father followed the stink. My stomach bucked in protest.

Damn it. The darkness knew. I should have left Mom asleep.

Dark blotches covered Dad's pants, his camo shirt plastered wet and black against his torso. A large clot of dirt fell on Mom's shining linoleum.

How in hell did I miss seeing the blood?

Coarse hairs around T-dog's muzzle and mouth were stiff with dried scarlet, turning his gray fur to near ebony. A red raw line marked one massive shoulder.

"Shit," I said without a thought for my language. "Terror's hurt. Are you?"

"I'm fine. His wound is shallow. He gave more than he got."

Relief oozed like honey from my tight-wound nerves. "I'll get the first aid kit for him." Then I realized I'd sworn in front of my father. "I'm sorry …." I said, lifting my gaze.

When I met Dad's eyes, normally snapping sparks of good humor, all I found were two dead black pools.

Shackles of iron gripped my throat.

"Trouble, Katie. Bad people scavenging the tower. And a lot of them got away – gone before I even got there. I never saw them."

"I heard shots …. What about …?" Another look at my father and I knew.

Mr. and Mrs. Wills – oh God, Todd – my bright shining key to the outside world. They are dead. Dead. Dead. Dead.

Blood thundered in my ears. A dark swirl clouded my eyes, I reached for balance. Found nothing. But I think strong arms caught me.

Next thing I knew, I blinked up at Mom's face. I lay flat on my back in the hall, my head in her lap. *She's pulled it together. Please God, make it last.*

"It's okay, baby. You just fainted." She stroked my face, crooning the soft comforting words of my childhood.

Too calm, she is. She doesn't know. And she can't. We can't tell her.

"Where's Dad?"

"Gone to the barn, then the basement. He had things to do. You okay?" Her forehead creased in concern. So incredibly normal. Just so fast, she again became the good-mother of memory.

"Yeah, thanks." I pushed up, shook my head to clear the fuzz. "Does he need me to help?"

"He said when you woke up, we should go under the house. He said bring your pistol and the first aid kit so we'll have one down there. He took care of Terror's shoulder. What happened out there?"

"I don't know, Mom." I rubbed my freezing hands on my shorts; swallowed hard. "Dad didn't tell me." *It's not really a lie. Dad never said a word.*

After lunch, Dad took T-dog and left to go hunting. "Try to get a deer."

My guess – he'd be hunting bad folk. I didn't have the nerve to ask and he didn't volunteer.

Mom's coffee perked fragrant on the wood stove. She'd gone under the house to work on storing our supplies.

I splashed water on my face, brushed my teeth and pulled my long hair back in a tail. "Out to do chores," I called, caught a muffled answer from the basement. *She'll probably try to make me stay inside.* I rushed out the back door and crossed the yard to the chicken coop.

The sun warmed me, it usually made me smile. I tried, but my face felt stiff. I told myself life wasn't so bad, really.

"What about the Wills'?" snarled the voice in my head.

"Well, things are bound to get better," I said. "They sure couldn't get any worse."

I'd just scattered a cup of grain for Mrs. Cluck and crew and turned them out into the small fenced pasture. In my basket were six fresh eggs.

Beside me, Lu gave a terrible growl, hackles raised, lips peeled back from her fangs.

Fear clamped an icy hand around my throat.

I flinched, pulled into a crouch. Unthinking, I clutched my basket, gave Lupine the hand signal meaning *run close to me.* Keeping in Dad's low soldier mode, I streaked for the porch.

I'd left the back door ajar despite Mom's constant nagging me to always close it. Good mistake to make – I didn't have to stop long enough to open it.

Something whizzed past my ear and thunked into the doorjamb just as we dashed through. My lungs froze.

Lu snarled, spun and tried for outside.

I grabbed a huge handful of fur, hauled her back. Slammed the door. Threw the bolt.

"Shit!" *Did someone just shoot at me? Where is Dad? Gun. I need a gun.*

My knees turned to water. I staggered, braced against Lupine and put the eggs on the floor. On automatic, I reached up and threw the second deadbolt. Giving my wolf the *down and guard the door* command, I crawled to the window and peeked out.

The nasty growl beside me escalated into full rumble.

"Oh God, oh God, oh God." *Mom, please stay in the basement.*

Three bearded men stood at the edge of the forest. Crude black barbed-wire tattoos covered a fat man's forehead, two sported full arm sleeves, and all three necks bore skulls-pierced-by-daggers tats. They wore prison-orange jumpsuits with the sleeves cut out.

Cold suffused my body; the inside of my mouth tasted like oily metal. *Where did they come from? Oh God, I was so careless.*

Ragged, dirty, carrying rifles, they advanced from the woods on an angle toward our house. Relaxed, cocky. Sure of themselves.

I watched them, needing to pee, my heart banging my breastbone.

"Get your goddamned gun," snarled the mindvoice.

"This is a decent place," one of the men said. "We could stay here easy."

"Did you see that girl?"

"Yeah, skinny little thing. Hope we can take her alive." The fat man's voice slurred, mouth slack, like saliva drooled. "Keep her for a while."

I felt his lust like a punch in the belly. *Where in hell is Dad?*

"Been lonely since the last one died." The shortest one said.

"In which case," the first guy said. "I hope your shot missed, you idiot."

My brain stuttered while it interpreted what they discussed. *Me? For a playing?* My stomach clenched. *Not a chance in hell.*

"She's got a big dog."

"They die easy with a bullet."

My *mad* roared awake. My vision went strange, like I looked through a sheet of red cling-wrap. *Threaten Lupine? I'll kill you.*

"Spread out, we'll rush the door."

Where is my Beretta? In my fucking bedroom. Stupid, stupid, stupid.

But on the table at my side, lay the little Jennings .22. Small, light, and loaded with hollow-point bullets. *Put enough of them in someone,* my father once said. *And they will die.*

I picked up the gun and noticed – as if it belonged to someone else – the trembling of my hand. No, the damn thing shook. I heard a high huh-huh-huh sound; realized it matched my panting.

"Katie." Dad's voice came low, pitched to carry. "I see you through the window. I'm on the far side of the house. I don't have a shot yet. If you do, go back to the kitchen and take it now."

Just his words, hearing his voice, settled me. My hands were still sweaty but they no longer shook. Palming the gun, I slid across the floor, crawled to my spot below the window. Peeked out.

The glass pane exploded.

"Don't kill her, Herman. You stupid bastard. We want her alive!"

I jerked back, felt blood run warm down my face. Brushing sticky strands of hair from my eyes, I led with the gun and looked again. The men were ten feet from the porch.

The leader spat on the ground, and I saw brown grotty stuff on his teeth. I gagged.

"Hey, girlie? Might as well open the door." the fat one called.

"When cows dance the cha-cha," I whispered and snorted at my wit.

Lupine lay beside me, like I ordered. But she vibrated, the unceasing growl vicious in its promise. *I can't let her out, they'll kill her. This is up to me.*

Arm quivering, hand trembling, I grabbed a deep breath. Held it. Dad said shoot. *I will not be taken.* I exhaled, controlled and easy.

Slowing my focus, I sighted in on the middle one's chest. The one who threatened my best friend.

Easy, easy, I heard Dad's voice in memory. *Just squeeeeze the trigger.*

My lips moved, I think I chanted, "you sonofabitch, you sonofabitch, you sonofabitch." Then I shot him.

I don't know which of us was more surprised when scarlet bloomed across his shirt front. My heart hammered, pounded in my head.

He gaped down at the big hole in his chest.

"Fuck you," I whispered. I gasped a single breath, controlled it. Then I sighted in on him again. I gave him two more, laid my bullets in the tightest triangle pattern I could.

He screamed, eyes fixed on his bloody mess of a chest. Then he folded, like a cheap plastic chair, collapsed in a lump on the lawn.

"Oh well done," congratulated the dark voice.

My insides started to quiver.

The others stared at him, their faces first chalk white in shock, then scarlet in fury. Two rifle barrels aimed at my window.

"Don't stop now," coached the voice in my head.

I had a better line on the short one. I sighted and fired, but my hand trembled so bad the shot went wide.

His shoulder twitched and the rifle arced from his hand like Lu's Frisbee when I threw it. Then I saw scarlet. *Winged him.*

Terror's deep growling bark sounded outside.

Brrrt. Brrrt. Red blotches stitched across the men's torsos – from left to right. Brrrt. Brrrt. Dad's silenced Uzi.

They crumpled, slow, like life-size deflating human balloons.

Phffft. Phffft. Dad's Glock.

Two burnt-red colored holes appeared in their foreheads. Then another pair of shots and holes. Dad double-tapped them, just like he taught me.

My guts turned inside out, shoved bile into my throat. I swallowed hard against it but I knew it wouldn't work. Clamping a hand over my mouth, I sprinted for the bathroom.

Chapter Nine

My father's arm around my shoulders, one callused hand cupping my forehead, I vomited everything I think I ever ate. In my whole life. *I killed a person. Oh God, oh God, oh God.*

Lu whined and shoved against my shoulder.

I threw up again. Strings of thin bitter bile and drool. Harsh dry-heaves racked me and refused to stop.

Somewhere in the background I heard, "Hoolah, loolah." Over and over and over. *Mom's tether on reality's slipped big time.*

I wiped my mouth. "Did she see?" I whispered. "Did she see what I did?"

"Never mind, Katie. I dragged two into the woods before she saw. I said there was only one and I killed him." Dad exhaled, deep and relieved. "Bonus, though. None of the three were sick – at least not showing symptoms. I'll go out later and bury them."

I couldn't get past my mother's craziness to process the good news. "Did she believe …?" Nausea surged again, I swallowed hard against it. "Will she forgive you? She … her religion … murder …."

"This is my fault." Dad's voice held regret. "I decided to detour and scout on the way home. I came in on the wrong damn side of the house."

From years of habit, I waved a negating hand at him. "You couldn't know …."

"God in Heaven. Hoolah, loolah."

My father cut his eyes toward Mom and his face twisted, a muscle leaping in his jaw. For a second, something terrifying passed behind his eyes. Then it smoothed, calmed and my self-disciplined father returned.

The *mad* struck. Tears of rage flooded my eyes.

"Dammit, Dad," I gritted. "I hate this. Hate being stuck out here in the middle of nowhere. Hate taking care of her. Hate being weak and stupid and scared. I hate you for putting me in this position." I burst into sobs.

"Your anger is understandable, Katie," my father said. "I'm surprised you haven't said anything before. But this was … is … the only way to keep you and your mother safe."

"Why?"

"Some time we'll talk. This isn't it." He squeezed the back of my neck, rubbed my shoulders. "You had to shoot. Never doubt it. Working through taking a life – especially the first time – requires time. It'll come right, you'll see. If I hadn't come back … well, you'd have handled them. Saved yourself – and your mother too."

One scarred hand wiped my face with a damp washcloth. I inhaled the fragrance of laundry detergent. *Heavenly. It blocks the stink of vomit.* A glass of water appeared in front of me. I gulped, rinsed and spat. Several times.

"Katie, I puked after my first kill. Everybody does."

So casual? My father didn't seem to notice my sharp intake of breath.

"It's hard, I know," he continued. "You are blameless, they forced you to it."

"I s-s-shot him, Dad." Searching his face, I found it set. A hard and unforgiving mask. But in his eyes, I saw approval. "I … shouldn't I feel awful?"

"How do you feel?" At another chorus from my mother he said, "Hush, Sharon. Everything is fine. Could you fix us a bite to eat?"

"Of course," Mom launched from the bathroom. "I'll go put something together."

Dad fixed his ebony eyes on mine and waited for my answer.

What was the question? Oh yeah, how do I feel?

"Sick," I said. "It was gross, all the blood." I gagged again. "But what they said, what they wanted to do. I guess I should be sorry, but I'm not. But I have to get my Beretta from my bedroom. Right now."

"Good girl," he said and patted my back. "Tomorrow, I have to begin teaching you … well, everything. Things I never wanted you to know – things no young woman should need to learn." Dad's mouth worked, then pinched like he tasted something nasty. "But for now, Katie, if you're up to it, we should go reassure your mother."

How? Even when her mind isn't quite right, she never fails to spot a lie.

Pans banged in the kitchen. Bowls clattered.

Dad took my elbow in a gentle grasp, and guided me into the kitchen. "Sit, Katie," he said and pulled out my chair.

I did. *He's acting like nothing happened. How in hell do I match that?*

Mom put three bowls of chili, a plate of cornbread and a basket of fruit on the table.

"Smells wonderful, Sharon," my father said and gave her a hug. He seated her; then himself.

I couldn't eat.

Mom and Dad did. Then, my father slipped her a pill and waited until she faded into sleep.

"Going to do a little housekeeping," he said. "It won't take long."

He was gone less than an hour. Dad went straight upstairs, and when he came back, he reeked of disinfectant.

"Phew," I said and looked the question at him.

"No rash, no symptoms anywhere on them," he said. "I think we're fine."

Then he took me into the woods and taught me things that twisted my mind. Far different from my former lessons. How to kill using ordinary objects – anything at hand. A shoelace or a piece of string. And, depending on what you needed to achieve, about a zillion uses for a knife and where in the human body to stick it.

"Jam a pencil into your assailant's eye, Katie," he said. "Hard as you can. He won't bother you anymore, and he could die. If not, he'll be distracted enough so you can shoot him."

He took me into the woods, chased me, taught me more ways to evade, how to set lethal traps for pursuers.

"Never, never, let anyone get hold of you, Katie. Ever." Then his face slid into those hard planes of muscle, and a wintry, detached soldier stared into my eyes. "But," he said. "If someone does, your elbow is the hardest bone in your body. It's lethal – use it in all those vulnerable places I've showed you. Your forehead, headbutted into another's face, is virtually indestructible. It will put your enemy out, and if you strike hard enough, it can kill."

At the thought of the three men, cold sweat slid down my spine and I reached down, laid a hand on my Beretta. For comfort.

Dad caught my shiver. "If Lu or Terror growls," he said. "Shoot first, to kill. No hesitation. The dogs know good from bad. Trust them."

For the next two days, when we could slip away from Mom, and during the night while she slept, I followed my father's relentless instructions.

Even with Lupine by my bed, exhausted from Dad's lessons, I couldn't sleep. The attack by the awful men filled me with terror; yanked me, mumbling and thrashing, from the lightest doze. My morning glances in the mirror reflected eyes too big for my face, ringed with dark circles.

The second morning after the three convicts found our place, Mom threw Dad and me out of the kitchen and started cooking.

"Let's go to the barn," he said. "There's something I need to do."

He gathered a few tools, and I watched – taking mental notes – while he disabled our International pickup, the Army jeep and the Kawasaki.

"What about the tractor, Dad?"

"It shouldn't appeal to people interested in moving through, or traveling fast."

Okay, that makes sense. I watched him remove the distributor caps and tires, helped him load them in the tractor bucket. I rode, standing on the back, while he drove into the woods, dug a hole and buried the tires. I memorized the location: the nearby juniper with Dad's knife nick in its bark and the tiny cairn of pebbles beside it.

It felt like we marked a grave.

"Why, Dad?"

"If we have to run, we need vehicles that work. Vehicles that can't be stolen." One of his caterpillar brows lifted in question.

Shit. What does he mean? He obviously expected me to figure it out. The little idea 'light bulb' flashed in my brain.

"Ah," I said. "They can't drive our stuff away without tires or parts."

"Right."

"But we can put them back together and they'll work just fine."

"Right again."

We headed for home and on the way Dad paused, gave me an enigmatic glance, shifted a pair of rocks and exposed a heavy-duty plastic container. He hid the distributor caps and the hand pump for our underground gas tank inside.

I had both keys and answers. *Why?* My heart dropped into my boots. Dad wanted me ready to take charge if something happened to him.

No, I won't. I'll be the one leaving.

For days, Dad drugged Mom and locked her in their bedroom with T-dog to guard.

For days we did strength training, jogged in the woods with backpacks, climbed the bluffs and scaled the rocky outcroppings and boulders in the Painted Canyon. *How will I keep this up without sleep?*

For days, we practiced martial arts and fighting dirty. I'd never been so sore, so creaky stiff.

"Can you get to your secret cave without me catching you?" The corners of Dad's eyes crinkled with his grin.

"I'll try." *I doubt it.*

He caught me half-way there. But the next time we tried it, I almost made it. With each outing, I knew I got faster, my reaction times increased.

How is this possible? I'm too tired to think. My mind felt disembodied.

"Fatigue induces endorphins," whispered the darkness inside. "You have reserves you haven't begun to touch."

"I think I'm going crazy. Bad as Mom – maybe worse," I whispered back. "What about that?"

"Pay attention to your father," it said. "He's got more to show you."

"He's got more to tell me, too," I snarled under my breath, then flinched at his voice.

"What?"

I lifted my chin, met his eyes. "Something happened years ago. I need to know what – you owe me that much."

"No," he said. "Trust me on this. Not yet."

"I don't believe you," I growled. "But never mind." The tops of my ears tingled.

He slanted a look, shook his head. "Katie ...." Concern colored the word.

"No," I spat. "Leave me alone. Get on with your lectures."

My father opened his mouth, closed it again. Drew one deep breath, then spoke. "You might have to run – maybe a long way," Dad said. "You have to be strong."

"Yes," I nodded. "I can, I am." *But what about Mom?*

A scrape sounded, startling in the quiet of the woods. Perhaps an elk or antelope hoof on rock. My father stilled, silent as death. He didn't breathe. Instead, on the instant, he blended, became part of the countryside. One moment he stood there before me, the next he ceased to be.

I have to learn this ... invisibility. I copied him, tried to melt into the bushes. I only moved my eyes, fixed them on T-dog and Lu. When they didn't react, I relaxed. Cutting my gaze sideways, I saw Dad did too.

When we sparred, it took all the control I maintained over Lupine to keep her from attacking my father. *Holy Christ, I think she'd kill him. Even though she knows him.*

Lu knew when each strike connected.

I swallowed my grunts, but she knew and it made her crazy. She'd lift, noiseless, from her belly on the ground spot, rising to crouch, powerful legs bunched beneath her. *All she needs is one leap to be on Dad. That I cannot have. For many reasons.*

"Down, Lupine. Stay." I reassured and reassured.

She whined and grumbled, but obeyed.

I acquired bruises on my bruises but I got fast ... and wary ... and good.

And one day, during our sparring, I scored on Dad.

Those furry caterpillar brows hitched toward his hairline.

"Gotcha," I snarked. My heart did a happy dance in my chest. *I really did get him. I really did!*

"Graduation day," he said and the corner of his mouth quirked. "Good girl."

We ran home, Lupine paced us, ranging ahead.

Dad never faltered, never tired.

I knew his goal, well, besides building my endurance. He needed to get home, get the bedroom door unlocked before Mom woke.

The man is inhuman. I refused to falter, or fall even a half-step behind. I flagged, fought for air and pushed through my fatigue. Pride forced me beyond my limits.

"Oh my," Mom said, coming down the stairs. She entered the kitchen where Dad and I sat at the table. Pushing her hair back with one small hand, she added, "Did I fall asleep again? What in the world is the matter with me?"

"Not a thing," Dad stood and kissed her.

She blushed, fluttered her hands and asked, "Leftovers for dinner, okay? Then I can start cooking again tomorrow?"

The unexpected smile on my father's face softened it, erased his formidable mien.

"Perfect, Sharon," he said. "I'm tired. I'd like to get to bed early."

"Sounds good," Mom said. And blushed.

I thought of Todd and how he made me feel. Opportunity and joy gone, I couldn't watch them anymore.

"Think I'll go clean up," I said.

Fatigue rode the marrow of my bones. I should have slept the second my head touched the pillow. Instead, memories of Todd tormented; my body throbbed with desire. When I managed to put thoughts of his kisses aside, worry about strangers took their place.

I fell asleep at three am and woke to Mom calling me for breakfast at six. I poured water from my bucket into my sink, washed my face, brushed my teeth and made a face at the pair of raccoon eyes staring back from the mirror. I pulled on clean clothes and headed to the kitchen. After we ate, Dad got the radio and cranked it up. When the emergency broadcast finally came, confirming Dad's worst fears, I wished we'd missed it.

A loud voice blared and we all flinched. "Stay in your homes," a man said. "Do not attempt to leave your area."

I looked at my father, saw his face sag. He shoved a hand through his hair.

"I'll have to try for Nyssa," Dad said, his tone resigned. "If it's not flooded. Buy anything I can, but mostly find information."

"Don, please don't go." Mom clung to his sleeve. "This whole thing is beginning to scare me."

It's just now beginning to scare her? I felt the old resentment stir inside. *Dear God, does she live in a bubble? I've been terrified for two weeks.* But something hard and mean was awake inside now. Instead of fear, I owned fury.

I helped my father replace the tires and distributor cap on the International.

Dad took money plus a lot of our spare change. He put his Ruger on the seat, laid the Glock beside it; settled his rifle and Uzi in the gun rack. Motioning Terror to the passenger seat, he drove down the hill, headed toward town.

We passed the time, my mother and I, mostly exchanging glances. I worried she'd do something irrational. We tried to talk but couldn't find a comfortable subject. I knew she worried for Dad. I did too. For once, she didn't quiz me or try to give me orders.

"Not that I'm ungrateful," I whispered to Lu. "It just makes me wonder what she's thinking."

"Consider it from her side," said my mindvoice. "She's helpless without your father and knows it. She has no idea how capable you are. No wonder she panics when he leaves. She thinks somehow she must take care of you because she's the parent. And she knows she can't."

I considered my mother with new eyes.

"I'm going to treat her better, Lu." Carrying my rifle, wolf at my side, I paced the yard, then worked the protective trees around the house. *I just wish someone bad would show up – I'm sick and tired of waiting and worrying about it. I'd like to get it over with – or maybe just have something to do besides be on high alert every second.*

"You are getting crazier every day, Katie," said the voice in my head. "You need sleep."

"Yeah, I know. I'd love to. What do you suggest, drug myself like Mom? Then who protects us, tell me that?" I snarled and felt the hardness in my mind shrivel.

"Katie?" Mom called.

"On my way."

"I need a few things from downstairs," she said. "Could you get into the survival boxes – get some canned things?"

"Sure, Mom. What do you need?"

"Butter, evaporated milk. Flour, salt, yeast and sugar. Some dark chocolate. That should do it." Mom grinned. "Making venison chili, some cream puffs with lemon custard filling, drizzled with the chocolate. What do you think?"

"Yum," I said. "Sounds wonderful."

"She's really upset," said the dark little voice in my soul. "You guys can eat for a week on all this."

Mom made us each a sandwich for lunch. I carried mine to the front porch and found a wolf eyeing it with interest. Then, Lupine stilled, head up, eyes focused in the distance.

Someone's coming. I'm ready this time. I set my plate on the little table, slipped into the house without Mom seeing me. I lifted the binocs from their hook, draped the strap around my neck and snagged the rifle by the door.

Cold fingers tickled my spine.

Lu watched the road – like me, she didn't know whether the incoming vehicle held friend or enemy. I perched on the top rail of the porch, glasses fixed on the truck. Our old pickup came into focus, then I recognized Dad's ballcap. Next to him in the passenger seat (if you didn't look too close) sat a large shaggy old man. I melted in relief.

"Dad's back," I called, poking my head through the kitchen door. The smile I got lit the room … hell, the entire house.

"Can't leave my baking," Mom muttered. "My cream puffs will fall."

"S'okay," I said. "He's still a ways out." I went back to the porch to finish my sandwich and welcome him home.

A different Dad crawled from our truck. He'd aged, terribly, in four hours. Rigid muscle under the skin of his face etched lines like an ancient man. One grim shake of his head and my father went inside.

My face and shoulders and heart drooped in imitation as I followed him.

Mom met him in the hall. "What, Don?" she said, voice rising in pitch.

"What is it?"

"The south part of Nyssa is still flooded. Most of the people I know are gone, taking their chances on the back roads, heading to California." Dad dropped into a chair, his movements graceless.

"Why?" Mom's big eyes were too wide. She pressed one palm against her cheek, the other clutched my father's shoulder.

"They're worried about wintering here without power or natural gas but they are more worried about the gangs. I asked about the blockades. They said the soldiers caught The Great Awful and died. No one is manning the checkpoints, there is no law enforcement. Not anymore."

So we're free to go? I opened my mouth, then shut it again. Upset and discouraged, Dad forgot he'd kept secrets from Mom. He'd just blurted it all out. *Maybe she won't catch on.*

"Is that good, Don? Should we leave too?" My mother's voice trembled, too high, too breathy. "What is the great awful? What is so awful?" She piled baking dishes in the sink, then stared at her shaking hands like she'd never seen them before.

"Nothing's awful, Sharon. And no, we shouldn't leave here," Dad said. "At least not yet We've got enough food for a couple of years. The folk who are staying have boarded up their places and stockpiled supplies." Dad picked up a piece of bread and began to tear it into small pieces. "They've already fought defending their homes."

"Say something to stop him, you stupid twit," snapped the mindvoice.

I can't think what or how.

"Defend from whom, Don?"

"Prison inmates, local boys, or men with a bad streak."

Mom made a small, hurt sound and wrapped her arms around her body.

Dad's eyes were faraway, reliving something we couldn't see. "Like the people at the lookout."

"God," I breathed and saw my Mom's chest heave, way too fast.

"Dad ..." I finally squeaked and saw his eyes cut in her direction.

My father's face changed, just so quick. An 'oh shit' expression crossed it, replaced by resolve. Calm demeanor back in place, he said, "Sharon, we will be just fine."

The furrow between her brows smoothed, her pinched face relaxed. She gave Dad a tremulous smile.

Okay, it worked for her. But he didn't convince me.

Chapter Ten

We sat around the kitchen table, coffee and muffins before us. My nerves jangled, my stomach pitched. Normally, I can't get enough coffee, but today it made me nauseous.

"We have a better chance way out here – far better than the townspeople," he said. "But we've got to get ready. And do it fast."

That part I believed. Oh yes, I did.

"We'll set up in the basement," Dad said. "We'll take everything we need there."

Dad went to the barn, came back carrying a large metal box painted Army green and grunted his way down the stairs. T-dog followed him, dropping hay straws everywhere.

Where was that hidden? What's in it? In the rush to create our safe area, I forgot to investigate.

Every scrap of food, our weapons and ammunition, linens, towels, blankets, medical supplies, the bags of dog chow – it all went below ground.

"Sharon, can you devise a way to make the basement half-windows invisible from the outside?" Dad asked. "Otherwise, we won't dare use the lanterns after dark."

"Let me think about it. Must be something I can do." She went to the barn, came back pushing the wheelbarrow. A roll of black tar-paper, heavy shears and Dad's industrial-size staple gun lay in the bottom.

Give her something non-threatening to do, something she knows how to do, and she's good. But when her mind wanders ... then it all goes to hell.

Mom tacked a double layer of the heavy paper over the little basement windows. Then she cut a dark brown blanket into rectangles and stapled those over the top. "Go outside, Katie. Tell me what you see."

I sprinted through the house, inspected carefully; vaulted back down the stairs. "Great job, Mom. Can't see a thing." She high-fived me – my parents' old adult thing. My heart jumped happy in my chest at her smile.

"We have to remember to check tonight, see if our lanterns show through anywhere," she said. "But I think it's good."

Dad gave her a huge squeeze and a kiss hard enough to make heat creep my neck. I thought of Todd and looked away.

"Okay, this is perfect," Dad said. "But, the windows could be broken."

Shit, he's right. They were half-size, true. No way a man large as my father could crawl through. *Problem is, I can and so can a lot of smaller people.* I did a quick count – three sides of the basement with four windows per side – a total of twelve.

"Dad? Could we board them up?"

"Then we couldn't see out, or shoot through them, if we needed to. Plus, it would be a dead giveaway that someone's hiding inside."

"Damn," I said, then raised my hand before she chirped. "Sorry, Mom. Sorry." *I've killed a man and I apologize for saying damn?*

"What do we do?" Mom's voice wavered again.

"We build a reinforced inner room with a heavy door," he said. "Don't worry."

Then we're trapped in here? The inside of my mouth dried like the Sahara. *Nonono. That's worse.*

"Stupid Katie," chided the dark mindvoice. "It's better than dead."

I hate when it's right.

Dad and I carried in timbers from the barn. The three of us built an ordinary appearing but solid reinforced wood wall across the back, right in front of the root cellar. Hiding behind it was a smaller room. Dad created a short narrow, triple-layer door using the zig-zag pattern of wood lengths to disguise it.

"Nail those 2 x 4's on the doorframe, Katie. Then nail the second layer crosswise."

"Holy Crow, Dad. It's heavy. Take a bomb to get through it."

"Not quite," he actually chuckled. "But close. It'll stop bullets. Exactly what we need."

He'd framed a spot in the bottom right corner of the wall for the door, with netting and ropes dangling from a ceiling hook to hide the hinges.

I edged close to my father and whispered, "We can't lift it. How do we hang it in the frame?"

"I have an idea," he said. Another trip to the barn, and Dad jury-rigged a pry-bar, ropes and a pulley and wedge.

Mom guided us. We got the door vertical. Then came the fight to mesh the hinge halves. Because of the weight, Dad used five sets – hinges on the door jamb, eyes on the heavy door. We got four sets perfectly aligned. But no way would the fifth slide in place. I swear the damn thing weighed more than Ferdinand, a local bull.

We were all huffing, short of breath when Mom said, "Hold it right there, just a second. Can you guys balance it?"

"Yes," Dad grunted.

She took off on a run up the stairs.

I didn't have enough air to answer. My muscles shrieked, still rock solid but tiny quivers threatened. The in-between place approached, the time where my will could no longer force my body. When muscles dissolve, go loose and slack.

"You're gonna drop it," breathed the darkness. "It'll crush your father."

I will not. I will not. My head sang from oxygen deprivation, but I didn't let go.

"Oh Lord," Dad said, taking the words right out of my mind. "I hope she didn't forget us."

Seemed like years before Mom raced back, Dad's sixteen-pound sledge hammer gripped in both hands. Squaring off, my slender mother grunted, lifted the hammer overhead and gave the resistant latch one hell-of-a-good whack. The door slid into place, smooth as anything and Mom drove the hinge pins home.

"There isn't much you can't fix with a sledge," she laughed. "Don, you said so yourself."

My lungs burned, heaving like bellows. I sneaked a peek at my father and saw he rested his head in his hands, panting like Terror in the summer heat. And then he laughed too.

"Good job, Mom," I wheezed. Breathing, speaking and chortling all at the same time.

The way her eyes lit, the grin threatening to split her face, broke my heart because it was tenuous. How long before she slipped away from us again?

But Dad guffawed, and distracted me. We congratulated ourselves, and did the high-five thing again – this time all around.

"You know, Dad," I wheezed. "If I didn't know the door was there, I would never see it."

"Thanks, Katie. Let me catch my breath," he said. "And I'll go get the chem toilet."

"Aw … ewww," I groaned and Mom snorted.

"Just in case, Katie." He winked. "JIC."

My mother settled sleeping bags on our three camp cots. They were comfortable enough except Dad's feet hung off the end. *Glad I'm shorter.* Three fruit crates, set on end, made nightstands, complete with flashlights. Humming *Somewhere Over The Rainbow,* Mom put our new home together. When she hit the refrain again, she winked at me and sang, *Somewhere under the Davis house.*

I lost control, laughed way harder than the joke deserved. So wonderful to have her mind right, have her happy.

Mom set up our card table and chairs, rearranged our supplies around the room's walls.

Dad came inside, saw she was good and waited. We relished Mom's company all through dinner, and for most of the evening too, before something twisted-up wrong in her mind.

I watched my father's face go blank and slack. Like someone cut the muscles and let his life leak away. His sigh, so deep and desolate, ripped me apart.

He gave Mom her nightly sleeping pill and tucked her in one of the beds.

We waited for her breathing to go slow and regular before we sneaked into the attic. All night we watched the countryside, cranked the radio and listened.

My heart thudded, beating way too fast. I realized both anger and fear now drove me. Before, our life wasn't perfect and I complained about things I couldn't have or do, but we'd been in control. Now we didn't even know what we battled.

Lu nudged me awake.

I heard Mom and Dad moving around in the kitchen overhead. I dug in my clean clothes pile, pulled on a pale blue tank and denim shorts, climbed the stairs and joined them for breakfast. We'd just finished eating and were sipping our second cups of coffee when Dad put the radio on the table and cranked it.

I choked mid-swallow when we heard a voice. News broadcast from a small station in Nevada.

"Chemicals and volcanic ash fallout have polluted both air and water in the quarantine section. The physical devastation of the plague has spread beyond one small corner of the United States. This flu is spread by contact or airborne, carried by the outrush of fleeing sick or exposed people. With the cordon failure, the plague has spread into the United States. Reports say it has crossed the Canadian border. I have had reports it has spread as far south as Mexico."

The announcer cleared his throat and continued, "Hospitals are overloaded with incurable people without anyone to treat them. Very few medical personnel escaped the first wave of sickness. Stay in your homes." The broadcaster coughed, and added. "Gangs roam everywhere, they are as dangerous as the plague."

"Jesus H. Christ," Dad whispered, wiping his palms on his pant legs. "It's Armageddon. We're on our own."

"What about your paycheck, Don?" Mom fretted.

"Least of our worries, Sharon."

"But how will anyone …." Her voice faded to nothing, and for the first time I realized the magnitude of the disaster. "The rest of the country …." She said, then stopped. "The rest of the world …."

A terrible thought struck me and my voice went high and breathy. "God, Dad. Can T-dog and Lu catch it?" I'd hoped for good news – I realized it now. I'd been clinging to the idea things would go back the way they were before. Tears blurred my vision. I stared at Dad in shock. Moisture coursed down the new furrows on either side of his mouth.

"Good God, Katie, I don't know." His head drooped, he shook it slowly. "But I don't think so. Around the military base, and all the way home, I never saw a single dead animal."

"What will we do?" Mom asked.

"We're only eighty miles from Boise. We're hard to find up here. If we're vigilant, we'll be okay." Dad laid a hand on her shoulder. "We have land, water and chickens. If wild animals survive, we can hunt. We already grow a lot of our food. Left alone, we'll be fine."

Stay here? Blood pounded in my temples. I pressed the heels of my hands against them making sure they didn't explode. *Stay here - maybe forever? No. I can't.*

Lacing his fingers, Dad first flexed, then cracked his knuckles. "We've got to assume more people will come. Either take our house or steal our food. We have to plan."

"Why would anyone …?" Mom's forehead creased. Something must have triggered a memory, because her eyes widened, then squeezed shut. "No. They can't come here."

Who? Future trespassers? Or ghosts from the past? Icy fingers caressed my body. *Whoever she means, no one will harm her while I live.*

"Take this pill for me, would you, love?" my father asked. "Katie and I are going to handle the chores. We'll weed and water your garden while we're at it." He watched to be sure she swallowed the Xanax. "Lay down for a bit. We'll leave Terror with you."

We went into the woods instead, Lu pacing quiet at my side.

At my raised brow, Dad grinned. "I didn't lie. We'll do chores when we get back. I have things to show you. Better she sleeps while we're gone."

I followed my father's broad back through the junipers and blue pines. His passage brushed and bent needles, releasing the sharp acidic tang of resin and turpentine.

"No scuffs," he said. "Don't leave a trail."

I tried. And failed. A surge of hot crawled up my neck and across my face.

"Don't blush," snapped my demanding little voice. "Concentrate."

The packed pine straw underfoot made it easier because it didn't hold indentations. I tried again.

"Vary the length of your stride, never walk a straight line." My father followed me, coaching. "Step up on that mossy rock, it won't leave a trace. Use the water but remember if you walk upstream in it, you leave a mud trail on the down side."

I stepped wrong, twisted my ankle on a stone, caught my balance with a hand on a boulder.

"Don't dislodge the rocks," came his implacable voice. "Exposed bugs will give you away."

I got better. And the ground I messed up, I brushed away with the pine bough Dad gave me. Sap oozed on my hand.

Dad saw me rubbing the spot and winked. "Makes good glue, Katie. If you ever need some."

The hot surge of love, the rush of pride, caught me off guard. Sometimes, it surprised me how much I cared. *Yes, Dad's a hard man. I hate his rules. But I'm sure he has excellent reasons.*

I made a vow, right then, to learn everything he taught – no matter how hard. Dad gave me the chance to live. Leaving, the thing I wanted most, might not happen as I'd imagined.

Whenever Mom slept, I trained with my father. Sniper skills to augment the shooting I already knew. I used his ghillie suit – camo covered with leaves that made it blend with the foliage – although it hung on me like an elephant's bathrobe. Before this, I'd never imagined so many ways to kill.

Suddenly, my father's scars made awful sense. *Who knew my loving Dad contained so much dark.*

"Why not?" whispered the black kernel. "You have me."

Dad pounded into me why, if threatened or I felt the slightest bit uneasy, I must never hesitate. "Kill them, Katie. Or be killed. The weak die."

Please God, don't let me murder somebody innocent.

After all this training, this knowledge, this darkness – could I find the normal life I wanted? Who would want the person I'd become? Cold, ruthless, calculating. A killer like my father? A man like Dad wouldn't want someone like me – look who he'd chosen. For sure, a college boy like Todd wouldn't. A shudder swept my body, desolation swept my soul.

Without explanation, Dad sent Lupine and me to a spot we'd walked three days before. "I'm going to catch you before you get there," he said.

"Unless I fool you," I laughed, motioned to Lu and took off. We backtracked, slid through the tumbleweeds. My wolf told me when Dad got close and we detoured. We made the designated tree without discovery.

"Great job, Katie!"

I leaped, my breath stopped.

Dad materialized from behind the trunk of a juniper.

My heart did a happy dance at my success, but he scared me so bad I crossed my legs to keep from wetting my pants.

After we stopped laughing, he pointed to a spot on the ground. "What do you see?"

"Nothing."

"Look again."

I shifted, just a quarter-step to one side, and in the dappled sunlight, I caught a tiny glint. I bent, brushed pine needles aside, and revealed a thick metal loop. I furrowed my forehead; waggled my eyebrows at Dad.

I got an exaggerated wink in return. "Closer scrutiny," he said.

I dragged a hand across the pebbled rocky surface, powdery ash gritted against my fingertips. "What …? They don't move …." Brushing at two larger rocks, the loose grasses and coarse sand, I found the outline of a man-sized circle. "Is this what I think?"

"Lift it," he said. "And I'll show you our biggest, best secret."

A metal ladder dropped down the side of a dark hole. At my father's nod, I grabbed the rails and began my descent. Three steps down, I stopped, asked, "How far?" I needed to know because I hate confined, dark places.

"To the bottom," he said, pretending to misunderstand.

I fought my heaving chest, fought to breathe, fought to keep descending until I set a foot on the floor. I sensed, rather than saw, a tunnel leading away from where I stood.

"Okay, I'm there." I stared skyward, saw Lu's silver head filling the opening. Her yellow eyes gleamed.

"Come on back," Dad said.

Out! Out of this dark creepy place. Quick as a monkey, I swarmed the ladder. Checking the inside of the manhole cover, I found four big slide-latches. *Aha.* If needed, we could lock this hatch from the inside. *I know what this has to be.* Crawling over the edge, I pushed to my feet and stepped clear. Tried to calm my galloping heart.

Dad closed the lid and brushed loose pebbles and sand back across the circle's edge; made it invisible again.

My father misses nothing. I didn't make a sound, I didn't move, but he knew my question anyway.

"Exactly a hundred feet, Katie," he said. "From this opening to the one hidden in our basement."

After Mom took her night pills, crawled into her sleeping bag and drifted off, Dad put T-dog and Lu to guard her. Placing a finger against his lips, he motioned me to follow.

A decrepit four-panel door separated our basement safe room from the root cellar. Inside the hand-dug storage area, wood shelving, baskets and bins holding onions, potatoes, apples and carrots lined the dirt walls. The earthen room stayed cool, even in the hottest summer days. On the shelves were rows of jars – canned fruits, vegetables. Mom even canned the rainbow trout we caught in the pond downstream. Strings of garlic and red peppers hung from the ceiling.

There is barely room in here for one person. I pulled air deep through my nose, let it out slow through my mouth. The smell of earth hung heavy in the air. *Damn claustrophobia.* My heartbeat refused to slow.

I watched him tug the lower corner of a narrow shelf on the back wall.

Hidden hinges allowed the entire section to rotate away from the wall. Smooth, quiet. I smelled greased metal.

Dad shifted, moved behind the section of wall.

"Feel here, Katie. Memorize what I do." Dad guided my fingertips across a row of bumps, just an inch above the seam where the wall met the floor. "Pressed in sequence, like this …."

Something clicked. A rectangular outline appeared.

Dad placed both hands on the left side of the door and pulled. It exposed a small concrete room, the ceiling so low he stooped. Passing through, we emerged on the far side, into a dirt tunnel. Again he motioned me to follow. He switched on a flashlight.

Why would we need this? Did Dad build it or was it here before? Or … is this the reason we live here?

My questions must have marched, one by one, across my face.

"This comes out below the manhole. With the tunnel, if we have to, we can leave or return to the house undetected. To hide in plain sight, we simply stick a broken padlock on the basement door and another broken lock on the safe room."

"But …?"

"Disinformation, Katie. People believe what they see – or think they see." The smallest of smiles pulled one corner of his mouth. "They will believe the cellar already ransacked. Empty house, empty basement, nearly empty root cellar. They will never search deeper, never find the tunnel."

"So it all looks abandoned and looters just go away … I get it. You are wily."

"Had a good teacher," Dad said. The corners of his eyes crinkled, then he sucked a breath, so deep I knew it came from his boot soles. "I'm showing you this for a reason."

A block of ice formed inside me. *No. Please don't say it.*

"I have to go foraging, Katie. Your mother is almost out of medicine – we can't have that."

"I won't stay behind. I'm the one who needs to get the hell out of here before I go crazy. If you don't take me with you, I'll leave after you go."

I don't know what showed on my face but Dad folded me in his arms and kissed the top of my head.

"God's truth, you know I hate to leave you. I'm sorry you couldn't have a normal childhood – but hiding was the only way to keep you both alive. I know you're scared. I'm terrified every time I leave. I don't have a choice,

Katie. I have to go. And you have to protect your mother."

I nodded, but the grain of anger rubbed the resentful spot in my heart. My ears sizzled. I pushed my *mad* away but couldn't help my thought.

It's always about her.

Chapter Eleven

Dinner over, Mom shooed us from the kitchen and washed the dishes. "We'll go walk the perimeter, Sharon. Okay?"

"Yes, yes. Of course, Don. I'm busy right here." Her bright smile and clear eyes reassured me.

"Not a good idea," said my mindvoice.

"Not my call," I told it.

Terror didn't want to stay behind with Mom, but he did what Dad said. Dark brown eyes reproached us for taking Lu and leaving him. We walked our perimeter, scouted for bad guys, practiced my hand-to-hand skills until my sweaty clothes plastered to my skin. Dad never appeared to tire. *He must be part machine. It's beginning to piss me off.*

We sat, side-by-side on a fallen log, to rest – more likely, he stopped to let me catch my breath. A gritty film covered me; I scratched my leg, snagged a drink from my canteen.

"What did you do before you married Mom? Military stuff? Is it what you still do?"

He turned his hooded look on me, searched my eyes but never said a word.

"Where did you go? All the times you left us here?"

His flat expressionless gaze no longer held the power to make me silent.

"Un uh." I gave him a dead eye of my own. "You got away with it until I saw what people were capable of doing to each other." I leaned in, broaching both Dad's comfort zone and mine. "How do you know so many ways to defend yourself ... or to kill?"

"Katherine Angela," his eyes fixed on something over my shoulder. Trees and boulders, things he'd seen hundreds of times, nothing new.

"Dad, you're staring at the liar's side. Look me in the eye."

"Fair enough," he said. "You know why I married your mother – besides the fact I fell in love with her. My life was ... is ... anything but innocent or full of fun. I've never regretted my choices. But, I knew, if I ever had children, I needed her goodness to balance what I am."

I don't know what showed on my face but he patted my arm.

"You're not like me," he said. "You don't have the dark … um." He'd slipped; it showed in his furrowed forehead.

Oh shit. The voice in my mind. Is this what he means? Of course it is.

"You're wrong about that," I said, and let my mouth twist.

Dad stared at me like I'd grown a third eye in my forehead. "You don't understand, Katie," he said. "This isn't like a bad temper. This is different."

"I do know, Dad. It's why I'm asking." I couldn't breathe, but I forced three tiny sips of air. "I need you to tell me, Dad. Because I've got a wicked thing inside. It's been talking to me."

"No," he whispered, swallowed hard, just once. "You can't be like me."

"I am," I said, calm and detached. Then I waited.

He went unnaturally still, and his ebony eyes searched mine.

It felt like hours passed. I refused to blink, willed my body motionless. I succeeded because eventually he nodded.

"Okay, Katie. Explain yours. Then we'll see."

Well now, there's the rub. How to describe what's inside? Before The Great Awful happened, I thought the voice was my imagination. Did it birth when I made my first kill? I don't know. But, right now, I have to find words for Dad.

"It's a cruelty, Dad. Or maybe a glee. It's the sarcastic, cutting thoughts I never speak. It's the part slicing through all the emotion, and laying out the solution – even when the answer is to kill someone. It's the rush when they die and I don't. I hate that I love it." The words came out in a flood, and I searched my father's eyes for any reaction. Disgust? Horror? *I wish I hadn't told him it talks to me.*

He gave me nothing.

I hurried on. "I know it's wrong to kill without cause, or inflict unnecessary pain. But is it wrong to love a fight? I thought I was normal. I'm not." I held his gaze. "I do know, Dad, sure as breathing, I have to understand how to control it. You have to help me because if you don't, I'm terrified it will rule me."

I never looked from his face while he sat in silence, his eyes tracking a pair of chipmunks chasing each other up the pinon trees, squabbling over the pine nuts.

"I guess what I'm trying to ask is … am I evil?"

"No." A muscle knotted in his jaw. "Not if it worries you. Some brains can compartmentalize – process needs or required actions – much differently than others so they don't eat away our moral compass or our souls. It's the survival gene in our DNA. In my case – and it seems in yours – we can do the necessary and not become monsters."

"But …." My brain tumbled, one thought tripped over the next but nothing emerged. "Dad, does yours talk to you? Kinda out loud, I mean?"

"Yes, Katie," my father sighed. "Never tell anyone. The military would suck you up in a heartbeat. I don't wish my career on you." He raked both hands through his hair. "If there is a military anymore …."

"What if I think I want to do what you do?" I raised my hand to stop his protest. "I might not, Dad. But there's a reason, I think, I decided on West Point. Please, tell me the rest. What you are, what you do, where you go?"

"I serve in a special capacity which I refuse to discuss. My darkness is why I was selected and trained for special missions."

Missions? I opened my mouth and Dad laid two thick fingers across it.

"No questions. As the tired old joke goes, Katie, if I tell you, I'll have to kill you."

"But …?"

"I negotiated our house, our anonymity, our safety. You and your mother were taken. We got you back."

Something passed across Dad's face, something so awful it turned my bones to soup.

"They hunted me, until we captured and locked them up." His gaze strayed to a point over my shoulder. The liar's side.

I narrowed my eyes at him, and he looked at me again. "That's the honest reason for the tunnel behind the root cellar."

"What prison …?" I started but he lifted a hand. Cut me off.

My father shook his head like Terror shakes out damp fur. "Enough chatter. We need to get back to your mother."

The pace Dad set for our run home told me he worried about Mom being alone.

"Maybe he's punishing you for making him talk about me," snarked my dark voice. "Maybe he's furious because you're just like him. And maybe there's more he doesn't want you to know."

I wanted to tell it to shut its big fat mouth, but the fast pace Dad set didn't let me speak. It took everything I had to get enough air to keep up.

We got home just as Mom put out cookies and lemonade.

The next morning my mirror showed me too-large, dark-ringed eyes in a thin face. *God, I need to rest. If I can't sleep when Dad's here, when can I?* I poured water in my sink, bathed the best I could and put on clean clothes. I brushed my teeth, combed my hair and watched from the back porch while Dad hand-pumped gas into our pickup from the big tank buried out past the barn.

He looks so different.

After he came home from Mountain Home AFB, Dad didn't shave. Now he wore a heavy, black beard. Maybe he hoped he wouldn't be recognized. *He won't.* Maybe he wanted to appear more formidable. *He does.* Or maybe he wanted to conserve on face paint. *Whatever the reason, he doesn't resemble my Dad anymore. My heart skips scared if I see him unexpectedly.*

Dad's rifle and shotgun hung in the pickup gun rack, pistols and ammunition lay in the center of the seat, close at hand. A cardboard box with Mom's special canned jam sat on the floorboard for barter, if he found a chance. His backpack and carrying sacks – for whatever he scrounged – lay on top. He'd hidden the Army Jeep with the hole in the windshield far back in the barn, under a pile of loose hay.

Terror waited in the truck in his usual spot, his head out the passenger window.

"Dad, I should go with you. Just once, so I'll know where to go, what to get, when I take care of Mom."

My father's brows pulled together over his nose. "No, Katie," he said and shook his head. "We can't leave her alone. Ever."

He hesitated, cocked his head, then turned and went into the house. He returned carrying his collector coins – the silver and gold ones.

Mom followed him from the house. "Don? What are you doing with those?"

"In case paper currency isn't good any more." He shoved the bag beneath the seat.

"Why not the new change in the jar, Dad?"

"Those coins don't really contain much silver. They'll be as worthless as paper."

"Where will you go?" Mom's voice quavered. "Adrian?"

"It's flooded, Sharon. I'll try Marsing or Vale. Ontario if I have to."

"Why don't you go back to Nyssa, Don? You won't be so far from us."

"Sharon, I won't steal from folks I know."

"Please don't leave. I'm scared to be alone." Mom grabbed him around the waist, clung like a limpet. He removed her hands.

"I don't want to, God knows. But I have to. You need things, we need

95

things. Katie and Lu will watch. You must be quiet and hide if anyone comes around." Dad held her shoulders, stared in her eyes. A muscle jumped in his jaw. "Sharon, I'm serious. I've been training Katie. Promise me you will listen and trust her. Promise?"

"When are you coming back?" Her shoulders slumped, but she gripped his forearms.

He gently peeled away her hands. "Promise me, Sharon."

"I promise."

"Good," Dad caught my eyes, held the gaze. I dipped my chin in thanks. He exhaled, and some of the tension left his body. "I might be back in just a few hours. For sure, fast as I can."

"Don't hurry because of us. We'll be fine." I found my voice but it came out strangled. "Don't take any chances."

"I promise." My father fixed his coal dark eyes on me. "Remember everything I said."

I nodded, couldn't speak. My throat felt like someone stuffed it full of fluffy pink insulation. Fear of being alone and in charge again coated my underarms with chill sweat. But behind my angst lay something else – almost an anticipation.

"Wanting to try out your new skills?" whispered the evil voice.

No. Maybe. NO.

Dad gazed at us for a long, long time.

Like maybe it's the last time he'll ever see us.

Then my father crawled into the cab, fired the engine and headed down the driveway.

Mom turned, went in the house and I heard banging pans. I stared at the dirty white top of the cab until dust billows obscured it, stared until my eyes burned and I couldn't see anything anymore. I paced the porch until my legs ached.

When the noise inside stopped, a little frisson of worry climbed my spine.

"I better check on Mom," I said to my wolf and opened the screen door.

Lu grumbled, went inside and a couple of minutes later she gave me a soft "wuuf."

I followed the direction of her voice and found Mom snoozing, curled in the corner of the couch with a dog-eared novel in her lap. Something in the kitchen smelled really good; I went to check the timer. Fifteen minutes until it finished baking. Fifteen minutes to use the telescope in the attic. I checked my watch, noted the time.

"Wanna have a peek around?" I asked my wolf. "While she's asleep?"

Lupine grinned; then rumbled a response which I took for a yes.

We climbed the stairs, settled in and I scanned the countryside, a full 360 degrees. Not a speck of dust to be seen.

"Dammit, Lu. Wish he was home."

"Wuuf," she said, and lolled her tongue.

I used the telescope. I searched. I saw nothing. I checked my watch.

The fragrant baking smells morphed into "done", headed for "burning."

"Let's go see," I said and headed downstairs.

Lu's claws click-click-clicked on the wood treads.

My mother bustled about the kitchen.

"Something smells wonderful, Mom. Whatcha making?"

"Molasses cookies. The great big ones. They'll be done soon."

"Then I'll do my chores and hurry back." Although Mom's eyes were red and swollen, I got a smile. *Good, good, good!*

I fed the chickens, gathered the eggs and swamped out the disgusting bottom of the henhouse. I walked to the stream, picked a bunch of asparagus and headed back to the house.

Mom wasn't in the kitchen. I found her in the rocking chair in the great room, a wadded handkerchief in her lap, her lovely face puffy and blotchy.

She cried herself to sleep – again. Like she does – every time he leaves.

I paced the porch.

When she woke, Mom built a little fire in the cook stove and fixed us scrambled eggs, fried potatoes and onions. My mouth flooded with the aroma, I swallowed to keep from drooling. *I hate that she cooks the most when she's upset.*

"Be honest," piped up the voice in my head. "You love when she cooks, whatever the reason."

"Shut up," I snapped. "I can't help it."

"When do you think he'll get back, Katie?"

I jumped. Gasped. Mom startled me, interrupting my internal conversation.

"Soon, Mom. I'm sure." *Only I'm not – I'm terrified he won't.* My stomach burned like it held battery acid. If Dad didn't come home, dear God, what would I do? "It's turning dusk, Mom. We better go downstairs and lock ourselves in for the night."

She didn't fight me – maybe because we were both so afraid. I carried the container of cookies and a water bottle. Mom took her Xanax and her sleeping pill.

"I bet he's here before we wake up in the morning," I said.

"Yes, Katie. I'm sure you're right. Sleep well."

"Goodnight, Mom."

I caught her watching me across the room, so I made a big show of getting into bed. Then, I peeked to see her settling in her own sleeping bag. She couldn't fight the drugs forever. I waited, patient as a cat on a mouse. When her breathing went deep and slow, I strapped on my holster and grabbed the rifle.

Lupine and I slipped up the stairs to the front porch. We paced and watched. Watched and paced. After an hour, we made our way through the gritty ash on top of dewy grass to the back of the house.

We'd been there an hour or so when Lupine whirled and raced to the edge of the porch, her eyes locked on the woods. The hair on her spine lifted, ridged high and stiff and she rumbled low and deep in her chest. Ears pinned flat against her head, lips peeled away from her gums, she bared sharp fangs.

"Oh fuck," I whispered. "Someone's in the trees." Terror coiled around my throat and squeezed. I gasped for breath. Then my *mad* took over. *How dare people scare us? Threaten us? How dare they?*

"You don't have to go," said the black voice inside. "You could lock yourself in the safe room with your mother."

"No," I whispered. "I can't. All her meds are upstairs. I'm not prepared."

"You should have thought about that," chided the darkness.

"It's probably just an animal," I whispered. *Please, please let it be so.*

I needed more firepower than the Beretta holstered on my belt. I slipped through the house, pulled the shotgun from its pegs by the front door. My hands and eyes moved automatically as I checked for chambered rounds, and thumbed safeties to Fire. A gun in either hand, Lu at my hip, I moved stealthy off the porch, ran in a low crouch across the grass and into the trees.

Lu cued me to the intruder's location with the direction of her muzzle. I'd have figured it out anyway – the person in our woods hadn't been taught by my father.

Branches popped underfoot, and I heard a man's voice muttering and swearing.

I slid behind a tree trunk; Lu ghosted at my hip. Peeking out, I caught a metallic glint. *Gun.*

"You know what your father said," my mindvoice commanded.

"What if it's a good person?" I whispered under my breath. "Maybe he will just pass by."

The man kept coming, straight through the trees.

"What the fuck am I supposed to do? I can't just shoot him."

"He can't know you're here – you or your mother. What if he's one of a band? Like the tower?"

"I can't just murder him." I stepped from behind the tree, Beretta in my hand.

The man sensed me then. "Who's there?"

I didn't answer.

"Who's there, I said." His voice came louder. "I see you," he said, and settled the gun stock against his shoulder. The barrel rose as he aimed at me.

I shot him. Watched him drop his gun, and crumple. Moved with Lu at my side to where he lay. I crouched, a gun in either hand. My penlight between my teeth, I shined it on his face.

"What did you do that for?" he asked in a puzzled tone. "Why'd you shoot me?"

My dry mouth couldn't produce a word. My heart hammered. My lungs seized. I couldn't speak – I just shook my head, side to side.

I stood, backed away and double tapped his forehead. My guts churned at the awful sucking sounds, at the blood, but I'd done the necessary thing.

When I turned my light beam on his rifle, I saw a BB gun. *God in Heaven! What have I done?*

I vomited the whole time I dug the hole in the woods, and buried him.

Mom woke, found me sitting in the porch swing. "Morning, Katie. I'll go start a fire in the cookstove. Want me to make breakfast?"

"Not hungry, Mom. Just coffee, thanks."

"You've dark circles under your eyes. Did you sleep well?"

"I did, Mom. Maybe too hard. Could be the reason?" *What a lie. I never closed them all night. I never left this swing.*

"Yes, I suppose it might. I'll fix the coffee."

My old Timex said ten when I took my mug and headed for the attic. Lupine hovered by my side, her eyes gold lanterns, tracking my every move.

"Stay with Mom," I said. "Protect."

She gave me a martyred eyeroll and flopped on the rug at the back door.

"Know just how you feel, Lu," I whispered. "Every time Dad leaves me behind."

Mom sang to herself, stirring up a batch of cornbread. "I'll start things for dinner. Your father will be hungry when he gets here."

The dead man's face haunted me. Every time I closed my eyes, I saw the two holes in his forehead. Heard his voice asking me why I'd killed him – it played over and over and over in my head.

My fingers were numb, my hands trembled. I pushed my hands through my hair, gripped and yanked it. I couldn't stop the fast blinking of my eyes, but I had no tears.

I'm a murderer.

Spaghetti sauce bubbled, fragrant with onions and garlic, over the tiny fire in the family room wood stove.

It should smell good to me, I love Mom's sauce, but the nasty metal taste in my mouth makes me want to puke.

The asparagus I picked yesterday lay piled near the simmering pot. Mom always sliced it in at the very end so it stayed crunchy. In the cookstove, two loaves of bread browned. The corn muffins were poured into their paper cups. They'd bake next.

My "Be right back, Mom" got me a cheery wave of her spoon.

Up the stairs, I went, put an eye to the telescope and recoiled.

Sweat slicked my underarms; I smelled the sour stink of my fear.

Dust boiled above the road. Although I tried and tried, the thick fog of dirt wouldn't let me see who came. *Oh God, please don't make me kill again.*

My mouth felt full of chalk, I couldn't swallow. *I'm terrified – bad as before. But this time there is one difference. This time I know what to do. And I know how.*

I ran for my guns.

Chapter Twelve

T-dog leaped out of the pickup window and watered every tree and shrub in the front yard.

Lupine kept him company, her tail doing quick happy waves. *If I had a tail, I'd wag it too.*

"Don! Oh, Don!" My mother flew out of the kitchen waving her spoon.

The kitchen timer brrriiinged.

"Oh no," she cried. "The bread." And raced back inside.

"Guess you know how important you are, don'tcha?" I said and felt a grin kidnap my entire face. He couldn't know how glad I was to see him – to give all the responsibility back. *I'm a murderer.* Felt my smile slide and disappear.

"Yup," Dad said. "Right after the bread, I come first." A chuckle tumbled out and he hugged me hard. "Everything good here?"

"Fine," I said but it stuck in my throat.

"Liar," he said but the words were teasing. "Then why is my favorite girl, too young to have bags under her eyes, wearing a double set?"

"Couldn't sleep."

"Couldn't or wouldn't?" Dad's inspection saw everything; his smile faltered.

"Couldn't, Dad. Honest." I watched him waver between calling me on the lie or waiting for me to speak.

Twin frown lines formed between his eyebrows, but he gave me a quick nod. "Okay, Katie."

He can't guess my secret – there's no way. But I need more time to decide. Should I tell him I screwed up? I don't want to disappoint him.

Mom tore through the front door, leaped off the porch and threw herself into Dad's arms.

"Fill you in later," he mouthed over the top of her head.

The news must be awful.

I nodded, turned to give them privacy and began unloading the things he'd brought home. Medicine bottles – the big pharmacy kind. Amoxicillin, I recognized. Mom's sleeping pills. A partial bottle of Xanax with someone else's name on it. She'd been out of one med for almost a week now. And he didn't get any of those. *Not good, not good, not good.*

My heart did a slow slide into my shoes.

Dried fruit, Twinkies, Hostess Ho-Ho's. Fried fruit pies. Extra clothing, sweaters, long johns. Hiking boots. Heavy socks. Extra parkas. Batteries, all kinds. Extra lanterns. Knives. Reconstitutable meals. Canned meats, fish, butter. Vitamins. Medical supplies. Generic painkillers, cough syrup. Bottles of liquor. Everything Dad could get his hands on.

Cigars and cigarettes? Mom would have a fit. Then I understood. For trade or barter. He took everything he found because it wouldn't be there next trip. *We're screwed.*

My pulse fluttered in my throat like a captured bird. My father prepared for a future without power, doctors or anything. Just us, hidden away up here. Alone. On our own.

So much for me leaving. I can't stay, I can't.

Then the realization struck.

I have no choice. I have to. I will.

The second the food got hot, we put out the fire. No need to make extra smoke – increase our chances of being noticed, Dad said. We ate Mom's great spaghetti, moist tender corn muffins, and everything else she'd baked during the day. Well, the two of them did. I moved the food around on my plate and tried to fool them.

"Great meal, Sharon," my father said, crunching an oatmeal cookie between white teeth. "I found some chocolate chips, but no fresh butter. I got more canned."

"I've been baking with it already."

"We have plenty," he said. "Plus I got more powdered eggs, yeast, milk, baking soda, sugar, salt and ghee. We're set."

"Hah," she said. "Always thinking of your stomach, Don." Her attempt at humor fell short, sounded brittle.

When Mom wasn't looking, I felt my father's eyes on me, questioning, evaluating. I tried to meet his gaze.

His dark ones narrowed, and mine slid away. *He knows something's wrong. Can I hide what I did?*

We sat on the porch, the summer night warm and dry, a sliver of moon in the sky. The dogs were relaxed and quiet – no one anywhere around. My watch said ten o'clock but it could have been midnight. Or three in the morning.

If Dad and I were to talk, Mom needed to go to bed. But Dad didn't rush her, and I sure wasn't in a hurry.

"Leave the bad news for another day. Maybe two?" asked the voice in my head.

Mom stayed on the porch another hour, sighed, yawned, and stood. "I'm tired. I'll leave you two night owls to it."

"Let me tuck you in," Dad said and took her hand. They disappeared into the house.

When he came out on the porch, I slapped my forehead with my hand.

"I can't believe I forgot," I said.

"What?" My father's voice held a riff of laughter. "What terrible thing have you done?"

Oh fuck, Dad, if only you knew.

"I put a six-pack of beer in the creek," I said. "Then forgot. I intended to give you one with dinner."

"Well, now's good. Where in the stream?"

"I'll go," I leaped to my feet. "I know right where it is." Lupine surged upright and I wrapped my hand in her fur.

"Take my flashlight, Katie."

"I've got a penlight, Dad. But I doubt I'll need it."

"Katie …," Dad stopped. "If you want a beer too, I'm fine with it. You've been a functioning adult since this mess began." His voice cracked, he cleared his throat. "Actually for a long time before, to be honest. I haven't said much, I know what you do. I appreciate it. You're a good, fine girl. I'm proud of you."

Tears rushed, uninvited. "Thanks, Dad," I said. Then I whispered a tiny add-on, "I don't deserve it." I moved down the porch steps. "I'll just get the beer."

I sobbed, silently, to the creek and back. The walk took a little longer than usual but I needed to regain control. Thanks to the dark, Dad couldn't see my face.

"You need to blow your nose," snarked the voice in my head. "You sound like an aardvark."

I held out the beers to my father. "Thanks for the offer, Dad, but you know I don't like the stuff. You can have them both. I brought myself a soda."

"The only law out there now is – there is no law," my father said, his words framed with sharp edges of fury.

I'd just asked him why there were criminals running loose, like those who'd murdered the Wills. *But there are others – like me. A stupid scared girl killing a man carrying a BB gun.*

"There are people out there, Katie. Hungry, armed, desperate. Everyone is foraging. Some of the most brutal have banded together. If those people captured you, you wouldn't last a day."

"What about the government?"

"The Federal quarantine is useless – the posts are unmanned. Survivors are mostly people like us, away from the damage, never exposed to the plague."

"What are they doing?"

"The man at the sporting goods store said most have headed for high country, hunting for places like this. Taking them from the owners if they're occupied." His throat worked in a hard swallow. "It's called survival, Katie. Nice people doing terrible things in order to live."

"That's wrong," I said. "They'll get a surprise if they show up here."

"They will, for sure. Unless there are too many. The guy told me there's a new gang in the valley – they hunt people for sport. Responsible for at least fifteen deaths."

"God," I whispered and my insides quivered. *So much for goals, for dreams.* My lower lip trembled, and I bit it so Dad wouldn't see. Could the man last night have been one of those?

"We might never be found – if we're careful. But we can't count on it and the Nyssa folk know I'm here. If one of the gang members asks the right questions, in the right way ...."

"What do you mean?" *God, I'm sure I know.*

"People can be persuaded. They always talk – eventually," he said, and his black eyes went hard and far away. "Someone remembered the lookout."

"God, yes. Who's over there now?"

"I talked to a guy headed for Canada. He hid and spied on them. Said they were a rough bunch with motorcycles and trucks and guns. If they bother with the telescope, they'll spot our roof. The tower's scope is far superior to ours." Dad bared his teeth in disgust, snarled his next words. "Why the hell, when I was there, I didn't shoot the damn thing or bring it here, I do not know. Pure stupidity."

"Are they bad? The people at the tower now. How can we know?"

"We don't," he said. "I doubt they're part of the first group – the ones who killed the people working the tower – but there's no way to be sure."

A thought struck. "We can't ever have a light at night, can we? With people at the lookout, I mean?"

"No. It's just a matter of time until they notice us. That means I have to go take care of this now. Prevent murderers creeping in on us."

"How many?"

"Maybe ten – loud and bragging about kills. Could just be talk. The store owner said the group robbed him. Just grabbed what they wanted, then trashed his place for fun. Told him they were setting up camp at the tower. Bastards." Dad spat the epithet like it lay bitter on his tongue. "At least they left him alive."

"So assume they're bad. I'll go with you. Against so many, we need two good shots." Inside, my guts were jello. So were my knees, but I held my voice steady.

Dad can't know I'm terrified, he has to trust me, believe I'm strong. I am. I'm a murderer. He can't do this alone – too dangerous. And, God help me, I have to get out of here – if only for a little while.

"Take Lu and go to bed," he said. "I'll handle the first watch."

I didn't want to leave the protection of my father's company – I needed to hear his voice, have the reassurance he was really here. Still, my insides shivered from fatigue and my breath whistled dry and white-hot in my throat. I wanted to talk to Dad but I also didn't want to talk to Dad. *WTF, Katie?*

I won't be able to sleep. But I didn't argue, I just went. I thrashed in my sheets, wide awake. At 3 am, Dad tapped my bedroom door. "Katie?"

"Yeah, Dad."

He stuck his head into my room. "Apologies for waking you."

"I wasn't asleep. What's up?"

"There's movement at the lookout, I'm going to solve the problem. Need you to guard."

"Can't I go?"

"Someone might come. Your mother needs you and Lu for protection."

"He's right. You know it already," said the dark voice. "A man did, a man died."

"Can't you just leave it alone?" I whispered. "I'm trying to forget."

"Did you say something?" my father asked.

Damn his ears! "Nothing, Dad." I swung my legs out of bed. "Go ahead. I'll be right there."

Lu and I slipped downstairs. I parked my butt in one of the Adirondack chairs on the back porch and she snoozed beside me. Hours passed, my head drooped.

Multiple explosions jarred me, yanked me to my feet, guns in both hands, spinning in a half-circle.

"Fuck." I sprinted to the rail, saw bright flames licking skyward. *The tower is burning!*

I needed the telescope in the attic. *I can't. Even with her sleeping pill, the noise might wake Mom. I have to make sure she stays in the house.*

I bowed my head and closed my eyes. "Please, God," I whispered. "Let Dad be the cause – not the victim."

My father and T-dog arrived an hour and a half later, smelling of blood and chemicals and smoke. Acrid odors, like burned electrical wires, clung to Dad's clothes and Terror's fur.

My nose itched and Lu sneezed.

"You hurt?"

"Nope. Not a scratch on either of us."

What happened?" I stared hard at my father.

"They blew up," he said, his face impassive. "No one will be living there again."

Oh shit.

Mid-afternoon, the dogs leaped to their feet, growling at the back door. A fast hand signal from Dad kept them in the house.

My breathing went from normal to the wheezing of an asthmatic.

Mom's face turned the color of chalk.

"Sharon, can you go down into the safe room?" Dad's words weren't really a question.

"Yes, Don," she said, turned and went.

"Walking the perimeter," Dad said. He buckled his gun belt – with his Ruger, Glock and Ka-Bar – around his hips. Carrying his Uzi, he and Terror went out the front door. I closed and locked it behind them.

Lu and I waited. I held my Beretta in my hand, rifle and shotgun on the kitchen table near my elbow. I peeked outside, then moved from window to window. Mostly I watched Lupine for clues. I breathed again when my father and T-dog moved low and fast across the grass.

Dad detoured around the house again and I ran to let them in.

"A big group coming. Too many for us, Katie. And they have kids with them."

"Basement? Or safe room?"

"Safe room, this time."

Mom waited in the big basement area. When she saw the four of us rush down the stairs, her blue eyes widened.

"Safe room, Sharon," Dad said. "Big group coming – we have to hide."

"I hate this," Mom grumbled.

"Me too," I said.

Grabbing my hand, Mom squeezed it and hung on tight.

Dad threw locks and latches behind us, all the way to the open root cellar door.

Terror and Lupine rumbled displeasure when footsteps thudded overhead.

Dad's hand landed soft on T-dog's muzzle and I patted Lu's head. The dogs stayed quiet but their bodies tensed, muscles hard, coiled like springs wound too tight.

I heard lighter faster steps, then a faint high giggle followed by a muted scream.

"The kids," I murmured. If I hadn't been furious at the invasion, I'd have laughed. "I think one just slid down the banister."

"Children?" My mother's voice quavered. "They must be hungry. We have plenty to share here. I have to go feed them." She jumped to her feet.

"Oh, hell," said the mindvoice. "She's gone again."

"No, Sharon." The edge of Dad's voice came sharp enough to etch glass. But the grasp of his hand on her arms remained gentle.

Mom collapsed like a puppet with severed strings, then she straightened, her eyes unfocused.

"But ...." she tried again. "I have to ...." She jerked against Dad's grip, yanked her arms until the skin where he held her turned bright red.

"No, Sharon. No. Please don't fight me. There may be children, and they could be sick. No way to know what the rest are like."

"You are an awful selfish person," she snarled. Throwing her head back, she opened her mouth to scream.

Dad covered it with his own. He kissed her with such gentleness, my heart wept.

My emotions quivered, shredded, raw. *I can't begin to imagine what this is doing to him.*

Hearing footsteps overhead, knowing they searched our house, knowing they sat on our furniture, I crouched in terror beside Lupine. *What if we're discovered? Then what? Fight and die?*

My *mad* stirred inside. Fury burned in my eyes, flamed in my chest. A roaring filled my ears. I picked up my guns, wanting to charge up the stairs and blow them all directly to hell.

"It's stupid, Katie," cautioned the darkness. "Suicidal."

I hate them. Someone might sleep in my bed. I placed my weapons back by my sides, took a deep breath. My nails dug into my palms, warm sticky liquid coated my skin.

Dad dug out a Milky Way and cut it into small pieces. He calmed my mother, buried a Xanax in one of her bites and waited for it to work. When her eyelids fluttered, he carried her into the tunnel and tucked her in her sleeping bag. Right before she went under, we heard laughter and the faint shatter of glass, of china.

The animals upstairs broke her lovely things.

White-hot rage flashed behind my eyes at Mom's whimper of protest.

"You can't put a stop to this," said the quiet deadly voice in my mind. "Pick your battles."

Memory surged; my throat swelled closed. I thought I'd never want to kill again, and yet ….

When Mom moaned, I turned to Dad. Mimed a gun with one hand and pointed overhead, lifted one eyebrow in question.

"Not worth it," he whispered. But his eyes were hard as two black stones.

Another hot flash of rage, on the instant, flooded my body, clouded my mind. *I think you're wrong, Dad. Somewhere we have to draw a line. Have Mom and I made you too careful?*

"Your father is many things, Katie, but he's no coward," whispered the darkness. "Trust him."

Chapter Thirteen

Hot and sweaty, I drifted in and out of sleep, listening to the intruders overhead. I panted with relief when I wrenched, awake and shaking, from a nightmare about BB guns. My eyes felt like someone had ground them with a belt sander.

Dad and I sat in silence, waiting and waiting and waiting.

I pointed at the ceiling. "Think they're gone?" I whispered. "How long ago did the footsteps stop?"

"Right after you went to sleep," he said. "About a half-hour." A frown creased his forehead. "Your nightmare – what was it?"

"Nothing, really," I said, saw his mouth twist in derision.

Okay, so I can't lie worth a damn.

Mom woke and the three of us sat, listening hard; watching Lupine and Terror. When they relaxed, I knew the people were gone.

"I'll go first, with Terror," Dad said. "Just in case anyone is still in the house. Give us a couple minutes, Katie, then you and Lu follow."

I nodded. "Okay."

"What do you want me to do?" Mom asked.

"Wait until I call you, okay?" He hugged her.

"Sure, Don. No problem."

"She's got it together," said the voice in my head. "Good deal. Now if nothing happens to derail her …."

Yes, I thought back. *Fingers crossed.*

The smell of smoke permeated the house. We went through the kitchen, into the great room. And found Mom's antique secretary, still smoldering in the fireplace.

"Nooooo," she moaned. Tears coursed down her cheeks. "The only piece of Mama's furniture I could bring with me." She scrubbed her face with her knuckles. "And I can't go get … they can't know I'm …."

"Sharon," my father interrupted cut her short.

Dammit! Damn you, Dad! He was never rude, never interrupted Mom or me. *What did she almost say that he didn't want me to hear?* The tops of my ears lit like blowtorches. *Who can't know …what? That she's … what? Alive?*

I evaluated the damage. The people – no, the pigs – burned her beautiful antique. Why? I saw dirty pans and two crusty skillets on the hearth. The bastards hadn't bothered with the wood stove. Mom's Oriental carpets were smeared with grease, soaked with oil. They cooked in our great room in the fireplace. Parked a motorcycle on her rug?

Blood rage – the hot red film of my *mad* – obscured my vision. I stumbled to the kitchen for the can of rug shampoo. Heard a low, murderous growl. *Lupine?* No. *It was me.*

But what I heard when I passed Mom's Thunder Egg display reverberated in my bones; a harmonic shiver crawled my spine. I tried not to look but my gaze fixed on the geodes. Like phosphenes on the back of my eyelids, the glowing crystals smeared blues, ambers, purples, golds, greens. Plus other colors I'd never seen. So far, the intruders hadn't disturbed them. But they might. The thought made fury rush hot. My blood boiled. *Should I ask Dad.* Just that fast the geodes went quiescent.

"Hide them downstairs?" said the dark kernel in my soul.

"Yes," I answered, shocked at my fury. *They are just a bunch of dumb rocks.*

"Maybe not," said my mind voice. "Perhaps not."

A chill rattled my teeth. "What do you know about these things?" I demanded and got no answer. But because the geodes scared me, and so did the darkness, I grabbed a box and some old newspaper. I wrapped the smaller eggs; placed them in the container and carried it downstairs.

"Dad?"

"Yeah, Katie?" Dad's face changed, just a fraction. His eyes narrowed when he noticed the empty shelves.

"Can you help me carry the two big ones downstairs?" *Do you hear them, Dad? Do they sing to you, like they do me?* But I couldn't quite make myself ask such a stupid question.

We didn't speak, just tucked Mom's geodes away safely below the house. But now I wondered if Mom's treasure had somehow become mine. And perhaps Dad's too. The darkness might know – but it wasn't talking.

In the other room, Mom whimpered like a small wounded creature. I grabbed the cleaner, and joined her. Saw her small hands working convulsively, crushing and twisting the hem of her tee shirt. When she glanced down, she flinched. "Oh," she breathed, and smoothed the worst of the wrinkles.

I moved to hug her, but Dad beat me to it. Instead, I cleaned the rug, gathered the dishes and cook pots, carried them to the kitchen and began to scrub.

Dad walked my mother into the kitchen, one arm around her waist.

"You okay, Sharon? I should go outside and look around."

"Yes, Don," she said. "I'm fine." She moved next to me at the counter.

From the corner of my eye, I watched tears drip from Mom's chin in a steady slow stream. One little strangled sob escaped; then she dragged a large mixing bowl from the cupboard. She threw in flour, salt, sugar, hesitated, then shook her head. "I'm going to the basement, Katie," she said. "I don't have everything I need to … bake."

"Sure, Mom," I said. "Yell if you need me to help you reach anything."

Her usual luminous smile lit her face – for a moment. Then it wavered and disappeared. "Thanks," she said and went down the stairs.

"Goddamn them all. May they roast in hell," I whispered. My insides twisted with a vicious hatred I didn't recognize as my own. *She doesn't ask much. She didn't deserve this.*

The next day, more people found our house.

Again, we hid in the safe room, holding on to our guns and our breath and our sanity.

Dad and I exchanged glances. His lowered brows told me he feared like I did, Mom might come unglued and give us away.

I'm on the edge myself. Ready to climb the stair and go berserk.

This time, the scavengers didn't stay. They robbed our house, our garden and our barn. And moved on.

The lid for the chicken feed barrel lay on the barn floor but the grain hadn't been disturbed. The trees were stripped of fruit, and I cursed, slow and furious, at the one with broken limbs.

"Some fat ass tried to climb it," growled my darkness. "Good thing your father hid the ladder."

"Yeah," I nodded, looked up. Peaches, apples, cherries, apricots, plums and pears hung overhead, out of reach.

I joined Mom in her garden. She uttered a small shriek and fell to her knees in the dirt. "They've trampled my lettuce, crushed the carrot and onion tops."

"Won't they grow back, Mom?"

"I suppose," she said. But her hands fisted in the ruined greens.

My hands clenched too, but I kept them close to my sides. I trembled with the need to hit something. Hard.

"This won't do," Dad said. He gave me a little head motion, and I followed him to the barn. "I need to go out again but I can't leave you so vulnerable. We need a major deterrent. One you can handle by yourself."

The only way I will escape this place is to die.

Dad's face morphed from hard to implacable. "I have something ... I didn't want to use it. But I have no choice. Katie, distract your mom while I get what I need."

"Can't I help?" *I want to see what you do.*

"I'll show you when I'm finished. After she's asleep."

Heat crept up my neck, annoyance surged. *Why not now? What could be so secret?* But when Dad got that look, well ....

I mumbled a string of terrible curses and went to check on my mother.

Dusk fell before Dad left the dogs with Mom and showed me what he'd done. I had a *Holy Shit* moment. My jaw dropped, and my mouth opened and closed like a landed fish.

"There are two rings of defense – mines and explosives – one six feet inside the other, fifty yards from the house." We walked both circles, pausing for explanations and instructions.

"Jesus H. Christ," I said. "That one is huge." The lethal things, so close to me, made my skin crawl.

"I decided to only use two of those," Dad said. "Watch close, Katie. I'm going to disarm one, then reset it."

"Okay," I said. *No, no, no. This is not okay.*

"Now you do it."

Oh fuck no. Freezing sweat coated my hands, soaked my underarms. "No," I shook my head. "I'll kill us both."

Frosty dark eyes pinned me. "You have to. Understand me?"

I sucked it up, scraped the pieces of my courage together. Despite my trembling hands, I did it.

"Good job," Dad said, casual as if I'd just put all my shots in the bullseye.

I tried to say thanks but all that emerged was, "Um."

My father ignored it. "Look carefully," he said. "Here. Here. And here."

We walked the perimeter. I memorized where he pointed; took mental notes. "The two big mines are surrounded by trip wires, but they can also be detonated by remote. The blow buttons are in the house under the south kitchen window sill. I'll show you."

"Okay." *Big ones? Bit of understatement, Dad.*

"See the trip wires?"

"Yes." I clenched my teeth to stop their chattering.

"This is the way most people would walk. I situated the one on the opposite side of the house for the same reason. I'll show you."

"Okay," I managed.

"Pressure plates here," he said. "See?"

"The dogs?" I worried.

"We'll activate the explosives when I leave. But, to answer your question – yes, Katie, Lu and T are heavy enough to detonate the mines. Keep them close."

My mouth tasted dry as chalk. "How do you know …?" I blurted. "Where did you learn to …?"

"Long ago, in a land far away," he said. His words were lighthearted and joking but his shuttered emotions and flat, dead eyes gave them the lie. Dad scared me then, for just a second.

My face told him something, because he laid a steadying hand on my shoulder. "Katie, I'm sorry for all this. You should have never seen, heard, or had to do the things I've asked. You should have been free to live your life, anonymous and protected at West Point." Dad studied my face, stared into my eyes.

"How long since you slept more than an hour at a time, Katie? Days? Weeks?"

I couldn't speak. *I will not come apart.* I bit my lip for control.

Dad saw and changed the subject. "I need a beer. You want a soda? Or lemonade?" He gave me his lopsided smile. "Then, Katie girl, you're going to bed."

Lupine whined and fussed until I woke.

I picked up my Beretta and went downstairs. The Coleman lantern still burned, casting a low golden glow through the room. My father sat in the kitchen chair, but now his elbows rested on the table, his forehead in his hands. He didn't move at my entrance. *Too still. Asleep?*

No need to wake him. I'll just check around, turn out the light and go back to bed.

Across the kitchen, Terror sat on his rug, eyes fixed on something I couldn't see. *No intruder problems then.* But T-dog didn't greet me, didn't get up. *Almost like he's been ordered to sit and stay?* I slid quietly into the room and looked where Terror did. A wave of gooseflesh coated my skin. *Oh, fuck.*

The kitchen door stood open.

"Dad?" I whispered.

Two things happened so fast I couldn't follow. First, my father launched from his chair, eyes clear and unclouded by sleep. Second, I stared into a deadly black hole inches from my face.

"Shit, Katie," he said. "Sorry." He lowered the gun barrel, his eyes scanned the kitchen. His body stiffened, and he whispered, "Oh Christ."

"Lu woke me," I said.

"Check our bedroom." Dad's voice sounded calm but a muscle twitched in his jaw. "I'll take the basement."

"Okay."

Please God. Please let Mom be in bed. Please, please, please. I raced up the stairs, my wolf ghosting beside me.

"She won't be," said the dark voice in my mind.

"Shut up. Just shut up," I said and threw open their door.

The covers were rumpled on Mom's empty side.

"Please God," I whispered and checked the bath. No Mom. A wave of cold swept me, my breath came in shallow rapid pants. I hurried downstairs, searching every part of the house as I went. I met Dad in the kitchen.

"Nothing," he said and shook his head. "You?"

"No."

"Then she's outside. How in hell did she miss the mines?" Dad glanced at his watch, his face sagged. "Can't have been gone more than an hour. Get your weapons and a flashlight."

"Be right back," I said. *He looks a hundred years old. He's terrified. Me too. I'm scared of what we'll find … if we don't find her in time.*

Dad swallowed hard, licked his lips and turned off the Coleman.

I followed him out the back door; waited while he locked it. We followed Dad single file – first Terror, then me, then Lu.

Once past the explosives, the dogs went noses down. I hoped the ash residue wouldn't damage them. A half hour later we saw a bobbing beam of light in a small stand of trees. We found Mom wandering through the junipers, mumbling about making a pie for breakfast. Thank God for a cool night and sleeping predators.

Between the two of us, we got her back to the house. She fought us, made three breaks for freedom before Dad finally gave up treating her like fragile china. He just gripped one wrist, I grabbed the other and hung on.

"Help," my mother shrieked. "They're kidnapping me. Help!"

"Goddamn it," snarled my father. "Be quiet, Sharon. You're fine."

But she wouldn't, maybe she couldn't.

Whatever is playing out in her mind is not what's happening here.

Mom screamed, and yelled. She refused to be still. When Dad gagged her with his bandanna, tears ran down his face.

I couldn't look at her then, because her blue eyes bulged, wild with terror. And the gutteral muffled noises from behind the cloth made my stomach writhe.

Dad carried her, the rest of the way home. Safe in the kitchen, he made her swallow an extra sleeping pill. He shook the bottles, glanced inside and a pair of deep vertical lines etched between his brows. "Here, Katie," he said. "Would you put these in the cupboard with the rest?"

My father pulled a chair close to my mother; turned it to face her. He sat, cupping her cheeks gently between his palms.

She couldn't turn away.

Dad's eyes locked with hers, and he held her gaze until she finally calmed. "Sharon, love," he said. "Are you okay now?"

She didn't answer and the icy expression in her blue eyes made the hair rise on the back of my neck.

Dad waited a few minutes; asked her again. This time she responded, but her eyes wandered, confused. And wounded. She tried to speak.

"I'm sorry, Sharon," he said, removing the gag. "You had a little episode."

Mom whimpered and turned her face away from him.

Dad sighed, so deep it had to come from his boot soles. "I'm going to put her to bed," he said. "And sit with her until I know she's asleep."

"Tie her in the goddamn bed," suggested alter me. "Put the gag back, too."

I didn't say anything.

"Oh, Missy Katie," said the hard kernel in my soul. "You're in deep shit now."

I waited in the dark kitchen and thought and thought and thought. The voice in my head had it right.

If Dad leaves again? If she goes crazy like this? What in hell will I do?

Chapter Fourteen

The next morning, I woke early. I listened but didn't hear voices. Lupine rolled over on her rug, grunted, opened one eye and closed it again.

I poured water into my sink, did a quick wash and brushed my teeth. Pulling on a ratty tank top – my only clean one – and tan shorts, I sneaked into the hall.

Terror rose from his rug outside my parents' bedroom door and followed me down the stairs. I heard his claws tick-ticking on the wood treads; then, behind him, I heard a second set of nails.

In the kitchen, I fed the dogs, started a small fire in the cookstove and put on the coffee.

"Your mother will have a fit," said the voice in my head. "You used new grounds."

"Yes, I did," I snapped. "I'm sick of weak, watery stuff from three-day's use."

Ten minutes later, Terror's head came up, turned toward the staircase. Lupine's ears twitched and my father entered the kitchen. Drops of water dotted his sleeveless tee; his wet hair neatly combed.

"Do I smell coffee?" he whispered.

"Yeah," I mock-snarled. "First use, too. I couldn't stand the old grounds another day."

"Oh good for you, Katie girl!" he laughed. "Oh, really good for you."

"Where's Mom?"

"Still sleeping. Much as I hate it, we need to talk. This is a good chance." An expression, so very sad, so very hopeless, drifted across my father's face.

"Oh God, Dad," I whispered. "I suppose we do. Can I get a couple of cups of coffee in me before we do the hard stuff?"

"Sure, Katie. Is it done?"

At my nod, he reached for the pot. "Then let me pour. You made it, it's the least I can do."

We sat in silence, inhaling the steam, the aroma and sipping.

I rolled the hot liquid across my tongue, swallowed slowly. "Ahhh," I said, savoring the flavor.

"Damn that's good," Dad said.

"Want a Blackcap muffin to go with it?"

"Do bears shit in the ... oops. Sorry, Katie." Red crept up my father's neck.

"For God's sake, Dad. Don't apologize – I swear too." I stood, opened the roll-up door on the wood bread box on the counter and got the bag of baked goodies. I put four muffins – two cornbread and two Blackcap – on a plate. Then I cut three big slices from the peach pie and set those out too. "One for me and two for you."

I refilled our coffee mugs; got two plates, two knives and forks, and the butter crock. I sat in my chair, picked up my coffee and made a toasting motion at him.

Dad clinked his mug against mine and said, "Let's eat."

We piled our dishes in the sink.

"Let's go out on the porch," my father said. "More privacy there."

"In other words, it's harder for your mother to sneak up on you and eavesdrop," said my mindvoice.

I couldn't argue. *The damn thing's right. Again.*

"We have to make some changes," Dad said. For the first time in my life, my father had puffy bags beneath his eyes. "She's getting worse."

"Yes," I nodded. "I've been thinking that too."

"It's taking a bigger dose of her meds to put her to sleep. She's going to run out of what she needs much faster than I planned." Dad knuckled the black circles around his eyes with both hands. "She's more devious, too. Twice, in the past week, I caught her spitting out her pills."

"Oh God," I whispered.

"As long as I'm in bed with her, I know when she moves," my father said. "But I can't risk falling asleep anywhere else in the house again. How in the hell I did, I cannot understand."

"Maybe you were exhausted?" I said. "You are human, aren't you Dad?"

I got the half-grin I wanted. "Besides, nothing bad happened, and we learned something. Don't beat yourself up. It's what you'd tell me. Right?" This time I got my father's full smile. Happy warmth rushed through me.

"Didn't realize how much you missed it?" asked the dark voice. "Not been anything to smile about lately."

"What do you want to do?" I asked but I really didn't want the answer. *I'm terrified. Scared I can't protect Mom, scared of Dad leaving, scared of bad people coming. Of The Great Awful, of dying with the plague. Of starving, of the power never coming back on. But mostly, I think, I'm afraid I will never leave this place.*

"… so because of everything, I think it's better if we all start sleeping there."

I'd been woolgathering and I'd missed the first part of Dad's sentence. Still, my inner voice caught enough to fill in my blanks. "So, starting tonight, we have to spend our nights in the basement?" I asked, and heard the anger in my voice.

"I'm sorry, Katie girl." Dad shot a sideways glance at me, and his words sounded apologetic. "In shifts, too, I'm afraid."

"Why?"

"I'm not sure about her anymore."

"What do you …?"

The expression – or lack of it – on Dad's face froze the words in my throat. "You don't think she would harm …?"

"It's something we must consider," he said. "You had to know that."

But I hadn't. Not for a second had I ever considered my gentle mother capable of hurting Dad or me. Bile boiled in my stomach. I coughed to disguise my gagging.

"Shame on you, Katie Davis," the bitter voice berated. "If the thought makes you this sick, what do you think it does to your father? Instead of being angry, you might try to help him."

"Okay, Dad," I said. "What do you need me to do?"

"Your turn for bed," I nudged my father's shoulder.

"I'm fine," Dad's eyes opened, and he yawned.

He'd been dozing on a chair blocking access to the cellar door – no way to get in or out without waking him. For the past three days, we'd slept one at a time. Mom's mind was nearly gone.

One of the meds that kept her on the rails ran out a week ago. Since then, Dad and I watched her slip over the edge – every day a bit more.

It's like a window. For moments – even hours – it's open and she's completely all there. Then, just when I dare hope she's getting better, the window slams shut. The person replacing Mom is unbalanced. Scary. We have to watch her or drug her. We don't have many pills left.

"Tie her up," said the resentful darkness. Then the voice turned angry. "No. Better yet, let her loose. An easy fix."

"Shut up. Go away," I said, but it refused to listen.

I know Mom can't help it and I try, oh God do I try, for patience. I watched Dad watch her, saw his face twist. He blinked too hard, rubbed his hand across his eyes.

He adores her. This just kills him. Me too. This stress is overwhelming. What can we do? There is no solution.

My heart felt shredded. I blinked back the wet flooding my eyes.

"Yes, there is," said my evil voice. "You know what to do."

"Shut up," I whispered. *Does Dad think about these things too?*

In the kitchen, Mom sang "hoolah, loolah" to the tune of some awful old song. Years ago, after we moved in, I'd found a record in the attic by Sam the Sham and the Pharaohs. I'd thought it funny; played it for a week. Now, somehow, my mother's mind remembered, and followed that track to the end. *She sings damn "Woolly Boolly" all freaking day.*

We turned the calendar, marked the day. July 1, high noon, and hot. The thermometer hanging on the porch – in the shade – said eighty one degrees.

A breeze whispered, then gathered strength. The wind came up, whipped through the trees. Made the weeping willow boughs lash the air. Black thunderclouds boiled in the sky. Lightning cracked, arced, and the water dumped like God used a bucket. Rain soaked the hot, parched ground, turning the layer of volcanic ash slick and treacherous. For almost an hour, the storm pounded us.

Mom stayed in, sitting in her end of the big red couch.

"Katie, you come inside. You'll be struck by lightning."

"I'm safe," I called. "I'm beneath the overhang. You know I love thunderstorms."

"Don," she shouted. "Make her come inside."

"No, Sharon," he said. "I like them too." Dad dragged a deck chair close to mine and sat down. "These monsters are like huge movie productions. Wild, beautiful, exciting." He raised his voice, shouted to be heard inside the house. "We're fine, Sharon. You come out."

"No. You're both crazy," Mom yelled and I heard the pout in her voice.

Dad rolled his eyes at me.

And, God help me, I laughed. Too much. Too long. Too loud. *But it feels so good.*

As abruptly as they arrived, the indigo clouds cleared, and the sky glimmered turquoise again.

I inhaled, pulled air through my nose to the bottom of my lungs and smiled. My favorite of all smells – the sweet fragrance of new clean rainfall on the sagebrush, the grass, the trees, the moist earth.

I spied through the door and saw Mom dump coffee grounds into the percolator to boil … again.

"I'll search extra hard for coffee my next trip." Dad read my mind, or more likely he saw the face I made at the pot on the stove. He headed inside, returned with his mug in hand, and rejoined me on the porch.

"We've still got a coffee stash," I said. "She's just conserving it."

"Or she's forgotten it exists," chimed my nasty voice.

If you're up there, God, if you're real, then fix my mother. She deserves better. So does Dad.

Our supplies were low – Mrs. Cluck and her brood helped, but the people coming through diminished their numbers. The older chickens were crafty; they hid from strangers but we lost most of the younger ones.

Dad sat in the porch swing, sipping his coffee, expression so solemn. The hard worried planes of his face, the new deep lines on either side of his mouth, the white knuckles of the hand gripping his thigh. All bespoke worry and unease.

I don't feel as sorry for him as perhaps I should. The thing making my *mad* boil – was that Dad got to leave. He got a break, got free of this place. And I didn't. Not ever.

"Whatcha thinking about?"

Broad shoulders lifted, shrugged, then collapsed.

"I've got to go …," he said. "Farther than before. I've got to find a pharmacy." One big hand waved at the area to the east and north of us. "Everything close is picked clean. I want to add to our stockpile of food – the non-perishable kind. For us and the dogs."

"Why? Can anything fix her now? She's too far gone …." I blurted, then clapped my hand over my mouth. "Oh shit. I didn't mean …."

He didn't respond. That told me more than any words. Then those dark eyes turned ruthless, assessing. Did he suspect how hard I fought to keep from snapping? *God, I'm glad I didn't tell him about the man in the woods.*

I watched my father's face. He held it carefully expressionless – like a poker-player. Did mine appear the same? Probably, because I felt like I wore a mask.

I'm different now. I don't want to be, but I am a murderer. Before The Great Awful, I wanted to meet and talk to everyone. That's all changed.

Around my heart, the secret place where I kept my most vulnerable part, now stood a high stone wall. I could see the barrier in my mind. There used to be nothing in the way. *The new me is hard, logical, protective. Focused. I don't like me much.* Did Dad feel this way too? He loved us – Mom and me, and the dogs – but he did what he had to. I understood him a little more, liked him a little better.

"You didn't build your wall on purpose," said the voice in my head. "It's necessary, that's all."

My father's words pulled me back into the present.

"The kind of drugs your Mother needs are stored at the base. Huge quantities of everything. If I don't go get them, we'll lose her – one way or another."

It always comes back to her ....

"No, Dad. Not Boise, not the AFB. You're AWOL. They'll put you in jail, never let you come home. Promise me you won't do that." I couldn't get a grip on my breathing. "What if there's a new kind of plague there now? One you're not immune to?"

"If he goes there," whispered my darkness. "He will die."

"No promises, Katie, except I'll try everything else first."

"No, Dad. If you go there, I have to go with you – watch your back."

The evil little voice spoke up. "You're not worried for your father's safety. You don't want to stay behind with your Mother."

"No," I shook my head at Dad but I spoke to the dark voice. "No. Please, Dad. Please let me go."

"You know you can't," my father's voice held fatigue. "Who would take care of your mother? Terror stays here this time. You might need both dogs."

The red sheet of *mad* stretched across my eyes. My ears burned.

"How the hell will I watch her?" I snarled. "Goddammit, I'll have to stay awake 24/7. This is not fucking fair."

I expected my father to slap me, to give me orders, to yell.

His eyes went sad and troubled, his mouth trembled, just for a second, before it firmed again.When he spoke, his words were soft. My heart cracked.

"Don't you think I know what I'm asking, Katie girl? Don't you think I know?"

"Oh shit, Dad." I couldn't hold my anger, my voice lost its edge. It quavered on his name. I squeezed my shoulder blades together, sat taller, tried to project composure.

"If I had a choice, I'd take you."

"You would?"

My mind leaped, happy at his words. It wanted to dissolve my anger. It tried. It didn't work. I felt better, yes, but nothing changed. I wanted to go and I had to stay – with my mother. *All her fault. Again.*

"When will you go?"

"Soon as possible – later today. I'll take the pickup and put your Kawasaki in the back – just in case I have to go off road or make a fast exit. Help me put them back together?" Dad searched my eyes.

I don't know what he saw but the smile slipped off his face like snow down a windshield.

He knows exactly what I'm thinking. Darkness recognizes its own. "Sure Dad," I forced a smile. "But what will we do with Mom while we work?"

His mouth twitched. "I'll ask her to cook food for my trip."

Four hours later, the pickup full of gas, motorcycle stowed in its bed, Dad laid his guns on the bench seat, hooked his 30.06 and Uzi in the gun rack. Closing the passenger door, he turned and embraced my mother. In the morning sun, her curly brown hair haloed his shoulder.

Mom's shoulders shook. Gasping sobs rocked her slender body. She murmured love, fear. "Please, please, Don. Don't go."

"Tracking pretty well, I'd say," said my evil voice. "She never once said hoolah, loolah."

I squeezed my eyes closed but the tears squirted like little jets from a watering hose.

His touch feather-soft, Dad detached my mother from him, turned to me. His hands wrapped each side of my face; he kissed the middle of my forehead. Then with a groan, he pulled me into a hard hug and walked me toward the truck.

"I love you, Katie girl. You'll find my back-up Uzi on your bed. I hope you won't need it."

I didn't know you had one.

"Hide it from Sharon. Take care of things 'til I get back. Probably be no more than a few days."

"I l-l-love you too." I swallowed hard, watched a shimmery glow surround Dad. I blinked to clear my eyes, felt his finger wipe my face.

Terror whined at my side. Lu thrust her cold wet nose into my palm, whuffed at my distress.

I held tight to their collars although I didn't need to. Dad's hand signal froze Terror in place securely as any chain. Lupine wouldn't have left me for any reason.

"See you soon," he said.

Turning away, he waved over his shoulder and climbed into the truck. One hand passed over his face before he put on his aviators. Cranking the motor, he stared at us a long, long time. The sunglasses hid his eyes.

At my side, Mom wrapped her arms around her body and whimpered. *I should comfort her. I don't want to.* Resentment burned like acid in my soul. *Who comforts me?*

With one final wave, my father turned the pickup down the driveway, headed for the main road.

I watched him go until my eyes burned from staring, until I no longer saw a hint of dust.

I tried very hard to ignore the darkness when it whispered, "You will never see him again."

Chapter Fifteen

The next morning

Mom seemed in great spirits, bustling around the kitchen, making breakfast and singing one of her hymns. I parked at the kitchen table; sipped a cup of tea.

"Bleah." I said. "At least it's hot."

"Katie, how about we run the generator for a bit? Do laundry, clean?"

"Sorry, Mom. Remember Dad said no?"

"Oh. Well, he's gone now. We can just do it."

Spooky. Normal Mom would never suggest going against Dad's wishes.

I shook my head. "We don't dare. It's not safe." I didn't tell her he dismantled and hid the parts to it, too. I poured out my tea, washed the cup in the sink, stuck it in the drainer and went up to brush my teeth.

I heard the kitchen door slam, peeked out my window. Mom stomped her way to the shed, jerked the door open, stepped inside.

"Goddamn her," I snarled. "She's out there unprotected." I snatched my Beretta and went down the stairs, hitting every third one.

Lu and Terror lurched up from their rugs by the back door, shaking off sleep. They followed me when I burst through the screen; flanked me across the porch. I took a second to study them. Their only concern came from my agitation. My mother wasn't in any danger.

I pulled the shed door open, saw Mom pounding on the generator with one small fist.

"Damn you, Katie. I'm the adult. I'm the parent. I give the orders around here," she snarled and burst into tears.

"Mom, the generator doesn't work any more."

"Well, why didn't you say so?" she snapped.

"I guess I thought you knew," I hedged.

"That's a lie." She sidled past me, went through the door, and stormed back to the house. I watched her go. *How long until she starts speaking to me again?*

"Just a wee bit irrational?" asked the voice in my head. "Getting worse?"

"Fuck," I whispered. "What am I going to do? Even if I told her the truth, would she believe me? Or would I just make her madder?"

The only bright spot I could see – thanks to Dad, now no one could spy on us from the tower.

I dropped the wooden ramp from the chicken house to the ground, scattered grain and laughed while they trooped down.

Between the garden, the chicken eggs, an occasional fryer and our remaining stores of food, Mom, Terror, Lu and I wouldn't go hungry. But I couldn't hunt or fish – Mom had to be watched. Every freaking minute of every freaking day.

Now I stood watch in the attic because my Mother decided she "wanted an afternoon nap in her own bed in her own bedroom." End of discussion.

Fine. When I saw she slept, I locked the door from the outside, left Lu to guard it, and went up to the attic.

Water bottle and rifle in hand, I watched the countryside. *Dad should be back by now.*

"Really?" snarked my nasty alter self.

"No, you stupid voice. He shouldn't – not if he went farther afield. I just want him back right now, okay? Happy?"

No response. Good. I needed sleep – lots of it. But all I'd managed since Dad left were small naps. My nerves were wound beyond tight.

Lupine's growl brought me to full alert.

Peeking out the attic vent, I saw two armed men, automatic weapons at the ready, moving from the forest, through the planted trees toward our house.

"Step on a mine, would you?" I whispered and hoped for the best.

They didn't. How they missed them, I couldn't understand. *Just lucky? Well, I'll change that.*

Swinging the louvered attic vent outward, I rested my rifle on the trim, and contemplated more murder. My cold hands were slick with sweat but they didn't shake.

"No hesitation," ordered my mindvoice. "Obey your father."

This is a video game, I told myself. *These are not people.* Then, one after the other, I sighted in and snipered them. Dropped them in crumpled unmoving lumps.

I didn't vomit.

"You have to bury them," said the darkness. "What if they're infected with the plague?"

"Would you shut up?" I snapped. "I have enough to worry me without that."

The two men hadn't come alone – I heard the child before I saw her.

A woman emerged from the trees dragging a little girl by one arm. The child cried and cried and cried. I trained my scope on them.

The woman yanked at the girl, dragged her onto the lawn. Snarled, "Shut up."

"I can't." The words escalated into a wail. "I don't feel good."

"I'll fix it for you, then." The woman's words came, malevolent and cruel. Before I sussed her intent, she pulled a boning knife from her boot, gripped the child by the hair, and yanked back her head. One slash made a red bubbling line on the girl's throat. Bright scarlet spray fountained. The second cut opened the artery on the opposite side.

"Bleed out in the grass, you baby," she said. "I'm sick of your whining. I'm gonna see what's to eat in the house."

My brain froze, refused to process what just happened. Then, I morphed into a chunk of ice.

"Shoot the bitch," urged my black thing.

"Absolutely," I whispered back.

The scope showed me a face distorted by fury. I sighted the rifle on the center of her forehead, sucked in a breath, held it. Waited for the in-between space of my heartbeats. I smiled, knew it for a detached terrible thing; squeezed the trigger. Saw with satisfaction, the back of her head disappear in a pink spray. She folded at the knees, fell sideways on the grass.

She was quite dead but I shot her again. Twice.

The first bullet – for the little girl.

The second – just for me.

I blinked away tears. Sorrow for my murder? *No.* It was sorrow for the child.

The double tap wasn't necessary. No. I shot her cold, and I rejoiced. Katie Davis, 16 years old, judge, jury and executioner.

Careful to avoid the mines, I dragged the bodies through the brush and into the trees. Later tonight, I'd bury them.

Mom woke up and fixed us each a peanut butter and jelly sandwich. *I should be upset, unable to eat. Instead, I'm calm, like killing that bitch released all my anger.* My mother and I ate in companionable silence, chatting about what we'd go pick in the garden. *This is incredibly normal – yet things couldn't be more wrong. Beyond surreal.*

"We've got enough yeast to last a while." She jumped to her feet. "I'll stir up a batch of bread."

Good to have normal Mom back.

She turned, and her eyes were wrong.

Oh Christ! She doesn't recognize me.

I backed away, out of arm's reach.

Mom's eyes narrowed, her mouth gaped and her jaw worked but words wouldn't come. Finally, she snarled, "Don's out stringing fence, over on our north forty. Some cows got out. He needs his lunch and I'm taking it to him. And you, hoolah loolah, can't stop me."

Somewhere in her tangled mind, my Dad became the single track she followed. From that moment on, day and night, Mom tried to sneak from the house, from me, to find my father.

"Lock her in the basement," suggested the darkness. "Tie her to a chair or in a bed."

"I can't," I whispered. "She's my mother. It's disrespectful … it's heresy." In my deepest heart, I knew the pragmatic dark spoke truth.

"How will you feel if you lose her?" asked the voice. "If someone gets her, hurts her?"

The darkness argued with the voice of reason. Cold. Hard. Logical. "If Don comes back and she's gone? Or dead? Can you live with it?"

God help me, I can't. And I have to rest – it's been seventy-two hours since I slept more than fifteen minutes at a time. I'm getting as crazy as she is.

Night came and I tucked Mom into her cot; waited until her breathing went slow. Grabbing my sleeping bag, I motioned to the dogs and we slipped through the heavy security door. I closed it, pushed the latch over the eye, stuck the hasp through and snapped the padlock shut.

I should sleep inside with Mom because if I'm killed out here tonight, she will starve. But I'm afraid she might murder me to get away. I'm so tired I can't think what else to do.

I checked Mom's medicine bottles – still quite a few. If I took every pill in every bottle could I go to sleep forever? Might be the only way I'd ever escape.

"Coward's way out," whispered the darkness. "You can't do it to your father. You won't do it to your mother. You won't do it to you."

I knew the voice spoke true. "But I'm so tired …," I whispered, moving toward the kitchen. The floor seemed to float, I swayed on my feet.

Lupine whined, propped me up.

I grabbed the door jamb until the dizzy spell passed.

I spread my down bag and stretched full length, with one arm stretched above my head. My hand rested on the Uzi, the other held my Beretta by my side.

Two great hairy bodies sandwiched me.

"If someone gets me, it's fine," I whispered. "In fact, except for you and T-dog, I almost wish someone would. Then I could sleep forever."

Resting my head against my wolf's thick pelt, I crashed.

The screaming woke me.

Who? I struggled to find my wits. *What? Where?*

The dogs whined, shifted on the sleeping bag. They wouldn't leave unless I said.

So tired. Fuzzy brain. I lurched to my feet, Beretta and Uzi gripped in my hands. Checked my watch. *Morning?*

The sounds of agony – from the back yard – shot ice shards through my veins. The only good thing – my mother still slept behind the locked door.

"With this racket, it can't last," whispered the dark place in my soul. "You'd best see what's happening outside."

A thumping, then violent pounding started against the locked safe room door.

"Kaaaaaty! Kaaaaaty! Let me out!"

Still the screams, the shrieks tore the air outside our farmhouse. *What in the name of God is happening?*

Lupine leaned against my thigh. Silent death, her muscles made steel bars beneath bristling fur.

Terror growled. Beneath my hand, his hair stood stiff, a huge ruffed ridge on his neck.

The heavy musk of agitated, angry dogs came off them in waves. They stood in front of me, protecting, side by side, facing the door.

I closed my free hand about T-dog's muzzle. Carefully, gently around the tender membranes in his nose. "Shhhhh, boy."

No question about it – bad, bad trouble happened right now, outside. My bodyguards confirmed it. And more trouble waited, screeching my name, locked in the safe room behind me.

"I have to think what to do." I whispered. "You stay, T-dog. Guard." With a gesture, I put him in front of Mom's door. "I'll be right back."

"Lu, with me." Tucking the Beretta in the back of my jeans, I crawled on all fours up the stairs. A bass drum pounded in my chest and echoed in my ears. But it didn't mask the shrieks from the yard.

My wolf moved beside me, her big silver body low profile like mine. Sharp claws tick-ticked on the linoleum treads.

I cracked the back door. The screams splitting the silence were monstrous, the stench that billowed into the kitchen turned my stomach inside out.

Black lips writhed, peeled away from lethal fangs – a growl rumbled deep in Lupine's chest.

Outside, in the back yard, something burned.

It wasn't wood.

I crept on hands and knees across the kitchen's pale yellow vinyl, crouched beneath a window and raised my head just enough to peek.

On the lawn, two men took turns on a spread-eagled woman. Beneath her body, blood puddled, darkening the grass to black. She didn't move or scream. Or breathe.

OhGodohGodohGod. She's dead, and still they torment her. Then I saw what cooked.

They'd buried one of our extra corral posts in the yard. It stood vertical, surrounded by clumps of smoldering sagebrush, piled tumbleweeds. The naked man tied to it shrieked each time the flames flared. His abdomen gaped, sliced from sternum to pelvis, spilling intestines down his legs. Fire licked at his body.

Fear and more clamped my chest like a vise, gripped so hard I couldn't inhale. Vomit splattered on the kitchen floor. Mine.

"They're burning him alive," the darkness said. "You and your mother will be next. Raped to death or tortured or burned. Will you allow it?"

"No, I will not," I snarled and went down the stairs for Terror and my Uzi.

The soundproofing of our safe room kept Mom's shouts muffled. I didn't hear her until I hit the basement.

"Kaaaaty! Let me out of here."

"I can't, Mom," I said.

Not now, for God's sake. I have to take care of things first.

So intent on their evil, the men never saw me edge sideways through the kitchen door.

Hidden by the porch overhang, flanked by Terror and Lupine, I shot the man atop the dead woman. *Brrrt.* A fast three-burst. In the back. He spread, boneless, across the woman's body, like a deflated balloon.

The second one grabbed his gun and leaped to his feet, head swinging. His eyes searched the yard, then he half-turned toward the house, his weapon leading the way. Still, no fix on where his danger lay, his frantic eyes rolled, passed over me, hesitated, started back.

Brrrt. I put a three-round-burst into his chest.

"I'm coming to help you," I shouted at the man in the licking pyre.

Got a stifled shriek in reply.

I retched, brought up strings of bile, kept dry heaving all the way to the porch. The water bucket sat in its usual spot outside the back door. On the picnic table lay an old towel and a butcher knife. I grabbed them all. Guarded by my dogs, I sprinted for the fire.

Teeth bared, T-dog and Lu braced the bad guys – making sure. But both were dead, I knew. Once you've seen death up close and personal, there's no mistaking the slack, empty shell completely devoid of any spark. Still, I almost gave in to the urge to empty the Uzi into the rapist's groin.

"Good girl," said my mindvoice. "Save your ammo."

I threw water on the flames, moved to the man and recoiled. A loop of bowel slid from his abdomen. I gagged, cut his wrists loose; caught his arms as he collapsed.

He screamed so horribly when I pulled him from the embers, I stopped twice, to vomit, before I got him on the grass. I couldn't make myself push his intestines back inside. Instead, I laid the towel over his ruined body.

"Thank you," he whispered. Then, eyes on the woman, his face twisted. "Could you pull that beast off my wife?"

God! In his agony, he still thought to put her first.

The air stank of perforated bowel, burned flesh, and a sickly-sweet ferrous stench. I knew and so did he – without an operating room and the best of trauma surgeons, he couldn't live. Even with them, his odds weren't good.

"Oooh," he groaned. "Oooh, oooh." Spasm after spasm contorted his body. He locked glassy bloodshot eyes with mine. "Kill me, please."

"Oh, no." I sucked air. "No."

"You killed them. Kill me. I can't stand the pain." A ragged inhale, a gathered effort to speak again. "My wife is dead. I could live days. Please."

"No, I can't."

"I just saw you …."

"That was different," I whispered.

"How?"

"Because you aren't bad …." *I can't murder another innocent person.*

"So I die hard and they died easy? Your idea of what's right? Or wrong?"

My head twisted up at his logic. *He's right, but I still can't do it. I can't.*

But the darkness reared in my mind. Its busy little voice suggested an idea.

"Can you pull a trigger?" I asked.

"I … yes."

"I'll leave my gun with you, take my dogs and go into the house. It's all I can do."

"T-t-thank you …," he wheezed.

I made sure the safety was off and handed him my pistol. I turned and rushed for the house.

In the kitchen, I filled a bucket with soapy water, got a brush. I scrubbed vomit off the kitchen floor, scrubbed and scrubbed until my knuckles bled. *No shot.* I scrubbed some more.

What if he can't do it? Then what? I tried to force my mind away from the horrors in the yard. But the smell overpowered everything, even over the aroma of good clean soap, and the stink of my own honest sweat. *God, the awful, ghastly smell.*

All the while, from below the house, my mother's screams increased in volume. The imprecations grew more irrational. More demanding. More insane.

A single shot cracked the silence.

"What if he missed?" asked the darkness. "Can you finish it?"

"No. Yes. How in hell do I know? Please, just go away." Lu and T-dog flanked me while I crossed to check the man.

The top of his head cratered like someone used an ice cream scoop on it. *Thank God, he did it right.* So relieved I didn't have to deal with another death, I didn't flinch at his missing skull and the glistening bone and gray and pink brains blown across the yard.

All I feel is numb. I must be in shock.

"No, Katie," the darkness said. "It's only me, separating things out. Your father's gift."

I dragged the man and his wife, then the two evil men, into the woods and laid them beside the other bodies.

I dug one grave and one bigger hole.

Wrapping the man and his wife and the little girl in sheets, I buried them, in the grave – with respect.

I kicked the bodies of the awful men and the woman until they rolled and flopped into the hole. I shoved a few large rocks on their corpses, threw in some dirt and spat on them.

Words should be said for the victims. I don't know any. I don't even know their names.

"Rest in peace, husband and wife," I whispered. "Rest in peace, little girl. God bless your souls."

My blood boiled. I wanted to scream, to rant, to rage.

"Quiet will keep you safer," whispered the black kernel in my soul.

"Burn in hell forever, you murdering fucking bastards," I said. "I wish I'd killed you slow, like you did them."

Chapter Sixteen

The dogs pacing on either side, I trudged back to the house. I heard my mother's screams when I hit the top of the kitchen stairs.

"Fuck me," I said. "I do not want to deal with this."

"Shoot her too," said the evil inside. "It would be a mercy."

"No," I whispered. "I can't. I won't." I went down the stairs, paused at the locked door. "Mom," I called. "It's me – Katie. I'm going to let you out now." I twisted the key, slid the hasp through the eye, flipped back the latch. *She's furious. She's going to really chew me out.*

The door blew open with the force of her shove.

"Damn you, Katie." Like a striking cobra, Mom sprang through the safe room door. Mentally, I was ready for her anger. I didn't expect her physical attack.

Her hand connected hard against my face like a hundred tiny hornet stings. "How dare you lock me in that room? I ought to belt you. You're grounded. What were you doing? Out running around all night, screwing boys?"

What? I gave ground, knees loose like oatmeal. The events outside were starting to register, I felt my mind bend. My heart did half-beat dit-dit-dits. I stood, paralyzed by shock, staring at my mother.

Behind me, my wolf snarled.

"No, Lu," I said, and tried to think what to do.

Mom's eyes wandered, unfocused and white spittle foamed in the corners of her mouth. She bared her teeth, made a fist, swung at me.

Mom's never struck me – ever. Until now. But, how easy, with all Dad taught me, to slip her blow, slide close and catch her wrists. And hold her helpless.

Fury rose inside me like a tsunami. The tops of my ears flamed as my *mad* fought to be freed. Instead of slapping her back, I shook her, stared hard in her eyes. Knew from her flinch, mine were cold and narrowed. Perhaps the same obsidian pools of rage like Dad's?

"Her mind is gone," the dark thing inside me confirmed. "Round-the-bend, looney tunes, insane. She'll get herself killed; you right along with her. Take care of her now. Just another grave in the woods."

She can't help it. I grabbed a deep calming breath. She needed to be protected – not injured. *I promised Dad.*

"He'll never know," whispered the evil thing in my mind.

I'll know. You shut up. I searched her face, hoping for rationality.

"Mom! There were bad people in the yard. I had to keep you safe."

"What a crock of shit," she spat, spraying saliva. Her lovely face twisted, cruel and harsh. Lines dug trenches by her mouth, in her pinched lips. Crows' feet radiated from her eyes. "You don't expect me to swallow your fucking lies, do you?" Her pupils dilated so wide they all but eclipsed her sky blue irises. Madness lurked. She fought, twisted against my grip, kicked at me. So anxious for freedom.

"She's no longer your mother. She'll harm you now," whispered the darkness. "Gone crazy as a shithouse rat. No better now than those outside."

"No, she's only confused," I said, but I knew it spoke truth.

Icy worms twisted in my stomach.

"You must deal with her as Sharon, the lunatic," said the dark. "Sharon, the threat."

The counselor in my head advised me honestly. Mom was gone. The stranger left behind in her place was certifiably crazy.

But I must keep her safe for Dad.

Resentment crawled my neck, up my face, in a hot sweaty flush.

"If I let go, Mom, will you listen to me?"

At her nod, I released her arm, stepped back a pace.

She laughed, a deep guttural thing; launched away.

"Fool," she mocked and flew up the stairs, through the house; out the kitchen door into the bloody yard. I followed.

She skidded to a stop. Turning, she hissed, "You murdered people here. I heard their screams. You locked me downstairs so I couldn't stop you."

"No. No, I didn't."

Mom's face went cunning. Morphed into skin-stretched-over-bone skeletal. "You abomination. Get away from me."

"Mom … Mom … please. Wait." I advanced, hands outstretched, palms up and open. "Please, it's not what happened. Please listen to me."

"Get thee behind me, Satan," she hissed, holding her crossed index fingers between us. "You are not my child. You are evil. Stay away, I warn you."

Beside me, T-dog whined and butted me with his head. But Lupine growled, low and deep, and advanced toward Mom. I glanced down to make sure of my wolf. The instant I broke eye contact, my mother whirled and raced for the woods.

"Goddammit to hell," I snarled. "I can't go after her with just a handgun."

Terror and Lupine paced me when I sprinted through the house for my Uzi.

The demented not-my-mother-creature never slowed.

Crushed brush, sharp scents of juniper, bent branches, fresh divots in the ash-coated pine straw underfoot made tracking simple. Flushed birds and scolding squirrels told me her location. T-dog and Lu ranged slightly ahead. *What will I do when I catch her? God forbid she stumbles upon evil people.*

"More killing," said the darkness.

"Yes," I said. "There would be. I'd have to protect her." *Maybe Mom's right – maybe I am the crazy one.*

"Always more killing," the hard little thing went on, almost sounding sympathetic. "Life's own truth. Always those who take from the weak. Someone must stand in the way."

Why does it have to be me? A knot of anger twisted in my heart.

"Why did it have to be your father? Think about it." The words of the darkness worked in my mind. "Those who can protect the weak and eliminate evil must do so. Like your Dad … and you."

Go away. I fought to stay just-Katie. *Stop talking.*

Then, everything went all to hell.

My mother's scream echoed down the canyon. The odd note in her voice, the pitch of her shriek stopped me in mid-stride. Not a cry of physical pain. This howl bespoke mental agony.

Goosebumps crawled my body.

Part of me said, *Charge in there, Katie. Save her.*

The other half, trained by Dad, said, *Reconnoiter. Be smart and save you both.*

"Let her go," argued the darkness. "Go home, save yourself."

Another cry stood my hair on end, stabbing my scalp like needles.

Running toward her voice, Terror at my left hand, Lupine on my right, I scanned the forest for threats. I didn't find a thing. Emerging from the woods, I saw my mother poised at the edge of the canyon bluff.

"Annelise Megan Crawford," said the voice of my childhood, the normal sane woman who raised me. "Stop right there. Go home."

Who is she talking to? She's delirious. I swallowed, spoke past the lump in my throat. "Not without you."

"I can't stand the hiding, the dark. The fear. I know what I've become. I won't go."

"Mom, Dad will be home any day. You've got to come with me. It's dangerous here."

"Katie, I have no meds. There's no hope for me and no help. You can survive by yourself, leave the house if you have to. It's me that's the burden."

"No, Mom. I need you …."

My mother tilted her head to one side, a small sly smile crept across her face. "I see you trying to slip closer. You think to grab me, take me home by force if necessary."

"Mom …."

"No. I love you, Leesie. Remember it always. I'm sorry. But the answer's still no."

The landscape, trees, fragrance of flowers, color of the sky, the brush of wind against my sweating face – all impressed forever in my mind – in slow agonizing motion, in acute never-forgettable detail. Because, before I could react, my mother turned to face the yawning canyon, pressed her palms together above her head and executed a perfect swan dive.

I jumped for her, a powerful leap, fueled by fear and adreneline. I sprang without thought for myself. My clutching hands felt the whiff of disturbed air when Mom's feet passed inches beyond my fingertips. I landed flat, knocking the air from my lungs, and skidded toward the bluff's edge. Loose gravel beneath me rolled, urging me on.

My head hung in blank space. My eyes stretched wide; I stared into absolutely nothing. Without the sharp set of wolf fangs clenched in the seat of my jeans and the glutes of my ass, I'd have gone over the cliff right behind my mother.

Rocks pinged, clods of dirt bounced, dust churned as Lupine braced all four legs and hung on. We skidded, slid to a stop. My shoulders joined my head, dangling over the edge.

Mother lay below, a disjointed broken doll, much too still on the rocky edge of the stream. Dead.

She just … jumped.

"So did you, you stupid, stupid girl," the darkness snarled.

Lu backed, pulling me with her. Four white-hot points of pain lit in my behind. Torn skin, torn muscle, oozing warm.

I didn't resist.

I failed. What … how do I tell Dad?

My lips tingled like they'd been zapped with hundreds of tiny volts; an odd singing, like cello music, filled my head. Blood rushed and pounded in my temples. I relaxed into it, strangely empty, so glad … *I don't have to worry anymore* …. Everything went black.

"Ewww." I regained consciousness to the energetic licks of sloppy tongues. I flapped my hands at Terror and Lupine. "Stop it, you guys."

Then I remembered. Springing to my feet, I bent over, rested elbows on knees and waited for the head spins to stop. Bile splashed the back of my throat.

I have to go get her. Take her home.

"There, there," a faint male voice drifted over the canyon's lip.

"Oh fuck," I whispered. "What now?" Feeling a strange pressure in my hands, I glanced down to find I gripped handfuls of gravel. Dropping the rocks, I brushed the coating of ash and dust on my hands against my shorts, knelt and crept toward the edge.

"Ain't you a pretty one? Are you my wife? I've lost her. It's just not right how you're laying, there with your face in the water. That can't be comfortable. Let me set you up."

I held my breath and heard something like scuffling of shoes on stones, followed by a hard grunt.

"Naw, you ain't her. But we can chat a while."

Terror and Lu guarded, superimposing themselves between me and the cliff.

Very plain they don't want me near danger. Maybe they don't trust me, either?

The smell of smoke wafted from below; I pinched my nostrils against a sneeze.

"Okay," I said to the dogs. "I'll be careful. But I need to see."

They didn't move.

Stretching full length in the dirt, I guerrilla-crawled, using my elbows, worked my way between them until I saw Mom. A set of sharp teeth again clamped the seat of my shorts.

"Ow, Lu. Dammit," I whispered over one shoulder.

She ignored me and clenched a bit tighter.

I bit my tongue to keep from screaming.

A thin unkempt man perched on a boulder next to my mother. His hair stood out like coarse white straw, patchy, like he'd lost it in chunks. Boils erupted on his face and arms, the skin sloughing away.

The Great Awful plague? Radiation from the military cache? Or pesticide plant fallout? He's walking death.

The man patted my mother's limp hand. He'd propped her against a rock but her head lolled on her chest.

"Come now," he said, a wide manic grin exposing missing key teeth. A cigarette dangled from his cracked lips. "Isn't this nice. Can I make you a cuppa tea?"

I watched the man gather kindling, and tumbleweeds. In a depression between the rocks, he lit a small blaze. Pulling two battered aluminum cups and a teapot from his bag, he filled the kettle from the stream and put it on the fire.

God! He's mad as a hatter. I felt a scream building behind my teeth. Chewed on my tongue to distract myself with pain, and tasted metallic copper. *Stop it, Katie.*

"You can't go down there," said my darkness. "You don't know if you're immune. Better you mind your mother one last time, and go home."

As if they heard the voice in my mind, my canine protectors whined and nudged me.

When the wind surged once more, carrying the smell of the fire up and over the bluff where I stood, I flinched and slid back from the edge. *Could the breeze carry the sickness from that man to me?*

I considered my options – *none* – and gave it up.

"You realize what this means," whispered the hard kernel inside. "You're free. The only obstacle to your leaving just removed herself."

"No, no, no. Now I can't leave until Dad comes home. I have to tell him how bad I screwed up."

"Do what I said," snarled the mindvoice. "Go home. Now."

Tears wet my face, soaked the chest of my tee shirt. My course of action came clear as the water in Succor Creek. I did what the darkness ordered and pushed to my feet. Braced between my two furry guardians, I plodded through the woods.

I don't remember the trek, really. I do remember stumbling and falling. More than once. I remember the dogs supporting me, one each side, while I twisted my hands in their fur. But little else. And I remember my heart pounding in my chest, remember thinking it might explode. Hoping it would.

I cried myself hoarse, until I hiccupped and dry-heaved. I think I fainted because when my mind began to function again, the sun didn't stand overhead, it lay just above the horizon. And Mom was still dead.

"How can I live without her? She is … was … messed up part of the time, sure, but she's my Mom. She can't be gone." My soul shriveled; disintegrated into tiny bits. "How can I explain this fuck-up to Dad? He trusted me to keep her safe."

I gave no thought to the explosives placed around our house and the darkness didn't remind me. Either sheer luck, or my subconscious prevented me from blundering into one. Or maybe the dogs recognized the smell and led me around them. On autopilot, I fed T-dog and Lu, scattered grain for the chickens. Everyone ate – except me. The thought of food made me queasy.

Curled on the couch, I sobbed – without tears. I'd cried myself dry earlier. *I've failed Dad. Failed Mom.*

"Not quite," said my darkness. "You're still alive. Your father wants … he needs that."

"What if I don't?" *Damn you, you fricking thing. Leave me alone.* "Now, for sure Mom doesn't need her pills. I can take them all and go to sleep forever."

"You're Don Davis' daughter – too strong, too brave for that. Stop thinking about yourself. Don't you care about Lu and T-dog?" The nasty voice asked. "Someone will shoot them. Sure as shit."

"I don't care," I snarled, propped my chin on my hands, shook my head. "Yes, I do." I ran my hands over their furry heads, patted sturdy shoulders. "I just hate all the death, all the killing. All the awful people. You're right. I'll wait here for Dad. Long as I possibly can."

"What if?" asked my inner voice. "He never returns?"

"Then," I said aloud. "For Lupine and Terror, I'll begin planning for the worst."

"Attagirl," the darkness approved. Scariest thing of all, it now spoke in Dad's voice.

What does that mean? He's not dead – is he?

The mindvoice ignored my questions. Instead, it ordered, "Clean and disinfect your injuries. You're covered with blood. But first, go check the explosives."

I wanted to tell it to screw itself. *Problem is the damn thing's right.* The bites in my ass throbbed and walking hurt like a bitch. *Set your priorities, Katie, and get going.*

I found four exploded mines and replaced them, my perimeter once again protected by death.

Back in the house, I got the med kit from the safe room. I hydrogen-peroxided my injuries, rubbed them with benzalkonium chloride wipes and covered them with band aids. Shaking two pain pills into my hand, I popped the top on a warm can of cola and swallowed. I locked the door, then laid face down on my camp cot and crashed.

At noon, I crossed today off the calendar. Only three weeks since the Great Awful happened but it felt like forever. In the past two days, I'd heard four detonations. Hard to know how many died. I refused to clean exploded people off the sagebrush, or fish body parts out of the pinon trees. Maybe newcomers would get a clue and go away?

A stiletto of remorse stabbed my heart.

"Huh," grunted the darkness. "Like they'd think twice about murdering you."

"Swell, you again. Tell me, you with all the answers – why do they hike all the way up here? Where are they headed when they leave?"

I didn't get a response.

Thanks to new trespassers, holes again gaped in my perimeter defense. Should I pack and go? No, I'd wait for my father.

"So why aren't you out replacing the explosives?"

"Shut up, damn you," I snarled.

But the voice spoke truth. I gathered my guns, my explosives, my dogs and went outside. My hands coated with slippery cold sweat, and they trembled, but I filled the empty spots. I exhaled a monster sigh of relief, and went back to the house for lunch.

The emergency radio gave little news and none at all about any safe places. I cranked and listened first thing every morning and last thing every night, plus each time I took a break.

I opened a can of soup, ate it room temperature from the can. The radio broadcast came so unexpectedly, I dropped my spoon.

"Boise is rebuilding," the announcer said. "A small community has formed, and all good, healthy folk are welcome. We're working, removing the ash and cleaning up the town. After that, our next priority is to get the power back on. We need skilled people, especially engineers and those with medical training, but everyone willing to work is welcome."

"Oh God," I whispered. "Possibly a place to have a normal life? Maybe other kids?"

"Is this broadcast truth?" The darkness asked. "Can you believe it?"

"I don't know. I can't assume it's safe. Maybe Dad is there." Then I realized one thing. "If he is, he's either too sick or injured to come home. Or he's a prisoner at the airforce base." Then I realized something else. "If Boise is such a good place to be, why are people still leaving?"

"What do they know you don't?" asked my mindvoice. "The ones leaving fast as possible?"

"They're fleeing the plague. Or they haven't heard. Or …. Quit with the questions. If you don't have answers, just shut up," I snapped. And I felt good about it.

"Still, all things considered," I said to Lupine and Terror. "Where could we go and be better off? Nowhere, I think. Besides, they might not want you two."

Tongues lolling, they grinned assent … or maybe they just panted from the heat. *Whatever.*

Each day I sorted through our supplies, sifted the critical from the nice-to-have's and began filling our backpacks. Just In Case.

Without warning, items triggered memories – of Mom, of Dad. Of Todd. *Never again.* Despair hammered me. My legs folded, dropped me on my ass. On the four punctures. I shrieked, rolled to my belly. Chewed my lip to keep from screaming again.

"I'll never go to West Point. Maybe never marry, have kids." I whispered. Only weeks ago, those goals, although requiring hard work, were attainable. Now simply staying alive from one day to the next took all my attention, all my effort. And I'd lost everyone except Lu and T-dog.

Did I actually consider life without my mother? How could I have wondered how much easier it would be? God, she knew – she said so. I am a monster.

My mind looped from thought to thought; then started all over again. I hugged myself for comfort because there was no one else to do it. Now, suddenly, I owned my destiny. I could go anywhere, do anything. *My long coveted freedom. But I don't want it. Not at this cost.*

Lupine and Terror whimpered, growled at my distress. They nosed at me, butted big heads against my shoulders, licked my cheeks. Then, they sat, like guardian Foo dogs, leaning against me, providing love and comfort.

I possessed no barrier against their pure caring. Wrapping an arm around each thick furry neck, I sobbed.

Chapter Seventeen

Two days later

Sunlight across my face woke me. I'd fallen asleep in Dad's recliner. I went to the kitchen, made a short pot of coffee and ate the last of my mother's bread. *I'll never see her, never hug her again.*

The kitchen glittered silver through the wet in my eyes. *How will I manage? I have no idea what waits out there. And I may be forced to go.*

"Imagine that, Katie Davis," sniped the hard kernel inside. "Not long ago you were dreaming about sneaking out."

"Shut up," I whispered through my swollen throat. "Just leave me alone."

I put the emergency radio on the table and cranked – more from habit than hope.

"C'mon, c'mon," I begged the radio. "Tell me again, tell me more, about the refuge city."

With each passing hour, my hopes dropped like a pebble in a pond. I must have misheard the broadcast. I couldn't do anything … until I got good data.

My eyes burned. I climbed the stairs, brushed my teeth, washed my face. I grabbed my hairbrush, looked in the mirror and recoiled. Bloodshot eyes stared back. Even in the safe room, with the dogs, I never slept deep enough to rest. How wonderful to live in a community with someone else in charge?

"How can you check? Know it's true?" whispered my dark devil's advocate.

"I can't," I snapped, and dropped into a kitchen chair. Leaped to my feet. Damn bites! Now they throbbed. I got my supplies, went into the powder room beneath the stairs and took a peek with the hand mirror.

"Oh shit," I snarled. "No wonder they hurt." I saw four swollen red lumps, trying hard to become infected. I scrubbed with the benzawhatever wipes, applied antibiotic cream, and fresh band aids.

"Time for a little help," I said. Back in the kitchen, I shook two amoxicillin capsules from the big bottle into my hand. I considered them, thought again, made a decision.

"No reason to suffer," I muttered and opened the bottle of painkillers. It took my remaining half cup of coffee to swallow the three pills. I drank more coffee and waited for the percocet to work.

Sometime in the night, either my subconscious or my remorse-free DNA, had reached agreement. No matter how much I grieved, no matter how much I wanted things to be different, the past was done. I couldn't change a thing. Instead, I needed to put it behind me, forgive myself and look to the future. Make the best plans possible for my dogs and myself.

"We don't have a choice, guys," I told my furry guardians. "I wanted to leave – I still do. But there's no better place to hide. It would be stupid to just head out." Loneliness ate at me, the silence weighed on my mind, kept me on hair-trigger. Everything in the house brought a memory – but no longer tears. "We'll wait for Dad."

"And maybe swine will fly," said the darkness. "He's not coming home. Ever."

"Stop it," I said. "You can't have it both ways. You don't want me to go – but you say Dad's never coming back. Just shut the hell up." An errant thought made my mouth go dry. "How long," I whispered. "Since I've checked the perimeter?"

"Two days," supplied my helper. "And there have been three explosions since then."

"How much longer since I scouted the lands beyond?"

"One week," snapped the darkness. "If your father comes home and finds your body? Will he be happy?"

I'm losing it. Inattention would get us all killed. Unacceptable.

"Damn straight," said the voice in my mind. "Get your ass in gear."

I put Terror guarding the kitchen door; Lupine at the top of the stairs. I went to the safe room, lifted the lid on the box of explosives and began to count.

My heart crawled into my throat. "I'm fucked," I whispered. "Running out of replacements. Then what?" I selected mines and other nasty items; stowed them in my backpack. I took T-dog, Lu, the Uzi, the 30.06, my two pistols and went outside.

I found five detonated sites, put the dogs to guard. As I began replacing the first one, I stopped cold. Could I afford to replace every one?

"No," said the darkness. "Be smart about this."

Freezing fingers skittered up my spine. How long could my

replacements last?

"A long time … if no one comes to set them off."

Which ones do I replace? What would Dad say? The answer came, clear as the creek below our house. *Fix the areas I can't watch.*

"Attagirl," applauded my dark adviser. "What about when you run out?"

"I don't know," I said. "But I have to know who's out there. I have to scout."

The sound of my own voice made me flinch – creaky-rusty and too loud. I'd whispered for so long, it was strange. "Lu, T? Maybe we should do a day hike."

Two tails wagged excited approval.

I went back to the house. By the time I arrived, I'd figured what Dad would take. Binocs, a compass, the little first aid kit with anti-venin. The emergency radio – if I made high country, the reception should be optimal. I stuck in my small flashlight, took it right back out. *If I carry one, it should be dual purpose. Dad's is big enough for a weapon.* I stuck it in my pack.

"Should I take food for you two?"

Lu and T-dog tilted their heads and grinned. Terror's thick stubby tail thumped the floor.

At their smiling faces, a warm rush surged through me. Such good, good friends.

"Okay, it's a deal. I'll even carry it." I put dog chow in a zip lock bag, some trail mix in another, and a dozen vanilla wafers in a third. Tossed in a couple of power bars.

I feel better than I have in days. A goal, being busy, kept me from thinking. From remembering.

It hit me and my mind froze in fear. *This is my first hike without Dad at home as my safety net. If anything happens to me, no one would know. Or come to help.*

My knees folded and I slumped on the floor, my head in my hands.

Two noses poked my cheeks, two heads butted my shoulders. Their message came perfectly clear.

"Okay, okay. It's just all of a sudden, I'm scared." I pushed to my feet, surveyed the things I'd assembled.

"What if you get stuck? Have to stay out overnight?" asked the mindvoice.

"Let me think on it." I rolled my light jacket and tied it on one side of the backpack, put the small first aid kit and emergency radio inside. Creeks and streams were everywhere, the water should be clean but I added a canteen and a couple of purification tabs. *If the fish are alive, it's safe.* I'd just scoop the clear above the settled ash. The backpack bulged but everything fit.

I gathered my Uzi, two spare clips, the 30.06, my Beretta and two knives.

My mind did an 'oh shit' at the weapons piled on the floor. *I can't carry them all. I won't leave them. Now what?*

I thought of how Dad scared me in the hallway; how he bristled with guns and knives.

I need a weapons harness.

"I changed my mind," I told Terror and Lu. "We can't go yet."

Two pair of eyes accused, ears drooped.

"I know – you're disappointed. Me too."

"That's a lie, Katie," said my mindvoice. "You're relieved."

"You shut up," I growled. Turning to my dogs, I said, "See, I just thought of something. What if we can't get home the same day? We need more supplies."

I can have the dogs carry their packs; strap the long guns on top.

"What if you get separated?" the darkness asked. "You need a gun and the dogs aren't with you?"

"Damn." Despair surged. I dropped into the closest chair.

"Make one."

"Make one what?" I wasn't tracking on what my inner voice meant.

"Make a weapons rig, you idiot," it snapped.

"With what, you moron?" I snarled.

"Try searching," it suggested in a nasty tone. "There must be lots of possibles around this farm."

Okay. For the first time since Mom jumped, hope soared. *Maybe in the barn?* Opening the kitchen door, I placed one foot on the porch, remembered the three convicts, and yanked it back inside. I picked up my Beretta … and hesitated. Handguns weren't accurate at a distance. If someone came through the woods, I'd need something to make sure they died instead of me. I grabbed the Uzi.

Lu, Terror and I headed across the back lawn – at a full run. I put the dogs inside the barn, one on each side of the door.

"Guard," I said, although it wasn't necessary. *They know their job.* I slipped inside and climbed into the loft. When Dad and I stacked the bales of hay and straw, he'd offset some rows to create hidden pockets. Intruders had scrounged the barn, but they might not have thought about that.

The stacks were undisturbed. I got busy moving bales around; found extra ammo, dog food and chicken feed. Nothing to help with my project. "Dammit!"

Back down the ladder, I searched the main floor. Hanging on wood pegs on the wall, I found three harness buckles, two pair of reins, Dad's extra leather gloves.

And a partridge in a pear tree, snickered the voice in my mind.

Leather straps from the reins might work, maybe buckled and hooked to some of my belts? Peeking out the barn's man-door, I checked with Lu and T-dog. They wagged their tails, no worries here. Still, my breath came in little pants when I scanned the yard and tree line for danger. The three convicts still terrified me. *Will I ever get over it?*

"Better if you don't," said the darkness. "Keeps you wary."

All clear. I headed for the back door, Uzi in one hand, Beretta and my finds in the other.

I didn't find a single usable thing in the house. My shoulders drooped; so did my heart.

I won't find what I need.

"Stop it, Katie," said the dark voice. "You can't know that. Keep searching."

On my hands and knees in my parent's closet, I found another box. In it were medical supplies – more like trauma surgery than a first aid kit – with more sterile benzawhatever wipes, scissors, saline pouches, IV set ups, synthetic suture/needle combos, advanced quikclotting sponges. Surgical stuff. *Who is my father, anyway?*

Where else to look? An epiphany struck. Memory of Dad and his metal army box popped into my mind.

I left the kitchen door to the basement open, let daylight stream down the stairs. Setting Terror to guard the top of the stairs, I took Lu with me. I carried the Coleman, but I didn't need it. Boxes of supplies sat on the metal army box. Moving things around, I lifted the lid.

Smells of gun oil, old paper, greasy money and leather boiled out into the room. My heart ping-ponged in my chest.

An eerie yellow pair of eyes peered over my shoulder.

"Yay, I smell possibilities." But hope evaporated when all I saw were used fatigues, a box of medals, and a handful of passports rubber-banded together. The myriad identities, in different names, from different countries, bore the pictures of my father and another man.

Why does Dad have so many passports? Memory stirred in the far recesses of my mind. *Why does this other man look familiar? I've never seen him.*

I dug deeper, moving stuff to one side. The fatigues unfolded, creating an untidy heap in the box.

"Dammit." I pushed them aside. Stopped as an idea tickled my brain. Picking up the shirt, I shook it, spread it across my chest – shoulder to shoulder, checking width and length. Did the same with the pants.

"The camo your Dad's?" asked the dark thing.

"No, too short ...." My fingers straightened fabric, brushed out wrinkles. "But, I can wear them." I refolded the uniform, set it to one side, found a matching hat, laid it on top of the pile.

I touched metal. Another handgun lay concealed by the fatigues. *God!* I held a silver, boxy Sig-Sauer fitted with a silencer. It made my Beretta look like a toy. I hefted the Sig, settled it in my hand. It fit like it had been made for me; the weight and balance were perfect. *Thanks to Dad's training, I'm stronger than a lot of men.*

Digging deeper, I found a box of Parabellum ammunition and two spare clips. *Definitely my new weapon of choice.* I dug in the box again, touched supple leather.

My lungs seized. "It's just a belt, Katie," I said aloud. "Don't get your hopes up."

My fingers traced a buckle. *It won't be. It can't.* A sharp pain in my lower lip and a warm trickle on my chin clued me. I stopped biting and focused on the contents of the box.

The bulky bunch of leather, wedged tight in the corner, took a couple of gentle tugs to free it. It unrolled in my lap.

"Damn, Lupine. It feels like ...." Moving into the daylight coming through the open basement door, I inspected my find.

My heart swelled like it would explode, the top of my head tried to lift off like a rocket. What I held in my hands was exactly what I'd prayed for. Exactly what I needed.

The weapons harness, beat-up, scarred and covered with dark stains, showed no cracks. It didn't creak, and from everything I could see, it seemed in good shape. It wasn't dry. Someone – *Dad?* – had taken care of it. *Too small for Dad. Who does it belong to?*

A small 'S' shape, about an inch tall on the left bandolier strap, caught my eye. The same kind of insignia I saw on Dad's harness when he went to fix the mess at the lookout. *What can it mean?*

I shrugged into the rig. My heartbeat throbbed in my eyes.

"You're holding your breath," growled my inner voice.

I exhaled, sucked in a lungful of air, assessed.

"Shit."

The length worked okay. But it wrapped me – well, not quite twice – but too big. For sure, if I tried to use it the way it was, I'd be tangled up.

The tops of my ears simmered, my *mad* wanted to break something. "Dammit, I need this."

"Cut it down to fit."

"Yes. Of course." Once again, the accursed voice spoke truth.

My emotions bubbled happy, rose too high, fell too low, doing the roller coaster thing. "Yes, I most certainly can." A half-chortle got away; I pushed off the floor. "I need tools."

Lu saw, anticipated my move, and now waited with T-dog at the top of the kitchen stairs.

They flanked me as I snagged the Uzi and streaked for the barn. I grabbed a hayhook, found a hammer. We sprinted to the house. I took Mom's poultry shears from the kitchen drawer.

"I'll set up in the attic," I told the dogs. "Besides excellent light, I'll have clear visibility on all sides of the house. Plus easy sniper shots."

By the time I'd cut the ends off all the straps, broken blisters covered my hands. *Blisters on calluses should not be possible.*

Hammering the needle-sharp hook through the leather to make new holes proved much easier. I just draped the belt across a joist and hammered until the point hit wood.

Years of Mom teaching me to sew came in handy.

"Measure twice, cut once," I muttered. "Do not screw up, Katie." I could always make straps shorter – as many times as I needed – never the other way around. Still, it took three tries, three sets of punches on each strap, before the rig fit right. It hugged my body but didn't bind. I swung my arms, twisted, turned. *Stellar success.*

I found the bottle of leather care Mom used on our couch and treated the surfaces. The bandolier proved noiseless, creakless, whisperless, even when I shifted and stretched. I did a happy dance in the middle of the room.

In the bottom of the box, I found four knife sheaths – two large, two small – sized for a man with arms and legs like tree trunks. Memory twitched again – something lay hidden, buried deep. But I'd never met any of Dad's friends.

I removed the blades. *Careful, careful, careful.* Any weapons in Dad's

148

possession would be damn sharp. In addition to the two knives Dad gave me: my Ka-Bar fighting knife and my 9-inch skinning dagger, I now owned a switchblade and one monster freaking scary thing. If my guess was right – the brute thing I held was a Ka-Bar Kukri machete.

In the box, beneath the knives, lay a huge blade in an old stained sheath. The sight of it made me pant in terror. Air whistled hot in my throat and my guts churned. *Why does it affect me like this?* The weapon twisted my mind; the little memory door cracked ever so slightly. *Maybe I saw it in a nightmare?* It didn't matter – I'd use it. This was one hell of a knife.

I shoved the questions away and went to work. I cut, punched, buckled on. *Damn.* Did it again. *Damn.* Adjusted the strap lengths, tried them on for size and ease of access. *Double damn.* Did it again, put it on, adjusted the placement on my arms and legs. Finally they rode like they'd always been mine.

I sat sucking blood from broken blisters. My fingers and palms were a mess. I studied the cut-off pieces of leather, studied the reins. *Can I use them?*

Another trip to Dad's workshop in the barn yielded his rivet gun. I tacked loops on the harness back. Made room for the 30.06, the Uzi, the shotgun, the Sig, Dad's Glock, my Beretta and the Jennings.

"You'll look like a porcupine," said the sarcastic voice in my head.

Yeah, maybe. But with the fatigues and hat, the bandolier, my hair in a tail, I might pass for a man.

"Attagirl," said the voice, and to my surprise, these words were laced with approval.

I felt a little smile ghost across my face. My hatchet fit perfectly in one of the larger loops.

"Why don't you load it? See if you can pick it up?" snarked the voice in my head. "Plus your pack? Even if you can, how far can you carry them? Fifty feet?" The damn evil thing chuckled. "Silly girl."

The accursed voice was right. Again.

How would Dad solve it? I could carry two handguns, the Uzi and the sawed-off. Then if I broke the other weapons down, I could strap them on Terror and Lu's packs. *Problem solved. We can go.*

I'm going to be out there … alone. My heart stuttered.

"This is what you've always wanted," reminded the snotty voice in my head. "Your freedom."

"I didn't want it like this," I whispered. "I just wanted to be a normal kid in a normal world. That's all."

"Well, this is the hand you've been dealt, Katie. Play it well."

A pent-up scream roiled behind my clenched teeth. *I can't lose it. I can't. I can't. I can't.*

I did. The howls burst from me, split the silence in the house.

T-dog and Lu whined, shoved at me with broad shoulders, butted me with their heads.

"Stop it, Katie. Right now," ordered my mindvoice. "Someone might hear."

"How do I hold it in?" I screamed. "Take Mom's Xanax? I never have. How much do I take? Maybe a half, or a quarter? One pill put Mom sound asleep all night. I could wake up dead. Or worse, someone's captive."

But I knew – even if nothing bad happened to me – I couldn't afford to fuzz my mind.

I just don't dare.

Chapter Eighteen

It took me an hour to pull all my pieces together. I fought the fear washing through me in cold waves, messing with my mind. Loneliness, another thing I hadn't anticipated, amplified in the total silence of the forest.

I talked to the dogs. It helped but it didn't fill the need for people conversation. When the evil little voice inside spoke, I felt gratitude. I remembered a fact on insanity and loneliness – something I'd read and disbelieved. I understood now, how madness could happen to me.

I cranked the radio and listened. Cranked and listenened. I did my chores, gathered the eggs and fed the chickens. I kept an eye on Terror and Lu – my living intruder alarms – hyper-aware no one now protected me … except me.

I sucked it up and picked an apple, a peach and an apricot from our trees for lunch. Sitting in the porch swing, I strategized with Lupine and Terror. "Way I see it, guys, we've got four things to do before we go. Even for a day hike to my cave – never mind an overnight."

The dogs twitched their ears and nodded, far more polite than my mindvoice.

"More than four, I bet," the darkness chuckled, the morbid sound of a creaking door. "But let's hear it."

"I need to set up Dad's abandoned house scenario. Second, I need to prepare our full-size packs for permanent departure and hide them in the tunnel. That way we can run at a moment's notice. Third, I need to practice with my new weapons and bandolier."

"You can't fire the guns," the damn mindvoice cautioned. "You won't know if you hit anything."

"I know that," I said, felt my *mad's* flush hot on my ears. "I'm not stupid. Do you mind if I finish?"

"Oh, please do."

"Fourth, I have to write a letter to Dad explaining where I've gone and leave it in the tunnel."

"Not bad, Katie," said the hard kernel inside. "But there's one more. A big one. You need to move everything of value from the safe room into the tunnel. You best get busy."

For the next two hours, in front of the full length mirror in the hall, I worked with the rig, the guns and the knives. I practiced for combat, trying to increase my speed in pulling my weapons, refining my aim. I memorized what gun, what knife was where. I wouldn't have time to look or think. Dad had drilled one thing into me during training – hesitation would get me killed.

"Using your weapons must be automatic as breathing," said the darkness, in my father's voice. "Fumbling isn't an option. Practice some more."

I did. Then I worried and worried and worried while I ran the stairs from the basement to the attic and back again.

The dogs watched, yawned, and appeared bored. After my first few trips, the only things moving when I raced by were two sets of eyebrows.

When I couldn't run another stair, I began filling our gone-for-good packs, keeping the weight light.

"We won't carry things we can find, scrounge or hunt," I told Lupine and Terror. "But, on the flip side, if we're on the run, in winter, without shelter – we best be prepared."

Compass? *Yes.* Water purification tabs? *Yes.* Reconstituted meals. *Yes.* In my personal pack, I put a quarter-box of ammunition and one clip. The four grenades, extra ammo and clips, I split between Lu and T-dog.

What else? We'd tried the GPS – useless before. I tried it again. Still no response. I hid it in the tunnel. Perhaps in time, we'd be reconnected – if the national systems ever came back on.

If we have to go. We're ready. Between my guns and the dogs running prey to the ground, we'd eat well. Lu and T-dog were fast, canny hunters, young and in their prime.

I converted my backpack to horizontal, settled it around my waist and loaded the dogs. We went beneath the house into the concrete room.

"C'mon, guys, we gotta take our supplies into the tunnel."

T-dog and Lu flat balked. Sat. Refused to move.

I ordered, I pleaded. I gave up.

I removed Lupine and Terror's backpacks, hooked theirs to mine, end to end. Dragging them behind me, shuddering and hyperventilating and covered in gooseflesh, I crawled into the long dark awful space and left them about twelve feet away from the house.

It took two more hours to move everything important from the safe room into the tunnel. When I carried the box containing Mom's prized Thunder Egg collection, my eyes went hot and blurry. *She'll never enjoy them again.* I put a throw rug on the floor and laid the biggest geode on it, pulled it into the tunnel and sat it upright. Went back for the other, dragged it next to the first. Maybe I should have been prepared for what happened next. I wasn't.

Waves of chills, then rushes of fever flooded my body. A strange scent filled my nostrils, cloyed heavy in my throat. Not offensive, exactly, just exotic. My head filled with otherworldly music. I heard snatches of a language I didn't understand. Terrifying, exciting. My heart was going like a hammer. My body hummed like I'd downed a dozen stimulants. It had to be the Thunder Eggs. The geodes twinkled like Christmas tree lights, their flashing colors rainbowing the tunnel. I braced a hand against the wall, another on the floor.

"God," I whispered. "Oh God." I backed out of the safe room, leaned against the door to close it. My knees went boneless and I slid down the wall. Collapsed in a puddle on the floor.

Lupine and Terror wandered to me, wagged their tails and sat. Lu yawned.

"Shit!" I said. "Some guard dogs you are. Here I am scared enough to drop dead and you're sleeping?" Then to my darkness, "You in there? What the hell just happened to me?"

Never any input when I needed it most.

Okay, I'll either live or die. I'm absolutely powerless against something like that.

"Maybe," the voice in my mind shocked me. "Maybe not."

"Talk to me, please?" I begged. "Explain this. I'm not going crazy?"

But, of course, it wouldn't give me anything more. I took another look around, checked my preparation. I left a single cot set up to use tonight. *I'm ready.* I heaved a monster sigh. Everything valuable now hid where it would never be found. My knees wobbled beneath me, but I pushed to my feet.

I fed the dogs chow, let them out for their evening walk and chewed a stick of beef jerky. *I'm too tired to eat anything else. Perhaps I'm finally tired enough to sleep.*

Lupine and Terror came racing back; we went to the basement, locking the kitchen door behind us. Then, once in the safe room, I locked it too.

Armed and dangerous, we should be safe. My stomach clenched and knotted, I tossed and rolled on the narrow cot. I didn't sleep one minute all night.

I crawled from bed when the luminous dial on my watch said 4:00 am. I couldn't lie there another second. I ate a handful of trail mix, drank some water and paced the floor.

Because Terror and Lupine were sleeping on their rugs, it meant we were alone in the house. I debated going upstairs.

"Why?" asked the dark voice, right on cue.

"View the night sky, okay? I'm sick of being cooped up down here." My guts coiled at my words, the very same ones Mom used just before she jumped. *I won't think about what that says about my current state of mind.*

I drank a cup of water, debated brewing a cup of precious coffee, decided against a fire. Instead, with the dogs at my side, I picked up the Sig and my Beretta, unlocked the safe room door and made my way through the dark up the stairs. Unlocking the kitchen door, I crept into the dim main floor. I led with the pistol, made my way to the front of the house.

One last glance at Lu and Terror – all good. Tails telegraphed their delight to be headed outside. I slid both bolts to unlock, pulled the door open and went to sit in one of the Adirondack chairs.

The tendons in the back of my neck were taut as steel cables. I groaned, placed my guns on the seat beside me, and massaged the knots with both hands. I flinched for no reason, patted the guns beside me for reassurance but I couldn't relax. *I should be able to – now that I'm out of that damn coffin of a safe room.*

Volcanic ash clouds blown away, the stars shone bright. I breathed in fresh air and savored it.

Lu and Terror toured the yard, took care of their business, then stretched full length on the deck. No one nearby, no danger threatened. Still, no matter how much I rubbed, my neck wound tighter. The muscles in my back charleyhorsed. I touched my right shoulder and found three big knots.

"I can't stand this," I whispered to the dogs. "I'm going to scream. You guys stay here. And say dog prayers there is something in one of those bottles in our plastic bin."

I found an old bottle of muscle relaxants – from when Mom hurt her back. I poured a glass of water, choked down one of the pills. "Good to have," I said to no one at all. "Hope they're not too old to work." I put the bottle back, reclosed the box, and rejoined my furry friends on the front porch.

"Today, I'll implement Dad's scenario for the house and practice with my weapons." I eyeballed the dogs. "Whaddya think?"

Heads tilted, both sets of eyes blinked, but they didn't say a thing.

"How about one woof for yes? Two woofs for no?" Lupine opened her mouth, displaying sharp white teeth, lolled her tongue.

"I'll take your woof as assent," I said. "Motion carried." *Glad I have them*

– otherwise I'd be chatting with the voice in my freaking head. Or to no one at all. And that's truly crazy.

"Maybe you are," whispered the darkness. "Appears to run in the family."

"Screw off," I snapped. But only because I'd been worrying the same thing for weeks.

When the sky turned light, clear and hot, I smashed two padlocks with the trusty five-pound sledge. One I hung one on the kitchen door leading to the basement. The second, I stuck sideways on the root cellar door. I *faux-* ransacked the basement and the dirt cellar – very deliberately. I opened the bins and left a few shriveled potatoes, apples and onions.

I took Terror and Lu, my Uzi and the sawed-off shotgun, when I went to the garbage pile by the barn. It didn't take long to find the white plastic kitchen trash bags holding Mom's shattered china, figurines, and glassware. At least I didn't have to paw through old smelly garbage. I hoped. *Please let me have enough broken things to be convincing – so I don't have to dig into the nasty bags.*

Emptying the broken bits into a cardboard box, I sorted out the pieces I wanted and carried them inside. My goal: make the house appear long abandoned. I scattered the debris with a critical eye. My heart hammering like a blacksmith on his anvil, I cursed steadily at the bastards responsible. White-hot rage seared through me. *I want to kill something.*

"You need more trash," said my dark. "You need more."

I refused to answer.

Black graffiti scrawled across our family portrait – the one concealing the wall safe.

Loss struck like an axe between my eyes. Dropped me to my knees. *Mom's dead. Dad's missing. No family ever again.* Huge racking sobs stole my breath, my voice. I gave it up, cried myself dry.

My furry friends tried to comfort me, whined and licked tears until I quieted. I blew my nose on a paper towel, hiccuped to a stop and got it back together. My knees wobbled beneath me, but I stood, lifted the picture from the wall and placed it on the floor. The safe appeared undamaged. How did no one discover it?

"Shit! How did I forget?" My skin coated with sweat. I lifted the picture from the wall and placed it on the floor. The safe appeared undamaged. How had no one discovered it? *I can't believe I forgot.*

"You never opened it, never saw the combination. Why would you remember?" asked the mindvoice.

"So where would the combo be?"

"Think like your father, Katie."

I tried, I really, really did. I searched every corner of the house, the downstairs, the saferoom, and the tunnel. Nothing. My heart hammered, made me cough and pant. I belted on my holster, checked the clip on my pistol and went to the barn. Nothing. I checked the distributor cap hiding place. Nothing.

"You'll need the flashlight," said my helpful voice.

I grabbed the Maglite from the kitchen counter; stuck it in my belt.

With the dogs at my side, I stealthed into the woods. Checked every place I could think of around the tunnel lid.

"Dammit!" My stomach squished into my throat. I had to do it.

"Lu. Terror. Guard." I put them belly down for concealment. My clammy palms slipped when I gripped the edge of the opening and lowered myself onto the ladder. I wiped my hands on my shorts and went slow, checking the walls for secret spots, for plastic or metal boxes. When I reached the bottom, I stepped onto the dirt, clicked on the flashlight and searched every inch of the area. Nothing.

"You're hyperventilating," said alter me.

I fought to calm my breathing, listened for canine alerts, sounds of trouble. All quiet.

I shut off the Maglite off, stuck it in my belt, gripped the ladder and swarmed up the rungs. I didn't slow at the top, just leaped out, went flat on the ground. Looked around.

The dogs were relaxed. Birdsong broke the silence. I gripped the manhole cover, lowered it into place, and brushed dirt, pine needles and rocks over the top.

"C'mon, guys," I said. "Let's go home. We'll have to wait for Dad to open the safe. Right?"

Two long pink tongues flopped, I laughed. We practiced creeping through the trees all the way back.

Back in the house, I started enjoying myself. I took old papers from the family file cabinet and threw handfuls in the air for random placement. *What fun.* Still, my next throught sobered me. *It's mostly the feeling of finally being in control of something.*

In my bedroom, I strewed costume jewelry across my dresser, and on the floor. In my parents' room, I did the same. Draping a necklace over the edge of Mom's nightstand, memory caught me by surprise. *Mom let me play dress-up with these. Oh, Christ. Mom's dead. My fault.*

Harsh racking sobs stole my breath, my voice. I sank to my knees, gave it up and cried. *Won't I ever run out of tears?*

T-dog and Lu nudged, whined, licked tears until I got it back together. I went downstairs, found some paper towels – blew and blew and blew. My breathing still hitched and hiccupped when I stood and fought for composure. Feeling more in control, I did a visual search. *What else needs doing?*

Dropping a few pennies, a dime and two nickels, I made a subtle breadcrumb-kind-of-thing trail toward the front door.

In my best cursive, I wrote Dad a note on Mom's fancy stationery and sealed it in the matching envelope. *Where to leave it?*

"The tunnel?" suggested the voice. "That's where your father will look."

"Good idea."

Upstairs in my bedroom, on my study desk, sat an antique paperweight, all ruby and gold Carnival glass cut in intricate patterns. *Perfect!* I carried it and the letter downstairs, placed the envelope in the middle of the dirt floor and held it in place beneath the heavy sphere.

Maybe when I get back, Dad will be here.

I didn't recognize the person in the full length mirror. The camo uniform and hat from the trunk were too short for Dad and too big around the middle for me. No problem. I cinched the pants with a belt, they worked fine tucked into my lug sole boots. The sage, tan and gray colors blended perfectly with the summer foliage, pine trees and dusty bluffs. I put a tan tank top under the oversize shirt and left it open. I pulled my hair back and put on the cap, evaluated my appearance. *I don't look like a girl.*

"Which is, I believe," I said to the dogs, "the desired result."

The stranger in the mirror began to shrug into the harness. *First ooops.* The loose shirt prevented a good fit, bunching and twisting beneath the leather.

"Wear just the tank, put the shirt in your pack," said my adviser.

"Fine." *The damn thing's right again.* I rolled the shirt, set it aside. Donning the bandolier and my gun belt, I adjusted my weapons. I strapped on the arm and leg sheaths; positioned knife handles and gun butts.

I pulled each weapon twice, watched in the mirror. *Too much thinking. Too slow, too jerky. This will take time; I don't have it.* I worked with the rig long past bedtime.

The next morning, I fed the chickens and leaned their ladder inside the coop. If we weren't back before dark they could put themselves to bed or roost in the trees.

"If you don't come back at all, they'll have a better chance to survive. It is what you're doing? Right?" asked the little dark voice.

I didn't answer.

What did I need for a day trip? Harness or backpack? I couldn't wear both. I didn't want to leave any of my guns behind. Not even in the tunnel.

Still, if I didn't, I'd have to break down the rifles, maybe remove the stocks to carry them. Not such a wonderful idea. Okay, I'd take the Uzi, the Sig, put my Beretta and the Jennings in Lu's pack. Extra ammo and a couple of grenades in Terror's. I strapped a small fanny pack around my waist, above my gun belt.

I eyeballed T-dog and Lu and grinned. I hadn't planned to have them carry anything on a simple day trip, but they could. Huge strong canines.

Lu read my mind – I swear it. She grumbled, low in her throat, and belly crawled out the back door. Terror's big dark eyes got round, and he went low profile right behind her.

I laughed, ran down the stairs, found the plastic storage bin marked Terror/Lupine, and snapped off the top. A quick dig through the contents produced their canine packs.

The day heated up fast. I sweated in the camo pants I'd tucked into my boots. I thought about shorts – no. I'd need long pants if we stayed out. Temperatures up here dropped dramatically at night. If I needed to blend, I'd put on the uniform shirt.

I packed replacement explosives in a small duffle while I waited for my furry friends. Although they'd fled, they wouldn't be able to stand it. Less than five minutes later, I heard the click of claws on vinyl, felt eyes on me. Took a peek at the top of the stairs.

Saw accusing, betrayed canine eyes.

"Hey, you can carry your own dog food. And a few things for me. Unless you'd rather stay home?" I did lunges up the stairs two at a time, knelt and split the contents of my backpack between theirs.

"Come, Lu. Come Terror."

A pair of yellow eyes and two cocoa ones evaluated the packs.

Evaluated me.

"Hey, you don't help; you don't go."

Lupine snorted, raised her head and stalked to my side. Proud, she stood stacked like a show dog. Acting like she'd thought of it.

"You haughty wolf. You don't fool me one bit." I laid the pack across her broad body, settled it comfortably, buckled it. Then I did Terror's. He whuffed at me, ran his long pink tongue over my face, left a broad saliva trail behind.

"Ewww, devil dog." But I forgot, just for a minute, all the bad. I just enjoyed the rush of feel-goods. We were leaving this place of such sadness – if only for a short time.

Joy, contagious and spirit-lifting, surged warm through my body.

Lupine peeled her wolfen lips back in a smile, sharp white fangs glistened. *Good thing I know her like my own soul. Otherwise, she'd scare me to death.*

One last glance around. My heart slid into my boots. *This is wrong. I shouldn't go.*

"Fear talking, not good sense," said the darkness.

"True. I have to scout. I need to make this trip." I left the house unlocked, of course. *What would be the point?*

Terror and Lu were delighted – leaping and chasing on the lawn like a pair of pups. Growling, showing hackles, mock fighting.

I forgot my worries for a minute, snorted at their antics. I called them close, kept them with me. I sobered at the task of setting the explosives on our way out. *Every time I do, I'm positive I'll lose a hand.*

Sweat coated my body, slid stinging in my eyes, rolled down my spine. The wide leather straps of my bandolier laid hot, trapping moisture and slithering against my skin. My hands trembled, slippery with sweat, like willow leaves in a breeze. Shook so bad I held them in front of me and stared at their quivering. I gathered all my bits of courage and filled the empty spots.

"Stop it," I ordered. "Right now." *No chance.* They trembled more violently. Nothing to be done for it – Dad's explosives terrified me.

"You could just skip the reload," said the voice in my mind.

No, I promised Dad.

"Think about it again," insisted the darkness.

I stopped, reconsidered. The voice had it right. *It makes better sense to save the replacements – set them after I get back.*

T-dog and Lu sidled toward the trees, sniffing at body remains.

I quickly called them back. "Not today. You could step on a mine. Sit and stay."

I refused to look. I hid the olive green duffle containing the extras high up in a tree, above lots of branches loaded with leaves. Anyone walking below would never notice my bag.

I took a fast surveillance of my surroundings. No breeze, no disturbances to indicate anyone or anything moved through the area. I blew out a huge breath, tried to slow my adrenaline rush.

I decided on Honeycomb Bluffs. From there, I could see everything, except the gorge floors. I'd be above any flood damage, and I could see what had happened everywhere else.

"We'll check the low ravine on Succor Creek, okay?" I asked my protectors. "If it's good, we'll cross there." The stream burbled and flowed fast but I knew all the deep spots and how to go around them. At least I used to.

Sorrow hit me then. I gasped, pressed my fingers against my lips. Massaged my temples. We'd be passing the place where I met Todd. *Now he's dead too – the one I dreamed would show me the world outside.*

About halfway out, I saw dog ears twitch, heads tilt. I slid behind a boulder, motioned Terror and Lu in beside me. Then I heard noises. A man and woman hiked up the trail. They weren't quiet.

"I'm tired already, Dave," said the woman. "And I think I have a blister."

"Well, it's not like we planned to hike to California," he said. "But it's better than dying down there."

"Yes." The woman's steps halted. "Let me put on another sock. These new boots are stiff. Can you reach in my pack and pull one out?"

"Sure. We're lucky, you know, that the store we found had any supplies left," he said. "It may take us a long time, unless we find a car and open road, but at least we're getting out."

I waited, silently, patiently, until the noises of zippers stopped, and the woman said, "There. That's better. We can go now."

When their footsteps faded, and I was sure we wouldn't be seen or heard, I motioned to my dogs. "Okay, you guys. We can too."

I headed up the hillside, the dogs roaming ahead. They knew our destination. We almost always stopped at my secret cave.

"Of course, there won't be anyone in there. No need to worry about bad people." A deep malicious chuckle laced the dark words. "Or if it hasn't collapsed."

160

"Damn you," I growled and hiked faster.

I've finally reached the point where there is nothing left to stop me from leaving. I am going from what is safe to what is unknown. Entirely on my own. Exactly what I've wanted for years.

I couldn't stop my shudder.

Chapter Nineteen

The same day

A good three hour walk-jog put us across two ravines, at the bank of Succor Creek. Beyond the gurgling stream, the borders of the porous lava bluffs loomed. I held my arms away from my body, let the aggressive breeze cool my sweat. The ash stirred beneath my boots, but the air was clear.

The dogs were already belly deep in the water. I felt a twinge of worry for the contents of their backpacks. *Ah, what the hell.* I stood, gazed across the fast-running stream and evaluated the bluff – base to top.

The Honeycombs were fun to climb … normally.

I loved the challenge … before.

Only three weeks ago, nature held all the dangers. If you paid attention, the possibility of injury by a snake, a four-legged predator or a hiking accident became so remote it didn't warrant using brain cells to worry. Now, my day-trip joy evaporated, burned away by the terrible events of The Great Awful. Now, I not only needed to worry about being seen while I climbed, but also about loose rocks, and cracks in the ground and bluffs.

"You have to do this, Katie," counseled the dark voice. "Get your head in the game."

From the top of the Honeycombs I could see the entire countryside. The only exceptions were the bottoms of the ravines, but otherwise with an hour or two of careful surveillance, I'd know if anyone moved within the vicinity of my house.

The stream gurgled, ran so clear I saw silvery scales on the trout and the mineral speckling on the stones in the creek bed. A fine layer of glass and rock lay on the bottom, filtered between the pebbles. Cupping a hand, I dipped cool clear water and gulped before it leaked through my fingers. Beside me, Lupine and Terror splashed and lapped.

"Yum." I scooped and drank until my abdomen pooched. The noon sun shimmered and scorched, stinging my arms, legs, and the exposed skin on the back of my neck. *Sunscreen. I forgot my freaking sunscreen.* I made a mental note to put it in our pack for next time.

"How about we stay here a bit longer?" *While I try and figure how to get to the top without exposing us.* I moved back from the creek, up the hillside and into the woods. Leaning against the trunk of a large pine tree, I sheltered in the shade. The furry ones joined me, woofed and flopped on the ground.

I fished the binocs from the pack on T-dog's back, slipped the strap around my neck and dialed them in. I let them rest against my chest while I allowed my unfocused eyes to roam in a broad random sweep. Just like Dad taught me.

My gaze moved across the spot … froze, snapped back. *Shit. There.* I heard my gasp, pressed my lips together to stifle sound. *Did I give myself away?* My heart hammered in my chest like a crazed flamenco dancer. The three of us saw it at the same time.

Lu rumbled. Terror's deep growl echoed. I felt, rather than saw them shift. Their ears perked and two pair of eyes fixed on a spot across the gorge. Two pair of fangs flashed white against black lips.

I saw something – the dogs confirm it. But what? Then, it came again, an unnatural movement, something tall, sliding between the trees. *There.* A human form silhoutted against the grain of the landscape.

I picked a ruined tree trunk, charred and split by lightning strike, for my landmark, whipped up the binocs, zeroed in on the stranger. *A second later and I'd have missed him.* Male, by the size. Seemed to be alone. My lungs heaved and burned. It took everything I owned to keep from sprinting away.

"You're doomed if you run," said the voice in my head. "Coward, too."

I watched the hiker's subtle movements. He went invisible, blended. Just like Dad.

My guardians' gazes never wavered, their head movements minute. We tracked the camo-clad man across the span of the gorge. Watched him take care, moving elusive down the hillside toward the water.

"Don't give yourself away. If he spots you, wants to find you – well trained as he appears – he can," whispered the dark. "Someone that stealthy can sneak up on you. Someone patient will wait between you and the house. You cannot evade a soldier this good."

"I have Lupine and Terror," I said, hating the quiver in my voice.

"Someone really good might get them too."

"You shut the fuck up," I whispered.

But the damn voice did damage. My brain fizzed, like little vessels exploding, filled with worry. No … not worry. *It's fear.*

What should I do? Hike around him, head him off? Kill him before he can me? God on toast, Katherine Angela Davis, you are contemplating stalking and murdering a total stranger. What if he's a good person, or like the man with the BB gun? What if you go and kill a possible ally?

I realized Lu, T-dog and I were screwed – trapped here in the woods. If we left now, he'd spot us. We couldn't go directly home – he could follow. Plus, I needed to know which way he headed. And I couldn't be completely sure of the terrain any more. The quakes had rearranged more than one tree and boulder.

So, we watch him. We wait. We see.

The dogs grinned when I gave them the hand signals. I swear it. We were going to do what they loved best. Stay in the woods.

We backed into the brush; moved to put a few trees in the line of sight between me and whoever traveled down the hill. Then we stilled, tried for invisibility.

The glimpses, strung together, revealed a broad shouldered male. When he crossed a clearing, I saw his dark sage camo blended seamlessly with the blue-gray-green of the high country pines. The binoculars showed me a man who might be anywhere from eighteen to thirty. The grim expression on his tanned face made him appear old. If he smiled, he might be okay looking. Short dark hair, clean shaven. *He's good. Moves smooth, efficient. His camo pattern matches Dad's.*

He wore binoculars slung around his neck. When he crossed from one stand of blue pines to another, I saw a weapons rig. Guns, rifle, knives … something sticking up over one shoulder. He bent, dodged a tree limb, gave me peek at what he carried. *Shit! He's packing a crossbow. Cool.*

"Better be careful of this one," said the darkness. "Probably military, but if he is, why is he out here?"

"Dammit, would you just be quiet," I whispered.

The man moved across a clearing and I watched and assessed. Taller than Dad, his shoulders were broad above a thick deep chest. Even with the loose camo, I admired the way his muscles bunched and moved. *He's strong. Is he alone?* I couldn't breathe. Bony fingers clamped my lungs. *He's scary as hell.*

"You find him interesting as hell," snarked the darkness. "Admit it."

"No," I whispered. "No, I don't."

Lupine and Terror kept steady watch on the man, their breathing a slow unexcited chugging.

They aren't worried about him – unlike others who've come. A good sign? Or is he just too far away for them to know?

The man moved down the hill, headed for the bubbling creek in the ravine bottom. Through the binocs, I saw his hesitation, the stealthy load of his bow, the smooth release. A gobble, a puff of feathers.

"I think he just bagged turkey dinner," I whispered.

Two tails thumped the carpet of pine needles beneath us, hopeful eyes begged.

"Not a chance." Then I felt bad because they wilted, right before me. "Depending on where he goes," I said. "We can sit right here and watch. No risk of him spotting us."

Like Dad, this guy never stopped checking his surroundings. Constant head turns, long listening stops, careful scans with the binoculars. Could he feel our eyes? My intuition said he did. *Why isn't he carrying a backpack? Is his camp close?*

"We watch until we know," I whispered. Waiting until the man moved downhill, I parked my butt on the ground and leaned back against the tree trunk.

Beside me, Lu and Terror shifted, then sat up on the pine straw. Their eyes never left the stranger when he made his way to the edge of Succor Creek.

He cupped one big hand, dipped and drank. Then sat, patiently waiting, fingers tickling the stream's surface. One grab, so fast his hand blurred, and the man held a silvery fish, flipping, struggling to escape. He smiled, murmured something, and stood. Backtracking to a stand of junipers, he disappeared between two large rocks.

Tingles of panic lit my fingertips.

Where did he go? Did he see me after all? All he has to do is cross the creek – fast. Or shoot me. I can't get away.

"Stop it, Katie," said the darkness using my father's voice. "He didn't see you."

A duffle in one hand, backpack in the other, the archer made his way back creekside. He laid two weapons close at hand, a rifle I didn't recognize and a large handgun. A quick peel of his shirt exposed a lean muscled torso crosshatched with random white scars. My breath hitched at his six-pack abs. Fishing a washcloth and a bar of soap from the backpack, he lathered and rinsed, head constantly turning, surveilling.

Dad's got more scars, but he's older. Why doesn't this guy just strip and bathe? My heart missed a couple of beats.

"Voyeur? Pervert?" said the voice in my head. "First look at a naked man?"

"No. Well, yes," I whispered and the dogs perked their ears. "Curious, that's all." Succor Creek's splashing melodies covered my words.

"Ha," snarked my mindvoice.

His quick wash complete, the man fished a clean beige tee from his pack and pulled it on. He increased his vigilance, whipping his head up, maybe a dozen times.

I bet his senses are telling him someone else is around. I bet he wanted a bath/ swim/shave but he doesn't dare. He'll be nothing but careful until he knows why he's spooked.

I watched the stranger search, sweeping my hiding place with his binocs, but he couldn't see me, on the ground, tucked away behind the trees. I spied while he cooked both the turkey and the fish, watched him sit, his back braced against a big pine while he ate. He listened to his radio but I couldn't tell if he liked what he heard. Or if he heard anything. *So where is his camp?*

When dusk fell, the archer tied the duffle to the backpack, slid the straps over his arms, and pulled a rope from behind tumbleweeds piled by the tree trunk. It hung from the pine's upper branches – virtually invisible.

My chin dropped, my eyes went wide. I watched the muscles of the stranger's upper body bunch as he went hand-over-hand up the rope. Even with my binoculars, I barely spotted his hideout. He'd stretched a deep green hammock between two big limbs, concealed from below by the lower bushy branches. *If I hadn't seen him earlier ….* A chill rippled through my body. *I could have walked right below him and never known.*

"The dogs would have smelled him," said my adviser. "Still, better watch overhead from now on, yes?"

"Yes." I stared in admiration while he wormed onto his bed, reeled in the rope, and settled for the night.

Nice! Now I thought about it, I remembered Dad talking about this. Because of Terror and Lu, I never considered it. But they normally slept on the ground – and higher would be much safer for me.

Obviously, the archer hid too. From what? Or who? Or perhaps just cautious?

"Maybe he's hunting someone?" suggested the mindvoice. "Or perhaps someone's hunting him?"

My veins filled with icy sludge. *Which way? Is he good or bad?*

Goosebumps rippled up my arms and legs. *How long has he been out here? What has he seen?*

"You haven't been diligent in your perimeter patrols, have you, Katie girl?" chuckled the malevolent dark thing in my head. "He could have been by the house already."

Oh shit. I needed to get between him and home before he saw me. I needed to keep him from seeing me. I needed to make sure Mom .... *Oh God! There's no Mom to worry about ... but ... maybe Dad's come back.*

If the man slept, and he probably would, I had to rest too. My fuzzy brain felt like cotton candy. My body ached with the need to lie down, stretch out.

I considered sneaking away after dark. What stopped me wasn't exhaustion.

"Can't use a flashlight," said the voice in my head. "And you can't move in the dark. You'll make noise."

"Yes," I whispered. "A step on a branch would sound like a gunshot. Might get me shot. Or I could stumble and fall. No, we have to wait for dawn."

"Here, guys." I unloaded the dogs. Unpacked and spread my sleeping bag by the tree trunk. The three of us lay side by side in the warm summer night.

I worried, and stewed, my viscera queasy and upset.

"Tomorrow," I whispered. "Tomorrow we go early. We slip away and we get back home and hide."

I slid from sleep, conscious of something hard stabbing my spine. My exploring hand found a rock beneath my sleeping bag. *Damn.* A light bright enough to sear my eyelids, pulled me awake. An orange ball, shot through with white brilliance, pierced a turquoise sky.

Memory struck. *Shit. What time is it? The stranger. Is he still in the tree?*

I sprang to my feet, whipped the binocs up, searched for his hammock. Saw his head move, saw a pair of field glasses zoom on my hiding place.

Oh fuck. Big screw-up, Katie. He's in the tree – he won't be for long. He saw you.

I stilled, angled my binocs to minimize any lens reflection, and tried for unobtrusive. *Maybe he just saw Lu or T.*

"No joy," chortled the evil voice in my head. "He saw you."

The morning sun glinted, threw a bright reflection near me. *The metal trim on Lu's pack.*

"Oh shit," I whispered, tried to pry it loose. It didn't budge. I spat on the ground, twirled my finger in the dirt and ash, scooped up mud, and covered the spot. *Do it better, later.*

I peeked through the glasses, found my eyes locked with the stranger's.

The man's mouth moved, his sculpted lips easy to read. "Hi." One large hand waved. "Matt." A finger pointed to himself; then to me. "You?"

Goddammit. Shit. Hell. My brain was mush. *Do I run? Yes. Can he catch me? Maybe ... probably yes.*

"Talk?" He tapped the finger against his chest; pointed at me again. He didn't try the hand signals Dad taught me – if they are military. *I'll keep that my little secret. For now anyway – maybe forever.*

I shrank back against my tree, kept the binocs on him. A shudder rippled my body. I'd seen his skill with the crossbow. The center of my chest itched, like it already bore a target.

"I won't hurt you," he said, turning his palm up, pressing it to his chest. *Yeah, sure. Everyone is so civilized lately.*

"I know you from somewhere." The dark heavy stubble on his face made him look like a pirate – maybe a bandit. Probably an escaped felon. He waggled his hand, then dropped his binoculars on his chest. "Please? Talk?"

"No." I shook my head. I wanted to break my gaze, but I had to know when he left the tree. I kept the glasses fixed on him, drinking in details. *Nice, actually.* Dark eyes, and dark hair in a military buzz cut, accented his chiseled face. He had blunt features and a generous mouth. He reminded me of my father – same look, unsophisticated and a little shaggy. The large square hand, moving his field glasses back to his eyes, bore scars – a competent working hand. Like Dad's. I knew he'd be tough, rugged, capable.

"Have to talk," he mouthed. "Me – there?" The hand signals, finger pointing made his intent unmistakable.

"No."

"Good protectors." He forked two fingers at Lu and T.

I trembled and watched him scan my hiding place, scan the dogs. Scan me. I squeezed my arms against my sides to hide my shivers.

"Don't let him see your fear," advised the mindvoice.

How can I not be afraid? He can hunt me down and kill me.

"Is that a wolf?"

"No."

"No? To which question?" he said and smiled. It transformed his stern face into a little boy's innocence.

I grinned back before I could stop myself. My body warmed before fear reasserted.

Damn me. I want to meet him. I don't dare.

I put my game face back on. "No."

"You," the finger pointed at me, then at his mouth. "Beautiful smile." He mouthed the word, "Safe." Pointed at me again, then himself, "You. Safe. With me."

"No." I gazed back through the glasses, found my eyes locked with his. When I focused on his mouth, I thought of kisses. The wave of longing hit me in the gut, a hard blow. I flinched, saw him do the same.

"What the hell?" His dark brows arced high toward his hairline. A wicked, sexy smile lit his face. "Wait. I'm coming. Talk."

"No." My lips felt too loose on my face, they quivered, made it hard to form the word. My heart pounded – from fear or something else?

I don't even think he's cute. Todd was cute. And he's dead. I don't like this man's looks. Yes, I do. He's sexy. But he's way too old for me. Dad would have a coronary.

"What is going on?" I whispered. But even in my naiveté, I knew the answer.

"Matthew Scavelli." The pointed finger at his chest; then at me. "You?"

"Nobody."

"Oh, you're somebody. For damn sure. *Bruja*, maybe? You just cast a spell on me? Wait. Please."

"No," I said, but he'd disappeared. I didn't get everything he said, but close enough. *WTF is a … bruja? A witch? Yeah, that's it.*

In the tree where Matthew slept, branches moved, shook and wiggled.

I watched the rope writhe, snakelike, against the pine's trunk. *Why am I still here?* I watched booted feet hit the ground, saw a puff of dust, watched the big man spin toward my hiding spot. I watched him lope down the hill, dodging rocks, fallen trees. He reached the flat, and leaping from rock to rock across the rocky terrain, raced for the creek. Close – too close.

My lungs worked like bellows, like I'd run ten miles. I had a roaring in my ears – excitement or fear? *I should be sprinting for home right now. Am I bespelled too?* My feet seemed fixed in concrete.

Matt didn't yell, but his deep voice carried across the musical babble of Succor Creek. "Talk to me. You are in danger – you need protection. I can help."

"No. I'm fine." I heard the quaver in my voice, hoped he didn't.

Except I'm not, I'm scared, I'm an emotional mess, I'm all alone. My legs won't work and I need to pee. My world is ruined, my head just got twisted inside out. I have no idea what's going on. Why am I just waiting, like the idiot girl in the movies, who stands and screams and lets the bad guy grab her?

"Move, Katie!" snarled the darkness in Dad's voice.

I stuffed my sleeping bag into Terror's pack, strapped both on the dogs, wrapped mine around my waist. Shrugged into my harness.

"Wait. Please. We have to talk," Matt said. I looked, saw him creekside, his body tensed like a coiled spring. He reached toward me in supplication. "Don't run. I'll still find you. You belong with me."

"No, I belong to only me." But my body vibrated, taut with needing … someone. Something.

"You lie,"the darkness said. "He's never even touched, but he owns you, sure as winter comes every year."

"This is a bad thing," I snarled.

"Maybe not. If he's good, he can help you." whispered the dark.

"Wait for me," Matthew pleaded, dark eyes holding my gaze. "Please."

"No." I moved sideways from the tree, kept my eyes on him.

"I'll find you," he said. "You'll have to kill me to stop me."

"I can do that. Should it be now?" I pitched my voice to carry, made it cold as death. The pit of my stomach jittered like it held ice cubes. But the rest of my body surged with waves of hot prickles. My knees wobbled. *I couldn't shoot him, couldn't aim a gun. My hands are shaking. Can I get out of here without falling down? Shit!*

"Can you kill me?" Matt scanned my body. I saw the binocs pause, move slow and deliberate over each of my weapons. "Perhaps you could."

Then his glasses paused on my chest. He startled like he'd been tasered. *What in hell did he see to make him react like that?* I watched him watch me. Studied his breathing. Like me, he struggled for control, labored for breath.

"Now," he said. "Now we really have to talk."

WTF? What just happened?

"Tell me one thing, pretty girl. Do you believe in love at first sight?"

My pulse throbbed in my throat. I faked an icy smile at this grown man.

"I don't believe in love," I said, knowing I lied.

"Oh yes, you do." The darkness mocked. "You're sixteen. You do."

"It's critical I talk with you." The full lips moved, his words carried clear across the creek. "I'd never harm you. I'll protect you with my life." One big hand stretched wide in supplication.

What just happened to make him go there?

"I protect myself," I said. But instead of running, I watched Matt, aware time seemed to slow, my senses alive to the point of pain and irritation. "I can't stay, Matt. I can't." *But I want to. Why in hell did I just use his name?*

The pragmatic inner voice saved me. "You better disappear. He'll be across the creek and on you in a minute."

"Perhaps later," I said to Matt. " Not now." It took every bit of determination, every bit of my Davis' stubborn streak, to turn away.

At my movement, Terror and Lu leaped to their feet.

I slid around the big boulder, knowing it hid my retreat up the hill and into the stand of pines. From there, it led to my escape route.

"No. Wait. Please. God damn it! I have to keep you safe." I heard him call. "I don't even know your name."

We fled.

Chapter Twenty

Terror, Lupine and I moved stealthy, noiseless and fast through the narrow rocky ravine, then cut across to the next sagebrush covered hill. A crack in the ground startled me, it hadn't been there before. I leaped it, and so did the dogs.

"We've got a lead," I told Lupine and Terror. "If he packs up his camp." *Shit! What if he doesn't? He'll be on us in minutes.*

I put on my happy whisper for the dogs. "We know where we're going, we won't leave a trail. He'll have a hard time tracking us." *Will he follow?*

"Certainly appears so," said my mindvoice. "He wants to talk to you badly."

"Will he find me?"

"Probably, if he's as good as he seems," it answered.

"God, please. Let us get away from him. God, please let us reach the tunnel and get inside without being seen. I promise I'll never do anything bad again – never even think anything bad again. I promise I'll never swear. I'll go to church – if I can find one. God, just let us get away."

"What in hell are you doing?" snapped the voice in my head. "Making promises you can't – won't keep? Kindly remember who and what you are."

I am Don Davis' daughter and I have the tunnel. A hot rush of pride made tears sting. Thanks to Dad, we were invisible for as long as we needed. Advantage – me. *If … we get home undetected.*

I refused to consider how I'd get Lupine and Terror down the ladder. We'd figure it out.

"Okay, you with all the answers. I believe Matthew's better than just good," I whispered. "He reminds me of Dad. He might find the manhole, even if he can't open it. He'll work out the connection to the house – you know he will. If he does, then what?"

When I wanted an answer, the damn voice stayed silent.

Still, two eerie yellow eyes, and two cocoa ones peered at me and Lupine snorted.

"You don't think anybody's that good?" I murmured and she whuffed again.

"Hope you're right," I mouthed the words, grinned and we moved deep into the blue-green pine forest. Keeping below the ridge, we worked our way west, toward home. An hour later, I heard a crack, leaped straight up, and bit my lip to squelch a scream. In the utter silence of the day, the noise sounded like a gunshot. *A snapped branch, I'm sure. Maybe Matthew Scavelli made a misstep. If he did, I'd bet my life he's back there cursing up a storm.*

The back of my neck prickled, I froze and listened. The dogs waited, motionless, their eyes tight-focused behind us. Heads tilted, ears cocked. I heard nothing, and I wondered if they did. I used my tongue, then my fingertip to investigate the bite on my lip. Both found warm viscous liquid.

"Ow," I swallowed the word, and swallowed blood.

"It probably wasn't Matt," I whispered. "A mule deer, an elk, a bear made the noise – actually, it could have been anything."

"Ha," said my inner voice. "You're a liar."

"Yes," I whispered. "Yes, I am. I know the man's hunting me." Question was: Why?

He wanted to talk. Then, whatever he saw on my chest made him determined. I don't have big breasts – that couldn't have been it. I stared down at my chest, at the bandolier. The insignia like Dad's showed plain – I'd left it because … well, I don't know why. I just did. Maybe because of Dad. *Why does this guy think he knows me?*

We needed to put distance between us. Lose him. At least confuse him. A quick motion sent Lu in front, Terror behind me. My breath came in small sips because fear vise-gripped my chest. We stayed beneath the low tree branches, stealthy on the carpet of dry brown pine needles, hidden from everything except direct line of sight.

A magpie scolded us.

I opened my mouth to scold it back, and felt chill fingers spider down my spine at my near screw-up.

"Just announce to the world where you are." The damnable voice in my head never missed a chance to twist the knife.

"I didn't, did I? Just shut it," I hissed.

I hiked and watched and thought. Tried to keep a grip on my panic, my terror and my sanity.

Matthew … well, I figured him an unknown, a wild card. He might be good – but he might not. *God! I can't believe I forgot. He could be infected.*

My breathing went hard, came in funny little pants. *I'll evade, like Dad taught me. I'll do all the right things.*

We didn't go straight home – not that I wanted to – just in case Matt spotted us.

About a mile out from our house, the hackles on the dogs bristled. Low growls rumbled in deep chests. A few yards farther on, I saw the garbage. *How dare they?*

Bits of trash, carelessly tossed, mixed with crushed silver tumbleweeds, orange globemallow, yellow and blue wildflowers. One of the weeping willows hung with new additions. Pink and gray, bits of bone and red stained cloth festooned the drooping branches.

"So," I whispered. "We've got company and it isn't Dad or Matthew. But at least one pig-person paid for the intrusion."

The red film of fury slid across my eyes, my *mad* burst through. I fought an impulse to charge into my house, subdued my rage because giving in would get the three of us killed.

Sneaking into the woods, we worked our way into the stand of trees close to the manhole lid. In case we needed to hide, I wanted the tunnel close. The thick trees and woods, and the giant clumps of rocks Dad piled around the area provided great cover. I might catch conversation – get information – if this bunch posted guards.

A land mine waited just twenty feet away. I kept Lu and T-dog close. *We're behind the boulders. Too far for any detonation to hurt us, close enough for a front row seat.*

I let an icy smile creep across my face while I waited. I hoped they would all die because there would be less I'd have to kill. *God bless me. When did I get so cold?*

"When others made you defend yourself and your Mother. Not your blame," assured my little voice.

Oh God, Mom. Gone, dead. I pinched my lips together, knuckled the tears from my cheeks. *And Dad? Where could he be? Is he dead too?*

Loud voices, moving in our direction, alerted me. My furry guardians rumbled, and I hand-signaled silence. They settled on their bellies, but their paws were well under them, ready to spring on the instant. I moved to peer past my rock.

"Last place I want to be," snarled the short fat man. His fringe of gray hair, caught in a greasy ponytail, only accentuated his baldness.

"We'll stay out all night?" asked the second sentry.

"We have to. I wouldn't cross Za for the world."

"Well, way I see it, we don't have to stand at attention."

"Agreed."

When I caught a glimpse of him, I muffled my laughter with both hands. The man resembled a bloodhound. I watched him run stubby fingers through his short thick hair until it stood on end.

They stood together, smoking and talking.

The wind came up, gusted, and blew the smells of burning tobacco and the stink of unwashed bodies in my direction.

I can hear every word.

The conversation ranged from the gang, their leader Za, and her escape from the maximum security military prison.

Are all of the people in my house criminals?

"What's her story?" The younger man asked. "I wasn't in prison. I need to know."

"I wasn't in there either – I joined them on the road. They said swear allegiance or die. I didn't want to die. Woman is a genius, one of those people so smart they don't care who lives or who dies." The short man's voice trembled. "You can't say I told you. She'll kill you – worse, she'll kill me. Thing is, she's a sociopath. She loves blood – other people's. You don't know what I've seen her do."

"I won't say anything, I promise." The mournful tones of the taller man were perfect for an undertaker.

"If you do, she'll kill us. It was beyond awful what she did to two guys who mocked her. I still have nightmares."

I motioned Lu and T-dog to stay quiet, moved to my knees slow and easy, peeked around a boulder.

The speaker's skin was pale as skim milk. He swallowed hard and continued. "The original six from the prison are loyal to the grave. Two are her brothers. They'll do anything to protect her. She knows this area, got them out before the plague came. Watch yourself – they sneak around, they listen."

"Oh, man, I sure will," the tall man's voice trembled. "If you're sweating just thinking about it – well, damn. I promise, I'll be careful."

"Be careful who you talk to, careful what you say. Some newcomers thought to get rid of her, take control of the gang. She killed them." I heard him make a hacking, gagging sound. "What they did to those poor people … oh God. She loved it. More they screamed the more she laughed and giggled."

The tall man shuddered. "What's her story?"

"Maximum security, military jail. You figure it out." The short man's pony tail bobbed with the shake of his head.

The taller man's jowls flopped when he nodded. "Terrorist shit, maybe?"

The way the short man's face twisted, it wasn't a good memory. "She's good looking, but she's hard on men. They don't last long with her. Rumor is she's hunting some soldiers – sworn revenge on them. And on their families."

The taller man snorted. "I'm glad she picked the stupid blonde boy for her plaything. He takes the pressure off the rest of us. Can't believe that piece of shit gave up his parents just so he could live."

He raked his hands through his hair again.

"Where'd he come from?"

"Oh, Jesus," whispered the bloodhound man. "You joined us after that happened? She skinned her old favorite alive. When we took the lookout, Tanner saw the boy as a threat; put a bullet in the kid. Mistake he made, he didn't kill him."

"Oh shit."

The taller man whispered and I had to strain to hear.

"She patched up pretty boy, then killed Tanner slow. When the kid woke up, she made him help. If you see her put on her ballcap and her sunglasses, you hide."

"Why?"

"Blood's going to fly."

"God! That big flashy necklace she never takes off? Is it real?"

"So I hear. Some reason for it, but no one knows. No one asks."

"If it is, it's worth a fortune."

"Yeah, and worth your life to ask. Be smart. Stay away from her, and don't ask questions."

The men moved and I slipped back behind my rock. I heard a shuffle of feet, someone cleared his throat.

"Her name is funny. Is it short for something?"

"Eliza. Don't mention that either." The short man coughed, added, "Hey, make sure you don't tell anyone what I said. Smoke?"

"I won't talk. Thanks."

The two men were quiet again, so I rose just enough to see where they were. They hadn't moved, just sat, leaning against a rock.

I slid back into my seated position and waited.

Two clicks, the rasps of a lighter. Then, again the acrid smell of burning cigarettes wafted past, carried by a puff of breeze.

Criminals and murderers in my house. Rage churned in my guts. Heat crawled hot on my ears – terror warred with anger but my training kept me still. *I won't kill anyone – yet. I won't spend my life cheap. I need to know how many people are in Za's group and where they are. If Matt finds our house, he'll watch, just like me. He can't sneak up on us – not with Lu and Terror.*

The dogs and I crept away, found a secluded spot in the woods. Still within earshot, but we could move without the men realizing we were there. Terror and Lu moved deeper into the forest to relieve themselves. I did the same.

We ate dried foods and fruit bars; I drank from my canteen. Lu and T ghosted away and returned with wet muzzles. Night fell and we curled together. Lu and Terror slept with one eye open. I caught catnaps, interrupted by sounds from the men. One had sleep apnea, and the other farted with regularity.

At daybreak, the men stirred.

"Let's go eat," the short one said. "Maybe the new gal, the one we grabbed on the way in, can cook."

"If she's still alive," pronounced the mournful one. "The line of guys waiting to spend time with her was really long."

Blood roared in my ears. The dogs read me. They shifted, prepared to kill something.

"Not yet," I whispered. Laid a cautionary, calming hand on each big head.

When the two men headed back, we shadowed – letting them make all the noise and distraction. I headed for the best spy spot – a thick stand of junipers and pinon pines butting up to the rows of planted trees closest to my house.

The men were greeted with loud voices and some bragging.

"Ben's got her now, but she don't look too good." The speaker's lazy eye wandered to the right, then rolled back to left of center. "Guess I was a little rough with her." A smirk, a glance at his audience, then he continued his laughing tale of how he'd tormented the woman. I marked him for a very special killing.

"Are you turning into Za?" whispered the darkness in my soul. "Be very careful."

"Only justice," I said.

"Are you certain?" The malevolent giggle in my mind gave me pause.

Am I sure of anything anymore? Really?

I put the dogs to watch my back, deep in the underbrush, two points of a triangle. I took the forward position, settled with the binocs and waited.

Mrs. Cluck and crew were nowhere to be seen. *God, I hope they hid.*

The group moved, drifted in and out of the house, like a seething nest of rats. Two men checked the vehicles parked by the house – two jeeps, a Land Rover, and several four-wheelers and motorcycles. Za was not a woman to walk when she could ride, it appeared. The men clustered in the back yard rose, moved away, each one working to keep at least one other person between himself and the kitchen door.

Za must be coming. No one wanted to be in front. No one wanted to draw her attention.

She doesn't look scary. The slender woman moved with confidence. She wore a green tee shirt, the short sleeves rolled up to expose muscular arms. Her tight jeans were tucked into cowboy boots. The bib-style diamond necklace flashed and glowed in the morning sun. It looked incredibly stupid with her casual western gear. And no one would dare tell her. *Maybe I will, right before I kill her.* Medium height, she looked about thirty, long blonde hair pulled back in a ponytail. She wore a gun in a shoulder holster, and two knives in sheaths hung from her belt.

"Remember," whispered the mindvoice. "She's mean as a rabid dog. And twice as dangerous."

Good advice. I made a mental note.

People shrank from her, tiny involuntary movements. *They don't realize it. I wonder if she does.*

A tall blonde young man, wearing only blue jeans slung low on narrow hips, followed the woman through the door, onto the back porch.

"Oh God," the whisper escaped me. "Todd's alive." My thoughts of clearing our house of the human garbage disappeared.

His blonde head dipped to catch her comment, one of his manicured hands reached and rested on her waist, the other clasped Za's hand. Rings sparkled on her fingers. Todd gazed adoringly, entranced. I watched him hang on her every word. *Like his eyes were placed in his head for one reason – to worship her.*

My heart collapsed, like a balloon stuck with a pin.

She preened, stretched like a lazy sleepy cat, caressed his chest with her cheek. Todd standing tall and beautiful beside a sick, evil serial killer in an obscene, ghastly pairing.

My mind went numb. I needed to make decisions. My frozen brain produced nothing.

The three packs, with everything Lu, Terror and I needed to survive, lay in the tunnel. Accessible from right here.

"Get them," ordered the dark voice in my head. "Grab your freedom. Go now. They'll never know you exist."

"You're right," I said. "I will."

I trained the binocs on Todd for one last look. My chance for freedom, for love – lost.

"Why, Katie. Do you enjoy pain?" demanded the darkness.

"No." I lied. "Wait. I see …."

Todd did all the right things: smiled, flattered, stroked, nodded, bent to listen, his eyes never left Za. But when her attention fixed elsewhere, his movie star smile disappeared. The dazzling white teeth and charming dimples were replaced by lips compressed into two white lines. His jaw jutted, hard and rigid; his slitted emerald eyes glittered.

He hates her.

My heart leaped, filled with hope. He only needed my help to get away.

I have to save him. He can still be my life partner, just like I planned. Together we can leave, start fresh.

"Consider carefully," whispered the little voice in my mind. "Who is he, what is he, really? Why are his parents dead? And he's not? What did he do to live? Didn't you hear what the men said? Couldn't he have escaped already?"

"He's a nice guy. A victim. That's all." I shook my head against the derisive chuckle in my mind. "He is. How could he fight them all?"

The darkess laughed in my head. "He could have escaped, couldn't he?"

"He doesn't know this area," I said, defending him.

My memories of Todd's kisses, his touch, sent a hot wave of longing rippling through me. *I don't know how and I don't care but I'll rescue him. I love him. He belongs to me.*

A scream, followed by cursing and more shrieks, ripped the peaceful morning. Heavy bumping sounds, followed by thudding footsteps, pounded inside our house.

Something went down the stairs. Something thrummed loud in my head.

The screen door flew open, propelled by the naked bloody woman thrown through it. She landed in a pile on the porch, covered her head with her arms. *The new one the guards discussed?*

"Look at her," shouted the boxer-clad man in the doorway. He smeared dripping red knuckles on his shorts. "Look close. She's got a red rash on her. The bitch infected me on purpose."

I would have too.

Bright red streamers of fresh blood gushed from the woman's nose. Dark spots of old bruising, plus the red lumps of new, covered her body.

People ran. Scattered in panic like our chickens when danger threatened.

Za didn't move. Turning to the hysterical man, her icy voice could have frozen gasoline. "Ben, take her to the woods. Shoot her. Bury her."

"No. I don't want to get close to her." The man backed away from his victim, waving his hands as if he could fan the germs from the air around him.

"You just spent hours fucking her. I don't think you can be any more exposed. If you catch it, you die. I'll forgive your lapse of obedience. But only once." The smile exposed tiny, pointed yellow teeth. She reached a forefinger, rubbed the front two.

Everyone who saw it shivered.

Za's blue eyes were expressionless, cold and dead as two glass marbles. She stared at the man. "Tell me no again and you'll die for sure. And it won't be fast."

The man shuddered. "Yes, Za. Right away." He turned, grabbed a pistol, and kicked the woman across the porch. He booted her down the stairs, onto the lawn. "Get up. You heard. Go."

Za turned to the short sentry, spoke behind one hand. Her lips moved. I didn't have to hear to know what she ordered. Then she giggled, a high brittle thing.

Her followers flinched at the sound.

The man nodded, slid his pistol from its holster. Walking down the steps, he kept his distance as he followed the two across the grass and into the trees.

Anger pushed hard through my veins. My mind didn't give the order but the Sig appeared in my hand just the same. I didn't dare use it. *Still, doing nothing, letting them kill that girl, is wrong.*

"No, Katie," cautioned my mindvoice. "Don't waste your life on one already dead."

I stayed in my hiding place, but I didn't holster the SigSauer.

Shame on me.

Because I was selfish, wanting to save Todd and be with him, because I didn't want to be exposed to The Great Awful, I planned to sit here and allow those people to murder a helpless girl.

I didn't like the new Katie Davis. No, I didn't like her at all.

Chapter Twenty-One

I waited in my hiding place and watched our house. I counted the guards, noted the activity.

The blood thumped in my temples at the damage done by Za's followers. My *mad* tried to take me – not because I wanted to stay there – *oh hell, no* – I wanted to leave more than anything. But fury raged because now, sick people infected it. If I needed to return, if things out there were so awful they forced me back home, then what? What made me maddest – these horrible people needed to be punished – *no* – destroyed for what they'd done to other humans. They didn't deserve to live, much less live here.

"At least your mother won't be a victim," said the voice in my head.

Memory stabbed like a blade. *I'd trade everything to have her back.* I took my sadness and grief and tucked them away.

So far, I'd seen no friendships. Like the sentries, no one trusted anyone else. Through the binoculars, Todd's body language betrayed how much he despised Za.

I'm surprised no one's noticed. Or they have, but know how she treats someone bearing bad news.

Backing from my vantage point, I collected T-dog and Lu. I knew every tree branch and stray rock and every one of the perimeter mines. Keeping the explosive defenses between Za's thugs and us, we spent the rest of the daylight hours watching, moving, making mental notes. I broke out the dog chow, fed my friends, wanting to keep them close. They could hunt another day. I ate a can of tuna and wished for a bacon cheeseburger and fries.

"Please God," I whispered. "Please let a bunch of them blunder into Dad's mines." A thought crossed my mind.

"And you," I snarled. "Goddamn you, mindvoice, you said I shouldn't replace the mines. If I had, I might have wiped out a big part of these terrible people."

I waited but the dark inside never said a word. *Fine! You coward, you always disappear when you've screwed up.* I shook my head, gave it up. To be brutally honest, I'd made the final decision.

I checked and re-checked our backtrail – five times an hour, probably more, making sure Matt didn't creep up on us.

Probably startle me enough to shoot, and that would ruin everything.

I found myself comparing Todd with Matt and it made me mad. Matt's a man, a competent soldier. I'd have to protect Todd. *It's okay, it's what I want, because I love Todd.*

"So what about your physical reaction to Matt?" asked the voice in my head. "More, much more. You felt it clear across the creek."

"I don't know, and I don't care," I snapped. *But perhaps I should? No, I should plan how to get Todd free.*

Twenty men moved in and around our house. I included the bitch, Za. Bloodthirsty, brutal, worse than most of her men. I considered counting her twice because she was so awful. *Too many for me to just pick them off one by one.*

There were women, maybe kids, inside. I heard female voices, smelled food cooking. I couldn't see them. I couldn't worry about them, either.

This is war.

So far, Lupine and Terror hated every intruder. They didn't growl because I placed them on silent mode. Hackles up, spine ridges stiff, their black lips rolled back, exposing long sharp fangs.

"You should leave," said the voice in my mind. "The dogs are smarter than you."

"Todd's okay," I whispered. "Give him a chance."

"You can't see past your infatuation. You'll be sorry." The evil snigger made goosebumps zip up my spine.

"Just wait," I told it. "You're wrong. I'll watch everything overnight – see how tomorrow goes." Maybe by then, I'd have enough information to figure how to rescue Todd.

"You stupid girl," said the darkness.

"I won't listen to another night of two nasty men snoring," I told Lu and Terror. "And I'm not cracking the tunnel opening and chance giving it away."

"You just don't want to sleep in a dark confined space," snapped my alter-me.

"You're wrong," I growled. *Damn thing is right but I won't admit it.*

Instead, the dogs and I backtracked the four miles to my cave. Even if I only napped, any rest I got would help. While we hiked, I worried. *Where is Matt? I could step around a boulder, or a tree trunk, and be face to face with the scary man.* Every odd noise, every movement made my heart stutter. I didn't settle until we arrived and slid inside. Safe.

Through the asymmetrical lava cave opening, daybreak arrived. The landscape outside emerged from deep night to periwinkle, subtle lavender, then pale blue. The blurry watercolor shapes of the terrain morphed into hard lines of rocks and land. The bright line on the horizon spread into a rising sphere, lighting the new day's sky.

I waited until I could see to move without making mistakes. Then we returned to the farmhouse.

"Lu, guard." I pointed to her spot. "Terror, guard." I put him across, the third point of a triangle. I checked line of sight angles, moved slightly closer to the house. Until Za woke and came downstairs, nothing happened. How Todd might react, if he recognized me? *Anyone's guess.* How he'd escape Za, if he decided to meet me? *Totally up to him.*

I worked my way closer to the back of the farmhouse, staying on the opposite side from the tunnel.

The shift of people away from the kitchen door warned me of Za's arrival. The woman emerged for breakfast. Short, compact, blonde hair in a pony tail. Today, she wore her necklace atop an orange tee-shirt. Brilliant stones in a formal setting. *She has to know how ridiculous it looks. She doesn't care.*

Todd moved, following close behind. He wore a green tee shirt tucked into his jeans, the graceful lines of his body stiff with hate. If yesterday's pattern held, they'd spend an hour or two outside on the porch, eating, holding court.

She appears bored. Wonder if she'll murder someone this morning?

I searched my surroundings for vantage points. I selected three locations – surely one would do the trick. *How can I get Todd – and only him – to see me? Make eye contact without getting caught.* If today didn't work, I'd be patient. With my hoard of supplies stashed in the tunnel, I could wait a long time – if I needed to.

Unless Matt showed up. *Dammit. A careful man, a focused man. He's not going to leave me alone until we have his all-important talk. What in hell can he want?*

Our wicker patio table and chairs sat in their usual place at one corner of the back porch. Todd pulled out a chair for Za, waited respectfully while she sat, then slid her in.

My pulse ratcheted a dozen notches faster.

183

Todd had seated Za with her back to the woods.

"Hoping someone will shoot her?" snarked the evil voice in my head.

Todd took the chair opposite, shifted his weight, then tilted it back, one knee against the tabletop.

"Shit," I whispered to Lu and T. "It's the chair with the weak leg."

A woman with a black eye, carrying a silver carafe and two mugs on my mother's favorite tray, slunk through the kitchen door.

Red fog clouded my vision.

"Katie," shouted my mindvoice. "Stop!"

Christ all Friday. I lowered the Sig, slipped my finger out of the trigger guard. Sat and shook. I'd almost fired. *Stupid, stupid, stupid.*

A young girl carrying two plates of food appeared on the porch.

My binocs showed pancakes, but no eggs. A laugh bubbled inside; I closed my lips against it. I hoped my crafty chickens were well hidden in the woods.

My hands trembled – bottled tension coupled with sheer terror. I unbraided my hair and shook it free. Fluffed it around my shoulders hoping it would catch Todd's attention. Keeping low, I moved to a more exposed spot and waited. When Todd's gaze drifted toward me, I pushed slowly to my feet, locked eyes with him. I knew when one knuckle rubbed his eye, he'd figured me out.

I didn't hesitate, I dropped to a crouch, slid away smooth and slow. I wheezed, sucked air, tried to calm down. I glanced around, checked for danger. No one but Todd saw me. *I did it. I got away clean. I think.*

Backing, working my way to the safe position, I collected Lu and T-dog. We moved away into a niche between two large boulders. I sat on a rock and waited, heartbeat triple-timing in my chest. Waited more. My pulse slowed to normal. *Will he come? Can he get away?*

Three hours passed. My eyelids drooped. A faint shriek of agony from the direction of home, ripped the stillness; yanked me to my feet. I tried to calm my galloping heart, ease the iron band squeezing my chest. I moved Lupine and Terror to a small recess farther away, safer, less likely to be seen. Last, I checked my weapons, loosened them in their holsters, and climbed a big blue pine. Settling on the lowest branch, I hid in the foliage and watched for two things.

First – to see if Todd came.

Second – to see if someone followed him.

Whoever came made so much noise, I swear I heard them from a mile away. Embarrassing to blunder around like that. *I hope it isn't Todd.*

It was.

He came alone – I watched his backtrail to make sure.

"Where the hell is she?" he growled. "If she isn't here, I'll hunt her down and …. I could get skinned alive for doing this."

He screamed like a girl when I dropped from the branch into the path before him.

"What the hell …?"

My joy sagged into my boots. Not exactly the happy reunion I'd imagined – *but, cut him a little slack* – he'd been the prisoner of a sociopath. *It's understandable.*

"Hey, Todd. Good to see you."

"Jesus Christ, you scared me." He eyed my bandolier, one corner of his mouth twisted. "Who do you think you are? Rambo?"

"I thought you were dead." *Why be so nasty to me?*

"I nearly was," he said. "I've wished for it a lot."

I don't know what he saw on my face, but he added, "Good to see you too … ah … Katie. I'm sorry … the horrible woman. She's cold, a murderess. Honestly. I have to be so careful."

"Jesus H. Christ, Katie," snarled the dark thing inside me. "The asshole nearly couldn't remember your fricking name. Dump this loser and get the hell out of here."

I ignored it, drank in my handsome young man.

"I'm sorry you've had such an awful time, Todd," I said. "I came to get you out. We can leave together, right now. I hear there's a sanctuary city in Boise."

"No, she'll find me. I have to go back in an hour or so. She's insane, she's jealous. She'd kill us both. Make it last for days." Todd's eyes went somewhere else, his chest heaved. A red flush crawled from the neck of his tee shirt, nearly obscuring the small patch of rash on his neck.

"See that," yelled my mindvoice. "A rash. He's got it – The Great Awful. Run away. NOW."

I cleared my throat.

"Hey, Todd. We can't stand out here in the open to talk. I have a place no one knows. Let's go there and figure out what to do. Okay?"

Todd just stood there, scrutinizing me like a stranger.

Why doesn't he touch me, hug me like he did before? I examined it from his side – he must have endured awful experiences. He needed time to pull it together. And all I could think of was what I wanted. *Shame on me.*

"Okay," he said, and something odd flavored the word. "Let's go to your place." Then he gave me the megawatt grin I remembered – the one which hooked me instantly.

My heart hiccupped, beat at double speed. I stared at my handsome, gorgeous boy, saw his glorious smile didn't touch his eyes. A little thrill of alarm sounded in the lizard-portion of my brain. *He's been brutalized,* I excused. *I need to make allowances.*

"Pay attention to your intuition," warned my dark kernel.

I ignored it.

"Follow me, Todd," I said. "It's close and it's safe. You don't need to worry now."

With a signal, I brought T-dog and Lu to their feet. Like before, Lupine crowded between Todd and me. Terror rumbled, his growl low and unhappy. *What in the hell is with you guys?*

Todd did a half-leap away from my dogs.

"Ignore them," I told him. And then to Terror and Lu, I said, "Shush. It's just Todd. You remember him."

We reached the ragged-edged access hole in the lava. Except for a small spot of daylight just inside the opening, the cave appeared a dark patch, nearly invisible until you stood right before it.

"Hang on," I said. "Let me sweep for unfriendly critters."

"If there's creepy things inside, I'm not going in." Todd waved a hand before his face. "What stinks?"

"Oh, um …" I sniffed, then knew what he meant. "Big cat scat. Don't worry, they won't come in here with two dogs."

I switched on my Maglite. The cave wasn't large, but I needed help to see into the back corners. Working my way around the interior, I brushed away stickery dried weeds. Last nite, I'd just fixed a spot for the dogs and me, but now I cleared a spot large enough for two people. Then, I sat, my heart hammering, and waited for the man I loved to join me.

Todd climbed in through the hole, made his way to where I waited. Then he just stood, looming above me.

Little electric prickles stabbed the ends of my fingers.

Patting the bare ground at my side, I said, "We're safe in here, Todd. Please, sit." Someone filled the spot, but it wasn't Todd.

"Lupine, you know I didn't mean you."

Yellow eyes reflected, eerie in the half-dim light. She blinked but didn't move. Staring at Todd, she didn't quite growl, more like a threatening chugga-chugga-chug breathing.

"For heaven's sake," I pushed to my feet. "Just a sec, Todd."

"Lupine, come." I pointed at T-dog. "You too." I heard claws on hard packed dirt behind me. "There," I pointed at a spot beneath a rock overhang outside the opening. "Sit. Stay. Guard."

Two pair of eyes reproached, but they sailed through the opening and sat in the shaded area immediately outside. Facing the inside, their unblinking eyes fixed on Todd.

Diffused sunlight turned the cave's interior a dim gray, cool and shady compared to the full summer sun outside. *Why is he just standing there?* I still sat cross-legged to the ground, waited for Todd to join me.

He didn't move.

I glanced at him for clues but the half-light hid his expression. Where before I'd felt desire, now I felt a tiny stir of apprehension.

"Talk to me – tell me what happened to your folks. What's happened to you? Or if you don't want to talk about it, tell me what you do want." *Tell me you want to go away, find someplace safe. Build a future, just the two of us.*

"You don't get it," he snapped, and moved enough for me to see his twisted features. "No one escapes Za. She gets rid of people if she's tired of them. Or if she thinks they are disloyal. People die, but no one gets free any other way." Todd spat the words, biting the end from each one. Then, he turned, took two strides, spun and came back. Shoving both hands into his glorious hair, he twisted, then pulled. Hard.

I saw his face and flinched. He reminded me of someone in a horror movie – maybe a space alien. His upper lip pulled back in grimace, baring teeth and gums. His eyes were stretched too wide, bulging, glassy; they stared at something I couldn't see.

"What did you expect?" the little dark voice said. "You'd better be careful. If this is what he is on the outside, what do you suppose is inside?"

"Todd, I know it's been …."

"You don't know anything, Katie," Todd yelled. Then it all came out in a rush. "They came. She came." He panted, chest heaving like he'd just run a four-minute mile. "My parents were professors, for God's sake. They thought they were so smart, thought they knew everything. It was all their fault – everything that happened to them. 'Self-defense?'" Todd's voice mimicked and sneered. He parroted, "'Not necessary, Todd. Guns? Oh, much too violent.'"

Todd gasped like a trout out of water, his fists bunched at his sides. His emerald eyes rolled like they couldn't find the proper place to look.

"When I asked about criminals or just bad people," he shouted. "They told me they'd negotiate with them. Reason with them." He twisted his hands in his hair again. "How well did it work with that bunch of criminals?"

"I don't know," I gave him the softest answer I could.

"Not well, not well at all." Todd paced the width of the cave, back and forth, his jerky turns at either end robotic, like a man possessed. "I watched them try. I hid in a closet, left the door cracked. The lookout is one big room. I had to see and hear everything."

"Didn't you at least try to defend them?"

"Hell, no, Katie. They should have protected me. They deserved what they got."

Chapter Twenty-Two

"Oh God." My stomach tilted, wadded into my throat.

"God was no help," Todd snarled. "Za let the men have my mother. Right there, they were lined up out the door."

I slapped my hand over my mouth to hold back the vomit. "And you just hid in the closet? I'd have saved my mother – or died trying."

"Oh, yeah," Todd said. He tilted his head, inspected my hand. "You think so? You wouldn't. You'd do what I did to live."

I shoved my other hand in front of me, palm out and shook my head.

"You would. Don't say different." In the half-light, Todd's wild-eyed grin turned his face into a gleeful skull. "That was the worst thing I'd ever seen right up until Za started on my father. She told him to get it up for her, told him what she expected him to do."

My lips went numb. "Oh my God, Todd."

"Know what happened then, Katie, my dear?" Todd's eyes were wild, only the whites showed. A manic grin possessed his face. "He couldn't," he snarled. "So she mutilated him. Right there in front of everyone. Oh, Za has a talent for managing blood loss – sometimes she cuts for days and keeps her victims alive."

"Why hasn't someone killed her? I know not everyone in her gang came from the prison."

"She has six from there – two are her brothers, evil, soulless men. They have a cause, and she's their leader. Some men – some special forces group – killed her brothers and she plans to murder them and their families. Her brothers would die to protect her."

"How is it you survived?"

"When they found me in the closet, Za decided to keep me as her personal possession."

"So you sleep with her and that's it?" *He'll be so happy I rescued him. We'll be normal again, together.*

"Not quite," Todd said. "The torture scenes? I always have to help her do it."

Oh God! How can his face be so blank, so completely serene. This is heinous, beyond bizarre. I couldn't hold back. I surged to my feet, ran to the side of the cave, vomited and vomited and vomited.

Todd either felt sympathy for me or he wanted to make sure I heard the rest of his story.He followed; squatted beside me. Kept talking while I wiped my mouth on a handkerchief from my shorts pocket, kicked dirt over my mess, and dropped cross-legged back in my place on the cave floor.

"She made sure I got the message," he said. "Cross her in any way, displease her in any way – I'd die. In the most unpleasant manner she could devise."

He dropped to the ground beside me, his face contorted. "After she killed my parents, she asked if I found her attractive. I knew what she wanted me to say, what she expected me to do. She sent everyone outside." Todd's lips pressed into a thin line. "And I did it. Right there, in their bed, with the cooling bodies of my mother and father in the same room." Todd bared his teeth. I think he meant to smile. I froze when he added, "Wasn't so bad, really. I just closed my eyes and pretended she was you."

"Shit," I whispered.

"Get the fuck away from this murdering piece of trash," snarled the dark voice.

Leave me alone, I thought back, hard as possible. *He's been traumatized. He must be confused – this couldn't have happened. I can fix him, make him well again. I love him.*

Todd yanked his tee shirt, the same emerald of his eyes, over his head. "Look." A healing wound, round and red and angry, marked his right shoulder.

"Why did she …?"

"She didn't. When we came outside, Ron, her current 'toy', shot me. He'd been watching us inside – God, she kept licking her lips – he figured I'd be replacing him. Based on Za's past performance, Ron knew he'd be murdered for entertainment – an awful, terrible death. So he took a proactive position and tried to kill me. He only wounded me. Za patched me up, then made me help her skin him alive. Two opportunities, she said. My revenge on him for shooting me, and a teaching opportunity for her. To show me how it was done. While she peeled him, she explained the rules."

"Sounds like there are no rules." I wrapped my arms around my body and stuffed my icy sweating hands in my armpits. The nasty taste of vomit fouled my mouth, its stench wafted from the side of the cave.

"Oh there are lots of them, Katie. All hers, all punishable by something vicious. And all change from day to day, minute to minute, depending on her whim."

"G-g-god," I said and even in the warmth of the high plains desert, I shivered like I'd been stuffed in a freezer.

"Your precious Todd's guilty as Za," said my mindvoice. "Actually worse. He didn't try to save his parents, he even dares to blame them for what happened. She tortures and murders anyone who displeases her."

I ignored it. *This is my Todd, my dream partner. He's sophisticated, a college man. He might be my last chance to get a piece of a normal life. He knows what it's like, knows how to function out there.*

Todd fixed glittering ice green eyes on me. "We ate him. Ron, the guy who shot me, I mean. Za ordered parts of him cut away and roasted. She kept him alive long enough to feed him some of his own leg. She made the slave women set out someone's good china, put vases of yellow daisies on the tables, use matching linen tablecloths and napkins. Then she made us all eat."

"What if you couldn't?"

"We were given a choice. Eat and keep it down. Or have a leg amputated and roasted to feed the group."

I don't want to know if it happened. "I'm so sorry, Todd. I don't know what to say." *Change the subject, Katie. Do it fast.* "Her name is weird. What's it mean?"

"It's short for Eliza. But she hates that. So we have to call her Za."

"She's only a criminal."

"She's a serial killer," Todd said. "Does it for fun. But she's also part of some terrorist group or something because she was locked up in a military prison at the airforce base."

"How did she get out?"

"It blew up in all the earthquake stuff," Todd snarled. "I got to the lookout to visit my parents two days before it all went to shit. Za told me she murdered a family, the police caught her; put her in an institution for evaluation – to see if she was innocent by reason of insanity. You should have heard her laugh at their stupidity." Todd's face twisted, he panted odd little huffs, then continued. "She said the murders were just for fun. Then the military came for them. She said there was a much bigger reason she and her brothers were in jail."

Todd leaped to his feet; resumed his strides across the packed dirt floor.

"She said when the building blew up, most of the prisoners died. Za's street smart and lucky. She took the survivors and headed west before the plague arrived, picked up members and supplies and weapons. Someone told her the lookout would be easy to defend."

"Why you? Out of everyone she could pick?"

"If you mean I can't fight, or shoot – stuff like that? You're right. She has men who do it. What she wants is me because I'm 'gorgeous', the type of guy who refused to date her before. Now, if I want to live, I have to anticipate her every wish, tell her the lovely lies – how beautiful she is, how desirable, blah, blah, blah – and make her believe them."

"Does she? Believe the lies, I mean?"

"No, but it saves face. And sometimes, I think, she almost convinces herself because she wants to. She isn't bad looking – just an awful person."

"Shit. You can't go back there." I couldn't catch my breath. It felt like an elephant sat on my chest. I pushed air out through my nose, tried to force calm. "She's right, though, about one thing."

"She's wrong about everything." Todd shouted, his last two words escalating an octave higher than the others. "She's evil. She has to die. I'll never be free until she's dead."

I shrugged at him. "We can kill her, if you want. Easy." Then I stared at him, smiled. "You are gorgeous, Todd."

He turned, searched my eyes. Deep, like I held all the answers. "I won't throw my life away. I want revenge, but I want it safe. And I want to take my time with her. You can help – I'll use it as your teaching opportunity."

"Okay," I said, although his words, coupled with his twisty gaze, made me squirm. *No, Todd. I won't do it. Ever.*

Todd paused and seemed to make a decision. He sat, scooted close, gripped my shoulders and kissed me. Hard and desperate.

I found I shrank, ever so slightly from his touch. *Why? When I want him so much?* It had to be because I needed to plan our survival. "I can help you. We can get away."

"Are you kidding? Guns are scary – see what these people do with them."

"I can teach you, Todd. It isn't hard, it just takes practice."

Something passed across his face, shifted behind his eyes. Todd opened his mouth, closed it again. I wondered what he almost said. *It doesn't matter – we will build a life together. Me and this beautiful young man.*

He kissed me again, and then again.

Warmth surged. My mind wanted him but my body wasn't quite as sure. *WTF?* I pressed my chest against Todd's.

A traitorous thought intruded. *Matt made me hotter than this and he didn't get close enough to touch. What would happen if he did? Spontaneous combustion?*

"Pay attention, Katie," said the voice in my head. "Todd is a big fucking mistake."

No, I thought at the mindvoice. *You're wrong. This is the man I want.*

I kissed him harder.

Todd's breathing turned ragged, he clutched at me, fabric tore as he ripped off my shirt, then his. Pushing me against the dirt of the cave floor, he laid across my body, skin to skin, his eyes closed.

I should be crazy for him. He's all I've thought about since we met. But ... it's just no good.

The shaft of sunlight through the cave opening highlighted the circle of weeping red rash on his chest. *Oh shit, oh shit, oh shit!* The small spot hadn't rung bells but this big nasty patch on his chest looked bad.

"You saw it," snarled my inner voice. "Stupid, stupid girl. You ignored me because it didn't fit with what you wanted. It will be the last idiot choice you ever make." The darkness cackled. "You'll be too dead to choose anything."

I remembered Dad's words. "Those infected and dying call it The Great Awful."

And now Todd's leaking rash smeared lymph on my skin. *No. No. No.* His hands were everywhere. Pinching, grabbing, groping.

The small heat in the join of my legs died at his first rough touch. Todd was hard, cruel – not soft and loving anymore. My heart fluttered like the wings of a trapped bird. No longer a gentle person ... Todd didn't ask, he only took. Big mistake, Katie. *Was he like this before? Did I refuse to see?*

"Your dogs did. You ignored them too." The words from my soulvoice stung – doubly harsh because they were right.

I grabbed Todd's wrists, pushed him away.

In his surprise, he let me do it but he shook free of my hands.

"I ... I want to stop now, Todd. I'm uncomfortable with this."

"Who cares?" he snarled, and I flinched at the venom. "I'm going to be in charge for once. I'm gonna fuck you blind without worrying I'll be killed if I don't please."

"But Todd ... I've never had sex ...." My lungs were two frozen lumps in my chest. "I thought we had something special," I said. Hot tears filled my eyes, spilled down my face. "I thought we'd make a life together, maybe even at our farmhouse."

"Why are you bawling, you stupid twit? I was bored, amusing myself with you. Why would I want a kid – especially a virgin. I've no patience for breaking you in – I want someone who knows what they're doing. All I need you for is to get me free."

I don't know what I said, I think shock at the magnitude of my misjudgement forced a whimper. I stared at this horrible person in disbelief. I'd believed my virginity would be a gift to the man I finally chose. How could I have been so blind?

"You wanted to be," said the mindvoice. "You couldn't know. So naïve, with no social skills, no yardstick. Your fault is you refused to listen: to your parents, to the dogs. To me."

Todd's eyes rolled wild and green. "You'll kill Za to keep both of us out of her evil, evil hands. You keep saying you can," he spat. "You'll be my bodyguard, and my sex partner. If any bad guys threaten me, I'll just trade you to them for my freedom."

"You're sick," I whimpered. "You're gonna die."

"Maybe," Todd said. "I only have your word for it, and you don't know much. If I do, I'm gonna die happy." He ripped at my shorts, popped the buttons, yanked them and my underwear down.

Something in the dark recesses of my mind stirred. Recollection … a memory struggled for recognition … just beyond my reach. Fear mixed with fury.

I grabbed for my clothes, pulled them back into place. I didn't expect the backhand across my face, didn't expect the sharp pain of a ring slicing my cheekbone. Didn't expect the spray of blood. The blow caught me full-on and drove me to my knees.

"Ahhh …." I grunted, then rage kicked in. I released my *mad.*

I used my legs, drove off the floor and let momentum carry me into Todd. My shoulder caught him in the hollow spot where his bones attached to his sternum. The crackling snapping sound and his howl told me I'd broken ribs.

He folded across my back like an empty suit.

My impetus carried us across the cave. I pushed hard with my legs, with everything I owned; ducked to protect my head. Smashed Todd against the sharp protrusions of the rock wall.

"Oooof," the only sound he made.

A growl, inhuman in its fury, jerked every hair on my body upright. My involuntary flinch, then instinctive duck, came from the snarling silver blur sailing over me.

Lu's face passed scant inches from my eye, black lips peeled back from vicious fangs. The wolf wasn't dangerous to me but she intended to kill my attacker.

Lupine's teeth closed around Todd's throat. She dragged him from my shoulder and onto the floor. Scarlet spurted as Lu readjusted her grip on his neck; then shook her prey.

A strangled scream ululated, bounced off cave walls. Todd's body kicked and fought in her jaws. The nasty rumble of another pissed-off monster told me the huge dark shape chewing Todd's flailing legs was Terror.

I heard a bony crunch, another high thin screech, and one of the legs went still.

Warm fuzzies danced through my veins. *My protectors, God love 'em for disobeying.*

Todd squeaked and wailed through damaged vocal chords and a ruined throat. He scrabbled on the dirt, tried to dislodge my enraged friends.

"Shall I let Lupine separate your head from your shoulders? She'd like it a lot, Todd. Did you know a wolf has the greatest biting power of all canines? 1,600 square pounds on her fang tips – like a shark, that's how hard. T-dog is a bit further down the bite-power list but he can still crush any bone in your body."

I babbled, trying to get my trembling and my wobbling voice, under control. *Mad* surged, chasing away my fear and shock, replacing it with steel resolve. I felt grateful.

Stalking the dim cave, I inspected the hysterical male, curled a disgusted lip. "Should I let Lu break your neck, or chew it in half? She'd love to kill you, Todd. She disliked you from the very beginning. Terror too. I should have paid attention."

My apologies to Lu, T-dog, and to my mindvoice. I've been incredibly stupid. I will never make a decision based on emotion again.

I walked to Todd, kicked him hard in the ribs. "You know," I whispered. "The only reason you're not dead is because they are trained to hold. I have to give them permission to kill."

Lupine loosened her bite for a second, then reset her grip.

He gave a muffled screech right before she clamped down again.

"Now I have to decide your fate. I really don't care how, you bastard." Even to me, my voice sounded blasé. Emotionless. Dead. The only way to prevent mistakes.

If I can just hold it together a few minutes more – until I finish this mess.

"Should I let Lu and Terror kill you, Todd?" I stalked the cave interior, kicked the cave wall. "Did you think me so weak? So helpless?"

"Nuuuh." Todd managed to say. His eyes rolled, flashing whites. His pupils dilated so huge they eclipsed the green.

"Oh, of course you did. You misjudged me – greatly. As I did you. So, do I kill you easy – which you don't deserve – or do I keep my hands clean and let my guardians do it? Or should I leave you here, tied up; let you die from the plague? Your choice."

"Lu-ive."

"No, you don't get to live. I've got things to do. So choose how you want to die. Now. Or I'll choose for you."

I hardened my heart against Todd's groans and strangled screams. I didn't tell my furious guardians to release their victim. I exulted in their growls and the flesh-rending head-shakes they gave him. I pressed my palm against the seeping warmth on my cheek.

"You'll have to decide. He won't – he's a coward," said the darkness. "You should have kept your promises to your father."

"I know, I know," I snapped. "If I had, I wouldn't be in this mess."

I'm going to die – Todd exposed me good. Unwilling to think I'd be dead in five days, I turned my mind to the problem of killing. *I can just shoot him. I have a silencer on the Sig.*

"There's worse ways if you want to punish him," my sarcastic mindvoice said. "Let the sickness take him."

A muffled scream from Todd's direction made me think of the gang in our house. *I hope the only one searching for me is Matt. I don't think he means me harm. With luck, I lost him. God, I hope so. I'll be sick soon – I don't want to expose him.*

"Yeah, you trusted Todd," piped my inner voice. "Still think you are a good judge of character? Still think Matthew's okay?"

"Will you just shut up and leave me alone?"

A muffled grunt from the corner of the cave.

"Not you. Pick the weapon, Todd." I pulled the Ka-Bar from its sheath, tossed it in the air, caught it by the handle on its way down. "Knives are quiet. I bet you know lots about them. Want me to cut your throat?"

A scream from the heap on the floor.

"Guess not." I resheathed the blade. "I'll give you a minute to come up with a better suggestion."

I wiped the slimy wet from my chest with my fingers, scrubbed it with a corner of my tank, and put my shirt back on. *Damn him.* The tear in my tee front went from the hem to just above my bra cups. I shrugged. *I'm decent enough to perform an execution.*

A hot throb, like an electric zing, in my cheek made me trace the torn flesh with my finger.

"Don't touch …! Ah shit," said my mindvoice. "Now you've really done it."

"What?" I growled, then I froze. "Oh fuck."

"Yes. If you were a guy, you just stepped on your dick. Big time."

I rubbed the stuff from Todd's rash into my open wound. Oh God. Oh God. Oh God. My mind kicked into fifth-gear, revved like my Kawasaki. *Just throw the door open, Katie, and invite the germs right in.* I scrubbed my cheek with the clean – maybe – tail of my shirt. *Probably just ground them in deeper.* Frantic, I tore open the first-aid kit, found a betadine swab. I scrubbed the wound. Cleansed with a second gauze. Then a third. Now blood flowed, warm and sticky, down my face. *It's too late, I know it is. Simple killing is too good for him. I need something worse for revenge.*

I paced the cave, stopped and stared down at my captive, spoiler of hope and dreams. The one responsible for my soon-to-come death. I allowed my *mad* to look out through my eyes. Knew from his recoil he saw hate and rage. Saw a merciless executioner.

"You're gonna die anyway," I told Todd. "I'll just tie you up. Leave you. But not in here."

Those gorgeous emerald eyes, which had ensnared me, now made me sick. They stretched wide, then beseeched.

"No chance," I said. "Between my dogs, the wild animals or the plague, I don't have to kill you."

"Plgg?"

"You don't know?"

A grunt from Todd morphed into a whistling sound when Lu clenched her jaws more securely around his throat.

The small trickles of scarlet dribbling from each point where Lu's fangs pierced his skin brought my cold, evil smile. The one that bared my teeth, and didn't touch my eyes.

Todd struggled in Lupine's grip.

"Ah … the earthquake … the explosions to our east? You *did* notice those?" My voice grated, heavy with sarcasm. I enjoyed his cringe from my anger. "There's a flu going on. And you get a red rash before you really get sick. We're quarantined from the rest of the US. People are dying like flies. It's fatal, and now you have it."

"Wyy?" He whistled through a compressed throat.

"Why? Any new additions to your gang?"

"Noo grrl …."

"How long ago did you pick her up?"

"Too dyss," bubbled through Todd's compressed airway. His free foot – the one T-dog wasn't chewing – pawed the packed dirt of the floor.

"Two days? Perfect incubation time. Only about one person in a hundred is immune. Bet everyone in your gang is already sick."

Even distorted, the low evil laugh and "oo too" came clear.

Something in my mind snapped. The white-hot lightning of my *mad* ripped through my body, surged and escaped. In two long strides, I reached him, turned, snap-kicked him in the ribs. Something, maybe several somethings crackled.

He emitted a high muffled shriek.

"Yes, Todd. Perhaps me too." My flat, emotionless monotone surprised me. *My heart's shattered and bleeding.* My insides quivered, but nothing showed on the outside. I stared at Todd like a piece of shit on my shoe. "I'll find a special way to pay you back."

I leaned against the cave wall, studied the person I once thought contained my whole world. *What do I do now?* I'd achieved a major goal – I'd rescued Todd. *Stupid.* I'd achieved another goal. *I'm out of our house. Now I just want to go home.*

"You can't," said the dark voice inside. "Now what, Katie?"

"What I really want," I whispered. "Is my father."

Then Lupine and Terror went silent, so completely still, I thought even their breathing stopped. No growling, no whuffling – just two frozen statues, hushed and waiting. They held Todd fast, but their gaze focused on something behind me.

WTF?

I side-stepped and turned, spun fast, fixed my eyes on the sunlit cave opening.

"Dad?" Soon as I spoke, I knew it for error.

This man stood several inches taller, more slender through the mid-section. He stood, completely still, a black silhouette backlit against the bright azure sky.

Chapter Twenty-Three

The sun blinded me. My heart hammered against my ribs. *Who? What? Somebody worse than Todd?*

"Now will you tell me your name?" a deep bass voice resonated, low and sensual.

Fear dropped me into a crouch and I clawed for my guns. *It's Matt. Oh God. I'm trapped. What do I do?*

"Use your brain?" growled the mindvoice. "Check your dogs."

Although their jaws cruelly imprisoned Todd, two tails wagged.

I snatched my hands from my weapons, grabbed my ripped tank and pulled the two halves together in front. *Shit, shit, shit!* Desperately, I stuffed them in the waistband of my shorts.

"What are you doing here?" My voice shook.

"Followed you. You're damn good at hiding your backtrail, by the way. But once you hooked up with Tanglefoot, it got easy." Dark eyes scanned me, took in every detail. "The bastard," he said, his voice soft, even and razor edged. "What did he do to you?"

"He … I didn't …ah …."

Matt stepped inside the cave.

"No, God, no. Don't come in." I tilted my head toward the back of the cave. "He's got The Great Awful and I've been exposed."

"I'm immune," Matt said and crossed the cave. He stopped when I took a step back.

"You still haven't told me your name." He waited. "I won't approach you until you permit it."

"I'm …uh … Katie. Katie Davis." *Is Matt really okay?* I sneaked a peek at my dogs. They held Todd in a firm grip. Lu's silver plume brushed the cave floor and T-dog's stub rotated enthusiastically.

The stench of blood, coupled with the stink of vomit, hung heavy in the cave. My knees wobbled a bit. *Stiffen, dammit,* I commanded them, *so I don't fall down.* I took two steps toward Matt. *I need to see his eyes, his face.* For that I needed the light streaming through the opening of my cave.

He extended his hand.

I turned, assessed Lupine. She didn't react. I reached to shake.

Matt's warm dry callused hand enveloped mine. Up close, he towered over me. *Formidable, yes. But not scary. I think he could be a friend, but this time I'll be careful.*

He didn't release my hand, and I found I didn't care. The interest sparking between us across Succor Creek ignited with his closeness. A slow burn licked between my legs, traced hot wanting down the insides of my thighs.

"What …?" *I thought I loved Todd. How can I feel this so fast for another man?*

"Did you say something, Katie?"

"Ah … no. Sorry, just mumbling."

"Who's the pile of garbage?" Matt flicked his gaze at Todd.

The dark eyes I saw through the binocs – *and thought they were brown* – were deep pools of sapphire.

Matt's other hand lifted, touched my face below the open cut on my cheekbone.

The contact turned my breathing irregular.

"Did he do this?"

I nodded.

Matthew's eyes went furious and hard, the marvelous blue turned to deepest navy. His body stiffened, waves of anger surged from him.

"He's done a lot worse – true evil. I'm going to kill him. I told him to pick how. He can't seem to do it."

The glare Matt sent Todd's way lifted the hair on the back of my neck. He raised one huge boot, considered the whimpering mess on the floor. "Want me to do it for you? Except it appears your dogs are first in line?" The joking words were delivered with a smile. *But he means it, oh yes, he surely does.*

"Yes. No. I mean, I can kill him myself – and yes, they want to help." I turned to my furry friends. "My wolf is Lupine. This is Terror."

"Hey, Terror. Hey, Lupine. You're good protectors. In fact, I'd bet you're so good, I'm amazed he managed to lay a hand on your lady." Matt's statement held a question.

"They wouldn't have, but I set them to guard outside the cave while we talked. They haven't liked Todd from the day we met." I shook my head. "Should have listened. Would have saved me some trouble. Actually a lot of trouble."

"Ah, yes. You've been exposed? You sure? Are you sick?" His sculpted dark brows pulled together in a vee, horizontal lines furrowed a smooth forehead.

"Not yet. After he attacked me I realized he had a bad rash." The words quavered, and my insides shook. I fought for control before I added, "He got lymph on me." I made a half wave toward my face.

"On your broken skin?"

"Yes. I was stupid about it." *Dammit, my voice is still shaking.*

"Don't feel too bad. The stuff is transmitted airborne too. You might have caught it anyway."

The gurgling sound – *Todd's laughter* – cut off abruptly, replaced by a wheeze.

"Lupine doesn't like the sound of his voice?" Acid laced Matt's words.

"She hates everything about him," I said. "It's worse now he's hurt me."

"Would you let her kill him?" The big man stepped closer to Lu, studied her. "Looks likes she wants to."

"She does. I don't know if it's a good idea." I tilted my head, gazed up until I stared him in the eye. "Killing in a fight is one thing. Having her do it deliberately is another. What do you think?" I quirked one brow. "She was just a wild pup when she found me."

"That surprises me," he said. "Seeing her, I'd have guessed hybrid domestic stock." He watched Lupine confine Todd while stealing glances at me. "You're wise, I think, keeping her boundaries where they are."

"You'll likely think I'm a little loopy – but from the beginning she read my mind and I knew hers. We're bonded." Then I locked gazes with Matthew, because he needed to know. "Honesty heard, Matt, she's still wild. Nothing's off-limits. She'd kill to protect me – even my parents. I never told them."

"Then for sure don't let her kill the son of a bitch," Matt said. He tilted his jaw toward the lump in the back of the cave.

"Thanks." The warmth surging through my body shocked me. *Do I need comfort or reassurance so much?*

"Watch it, Katie," chirped my inner me. "You don't know this guy."

"What would you do with him?" I asked, rolled a shoulder toward Todd.

The tilt of a dark head told me Matt considered my question. "He's gonna die anyway. You could let it happen. Or just shoot him?"

"What he did – shooting's too easy. Maybe too loud." I snagged a ragged breath. "I have a silencer on my Sig. Whaddya think?"

"I think I'll stay on your good side. Is this a multiple choice question?"

I sneaked another glance at Matt. Saw a rough, scarred, dangerous man. Yet a gentleness touched him. *Perhaps because he's so strong, so capable and secure, he doesn't have to act tough. He just is?*

Matt waited, relaxed. He patiently watched me think.

I caught him cruising my legs.

He knew I saw and scarlet crawled up the back of his neck. For the second time in fifteen minutes, Matt Scavelli not only eased something inside me but twisted me up in another way. *Matt's real.* Todd was the made-up-dream-boy in my mind.

"Options," I said. "Multiple choices like you said." I felt a tiny grin tug the corner of my mouth. I held up my hand, ticked off each point on a finger. "Shoot him. Gag him, tie him up and leave him – but not in my cave. Cut his throat? Stab him about a billion times. March him out in the desert and leave him. What do you think?"

"I think you're the one he attacked, the one he exposed. If I heard you right about other things he's done, none seem harsh enough. You could let me play with him." Matthew faced the sunlight and what crossed his face turned it the same sardonic dark as Dad's. *He scares me – same way Dad does sometimes.*

I don't know what he saw in my face because Matt shook his head. "That reduces us to his level, doesn't it?" A muscle jumped in his jaw; he murmured something about me not thinking ill of him. Then his expression eased. "Katie, whatever you decide is fine. Meanwhile, we should talk."

"With an audience?" I raised a brow, inclined my head toward Todd.

"Why don't I put him to sleep for a bit?" Matt took a step, pulled his big Heckler & Koch and moved to the back of the cave. In one smooth motion he reversed his grip on the H & K, leaned down and smashed Todd on the temple with the butt of his gun.

Lupine relaxed her jaws, gagged and swallowed like she'd tasted something nasty. Stepping away from Todd, she hacked. I swear if my wolf could have pursed her lips, she'd have spat on the dirt. Lu crossed to me, butted me with her head. *Oh God! What if...?*

"Matt," I said and the quaver in my voice brought him fast to my side. "Matt, can dogs catch the flu?"

A dark shadow crossed his eyes. "Katie, I just don't know. But I traveled here, across the valley from the airforce base. I saw cars and trucks with dead people, just sitting. I saw abandoned houses, and livestock knee deep in water heading for high ground. I haven't seen one dead animal with any symptoms of the Awful. And I looked."

"So how did you get here?"

"I went to get the helicopter, but it was gone. I took a Hummer from the motor pool, but didn't get far. The ash just eats motors – ruins them in nothing flat. Between the huge crack in the valley floor and the wrecks and blockages, I had to leave it. I found a motorcycle, but it was out of gas in the middle of nowhere. Then I reached the flooding, and climbed to higher ground. I hiked about half the way."

My heart lifted, I found I could breathe again. My next question was why Matt was here at all, if it concerned Dad, but I never got it asked.

Terror let go of Todd's ankle, beelined for us.

Matt bent, rubbed T's big head and didn't straighten quick enough to elude the sloppy lick laid on his face.

"I believe you must be okay," I said. "They're never wrong."

Just so fast, the relief at having help I could trust, someone else to share the burden of survival, my body relaxed, my knees dissolved. Before Matt reached me, I turned into a puddle on the cave floor.

My head didn't bounce on the ground, a callused cushion shoved between it and the rocks. When the dancing fuzzies in my brain and the tingles in my fingers receded, I found I leaned into an arm solid with muscle.

I should move, this will give him the wrong idea. It's giving me ideas too. But I haven't felt safe in so very long.

"Not fair, Katie. Sit up, be strong," the darkness advised.

The damn thing's right.

"Oooh, thanks," I said, moving away. "I'm not a fainter, but for some reason …."

"I'm sorry I couldn't move fast enough to catch you."

"You saved me a headache." I glanced at him. "More than good enough."

Matt studied me; his intensity made my breath hitch. He smiled and it tugged hard, low in my belly. If he noticed, he didn't show it. *Oh shit. Am I ever in trouble.*

"Your face is still oozing," he said. Turning my chin into the light, he scowled.

I flinched, and he blushed. "Sorry, this just pisses me off. Will you let me bandage it for you?"

"Sure, thanks," I said. "It's bad, then?"

"Needs butterfly closures," he grumbled. "I'll clean it, do the best I can, but it might scar."

"The least of my worries, Matt."

His low chuckle stirred my blood, heated my body. "Your injury isn't what's funny, Katie. It's just exactly what Don would have said." He sponged the torn flesh, disinfected, and muttered some awful swear words. They were great – I took mental notes.

"I know why I thought I knew you," he said. "Across the canyon, I mean. I'm sure who you are."

"How is that possible?"

"You're a feminine version, although much prettier, of Don Davis. I know him well. Plus, there's another unmistakable clue."

"What clue? How …? No one knew …." I stared at my hands, found I twisted them in my lap.

"You're right," Matt said. "No one did know. But one soldier drove the base transport vehicle to pick-up and deliver your father. The same soldier flew the chopper."

Ahhhh. The light bulb switched on. "A dark-haired man, always the same one, I think. Spy hard as I could, I never saw a face. Was it yours?"

"Yes. I looked. In direct violation of my orders. I suspected someone else lived in Don's house. I caught glimpses once in a while, but never saw you." His head came up, his full lips parted just a bit and he gave a small nod. "No," he said. "That's not quite right. We locked eyes once, didn't we? Just for a second?"

"Yes," I nodded. "We did."

Lupine nudged her pack, whuffed.

I raised my brows and said in a mock stern voice, "Lupine, I've been feeding you, and you've hunted on your own. And still, you act like you're starving?"

She grinned, long pink tongue hung between bloodstained killer teeth.

Matthew laughed, nice and deep and companionable.

Then, since Lu brought it up, Terror decided to beg for lunch too.

"Fine," I said. "We can all eat. Hungry?" My glance at Matthew, then at the back of the cave, brought a nod.

"Your prisoner's out for at least an hour, Katie. Maybe longer. We can relax."

"Okay, fine. Great," I said and shared my food, spread dog chow; handed out juice boxes. But I couldn't stop peeking over my shoulder, back where Todd sprawled.

"What?" said my inner voice. "You expecting him to rise, and jump you?"

My worry, exactly. It made my knees wiggly. My stomach flipped, queasy and my hands trembled when I passed out the food.

Matt used the wicked knife he carried to slice his turkey into shares. At my involuntary sound, he laughed. "I shot and cooked it this morning, Katie. It's fresh." When he moved just right in the sunlight, my heart hiccupped. Branded, or carved, in his bandolier, just over his heart, I saw a symbol. An 'S' with an arrow crossing the center, and a knife blade on each end.

Same emblem as I have on my weapons rig. My brain locked up, went round and round, and couldn't come up with a response. I swallowed hard, scrutinized it again. *Okay, there's history here. I just need Matt to tell me.*

Lu and T-dog vibrated in place smelling the leftover bird. They ignored their dry kibble until Matt hand fed them, slicing turkey and handing chunks to each in turn. They gobbled every sliver. No pride.

Hoo boy! The turkey made my mouth water. I hung onto my manners, ate my share like a lady, but it was a fight.

"You've stolen my dogs," I complained, but I didn't mean it. "They'll work for you."

"Basic hand signals?" Sapphire eyes caught mine. A hot thrill stirred deep inside.

"Dad taught Terror. I taught Lu. They know much more than the basics."

"I'd like to team with you," he said. "We'll have a better chance surviving together. Maybe find others like us."

Here's my dream – my chance to get away. To go out there with someone who knows how it all works.

A wave of heat crawled my body, goose bumps rippled. *This isn't desire.* My brain froze. *This is sickness.*

"No, Matt. You can't hook up with me. I'm getting sick – I'm sure of it. I'll be dead in less than a week."

"I refuse to let you, Katie. I absolutely refuse."

Something in the intensity of his gaze, his absolute avowal, nearly convinced me.

"Katie, you fucking whore. Get your ass back here and untie me." The vicious words from the back of my cave said Todd was awake.

Todd knows I'm a virgin. But Matt might believe his lie. My *mad* torched my ears, burned a hole where my logical reason usually lived. I grabbed my Sig, reversed it so I held the gun by the barrel, stomped to where he lay, and fetched him a hard rap on the side of the head.

"A little bit harder," whispered my evil dark. "Just a bit more force and he'd never wake."

Why didn't I do it? Worried what Matt might think?

I kept from staggering when I rejoined Matthew at the cave mouth. I saw his body tense, and when he reached a hand to help me sit, I took it. I didn't need it – I just wanted to touch him.

"Tell me why you're out here instead of at home? And what's the story on him?" Matt stabbed a thumb in Todd's direction.

I gave him everything about Todd, Za and the gang in our house. I watched his face shift from open and friendly to all hard angry planes. His sapphire eyes turned navy, then black. I watched him think, process it all.

"But now it's your turn," I said. "I know you drove Dad, but if I'm right, the stripes on your shirt make you a Captain. Privates do chauffeur duty. You work for my father. Is he okay? Where is he?" I grabbed a deep breath. "What's the connection between you two?"

"I haven't seen your father since two days after the earthquake. He's EE Command – and I'm just a grunt. After Mountain Home blew up, I stayed to help with the sick and injured. I hunted for Don and finally one old sergeant told me – on the QT – he'd headed for home. When everyone died, with nothing left to do, I figured here would be my best shot to find him."

"What's EE?" *I finally get to find out what Dad does.*

"An elite 'evaluate and execute' squad. Make the right decisions in a split second, without emotion. Even the awful stuff. We share a genetic trait – what we have to do doesn't change us. I'm under a gag order about it – but what can it matter now?"

I nodded, sat waiting while Matthew studied me more closely.

"Don trained you, didn't he?"

"Yes," I nodded, then held his gaze with mine. "And he gave me something more, besides. You know, the special thing you guys all have."

Matt's eyes went wide, his jaw dropped. "You can't mean …?"

"Yeah. I got that too, the little bit of DNA. You can trust me to do what needs doing."

"Does Don know? How does he feel about it?"

"He knows. He hates it. He accepts it. What else is Dad to you – besides your Commanding Officer?"

"My godfather. My mentor. My father and yours came up through the service together. Close friends in school, in West Point, in the Army, then into Special Forces."

"Matthew?" I know he saw something in my face because he seemed to brace for my question. "There is an insignia on your weapons rig. And the same thing on the one I'm using – but I know it's too small for Dad. Do you know whose it is?"

"My father was critically wounded on a mission two years ago. Sabotage and leaked information." Matt said the words in a calm voice. Too calm – it told me much. Muscles knotted on both sides of his face, like he gritted his back teeth.

"My Dad was there?"

"Yes. Badly wounded himself, he carried my father out. Dad …" Matt's voice trailed silent. His jaw clenched and he said, "My father lived almost another day but they couldn't save him." Twin silver streaks slid down Matt's tanned face, dripped from his chin.

I wanted to wipe them away, give him comfort, but I sat frozen, unsure he even knew they were there. Unsure he'd even want me to touch him or acknowledge his pain. But I could change the subject – maybe.

"What does the emblem on the weapons harnesses mean? And why did I find one stored in Dad's footlocker?"

"The special forces men, our fathers and those serving with them, adopted it. The 'S' for 'special', although my Dad said it stood for Scavelli." A half-grin twisted Matt's full lips. "Your Dad said it stood for Snake, his nickname. We all have one."

I sucked air, nodded. *Wish Dad had told me.* But, given the way he slid through the woods, the name didn't surprise me at all.

"The blades at each end of the 'S' are knives; the arrow crossing the center, making the 'x', denotes our bows. We always joked that the 'X' stood for death – you know the cartoon characters with 'X's' in their eyes?" He waited for my chuckle.

I gave it to him, but my brain struggled with something. Information beat frantically in the back of my mind. I was missing something … but what?

Then I knew.

Oh shit, oh hell. What must he think? I'm wearing his father's clothes, using his father's guns and knives. I cut up his father's weapons harness.

Chapter Twenty-Four

The sun dropped to the horizon, then below.

Matthew spread his sleeping bag on one side of the cave; then did the same with mine on the other.

I felt a slow sapping of energy throughout my body, my skin too warm. My nerve endings twitched.

Matt and I sat in silence broken only by the sniveling, groaning and coughing from the back of the cave.

I thought and thought and wondered but my brain malfunctioned. Cotton balls stuffed my brain. I tried to use logic but I couldn't reach a decision about Todd.

"Quick will be a mercy killing," whispered the dark kernel in my soul. "Shouldn't he suffer?"

"Do you want to handle the mess in the back of the cave tonight?" Matthew's voice posed my thought. A hard edge accented his next words. "Remember, I'm happy to do it for you. No problem at all."

"I can't decide," I said, hating my indecision.

"You look exhausted, Katie. You've had a bad day. Sleep on it?"

"No, I think this needs to end now. Otherwise, I don't think I can sleep. I'll do it when he wakes up." I sat on my sleeping bag, leaned my head against the cave wall.

A nasal whine pulled me awake. *Time to kill him. I don't want to. Yes, I do.*

I heard Matt say something vicious, coupled with several profanities. I almost hoped he'd shoot Todd, so I didn't have to. *But, it's my responsibility.* I pushed to my feet, clicked on my Maglite.

Matthew simply moved to the cave opening, waiting. He didn't say one word.

Lupine and T-dog ghosted me on either side. I walked to Todd, my steps measured and firm. *I am an executioner.*

Todd lay awake, sweating, shaking, his eyes shiny from fever, and watched me come.

"What's it gonna be?" I snarled. "I told you – you decide. Fast easy way? Or something else? All I have to do is leave you here. You'll die in two or three days. Even untied, you're in no shape to walk out. If anyone saw you, they'd run screaming or shoot you like a rabid dog."

"You bitch. You were my ticket out of there. Your fault." Even through his damaged throat, I heard rage, defiance, frustration but mostly fear.

"You aren't going anywhere with The Great Awful in your body. How do you want to die?"

"Don't shoot me."

"Okay. No problem." I checked Matt's knots, tugged the two hitches of cords around Todd's wrists, made sure they were snug. "I won't have you die in my cave." I cut the ties off his ankles. Sniffed, lifted my lip in disgust. "You stink."

"You would too if you'd been thrown in a corner like garbage."

"You are garbage, Todd. Your soul is rotten. You let people kill your parents rather than dying like a man trying to protect them. And blamed them on Za. Get up."

"I can't," Todd snarled. "I won't."

"Pitch him over the edge, into the ravine," rumbled Matthew's bass voice at my side.

"Good idea. Quick, merciful. Instant death. Much too good for him, but it works. Would you help me get him outside?"

"Sure thing." Matthew grabbed Todd's shirt in one hand, his belt in the other. An effortless lift pulled the cursing, struggling man from the dirt. Matt propelled him across the cave, through the hole in the lava honeycomb. I shined the light on Todd and then I saw it – something from my worst nightmare. Weeping crimson rash covered his body.

"Oh shit, oh fuck," I breathed and felt the world do a tilt-a-whirl around my head. *That's what's coming for me.*

Dark all-over bruising and blood pockets dotted Todd's yellow-green skin.

"Where does he go?" Matt asked.

"This way." I heard the whistle in my voice, steadied my courage. "Off to the side of the trail and over the little hill."

"Hey, wait," Todd said. "That's a canyon ...."

"Yes, it is," I said. "But there's a niche in the rocks. At least there used to be. We'll leave you there. If you get up and stagger around, you'll fall over. I promised not to shoot you, Todd. I want to, but I won't. So I'm leaving you here instead." I turned to Matt, "Hold him for a second, would you?"

"Sure," he said. "But you should kill him."

209

"Damn betcha," I agreed. "But the wild thing in Lupine I don't want to encourage? I think it goes for me too. So I won't kill the murdering rapist – he's dying anyway." I sliced the rope cord ties off Todd's wrists.

"This is better than you deserve," I said. "I promised not to shoot you. I bet you'll wish I had."

Todd made a dive for me, grabbed a handful of my ripped tank top.

I dropped the flashlight, it flickered, and went out.

Lupine's jaws crunched his wrist, forced his hand open. Terror's big body crashed against Todd.

Matt wrapped one arm around my waist, backing fast, dragging me with him. The force of T-dog's hit sent Todd cartwheeling off the bluff's edge, plunging into the canyon.

I huddled in the hard curve, the safety of Matt's arm. And shook and shook and shook.

Below us, somewhere in the dark on the canyon floor, Todd screamed and screamed and screamed.

"I don't even have a goddamned shot," Matt growled. "Or I'd put him out of his misery."

"Fuck," I moaned. "Why didn't I just kill him?"

"Anyone within a couple of miles will hear," Matt said.

"He should have died instantly," I snarled. *I didn't cause his suffering, but he deserves it.*

"Cowards never die like men," Matt said, and his full mouth twisted. "No pride."

"Stupid girl," said the little dark kernel. "Tit for tat. He's killed you with The Great Awful. You owed him one."

"I should have gagged him." Matt's tone held disgust.

But the screaming tapered, faded, then stopped. I hated myself for the relief I felt. *Who am I, what am I becoming? Todd's dead. The end of my teenage dreams. What do I do now?*

I woke in my sleeping bag, a huge furry body snuggled tight on each side. Keeping my eyes closed, I stayed still and tried to determine if Matthew slept. My rest came in fitful intervals; the fever came and went. Matt got up and went outside the cave. Half of me remembered how his body felt against mine when he kept me from going over the cliff. Secure, protected, safe. I wanted it, wanted it bad – Matt lying next to me so I could sleep without fear.

"But the other half of you wants something else, doesn't it, Katie Davis?" The sarcastic mindvoice had it right.

Matt's movements made me burn, waves of desire flooded my body. I wanted to squirm in my bed, wanted to crawl in his, and I didn't dare. *This feeling is so much more intense than what I felt for Todd. Desire, yes. Lust, yes. But Matthew is a gentleman, a caring, unselfish person. How could I have been so blind? So stupid?*

"You didn't know any better," offered the little voice in my head. "You should have listened, yes. But don't beat yourself up too much."

"Comfort?" I whispered. "From you?"

I must have slept again because when I sat up, I almost puked at the pounding pain in my head. "Jesus H. Christ," I moaned, grabbing my skull with both hands.

"What?" Matthew materialized by me. "What's wrong?"

"My head," I snarled. "I'm sorry, that sounded cranky." I pressed my palm against my forehead, found it burning. "I might have a fever." My eyes shimmered, blurring my vision. "I'm scared, Matt. What if you catch it?"

"Don't worry," he said. "I've taken care of lots of people who've been sick with it." White teeth flashed against his tanned face. "I didn't so much as sneeze. Probably you just have a cold, or the flu."

"I'm never sick." But I dug in my backpack.

"What do you need?"

"Headache," I said. "Bad." I found a bottle that rattled the right way. Pulled it out.

Matt blinked, pursed his lips. Almost grinned.

I frowned, looked at the label. *Midol.* A hot blush covered my face. "I didn't .. ah. I'm not … I mean …."

"They're good for pain. Take two," he said with no expression at all. He pressed one big hand to my forehead, a vee appeared between his eyebrows. "If you're coming down with it, we need a better place. This cave won't do." Matthew shifted his weight from one big foot to the other. "We need to get going, Katie."

"Okay."

"The farmhouse?"

"It's full of terrible people," I said. "Really terrible."

Matt's face stilled. He tilted his head, narrowed his eyes. "What do you mean?"

"An awful woman leads the group. I heard the sentries talking about her. She tortures people for fun – she killed Todd's parents."

"Do you know her name?" Matt seemed to be holding his breath.

"The men called her Za." *Why does he care? What does he know?*

Matt's mouth opened, then closed. A muscle jumped in his jaw. He didn't breathe for what seemed forever. Then something terrible passed across his face; something deadly moved behind his eyes.

My heart stopped beating, just for a moment. *I saw death.*

"Is there another place within a few hours walking distance?" he asked. So natural, I questioned if I'd seen anything change in him at all.

"No."

"Then it has to be your house," Matt said. "How many people does she have?"

"No, no," I said. "There are a lot of them." My face must have given me away. "I just got free. I can't go back."

Matt's blue eyes deep-gazed mine, a half-smile softened his face. "I think I understand, Katie. I think I do. But we have to go there."

"No," I crossed my arms on my chest. "I just … no."

"We have to, Katie. And we need to travel today while you still can. I can carry you, but we need all our gear, all our weapons too. If the people there aren't sick or dead, we'll have to fight our way in."

I lifted one brow, quirked the corner of my mouth.

Matt's eyes squinted at me in *faux* annoyance. "We won't have to fight our way in? Do you know it for sure?"

"Not really, but it's a good bet." I gave him a sly grin. "See, Dad did something extra."

"Ah," Matt's wide smile lit a flame in my heart. "Of course he did. I should have known."

"How good a medic are you? The people you cared for – did they get well?"

"Not the ones with The Awful. I've never seen anyone recover from that, but Susan, the lady doc at the base, said she had two patients who did."

Great news. Matt's looking at me like he wouldn't take it well if I died. Hell, I wouldn't take it well if I died. Don't think either of us wants to be alone any more. My head aches; I don't feel good. I really don't. We've got to go. Now.

Matt read me well. Within a half-hour we'd struck camp, packed the dogs and packed ourselves.

I took the lead because Matt didn't know our cross-country shortcuts –

provided the dam flooding, or the earthquake changes hadn't messed things up. I told him where we were headed, gave him the compass and longitude and latitude, just in case I passed out or something. He'd been to our house several times, but always driving on roads or flying the chopper, from a different direction. He'd never traveled cross-country, on foot.

I set the pace fast as possible, without being reckless and getting spotted. *That would be a disaster. We don't need to fight our way there, fight to get inside, then fight to stay. All for something I don't want.*

The sickness crept through me, drifting along my veins, stealing strength. A boulder sat on my chest, I struggled to breathe. *Fluid in my lungs?* A glance at my arm showed me the little red rash covered more and more of my sweating skin. I fixed my eyes on the next landmark, then kept my eyes on the ground, concentrating on placing one foot ahead of the other.

When I staggered, Lu and T-dog took their usual spots on either side. They braced me with their big bodies, I wrapped my hands in their neck fur, and we went on.

"How are you doing?" Matt put a hand on my shoulder. Evidently I'd missed his questions.

"I'll make it," I husked. "You look funny though. All shiny around the edges. How did you get so fuzzy, and blurry everywhere?"

"Shit," he said, bent down, inspected my eyes, laid a freezing hand on my forehead. "We've got to hurry. Can you still walk?"

"Of course I can. Probably carry you if I had to." I snorted at my wit, but Matt didn't laugh. Instead his black brows pulled together in a frown. *Why on Earth is he so upset? The rash is worse, but I don't think he's noticed.* I felt a surge of strength. *I'm getting better.*

I picked up the hiking pace, moving faster than before. A while later, I scraped my knees on the trail. How it happened, I couldn't say. All of a sudden, the damn ground rose straight up in the air and tore off my skin. *WTF?* I checked my palms. *Damn, ripped and bleeding there too.*

A tall, dark haired man held me by the elbow, helping me to my feet. *Nice of him. Good thing he happened along.*

I introduced myself to him and expressed my thanks. The look he gave me made me wonder if I'd said something strange.

Lupine and T-dog whined, poked me with freezing noses. They made me shiver, gave me gooseflesh. *Brrrr. The sun's out, how can it be so cold? Why am I in shorts?*

"Can I have my coat, please?"

"Oh, shit," said the man. "How far to your house, Katie? Can you tell me?"

I gave him a sideways glance. A stranger asking the way to our house? No one is allowed to know. I gave him Dad's answer. "I could tell you … but then I'd have to kill you."

The man didn't laugh at this joke either. Didn't he have a sense of humor? That was funny.

I chuckled, smiled to see if maybe he'd catch on. But his arching brows lowered, hooding his eyes. It made him seem … scared?

Is this the same man from before? I shook my head, side to side, tried to rattle my memory loose – but nothing came. *This one is nice, the dogs like him. Maybe it's okay to tell him.* I wanted really, truly, to lie down in my own bed until I felt better.

For a second, the wind blew hard, cooling my skin. My hair whipped around my head, slapped at the bandage on my face.

The fog in my mind lifted and I talked fast to get it all out. "We go northwest, through the gulley, then up and over the next bluff. Straight as the crow flies. When we get there, I'll direct us in. Depending on what we find. Who, how many, and what they're doing." I rushed my last sentence because I felt it coming. Then, the mist billowed through my mind, obscuring my clarity.

"Maybe they'll all be dead," the man said.

What an awful wish. I don't understand. Why would he say such a horrid thing?

"Whoopsie," I said, laughing like a crazy person.

"Shhh," Matthew said over my shoulder. "Aren't we getting close?"

"Oh, yeah. Sorree." Then I imitated the laughing sound of our local birds, the chukkars. "Don't step there. See?" I staggered a bit, pointed out where the explosive waited, ready to detonate. "Be bits of you all over. We wouldn't want that."

"Good Lord," the man whispered, his dark blue eyes stretched a bit too wide. "Are there more of those?"

"Yup," I giggled. "Unless we have lots of people pieces. Watch out for the inner ring. Lu, Terror, stay close to me." My feet headed the wrong direction. It took a few seconds for my brain to get control. *If I'm right about this, I just staggered in a full circle.*

"Did you set the mines in this perimeter?" The dark-haired man's eyebrows pulled together over his nose.

"Yeah. Well, Dad set it up first. But since he's been gone … oh, oops. I shouldn't talk about Dad to anyone." I tilted a bit when I tried to see his face – *he's just too tall* – lost my balance and braced on Lu's back. The blood surged in my head, beating so hard it sounded like the ocean surf. My vision blurred; I saw white sparkles against a black background. *I should be seeing trees. What's wrong with me?*

The man's big hand steadied me by my elbow.

"Anyway – I've been reloading the exploded ones. But I'm almost out." I frowned. *I shouldn't have told that either. I can't remember.* "I think I just blabbed everything I wasn't supposed to."

"It's okay, Katie. I'm your friend. I work for your Dad, remember?"

"God, I'm sweating. Why am I wearing this extra shirt? It's not even mine. I'm way too hot." I wobbled a bit, grabbing for the sleeves, but I managed to peel the extra layer. I dropped it on Lupine's back. Out the corner of my eye, I saw the man fold the shirt and replace it in his pack. *Why am I wearing his shirt?*

My arm. Oh God. A heavy red rash coated both my arms and my lower legs. *If I had a mirror, I know I'd see it on my face, neck and chest. The Great Awful. The plague. I have it. So why haven't I died? How long have I been sick?*

The wind kicked up, blew an awful smell past us. The unmistakable stench coated the back of my throat. I heard the stranger cough.

"Dead body," I said. "Maybe more than one." And the fog in my mind lifted again. "Maybe we'll be lucky and all those terrible people will have died. We're close to home now."

"How far?"

"The other side of this stand of pines, through the windbreak of planted trees to the edge of our yard. I don't know how many people are left. Originally, I counted about twenty but I don't think I saw them all." I flushed, heat ran up my neck but the Great Awful didn't cause it. "I'm sorry, Matt. I'm so embarrassed. How long have I been out of my mind?"

A shake of his head. "No need to apologize, Katie. I'm astounded at you. Sick, delirious, running a high fever, and you've stayed on your feet. Walked the entire distance from the cave. In the right direction."

"How long have we been at it?" I shot him a glance, saw nothing but admiration in his midnight blue eyes.

"Close to four hours."

"Oh. I got off course."

He shifted his shoulders, just a little. "I'm not quite sure," he hedged. *I did.* "And did the dogs make sure I got back on track?"

"Yeah," he smiled, a little sheepish I'd caught his white lie.

"They know where they live," I stroked the two sturdy backs. "Even if I don't."

The reek intensified. We found bodies on the lawn, swelling in the summer heat like grotesque blow-up dolls.

I won't look. I won't look. I won't. I did. I had to. *Because this will soon be me.*

"What do you think about our odds, Katie?"

"Okay, Todd's dead, plus these two. That's three men out of twenty. I counted the head bitch as a man. I considered counting her twice, she's so vicious. I saw one female slave, but I heard other women and kids."

"Seventeen men then, plus or minus." Matt's whisper rumbled behind me. "Now we start being very careful. Let me reconnoiter, Katie. You're unstable on your legs."

"The explosives – at least any still left – are set in a circle, inner ring is six feet from the outer. Stay inside, in line with this position and you'll be fine." Something nagged at me, then I remembered. "Oh yeah, we already passed those, didn't we?"

"Yeah, we're all good." He fished his wicked Ka-Bar from its sheath. "You okay to hide, or should I settle you in a safe place?"

"I'm fine, Matt. Thanks."

I watched him go. The monster pistol in his right hand, nasty blade in his left, Matt did the invisible thing – *just like Dad* – and melted into the trees.

I got the Beretta and the Jennings ready. *The two lightest guns I have and my hands are shaking. I'd lose a fight, for sure.* I left the heavy Sig holstered, felt naked without it. The dogs and I backed into the trees, found a place surrounded by heavy brush and slid down, tucked tight agains a tree trunk. My heart beat erratic, made me cough. Muffling the noise, pulling cover around us best I could, I sighed and settled between my two protectors to wait.

Gunshots woke me. *Did I sleep or just pass out?* I heard shouting male and screaming female voices, then more shots.

Beside me, Lu and T-dog stood, posture aggressive, ready to protect. I saw their heads tilt, ears forward listening hard to something I couldn't hear; their eyes fixed on something I couldn't see. *Where is Matt? Which is he – shooter or shootee? God, let him be okay.*

Gooseflesh coated my bare arms and legs. Red with rash, the ripples showed white peaks for each blonde body hair. *Fever or fear?* I pulled my jacket from my pack, spread it over me. My palms coated icy with sweat. I labored for breath, each slow effort came hard.

It's fever, I'm doomed, flew through my mind and I slipped unconscious again.

A hand on my shoulder roused me.

"G'way." I mumbled and snuggled into Lu's side. Then I leaped, swallowed a scream and scrabbled for my guns.

Matthew slid into my hiding place. "Shhh, Katie, it's me," he said. "I just came to check on you. I've got maybe two more hours to clean out the house before I can take you inside." He placed a hand on my forehead, muttered something. "Go back to sleep. I'll return soon as I can."

"There's the tunnel, Matt. We could be in it."

"Where is it? Is there water? A bed where I can rig an IV?"

"Nooo…," I said. "But there's a …." Then black fuzz formed around my vision, closed in until the white dot before my eyes went out.

"Wake up, Katie. I've accounted for … ahm … nearly twenty of the fuckers. We gotta get you inside, in bed."

"You sure? Swept the house? Checked the basement?" I heard my voice rising, hysterical. "Did you check the attic? The safe room – did you even see it?"

"Safe room?" he muttered, but then his low voice rumbled, reassuring. "Yes, Katie, the house is clear."

"The head bitch?"

"Gone."

"Dead?"

"She is by now." Matt's blue eyes were flat, bleak pools.

"Good." I tried to stand but my knees seemed made of Vaseline. My body shook, trembled like an old woman's.

A hard hand gripped my elbow, levered me upright.

"Thanks, my balance is off." I took a step, lurched, grabbed dog fur.

Matt moved behind me, gripped my waist with both hands.

He's got the dogs loaded, he's reholstered my weapons, he's carrying both packs, and supporting me. Pride demanded I walk to the house, even if I required help every step.

Hot rushes of nausea, cold sweat, a headache pounded – sharp and spiky –

in my brain. My body shuddered, shivered. I panted but air wouldn't come. Panic drove my efforts to breathe.

I sneezed; the stink of cordite filled the air. *How many did he shoot? Does it bother him? Probably not, they were all bad. No, not the victims. Maybe they just died.* I focused on the pine straw carpet, focused on placing one deliberate foot before another, focused on watching my steps proceed across the ash coating our bright green grass. *If I stumble, if I fall, I won't be able to get up.*

My insides quivered – weak, so very weak. The back yard seemed miles long, the kitchen door so far away. *God, I don't think I can make it.*
I can.
I will.
I refuse to be carried.

Chapter Twenty-Five

I opened my eyes, saw a familiar pale yellow ceiling, recognized the floral striped wallpaper. My bedroom at home.

"How …?" Hazy recollections teased, just out of reach.

Wild thumping greeted my words. I heard claws on hardwood. Two big bodies bumped each side of the bed.

My heart beat hard in my cheek. "What …?" I reached a questing fingertip, found a patch of gauze taped over the bone. Memory stirred, blood heated in my veins. *Todd – the bastard hit me, broke the skin. Shit. The Great Awful. I'm dying.*

"Katie?" A big warm hand gently encircled my wrist, moved it back to my side. "Please don't touch it. It's swollen, infected." Matt scrubbed his hands in his hair. "Plus, Katie … I'm so sorry … I had to lance it."

Who is talking? I moved my fingers outward, reached and found furry heads. "Lu, girl. T-dog, how you guys doing?" A pair of cold wet noses pressed into my palms, made more shocking by the following contrast of warm wet tongues. "Hey, I'm glad to see you too. Been taking care of the place?"

A man's face swam into partial focus above.

Odd. Are those glinty things in his eyes tears? I blinked to clear my vision. I should recognize him. Shouldn't I?

"I'm so afraid it will scar, Katie." The man's words tumbled over each other, desperate to explain, to make me understand. "I tried everything first but the wound filled with pus. I didn't have an option, I had to open it. God, I'm so sorry. I didn't want to."

"It's okay," I said. *Matthew – I think that's his name.* "It's okay. About my cheek. It was already split."

"I might have to lance it again," he said. His face twisted, he looked so miserable, I wanted to hug him. Comfort him like a puppy.

"If you do, you do." I nodded. "Oooo." The motion sent a spike of pain from my cheek skewering into my brain. I muffled a scream. Turned it into a "mmmph" so … *Matt … yes, for sure it's Matt …* wouldn't know. *My head feels like a monster's hand ripped it from my shoulders, then stuffed it back – the wrong way.*

"Matt?" My dry throat rasped like a pipe-smoking ancient crone. "I have pain meds in my med cabinet. Can you get me one?"

"Tylenol?"

"Stronger. I need a perc."

"Sure, can you wait there a sec?" One deep blue orb viewed me with suspicion. "You won't try to get up and fall out of bed? Dislodge your IV?"

"No," I croaked. *IV?* Rolling my eyes, I surveyed my arm where it stuck out of the sheet. Saw the rash. *Is it less red than before? Or am I just hoping?* I spotted a tube snaking up the pillow, followed it to the makeshift coat hanger tree suspended on a hook from my bedroom ceiling. Two plastic drip bags full of saline and antibiotics. *From Dad's trauma box – or Matt carries his own. Why would he?* I couldn't think. My brain felt full of oatmeal

I don't remember getting here. Well, not much, anyway. Snatches of this and tiny bits of that popped in and out.

Busy hands pushed pillows around me, wedged me in place. Every spot the pillows pressed lit up my nerve endings like acid burns. Zapped the hairs on my skin like electric sparks.

"God," I whispered. "I'm on fire. Could you please hurry with the pill?"

"Shit, what am I thinking?"

Three long strides put Matt across the room, sprinting down the hall into the bath. He rushed back with a bottle and a glass of water.

My free hand wobbled. I frowned at it, commanded it to hold still. Damn thing trembled worse.

"Here," Matt shook out a pill, placed it on my tongue and held the glass for me. The pill stuck. I gagged, and gulped more water. At its slide down my throat, I nodded, heaved a sigh of relief. "Thank you."

"Welcome." The smile, so unexpected, so warm and unguarded turned his stern face into that of a carefree young man. "Can you handle soup? Otherwise the med may play merry hell in there."

"I'm so hungry my stomach is glued to my spine."

"How's your balance?" Matt held his face too still, expressionless.

He's holding back a laugh. What the hell have I been doing? I gave him a hard eyeball and a question. "Did I fall out of bed already?"

"Twice," he said, and a pair of long dimples made my heart do a funny hiccup. "Both times immediately after you insisted you were just fine. You gave me hell for worrying unnecessarily." The corner of his mouth twitched.

"Ha. So you feel justified in being suspicious?"

"I'd say I do. Should I tie you down until I bring the soup?"

"I'm fine." At his raised eyebrow, I let my tiny smile broaden. "I'm pretty secure in this pillow pile. I'll stay put."

"Okay, I'm gonna trust you. But dammit, Katie, I don't want to hear a thump from up here while I'm in the kitchen." His deep chuckle pulled an answering snort from me. Even though it hurt like hell to laugh, I enjoyed it. A lot.

Hearing pans bang downstairs, I surveyed my bedroom. Binoculars on the windowsill, a rifle on the floor under it, a sleeping bag laid across the floor in front of the door. Using the hand unhampered by the IV, I lifted the sheet. I wore one of Dad's clean tee shirts – or one of Matthew's. The sheets were clean – but damp. I felt my sweaty forehead – feverish.

How long have I been sick?

A chilly wave of gooseflesh rippled across me, up my body. My hair stood on end. The pain made me open my mouth. I slammed it shut against a shriek. Matt would run all the way up here thinking I was in trouble. I grunted, panted through my nose. *God, even my hair hurts! Please let the pill work, fast. Please.*

The hand, laid so gently on my shoulder, jerked me from sleep. I uttered a half-scream.

"Wuuuf." Lu acknowledged Matt, but she didn't stir from her spot by my bed.

"I didn't mean to startle you, Katie. Your soup is hot."

"Shit, Matt. Sorry. I drifted off." *Praise be, the pill is working. The pain's dialed back to bearable.*

"Wanna try to drink it, or should I spoon-feed you?" The sapphire eyes held a wicked gleam, a teasing challenge.

"Gimme it," I said. "If I spill, do I have to do laundry in the creek?"

"Nah, I'll let you get by with licking it off the sheets." His bass rumble of laughter caught me off guard. He held out the mug, wrapped in a dish towel to keep its heat from my rash-covered skin.

Beneath the sheet, my hand trembled against my thigh. *You will be strong and steady,* I informed it. Working it free, I ordered it to rise and grip the cup. It wobbled, it shook, but it obeyed.

How long since I ate? Sure the IV's replaced some nutrients, but there's no substitute for food.

Lupine and Terror watched, but they knew. They didn't beg and they didn't begrudge me a single swallow. Ravenous, I drank it all. Prayed I'd keep it down.

I stifled a burp, murmured, "Scuse." *After the intimate care he's taken of me, why bother? Because now I'm conscious and in my right mind. That's why.*

The fever returned with a vengeance. I flashed in and out of delerium. Sometimes I knew when Matt came and went. Sometimes I heard, or thought I did, shots, screams, explosions. Heard Terror and Lupine growl. In a single moment of clarity I thought, *There's trouble, and I'm helpless in this damn bed.* Then I passed out again.

I came to in mid-scream. Flames licked at my cheek, pressure surged against the bone. With every heart beat, a knot of pressure throbbed; tried to explode through the skin of my cheek.

I felt another person in the room, but Lupine snored by my bed.

"God help me, Matt. What the hell?"

"Your cheek is full of infection, Katie. I'm so sorry, but I need to lance it again. It could mean either one bigger scar, or maybe two."

"Screw the scars, Matt. If you have to cut me in half to fix this, do it. I don't know how long I can stand it."

"I have some morphine – I can put you to sleep. But I should restrain your hands, just in case you wake or move accidentally. What do you think?"

"I trust you. Do what you believe is best, Matt. I'll try to lay still, even if I come to." I watched him fill a syringe from one of Dad's medical supply bottles, then inject it in the IV shunt.

"Good night, Katie. I'll do my best not to make a mess."

"Matthew, if I live through the plague with only a scar, you won't hear me bitch."

Just as I went under, I thought I heard him whisper, "Katie Davis, you are one remarkable girl."

I tried to smile.

"Wha …?" I swam up from nightmare, stared at the … ceiling … of my bedroom? *But I left. I don't want to be here. How did I get in my bed?* "Who? Oh."

"Matthew … remember?" the mindvoice prompted.

Memory struck. *Oh … yes. He lanced my cheek. How long have I been out?*

Lu lifted her head from the rug, stuffed her wet nose in my palm.

I stroked her silver fur, raised my other hand. Almost afraid to check, fearing what I'd find, I touched fingertips to my face. Tracing a fat wad of gauze, I found no seepage. And best of all, no pain. I glanced at my arm. No IV. Just a ball of cotton taped to the inside of my elbow. *I'm better! Or I'm gonna die and why bother anymore. Damn.*

I lifted the sheet, saw my pink pajamas. Before, I'd been wearing one of Dad's tee shirts.

My mind put it all together, recoiled from the obvious. I felt the blood creep, bathwater warm, up my torso, my neck, surge across my face. The tops of my ears tingled. *Matt put me to bed. Cleaned me up — maybe, probably, more than once. How embarrassing.*

"Well, what did you expect him to do?" asked the darkness. "Leave you in a mess?"

"Well, no …," I whispered. "But …."

"Would you have taken care of him?" The damn voice bored right in.

"Well, of course I would but …."

"So, shut up and be grateful he was there."

Fine. I hated it when the dark little part of me was right.

I struggled to sit, and my head did slow merry-go-round revolutions. Lu tried to help but she didn't have the leverage. I waited until the violins between my ears quit playing symphonies and tried again. One elbow under me, I rolled toward the edge of the bed. My head hung over and down like my neck was silly putty.

Lu came to her feet, sidled close, and stood still. I slid an arm around her neck, but no joy.

The pine planking danced, or perhaps it was my eyes? When I straightened my neck, my double vision stabilized into one. I grabbed two handfuls of black-tipped silver fur. Sliding a foot out of bed, I planted it on the floor. *That's one.*

"Well, Katie." The bass voice made me squeak.

I jumped and nearly fell on my head.

A big arm, hard like soft skin over a steel bar, caught me, slid me back into bed.

"Appears you're better. But, since you haven't eaten for thirty-six hours, you might have some soup before you try to walk." A light teasing flavor to the words made my insides flutter, but it wasn't from hunger. "I'll go fix lunch."

Matt stopped in mid-step. "Lu, Terror. Keep Katie in the bed." Just so fast I had a hairy bedrail on either side.

I gave Matthew a mock scowl which earned me a wink before he left the room. His footsteps headed down the hall, stopped, returned. His tanned face poked back through the doorway. "How do you feel, by the way?" The corners of his generous mouth curved up, his dark hair tousled like he'd just crawled out of bed.

How did I ever think Todd gorgeous and Matthew plain? This man is handsome. I realized I stared, speechless.

"He's waiting for an answer, idiot!" snapped the darkness.

Oh, crap. Couldn't you go away and stay, I thought at it. *No need for Matt to think I hear voices and answer them too.*

"I … ahm … pretty good, actually." Then embarrassment made me blurt, "Oh, God, Matthew. You've been taking care of me?"

"Who else, Katie? The dogs are very protective, but they know I'm no danger to you."

"But you … I …." Speech failed, I waved my hand over the bed, over me.

"Katie, I'm military with paramedic training. I've seen and done everything. It's fine."

"Maybe to you." I tried for calm words, but the rest came out in a wail. "But not to meeee." And tears spurted.

"Don't cry," he said. "It's okay, honestly. I never opened my eyes." And a tiny snort escaped him.

"Oh shit," I said, and laughed. "I'm so embarrassed."

"I'm not surprised," he said. "But it's fine. Let me get you some soup, and then if you're up to it, you can fill in the holes in some of the things you've mentioned over the past couple of days."

"Oh no." *Please God, in my delerium, please don't let me have told him all our secrets.* But then my stomach growled, and Matt chuckled, a wonderful easy sound. Nothing smarmy shifted behind his deep blue eyes. *This is a trustworthy man.* "Could I maybe have some coffee, too?"

"Sorry, Katie. We're out."

"Matthew, I think I maybe told you things I shouldn't have. If I told you about coffee, then it's true. I stashed some in a safe place before I left home to scout."

"Well, now, you did mention coffee. But I wrote it off to your fever."

A flash of white teeth, the wide grin, set my pulse pounding in my head, and several spots further south.

"It's true," I said, trying to hide my panting. "And I'd kill for a cup. Fast as I'm able, I'll go fetch it."

"No, I will. You have to stay still, get better. God, you were so sick. Every minute I feared you were going to die. But you never formed buboes and it gave me hope. I don't know how you beat it – I can't take credit – although I tried everything I could think of. I kept thinking about the two people who lived through it, prayed you might, too."

"Dad said he was immune. Maybe I got a partial thing? The Davis family is tough, and stubborn." Then I clapped my hand over my mouth.

"Damn me for loose lips."

"I know you're Don's daughter. We discussed it in the cave. But that fucking asshole … er … sorry, Katie. That guy smacked you pretty hard. Might have concussed you a bit. Or maybe the fever …. Still, you could be a twin …" He stopped, swallowed.

I wondered what he saw on my face.

"I mean you look … erm … act just like Don. Oh, sorry. I meant to say you're much prettier."

A half-wink, a quirk of his lips pulled a smile from me.

"He trained you, didn't he? I saw you move through the woods; I saw the perimeter defenses. "

"Yes. Matt – soon as I can travel, I've got to find him. There is something he has to know. He's been gone too long. I worry something's happened to him."

"We'll talk. We did a little, right when you were getting sick. I doubt you remember most of it. We need to plan, to decide what we'll do. We've got to be ready for more bad people. That is, if you want to partner with me?"

I heard an undertone in his voice, his words came rushed. Something else bothered Matt, but what? Some extra danger? Stuff he knew and I didn't?

It can't be he likes me and doesn't want me to know. It can't be fear I might want him to go on his way and leave me alone. I'm not like my Mom, the kind of girl boys want – dainty, blonde, petite. Never mind a grown man, already a captain if I read the stripes right – although he looks too young for that.

He backed into the hall, then stuck his head around the corner. "Let me get your soup. Umm … do you need to go …," Matt inclined his head toward the bathroom.

"No, not yet." And the heat crawled across my chest, up my neck and over my face. *Why in hell do I have to blush?* I coughed to cover my embarrassment, added. "Let me see how strong I feel after I eat?"

The chicken noodle soup tasted wonderful. I ate two big mugs full plus a handful of saltines.

"Ready?" I asked Matt. "Let's go get the coffee."

He supported me down both sets of stairs, into the basement, then into the saferoom.

"In here," I pointed to the trashed room. "Lu. Terror. Guard. Did you bring the flashlight?"

The dogs lay down by the door, facing the basement stairs.

"Of course I did, but hell, Katie. There's nothing left, I told you so. You wasted your strength."

"Have a little faith in your new partner, Matt." I shot him an evil glance, gave him a matching chuckle and staggered to the back of the cellar. "Don't just stand there, you coward. Come on in."

That tore it – I knew it would. I figured nothing outside of a challenge or sweet talk could get Matthew Scavelli inside a falling down root cellar. And I doubted, the way I must look – not to mention smell – I'd be able to sweet talk Lupine into eating a treat, much less convince a man to do something.

"Here … whoops!" I did a sideways stagger. *Well, it worked. Unintentional, but it got the man in the root cellar just like I wanted.* "Matt, I'm weak. I need you to grab this edge and pull it away from the wall."

He couldn't stop his involuntary flinch when the entire section swung toward him. "Well. I'll be damned," he said. "More of Don's trickery?" He switched on the flashlight.

My laughter came out in a burbly-kind of thing. Moving inside the concrete room, I made my jerky way to the back wall, dropped to my hands and knees. "Here," I said and found the bumps of the lock. "Here – at the juncture between the floor and the wall."

He needed to get close to touch where I did. My body went into overdrive, heated at his nearness. Warmth flooded the 'y' of my legs and my breathing went ragged. I knew he knew – he couldn't miss it. From the sound of it, Matt suffered the same problems getting air.

"Put your fingers on top of mine. See how it's set up. Then press these buttons – in the sequence I show you – then wait."

Matt leaned over me, his chest touched my back, but he bridged on his fingertips, careful to keep his considerable weight from pressing on me. I knew he concentrated; memorized the pattern.

"Got it?" I asked.

"Got it."

"Do it, then. And let's go make coffee!"

The muted clicks, the snick of latches, and Matt pulled open the tunnel door. Shined the flashlight inside, whistled softly. "I'll be damned."

"About four paces inside – on the right in the plastic tub. A can of Folgers, and it's already open."

"Oh, Christ, Katie. I've got it – real coffee. God, I'm drooling."

I laughed, a low delighted sound of anticipation. "Know just how you feel, Matt. My mouth is watering too."

"How do I lock up?"

"Just push the doors closed, the mechanisms will do the rest." I backed up, on hands and knees, until I hit the basement stairs. Levering myself to my feet, I panted like I'd run a marathon. *I can't have him pushing me up the stairs. If he touches me, I'll turn around and grab him. Maybe not the best idea – especially right now. Be cool, Katie.*

Claws scratched and clicked as Lu and T-dog scampered up the steps. Covered with rash, feverish, my body shook and quivered. I put my hands on the treads, pulled and pushed and crawled up into the kitchen. I shoved to my feet, made it to the kitchen table. My coordination was shot to hell. It wasn't pretty but I did it by myself.

I stood, hanging onto the chair back, trying to pull it from beneath the table, so I could sit. Then my knees dissolved.

My hands went numb and started to twitch. I heard quick steps on the stairs, gripped the chair, felt my balance shift. *I wanted to do this myself. Instead, I'm going to faint.*

Matt was there to catch me. And independence be damned; I let him.

227

Chapter Twenty-Six

I must have passed out, at least for a few minutes. I came to, seated in a kitchen chair, my face resting on my arm on the table.

A steaming mug slid past my nose; the heavenly fragrance of fresh brewed coffee drifted into my nostrils.

I sniffed, opened my eyes, cupped my hands around the hot cup. "Ahhhh."

A huge slurp, then I said "Ahhh," again but this time because I'd seared the roof of my mouth. *It'll blister. I don't care.* I sipped again, only a tiny bit more carefully.

"So which of the things I told you, when I was out of my mind with fever, didn't you believe?" I crinkled my eyes at Matt; got one of those rare little boy smiles in return.

"What I just saw explains the escape tunnel, the extra food, the extra weapons. I think if I follow that tunnel, knowing Don, the other end is hidden somewhere in the woods far away from the house."

"How do you know Dad? What were you doing at Succor Creek?" *His eyes just darkened a little, the corner of his mouth twitched. I bet he told me all this before but my memory is so fuzzy.*

"He's my commanding officer," Matt said, straight-faced, like he and I hadn't talked about this. "I'm searching for him too – not on behalf of the military – just for me. I knew, as his assigned driver, Don lived out here. I didn't know – but I suspected – he had a family. We were together when we were exposed to The Great Awful; neither of us caught it. So, I figured the odds were good he'd still be alive."

Matt's eyes fixed on a point over my shoulder, a grimace twisted his face. He breathed once, sighed heavily, and continued. "Then, more people died. Many buildings, including the prison blew up. Some very dangerous people escaped. When the whole situation disintegrated, Don went missing. I searched everywhere. Then I got worried, decided I needed to find him and figured my best chance was to start looking here."

"He got home okay," I said. "He was shot, plus beat-up pretty bad – but the real problem was Mom's meds." Guilt stabbed, a gasp got away from me. I held my breath against the pain until I could manage speech. "She was nearly out. Dad went out to forage." I added. "He never came home."

"Where is your Mom, Katie?" Matt said it so soft I wondered if I really heard it. "Did she get sick?"

The tears came. *Oh God, it couldn't be just a few.* No, this was a flood, accompanied by great tearing racking sobs.

"Dead. My fault, Matt. How can I tell Dad I lost her? He won't understand. He won't be able to forgive me this." *You won't either, when you know the truth.*

Strong arms folded around me, I felt tiny and protected against his broad hard chest. He pulled me from the chair, sat, lifted me and folded me into his lap. Then he laid his cheek against the top of my head and let me cry. He rocked me like a child, murmured something comforting, handing me paper towels to mop up and blow.

Don't get used to this, whispered the voice of the darkness. *He'll dump you fast when he finds out how you failed.*

I cried harder. Then, when I ran out of tears, I finished with dry sobs and hiccups. I blew and blew and blew.

"God, I'm sorry. Look at you." I blotted the soaked chest of his shirt with a paper towel.

He laughed, murmured something and brushed aside my fretting.

I missed what he said, glanced up and quirked an eyebrow in question.

He leaned down to tell me.

I lifted my chin and we collided.

We muttered mutual apologies; Matt kissed the red spot on my forehead. Then he sucked a deep breath. And kissed me on the mouth. A soft, easy thing.

I slid my arms around his neck, hung on like he was a lifeline, and kissed him back. *Oh yes, oh yes, oh yes.*

His big body bowed, protective arms encircled me and for the first time since Dad left, I relaxed. Leaning into Matt, I took comfort, took warmth; took a deep breath from my very core.

Matt's a strong capable person, but so gentle. Safe. I'm safe.

He trembled against me, his breath hitched. *He needs human contact as much as I do. We're both starving for it.*

The second he realized he'd tightened his grip, his touch lightened and his hands fell away.

"Damn me," he said. "You're sick." He stood, taking me with him, slid one arm around my back, the other under my knees. "You belong in bed. With another cup of coffee. We still need to plan. And you need to get well."

Shit! Hell! I need to be in bed, yes, but it's not with a freaking cup of coffee!

Matt carried me up the stairs and into my bedroom. Two thumps and half-grunts pulled my attention. Lupine and Terror were now stretched full length on the floor.

Matthew deposited me in my bed, covered me with the sheet. Deep exhaustion owned my bones. Everything ached. My skin drove me crazy – raw and painful in some spots, itching furiously from healing in others. I ground my teeth. *I don't have to be a martyr.*

Matt brought two cups of coffee. I watched him set both on my nightstand, place his pistol beside them.

"Matt?"

"Umm?"

"Before you get comfortable, could you bring me a pain pill and some water?"

"Sure."

I swallowed the med and gulped all the water.

He pulled my old chair and ottoman close to the other side of the night table. He sat, shifted until he got comfortable. He relaxed, exhaled a big breath and lifted one dark brow. "Where do we start?"

I asked the question he never expected. I know because his jaw fell; his full beautiful mouth gaped, chin almost resting on his chest.

"How old are you, Matt?"

"Twenty three."

I wasn't prepared for his answer. My brows arched, my eyes stretched wide. "Whaaa?" My face did the involuntary shock thing.

"Why, Katie?" His finely sculpted brows rose to a high arc, then furrowed to a vee over his nose. "What's wrong?" Concern laced his words, "What were you expecting?"

"I dunno. Sometimes you seem and act so old – like my Dad. And then sometimes, like when you're sleeping, you look about twelve."

"Okay, it cuts both ways." He laughed. "So how old are you?"

"Sixteen," I said. And I honestly, truly wished I'd lied.

Matthew recoiled, leaped from his chair, mashed his back against the wall. "What?" He backed around my bedroom, body pressed against the walls. As far from me as he could get. "S-s-sixteen?" he hissed. When he reached the doorway, he sidled backward into the hall. "Oh, fuck."

"What is wrong with you?" I snapped. "It's not catching. Age isn't terminal unless you're about a hundred."

"Christ on a motorcycle, Katie. You're Don's daughter."

"Yeah, so? You knew that already."

"So?" he said and his bass voice rose until it squeaked. "I took care of you, saw you with your clothes off. Christ, I kissed you!" Hysteria tickled the sharp edges of his words. "If you weren't so sick, it might have gone further. Oh shit! Oh, God, I'm so fucked."

"Would you calm down?" I snapped. This reaction, totally unexpected, was also totally unbelievable. "So what? To all the above."

"You're a minor," Matt's teeth chattered. "I'm not. You're a kid – I'm a soldier. This will get me thrown out of the service with a Dishonorable Discharge, get me thrown in jail. My life is ruined. Your father will flat kill me for touching you." The whites of Matt's rolling eyes showed. He stared at me from the hallway like I'd grown a second head.

"Would you settle down?" I asked. "I don't understand your problem. Get your ass back in this chair."

"No. Oh no. I'm staying the hell away from you. In fact, I need to get out of here." He darted into the bedroom, snatched his pistol from my nightstand. Retreated to the hall.

"You can't run away," I said. "You're not a coward. Scared, maybe. The victim of unintended consequences, victim of doing the right thing, maybe, but no coward. You couldn't have known." I heard the conviction behind my words. "And I don't care."

He heard it too. His eyes refocused, his chest stopped heaving.

"I'm sick, I still need help. Look at me …."

"No, never again."

"Think about it, Matt. You saved my life, you got me home. You eliminated Za's gang. I'm betting you buried all their bodies and cleaned this house before you brought me inside. I think I'm getting better. I'm Don's daughter - you can't abandon me." I lifted my arm, watched my hand shimmy at the end of my wrist, let it drop heavy to the bed. "See that? The trip downstairs took all my strength – right now I couldn't even make it to the bathroom alone. You know I'm in no shape to fight. T-dog and Lu will die trying to protect me. Do you want that? Will my father thank you if you run? What if I had a relapse?"

He processed it all, drooped his head in defeat. Darting inside my bedroom again, he snatched his sleeping bag from the floor, dragged it into the hall.

"Damn you, Katie. Teenage girls aren't supposed to be so logical."

"I haven't been a teenage girl for about three weeks now," I said thinking of all the murders, all the awful people. *God! People I killed.* Thinking of Mom. I don't know what story my face told, but Matthew softened.

"Okay," he said. "You win. But I'll be sleeping on the red couch downstairs from now on."

Well, shit. An impasse. Does it mean I have to wait two more years for him to kiss me again? With his moral compass, I guess it does. Damn it all to hell.

Golden beams of sunlight streamed between the blinds of my window. The banging from below said Matt worked in the kitchen. I realized I needed the bathroom, like right this instant. I crept from bed and down the hall.

Lu watched me go, but stayed on her spot on the rug.

I washed my face and hands, brushed my teeth, then poured the water into the toilet, and flushed it. I headed back to my room and dressed. An odd thing had nibbled at the edges of my memory all night. When I sat on the edge of the bed to put on my shoes, it surged to the fore.

"Matthew!" I yelled, then realized what I'd done. "Oh no."

I wasn't wrong.

The sound of running feet on the stairs preceded the wild-eyed man who burst through my bedroom door.

"Katie! You're up, you're dressed." His usual deep voice sounded an octave too high. "What's wrong?"

"Oh, shit. Matt, I'm sorry," I blurted out. "I needed to remember something and couldn't. I finally did; I called your name without thinking. I didn't mean to scare you."

"It's okay," he said. "But I may have burned breakfast. I'll be back in a second with coffee and, fingers crossed, a pancake." A few minutes later, he returned with a tray. Terror followed, tight on his heels. We settled in to eat.

"So what important thing did you remember?" Matt lifted one dark arched brow.

I felt warmth creep my neck. "Sorry about scaring you, I really am. I wanted to ask you about the safe."

"What safe?"

"Ours." I studied him, the planes of his face, the dark shadow of his heavy beard and my heart hiccupped. *Damn! I almost forgot again.*

The corners of Matt's eyes crinkled, a grin nearly escaped.

He's trying not to laugh at me. I told my momentary irritation to go away – the man had every right. "There's a safe downstairs," I said. "I couldn't get it open, or find a combination anywhere and Dad never gave it to me. It could be empty – but I don't want to leave anything important behind. What I thought was – you might be able to help?"

"Well," Matthew's deep chuckle rumbled. "You've come to the right person. Where is it?" He pushed to his feet. "I'll go investigate."

"I'll show you," I said. "I need to start walking. Building strength again."

We descended the stairs, Lu and T-dog at our heels. My bare feet made no noise, Matt's boots whispered on the treads, and the dog's claws quietly ticked on the wood. I led him into the great room and took our family portrait off the wall.

"Ah," Matt's said. "Rotary combination lock on a Diebold safe. Top of the line. Don would do no less." His perfect black brows pulled together over his nose. "Much more difficult to crack, of course," he growled.

"Can you do it?" I tried to keep the eagerness out of my question. I failed.

Matt palmed the lock, spun the dial, listened, rested his ear against the safe, spun some more. Twisted the knob, pressed, then wiggled the lever. "Hmmm," he grunted. "Let me get my tools."

Tools? WTF? Maybe he wasn't kidding about him being the right person? I perched on the arm of the coffee table and waited until quiet steps signaled Matt's return. In one big hand, he held a black duffle which he placed on the couch. His other hand gripped a weathered leather envelope folded in thirds.

When he opened the brown case, I saw rows of shiny metal instruments.

"Matthew?" I heard the accusatory note in my voice. So did he.

"This is a part of everyone's training, Katie. Your Dad gave me one of my nicknames."

"What?"

"You know – like we call your father Snake?"

"Oh – sure. So what's yours?"

"Fingers." One corner of Matthew's mouth quirked. He opened his hands, palms down and wriggled his fingers at me.

What is he doing? Then, I clapped my hand over my mouth because my lust-fired imagination went right into the gutter. Or perhaps just into wishful thinking. *Whatever.*

I watched a scarlet stain creep up Matt's neck into his hairline. Saw it cover his face. A thin film of moisture beaded his forehead and upper lip. He didn't look at me, not even a side glance. Instead, he fixed all his attention – more than necessary, I'm sure – first, on the safe and then, on selecting his tools.

Why does he have a dental mirror?

"There are a few basic things we always try first," Matt said. "And hope we get lucky. Knowing your Dad, I'm sure we won't. Still …." His voice drifted away as he slid the mirror behind the lever lock handle.

"Nope," Matt shook his dead. "He filed it off."

He did glance up, then, and caught my arched brow.

"Some manufacturers put the combination there." Matt replaced the tool. "It's gone, so now we work our way through other possible solutions. This is a Sargent and Greenleaf lock – we studied their try-out combination systems."

"Meaning?"

"Meaning the companies used the same beginning combination for each type of lock. They called them 'try-outs. Military had copies of all the lists. I remember some – but if none work, I'll have to guess. Hope I get lucky." He bent his head to the safe, concentrating, listening.

"I know what you're thinking," snapped the mindvoice. "Let him work."

I want to know, I sent back at it. *He brought it up.*

"Matthew," I said. "How many other nicknames do you have?"

He paused, took a deep breath. He didn't swear. He didn't seem surprised. I gave him points – his answer came smooth and friendly. Almost amused.

"Just one," Matt said.

"What is it?"

He shot me a sly look and his mouth curved in a wicked smile. "My Dad trained me in his specialty. They call me Nitro."

Chapter Twenty-Seven

Matt worked at the lock.

Lupine and Terror parked on the family room rug.

I picked a spot in the middle of the couch where I could watch everything Matthew did. Then I picked up a magazine, pretended to be absorbed in an article, but really I just spied. I sat and admired the play of lean sculpted back muscles, the restrained power beneath his thin tee shirt. Watched his delts, tris and bis working and flexing, releasing restrained power into big dexterous hands.

"Shit," he snarled, straightened and leaned to stretch his back.

I yanked my eyes off Matt's body and glued them to the book in my lap. Pretended to look up for the first time. "No luck?"

"Nope." Matthew unzipped the black duffle, fished through the contents. "Okay," he said. "I'm going to go gather a few things. Be right back."

Terror shoved to his feet, moved close to Matt and shadowed him out the door.

About five minutes later, I heard the whisper of footsteps on the back porch, then the ticka-ticka-tick of T-dog's claws on the kitchen floor. The smell of crushed green came with them, scents of grass and pine carried on Matt's boots and Terror's paws. The air suddenly smelled fresh and wonderful.

How long since Lu went out? Does she need to? Usually, she just shoved the door open and left, or asked me to do it – but lately she'd stayed very close.

"Lu?" I asked. "Outside?"

She whuffed and put her chin down on the rug. A definite no.

Selfish, but I got a little wave of warmth because now I got to watch everything Matt did without any guilt.

He'd brought Dad's cordless drill and a couple of bits.

"If I can find the weak points," he said, waving the drill like a laser pointer first in my direction and then at the lock. "I might get lucky. I don't know how much juice is left in the battery. Fingers crossed." He slanted a glance at me. "Pun intended."

I snorted a laugh. "There's always the generator, but …." I flinched at the thought of the noise.

Matt did too – I saw it. "No," he said. "Not even an option. There's other ways – like jam shots. Or Semtex or C4. I didn't have any explosives, but I found your Dad's stash."

Jam shots? I intended to ask but my mind flooded with pictures of Matt. In pieces. Bloody ones. My breathing halted mid-inhale and I coughed. I don't know what showed on my face.

"Not to worry, Katie," Matt said. "There is a reason they call me Nitro." Again he flashed his snarky cocksure grin. *But when he does it, I know he's just teasing. He's not arrogant like Todd.* The hot prickle of embarrassment's needles stabbed my face. *God, I'm so stupid.*

"Naïve, yes," whispered my voice of truth. "Stupid, no."

"Take the dogs and go out on the front porch, okay?" Matt lifted his gaze, checked for my assent. "Until this is done."

I nodded. "You?"

"I'll be right there," he said. "Should be okay to stay in the room, but better safe than …."

"Yeah," I said and gave him a hard stare. "Make sure you do that."

"Which one?" He chuckled, tried to make me laugh.

It didn't work. I lowered my brows, slitted my eyes at him. "You join me and be safe. That's an order."

"Yessir," he said and snapped me a crisp salute. "Yes'm, I mean." The corners of his eyes crinkled and took away the seriousness.

"I mean it, Matt. I wouldn't do well if something happened to you."

"I know, Katie. I feel the same."

I turned away quick, nearly ran through the house, Lu and Terror by my side. Tears spurted, flooded my eyes. *God, I hope he didn't see. What is wrong with me?*

Behind me I heard the screen door creak open; I turned to face Matt. *Kerwhump.*

He spun; now all I saw was his back disappearing into the house. Terror followed, right on his heels.

"Not much noise, Lu," I whispered and remembered to exhale. "Or smoke either. Hope that's good. Let's go see."

"Ha," said the safecracker, peering at the wall. "A fine job I did." A deep satisfied laugh followed his words. "So what is it we're searching for?"

"I've no idea," I said. "I've never seen inside. It's a fluke I even know it's here."

"Got a plan?"

"How about we carry whatever is in it downstairs; sort the contents there? If any of it can help on the trail, we'll take it with us. We can leave the rest safely in the tunnel." I watched the last of the smoke dissipate, peered around Matt for a peek. "Are there things in it?"

"Yeah," he said. "Looks pretty full, actually."

"I have an empty duffle downstairs. Lu and I can get it while you unload the safe? Or is it too hot to touch?"

"It's fine," Matt said. "Good idea."

The navy nylon bag was in a plastic bin stacked beneath two others, both filled and heavy. I grunted, rearranged, dragged the container I needed into the room and popped the lid. Dug until I found the duffle, set it aside; then put things back the way they were.

My heart hammered against my ribs and I gasped and panted. *I'm scared what we'll find.* I gulped three deep breaths and sprinted up the stairs.

T-dog whuffed at our return and Lu waved her silver plumed tail.

I placed the duffle on the couch, ran the zipper down and spread the bag open, patted it flat. "Ready," I said. "Whatcha got?"

Matt handed me a jewelry box, another heavy container made of burled oak and several legal accordion file folders. Then he handed me a silver metal envelope. "At first I thought this was stainless steel," he said. "But I checked it again; I think its titanium. Gotta be something priceless."

The cold fingers skittered up my spine, clutched my lungs. *I don't want to open it.*

"You've been bitching about answers, Katie girl," the relentless voice in my head bored in without mercy. "Now you're scared because you might get them? Suck it up, you baby."

I did the only thing I could. I dished off the decision to Matt. "Where do you think I should start?"

"Oooo, such a brave thing to do," snarked my darkness.

"As you said, let's get it below – pick out what you want to take. Jewelry, money? Pack it."

"Yes, absolutely," I said. "Thanks. I'm a little befuddled."

"Totally understandable," he said. "I think you need an idea what's here –

like, say the title to this house or whatever. Then you'll know what you're coming back to, or back for." Matt's forehead creased in a frown. "If you ever want to."

Matt slid the last part in so easy, so smooth. To placate me, I knew. But right now I no longer knew what I wanted. Right now, I wasn't sure of anything at all.

We packed everything except the wood box in the duffle. I shuddered again when I picked up the metal envelope and put it in the bag. *Not exactly a bad premonition – just a reaction. Like it's important. I should open it right now and get it over with.*

"Act like a grownup, Katie," snarled my other half. "Get this downstairs to safety."

I slid my arm through the duffle straps and stood.

"I'll get this," Matt said, pointed an elbow at the wood box. He held his repacked safecracking bag in one hand.

"Good deal," I said. "Thanks."

Lu moved out in front, I followed and heard Matt behind me. The dogs' nails clicked on the kitchen vinyl and we all headed for the stairs and the saferoom below.

While I touched, with reverence, each piece of jewelry in the box, Matt sorted the papers. Dad owned the house and the surrounding hundred acre parcel.

Where is Dad? Is he okay? And Mom. My eyes burned, shimmered and I bit my lip for control.

Nearly all of the beautiful jewelry was gold, and much of it seemed old. I scanned paper currency, bearer's bonds, stock certificates, tipped open the lid on an oak box full of gold and silver bullion.

"Matt, we can't take anything except maybe some of the gold and silver. It will all be safer here. But I want to wear this," I said, my hands caressing an antique gold locket. I held it out, showed him the pictures of the man and woman inside. "Even if I don't know who they were."

"Could they still be alive?"

"I doubt it, see the styles of their clothing. Gotta be a hundred years old – or more. Plus with The Great Awful …."

"Yes," he said and an odd expression crossed his face. "I doubt it, too."

Who does Matt have out there? I won't ask.

"This is the only thing left, Katie." Matt's voice held a question and I wondered if he knew I'd been avoiding the metal envelope. He handed it across the space between us.

"Of course he does, you dimwit," snapped the voice in my head. Silent for a long time, it startled me. "Matthew doesn't miss much."

"Okay," I said, but I spoke to Matt. I reached; took it from his outstretched hand.

It only took a few seconds to figure out the clasp, it wasn't locked. Inside were three sheets of paper, I slid them out, fanned them on the little table before me.

Three different sheets of paper, three different color hues and three different weights.

"From three separate origins," whispered the darkness.

"They're birth certificates, Matthew," my voice choked and quavered. "But whose?"

"I can guess," he said. "But then, you can too."

I stared at the names, the birth dates. The years matched Mom and Dad and me but the months didn't. Made sense, to change those if we were in hiding with new identities.

Elaine Anne Spurling – she would be thirty-six, William Philip Crawford – he would be thirty-eight and Annelise Megan Crawford – would be seventeen. Close enough. She would be me.

"Matthew …," I said and then the room did a merry-go-round thing. I felt a gentle hand on the back of my head, pushing it between my knees.

"Breathe deep and easy. It's a terrible shock, I know."

Two big hands wrapped their warmth around mine.

"Take your time, Katie," Matt said. "We'll figure this out."

"I'm pretty sure my name is Annelise." My eyes burned, and the world shimmered silver and out of focus. "See, Mom called me Annelise Megan right before she … before she died." I felt two trickles of warmth down my cheeks.

Matt let go of me and moved away. When he returned, he put a glass in my hand. "Drink this," he said.

I did. And coughed and choked.

"Want me to hide this in the tunnel?" Matt pointed at the duffle and the wood box full of gold and silver.

"Please. Deep, okay?" I held the now-empty shot glass. My mouth and throat burned.

Matt plucked the glass from my fingers, refilled it, handed it back. "One more," he said. "I'll hide your things, we'll have a bite to eat. And then get back to work."

I didn't argue, just nodded and downed the shot.

Matt took hold of my shoulders, stared deep in my eyes. "You're wobbly, you need to be back in bed."

Again, I didn't argue.

Matthew nodded, let go; picked up the duffle and the oak box. "Just let me do this, and we'll go upstairs. Be right back," he said and disappeared.

When the mine exploded, its huge concussive boom amplified by the deep quiet of midnight, I flew from bed, Beretta in hand. The gun muzzle kept dropping toward the floor. *Damn pistol didn't used to be this heavy! Yes, it was. I'm that weak. God!*

Crouched by my bedroom window, Lupine at my side, my mind finally caught up with my body. *What direction? Was it an animal? Or marauders?* I leaned against the window, rested the gun's weight on the sill.

"Matt?" I whispered but he didn't answer. No T-dog. Hunting with Matthew then. Whatever tripped the explosive, they'd soon know.

"Katie," his whisper, pitched low to carry, drifted up the stairs. "We've got incoming. Six, maybe seven men, all armed. Can you make it downstairs? With all the weapons and ammo?"

"I can," I said, and hoped it wasn't a lie. Piling the guns across Lu's broad back, I balanced a hand on them, held the banister with the other. She seemed to know just what we needed to do – but then she'd read my mind from day one.

"Matthew?"

"Here, Katie. How ya doin'?"

"Little shaky but I can shoot. About the other thing – I'm fine." I gave thanks for the darkness. *Unless Matt's sense of smell is extraordinary, he won't know I'm coated in cold sweat.* Not from fear – just from the damn effort of coming down the stairs. I couldn't fight a child. I almost cried tears of relief when he spoke again.

"I think we'd be wise to take refuge in the tunnel. I've been watching them work in closer and I think they've mostly all got military training. The two of us, even with you at your fighting best, plus our two furry warriors, are no match for these guys."

"How fast can we get our critical supplies into the saferoom?"

"The bulk of them are there, Katie. I've been moving stuff for a couple of days. I had a bad feeling."

"I should have known," I said, shooting him an apologetic glance he couldn't see in the dark. "Let's get the rest and go below."

Matt had made the concrete room comfortable as possible: Mom's prized Persian, grease, holes and all, covered the floor. He lit the Coleman, I saw burgundy and sucked air.

"Goddamn it, Matt. You're hurt. Why the hell didn't you say?"

"Just a scratch, Katie. Nothing major."

"Bullshit," I whisper-snarled. "That's a big blotch of blood. Let me see."

"I can do it," he muttered and reached for the first aid kit.

I snatched it from his hand.

"Sit," I said, pointing at a cot. "Hold still."

I peeled off his tee shirt with trembling hands.

"Enjoying him without his shirt?" the mindvoice twitted me.

I hoped Matt figured it for weakness from the plague and not from desire. But honestly, seeing him bare from wide shoulders to narrow tapered waist did interfere with my breathing. *God, I wish I knew what I babbled in my delirium.*

"Please tell me I don't need stitches, okay?" Matt said. Then he whispered, "I hate fucking needles."

"Let me see." I held the lantern close, dabbed at the wound with a pad of gauze soaked in betadine. A shallow trench, oozing red, crossed his back from spine to left shoulder. "Nah, I think I can butterfly it."

Matt's entire body relaxed, and I hid my smile. This big tough soldier – afraid of a needle? Although admittedly stitches were a far cry from a single injection. I disinfected, I cleaned, I ignored a muffled groan and the sounds of him breathing through his nose. I pulled the edges of his wound together, pinched and secured them with the plastic sutures. Topped the whole works off with plastic skin sealer.

"Here," I said. "Your turn." I held out a percocet but he shook his head.

"No," he said. "Much as I'd like to. I need my wits about me."

"Go ahead," I said. "I'll stand watch for the first shift."

"You're a good field medic," he said. "I'll take your advice." Because he didn't argue, I knew he hurt. When he stretched out on the cot, pummeled the pillow into a comfortable shape, I waited. Listening to his breathing, I knew when the pain lessened, knew when he faded into sleep.

I heard the faint resonances from the Thunder Eggs, felt their vibrations. I wanted to ask Matt if he heard or felt anything strange. But if he didn't, I sure didn't want him thinking I was crazy. *Wish I'd asked my father when I had the chance.*

I peeked at Matt lying on the cot and wanted to laugh because his feet hung off the end just like Dad's. Only further.

But my moment of happiness faded when the here-and-now reasserted itself. *I hate this, I fucking hate this. Stuck down here in the dark, again. I'm already supposed to be gone – out there – somewhere.*

"Ah, Katie," said the darkness. "Remember what happened the last time you headed out?"

"Yeah," I murmured. "You're right. Plus, now I'm not alone either. It's all good."

Still, claustrophobia danced and teased and poked the edges of my sanity. I kept my eyes and my mind fixed on Matthew. *Because he is my only tether on reality.* But sometimes I slid too close, too scarily close, to the border where insanity lurked.

The incoming men arrived, made lots of noise. Did a cursory search of the area outside our hiding place, and decided the house was abandoned. They went back upstairs.

Terror and Lupine slept, grumbled, ate, drank, and used the back corner of the room for their latrine. I used the chem toilet and a small hole I dug to manage their waste. Restless and upset at the noises overhead, they hated our confinement. We all seemed to be holding our collective breaths.

Three days and nights we spent in the little saferoom. I knew, after such close quarters, when Matthew lay awake; when he tossed, restless in dreams. *Just as he knows the same of me. We've got to do something – it's killing me, hiding down here, listening to the heavy footsteps, the laughter, the fights overhead. And the close proximity, the hot torment in my jeans.*

Sexual tension hung heavy in the tiny room. From waking to bedtime, we avoided each other's eyes, avoided looking at each other's bodies. *The fact is, I want him to touch me. It's almost more than I can stand. And he won't. His goddamned code of honor.*

The morning of the fourth day, I made up my mind. *I have got to get out of here or go crazy. I'm ready to start snapping at him for being a good, honorable guy. Not fair, Katie.* We needed to be out in the fresh air, hiking, wearing ourselves out. Moving. Doing something. Accomplishing goals.

"Matt," I said, swallowing the last of my beef jerky breakfast. Lu and

Terror begrudged me every bite. "We've got to make a decision. I'm nearly well – I'll be a hundred percent before too long. I'm able to travel now. Your back is sore, but it's scabbed and mending well. I think we should leave this place while the weather is still good."

"But where, Katie? What are you thinking? Do we head for California – hope the sentries don't kill us when we try to cross the border?" Matt's brows pulled together, a muscle in his jaw twitched. "I admit it damn near kills me to be skulking here in the cellar – hiding from the men upstairs. But where could we go that's better?"

"The last broadcast I heard – right before I hooked up with Todd – said a sanctuary city was rebuilding in Boise. Supposedly, a bunch of good people. Said they were cleaning up the ash." I shrugged. "Maybe Dad's there – injured or something. Do we dare trust it?"

"No. But if it's true, there'd be safety in numbers." Matt's sapphire eyes turned cobalt in the light from the hooded lantern. "If they've started a community, there might be some skilled folk – medical, maybe. Or engineers who have the basics working – like power and water." He tilted his head, and sighed. "If Don's alive and able to travel, he'd be here checking on you and your mother. Keeping you safe."

"But he's not – and he's been gone too long. I don't think he's coming back." I waited, my heartbeat pounded in my temples. *Speak to me, dammit. Say we can go. Please.*

"Okay," he finally said. "We could – we can do it. We could use any vehicles we find along the way." He stopped, like a thought struck him, then said, "Do you know horses? Know how to ride?"

"No," I said. "Neither Mom or Dad knew anything about them and I never had the chance. How about you?"

"Not a thing," he said. "Sure would make it easier, but that's out. We can hike if we need to, then surveille Boise from the neighboring hills. You know the local weather patterns – I'll trust you on this." Then a bleak expression erased the animation from Matt's face. "Unless they're disturbed by recent events. If snow comes early, or things are bad out there, we'll still have time to come back and prepare for winter before it hits. We can make it through with the food stashed here."

"We can scrounge," I said. "And hunt. But at least we'll be doing something."

Matt's broad smile pulled one from me. The dogs knew what we said, their smiling faces, lolling tongues and happy tails confirmed it.

"Leave before dawn in the morning?" I asked. The plea I heard in my words made me wince.

"Sure."

All my life, I wanted to go see the world. I just never dreamed it would happen like this.

Chapter Twenty-Eight

The luminous dial on my watch showed 4:30. I'd catnapped, tried to lie still, not thrash on my cot and disturb Matt. The small inner concrete room stayed too warm with the four of us crammed inside. Terror and Lupine lay between us. I knew from his breathing Matt hadn't slept much either. The closeness of his body kept mine in a constant state of heat.

Slithering from my sleeping bag, I tried to ignore my desire, but I heard my panting, rough and uneven. My nipples pebbled tight like tiny wild raspberries. They rubbed against my clothing, made the sensation even more intense. My lower body, the juncture of my thighs, was swollen and the center seam of my shorts pressed both delicious and painful against my pleasure points. I moved oh-so-carefully to prevent it. *Don't dwell on it. Get your shit ready to leave.* I wondered if Matthew suffered like I did and wondered what, if anything, he did about it. *I can't ask.*

From nowhere, I thought about the wrapped and stored Thunder Eggs I'd gathered for Mom. *I can't leave them all here. I might never come back. God, I almost hope I don't. And yet, it's home and all I have left of my parents.*

I rooted through the stacked boxes until I found the right one. Searched until I found Mom's favorite geode. I rewrapped it in newspaper. I pretended it didn't change color and glow, pretended it didn't warm in my hands, pretended it didn't vibrate and send little throbs of electric current up my arms. I stashed it in the bottom of my duffle. Swiped away the hot moisture running down my cheeks.

"You've never shown those to Matthew," said the kernel in my mind. "He'd probably enjoy them, unlike that nasty bastard Todd."

"I will, I will. Just not now." I whispered back.

"You worried, Katie?" Matt's voice floated out of the dark, from his sleeping area in front of the door to the house. "I know you didn't sleep."

"Neither did you." *If you weren't a member of the morality police, Matthew Scavelli, we'd both have slept just fine. And I wouldn't be such a mess. But I can't say it – it wouldn't be fair. And one of the reasons I want you is because of who you are.*

"I'm concerned, I admit it. But not really worried." My voice cracked, my throat dry from desire. "The bastards upstairs may have people in the woods."

Lupine's cold nose stuffed into my hand, and I stroked her head. Then I dug my fingers deep into the thick silver ruff around her neck. She groaned in ecstasy, opened a yellow eye, gave me a sloppy lick, then rolled over best she could in the confines of our small space. I used both hands, my clawed fingers raking deep in her fur. T-dog grunted, shifted and gave her some space.

A click from the Coleman, muted light flared. I didn't need to see, the rustle of nylon and movements from Matt's area told me he rolled his sleeping bag for stowage.

"Should have sentries. If they're smart, they do. Can they shoot us coming out?"

"If they see us, sure, but I doubt it, Matt. It'd have to be pure bad luck. Dad placed the exit well."

"He's Don Davis. Of course he did."

"My watch says 4:40. Ready? You're gonna hate this, Matt, big as you are."

"Nah, I'm not claustrophobic."

"Damn good thing," I snarled. "Because Terror and Lupine both despise the tunnel. And so do I."

"Found something that scares you? I'm shocked." A flash of even white teeth told me he joked to take my mind off the upcoming ordeal.

"There is something you can do, though. Because you are such a large strong man …."

Dark eyes, the color of the ocean depths, fixed me in suspicion. "Hmmm. And what might that be? You normally don't indulge in flattery."

"You can drag yours, T-dog and Lu's packs. I'll bring my own but I'm gonna have to make them go through."

"Hell, Katie, I'll take yours too. Then you'll only have your bandolier to carry and your furry friends to persuade. Do I go first?"

"No, Matt. Let me. Maybe, sandwiched between us, the dogs won't give me so much grief. They absolutely refused to enter the tunnel before." One last scan around, then I latched the saferoom door.

"Will you lock up after we're all inside this goddamned tunnel?" In my voice, I heard hysteria, barely held in check. *Please, oh please, don't let him know I'm such a coward.*

I dropped to all fours, moved into the tunnel's darkness. Tried to make my body move. My knees stuck, like they'd been set in concrete. My heart pounded against my ribs and I fought to slow my breathing. *This won't do.* I clicked on my Maglite, pointed the bright beam before me, and began to crawl. One hundred yards – didn't Dad say? *How fast can I go?*

"Katie?"

"Yeah?" I hated the breathiness of my voice, I hated that it quivered like I'd sprinted a mile.

"Lupine and Terror won't budge." Matt's voice held frustration.

"Well, shit! Lupine. Come." All my fear came out, ugly and harsh, in my command. *Damn it, she didn't deserve that.*

Ears flat against her head, my wolf's entire body drooped, shamed she'd failed me. Dropping to her belly, she skulked into the tunnel, crawled to my feet. Licked my hand.

"Oh, Christ, girl. Don't cringe. You're good." One small thump of a tail on the dirt floor. "I'm sorry, Lu. Let's go." A glance behind showed Terror crawling toward us, cocoa eyes wide, but he came. And right behind T-dog, broad shoulders scraping loose dirt from the tunnel sides, crawled Matt.

"How in hell can you be so relaxed. God!"

All I got was a low throaty chuckle that lit a fire in my pants. *I'll crawl fast while I'm distracted by sex.*

"You will probably die a virgin," chuckled the darkness.

"No," I whispered. "Why didn't you stay gone? You're the last goddamn thing I need. You're not even real."

But I knew better. *The evil part of me is back, it just took a sabbatical. Makes no sense – the way the damn thing comes and goes.*

"You'll never be free of me," the blackness whispered.

"What did you say, Katie?" murmured the low voice behind me.

"Nothing, Matt. Just cursing." The tips of my ears flamed, red hot, from the lie. And for once, I blessed the lack of light. *If Matt has the darkness too, why would he want me? Wouldn't he want someone without it, like Dad did?*

Crawling through the dirt tunnel creeped me out. My chest tightened, like steel ropes cinched tighter and tighter. The closeness, the confinement terrified me. But the hard little kernel living in my soul scared me far worse.

Bonngg. I bashed at full crawl speed into the bottom rung of the metal ladder. In the silence of the tunnel, the reverberations sounded like a huge bell. A searing pain made tears spring from my eyes, my heartbeat thumped in the fast-swelling lump on the top of my head. A warm stream trickled down the right side of my face.

"Christ, Katie. What the hell?"

"I screwed up, Matt. I'm sorry. I put my head down, closed my eyes and crawled fast as I could. I ran smack into the ladder. In case you didn't figure it out."

"How deep are we?"

I knew why he asked. The noise could have been heard.

"And if it was?" chuckled the malevolent voice in my mind. "Well, Katie-girl, if it was, and anyone's near? You might just have screwed the pooch."

You shut up! I thought at it.

"Katie? How deep?" Matt whispered.

"Um... Maybe twelve feet, give or take."

Matt sucked air, and never said a word.

I knew why he asked – weighing the pros and cons – even though he didn't voice it. So I did. "I'd say we have a fifty-fifty chance no one above ground heard or felt it."

"If we're freaking lucky." Behind me I heard the rack of a slide. *Fuck.* I settled my harness, checked my guns, flipped safeties, loosened my knives in their sheaths. "Going up to have a peek, Matthew."

"Question, Katie."

"Yeah?"

"Can T-dog and Lu climb a ladder?"

"Shit," I whispered. "I don't know." Then I thought a second. "Can you work your way to right here behind me?"

"Let me see," I heard rustling, squirming, grunting.

"Sorry, guys. Stay."

Matt's shoulders nudged me, and my treacherous body heated, went into hyperdrive.

"What's in your devious Davis mind?" he whispered, his breath warm on the nape of my neck.

"You can cover me from here, right?"

"Yeah, but I go first."

"Not this time. I know what's out there; I know the terrain. You don't. But about the dogs – if you and I are outside, and there's trouble – Lupine and Terror will climb that sucker to get to us. No question."

I didn't have to pull the ladder down – it was already there. *The freaking goddamn reason I smacked it with my head.* Which hurt like a son of a bitch, by the way. I touched the lump and found sticky, clotting blood. No surprise. *Time to go.*

Pushing to my feet, I shrugged to adjust my clothing, my weapons rig, and brushed away loose tunnel dirt. Then I swallowed a groan at the spike pounding through my skull into my brain, grabbed the ladder sides and began to climb. The damn thing moved and rattled. And then it didn't.

Two big hands clamped and held it solid, and mostly noiseless.

"Thanks," I quiet-whispered, then startled at his murmured "Welcome." *There's no way he should have heard. Man has ears like Dad's – like mine. Like a bat. Maybe it goes with our DNA gene?*

I paused, reached overhead, found the latches locking the lid in place. I didn't unlock them, I just traced their outlines with my fingers. Moving up another rung, I pressed my right ear against the manhole cover. Listened so hard it made my head ache – *or maybe it's the bash on my skull.* I couldn't hear a thing.

"Katie?" The voice ghosted up from below.

"Shhh, I'm listening," I said, soft as an exhale. I waited, my heart hammering so hard in my ears I really couldn't hear a thing. I listened a little longer, then whispered, "Going to lift the lid now, Matthew."

The smooth metal on metal movement of the four locks proved noiseless. Dad's continual maintenance paying off yet again.

"Take a lesson, Katie," snarked the darkness. "You got lucky here. You haven't done shit for weeks."

I know, I know. Shut up and let me do this without distractions.

The metal cover, with its permanent camouflage of gravel, pine needles and rocks, proved damn heavy. Plus I wanted to be so very careful. *What if a bad guy is standing right on top?*

To my ears, my fast breaths sounded like a wind tunnel. *Nerves, dammit. Just nerves.*

I pushed a wee bit more. Dad's well-oiled single hinge lifted, a tiny crack, silent as death. Enough to see almost all the way around.

Fresh night air, moist with damp grasses and weeds, threaded through the opening. I wanted to throw the cover wide, gulp lungfuls. Remembering my training, hearing Dad's voice in my head, I instead breathed easy and quiet through my nose. I listened, heard nothing, took a chance and pushed the lid up a couple inches. Searching the pre-dawn dark for anything other than night creatures, listening for any sound other than nature, I found no danger.

I waited, and waited, my arms beginning to complain at holding a heavy weight so very still.

"Were you planning on doing something before it gets light?" the damn dark voice asked.

"Fine," I whispered, stepped up another rung and pushed the

manholecover vertical. No noise, no sentries. I eased the cover to the ground, rose from the tunnel in a low crouch, gun in hand. Scanned the pines, the surrounding boulders, a slow 360.

Leaning my head over the tunnel opening, I whispered, "All clear. Come on up."

Lupine's low whine echoed up the dark shaft.

"Katie, I've got a big unhappy wolf down here. What do I do?" Matt's low words held a thread of … near-fear? *I didn't think him capable.*

My stomach knotted, then relaxed. *Lupine will never hurt Matthew.*

"Whatever it is," floated up to me. "I need to do it now."

"Matt, can you give her a boost? When I call her?"

"If she'll allow it. How about we try with Terror first?"

"She won't like it since I'm up here."

"Okay …," the following words trailed away. I heard a shuffling below, then Matt said, "Got her at the bottom rung. Call her."

"Lupine, co …."

The ladder bowed and I feared for the welds holding it to the manhole ring. Assaulted by a hundred eighty pounds of anxious wolf, the metal rattled and whanged. I knew when Matt gripped it, the noise lessened. But she still made a freaking load of noise before she clawed her way out of the hole and exploded all over me. Whipping my gun to ready, I scanned the surrounding area. *If there's anyone around, they heard.*

"Jesus Christ." A muffled curse from below. The metal ladder shook, groaned, metal rubbed metal, then quieted.

Matt grabbed it again.

A huge hairy *Bouvier* launched from the tunnel, landed a good three feet from the hole. *Well, obviously they can climb ladders just fine.*

Except for one tiny bit of creaking metal, Matt climbed the ladder, stealthy as a burglar.

"Congrats," I said when he poked his head out. "Compared to those two, you're a ghost."

He slid up and over the edge, pulled to a crouch, surveyed our surroundings.

"Shit," he said, brushed at his arms. "I've got claw marks all over me. Neither of them waited for a lift. And they sure didn't want to be separated from you. Damn good dogs you've got, Katie."

"Yeah, they are, but they made one hell of a racket coming up the ladder."

A short, quiet chuckle escaped Matt, and my body heated with the wanting. "I can well imagine," he said. "It was deafening down below. Dawn's close. Let's close this hatch and get gone."

I wanted to, yes, but I hated leaving our house this way. Hot silvery wet blurred my vision. *If I ever come back, what will I find? Stay or go, I can't control what happens here. I want to be with Matt – even if he's got something he won't share. What is it? Should I ask?*

"You want to leave, right?" asked my dark voice. "So what's your problem?" *Yes. Matt wants to go. And, so do I. Okay, then.*

We closed the lid, brushed dirt and gravel over it. Then, we spread out and moved silent as mist, carefully placing each footstep on the carpet of pine needles, carefully avoiding false moves. The sky lightened, deep purple streaking with gray-blue, paling to apricot, then pink-spattered peach. With the light came vision. *We can see others – and they can see us.*

The snap of a twig, to my right cracked loud, creasing the silent dawn.

"Fuck," a male voice snarled.

The sentry stood so close, just on the far side of my concealing boulder, it brought the hair on the back of my neck into hard painful points. I froze, knew Matt and the dogs did the same. *If there's one, there's more. And I'm in position.*

From farther away, I heard a second voice. "Don't sweat the noise. There's not a soul out here to hear us."

I intuited, more than saw, Matt's beginning movement for the crossbow on his back. *He's too far, he'll be seen.* I turned my head, stared him in the eyes. Hard. Wagged my index finger, waved him off. Pointed at myself. Mouthed "mine".

I got a tiny negating movement of his head.

Matt doesn't want me to make this kill. Maybe he thinks I can't. I need to prove my ability with close knife work. Maybe Matt doesn't want a stain on my soul. He doesn't know what I've already done.

"Maybe, if you want him, you should keep it that way," snarked the darkness in my mind.

I ignored it. I didn't hesitate. I didn't want Matt to interfere. My brain worked so fast, the lightening process of figuring angles, which weapon, how to approach. Odd though, paradoxical, because time also slowed to a crawl.

I have to take this kill. For Matthew to do it made no tactical sense. *I'm less than six feet away – Matthew's over twenty.*

"Don't screw it up, Katie," said the gleeful whisper in my head.

Chapter Twenty-Nine

I down-chopped my hand and waved Lu to my side.

Her black lips peeled back, exposing huge sharp fangs. Ready. Lethal.

I ignored Matt's signaling and moved before he did. Crept around my concealing boulder for a better view.

Sloppy, truly sloppy for someone on guard duty. The heavy-set man sat on a rock, leaning back against a larger stone. His rifle lay propped some six feet away from him, out of reach, resting against the boulder I hid behind. *Bad for him, good for me.*

I watched while he removed a pouch of tobacco, then a packet of papers from his shirt pocket. *Relaxed, rolling a smoke. No better time.* I put my hand on my silenced Sig. No. He wouldn't be out here alone. *Knife work.*

I studied the guard. About my height, maybe a bit shorter, a spare tire of fat hung over his belt. *Slow, but possibly very strong. I can't give him any chance at all.* My heart pounded. My mouth tasted like metal.

"Go, Katie. Quick," ordered the mindvoice.

I slid the Ka-Bar free of its sheath, sent Lu around the far side of the boulder, in case I needed her to take him down. Every nerve, every sense, focused beyond tight, I slid behind him, then eased forward.

My brain noted, in the collection of minutia, the acrid almost-fragrance of burning tobacco. Heard his first exhale and grunt of pleasure. Then he grunted in primal panic. My arm wrapped his forehead, dragged it back, leaving his throat open and exposed.

He thought to scream, then forgot when my blade kissed, then sliced, into his flesh. He couldn't help his involuntary reaction to the knife. He stretched his neck up and arched it back to evade my cut. His legs thrashed, his body twisted in the strongest human emotion – the drive to live.

Totally focused, I gripped the man harder and took him to the ground. He fought from terror; I wielded my anger, my grief. *I will not fail.*

A silver bullet hit and pinned his lower half while I sawed through his trachea, disabling vocal chords and severing his jugular. The sentry's violent struggles slowed; then ceased as he bled out.

"Good girl," I patted Lu's big head. Frowned at the scarlet smear on silver.

I inspected my hands, noting in a distanced kind of way like they belonged to someone else, that they were covered in thick red smears. I frowned at their trembling, clenched my teeth in annoyance because, to be scrupulously honest, the damn things shook.

Lupine's muzzle bore smears of red, but I didn't worry. The blood came from the bites she'd used to subdue the sentry and the sprays from my knife work. Her long tongue extruded, slurped the stains from her face, and I swear she grinned at me. I grinned back, and my hands calmed.

Wiping my knife and my hands on the dead man's shirt, I made damn sure no traces of my kill remained on the blade before I returned it to my leg sheath.

To ease Matt's mind, I pushed up from my crouch, gave him a jaunty thumbs-up and made a show of leaning against the boulder. I rolled my shoulders, feigned relaxation. Inside my guts juddered, nausea roiled at the coppery reek. My wolf all but glued to my leg, we crept back around the boulder and melted into the woods to join Matthew and Terror.

"Good work," Matt said. "Quiet and quick."

"Thanks," I said. "Lu's a great asset."

Matt nodded once. Silent and smooth as ghosts, we disappeared into the brush beneath the pines. That is, Matthew, Terror and Lupine did. My knees seemed filled with jello, they didn't obey my commands. Instead, they knocked together in strange jerky motions.

"So …," mocked the darkness. "You're pretty tough? Why are you staggering?"

I've killed before. WTF? Then it hit me. Yes, but I killed from a distance. Under attack. Morally acceptable.

"Be honest. You shot that man – and all he had was a BB gun. And the woman in the yard." The darkness evidently decided to be my conscience too.

"I did – but she murdered that poor little girl." The evil part of me spoke true – I had killed the woman. True murder, unemotional and premeditated.

"Does it bother you?" asked the darkness.

Sometimes.

"Would you do it again?"

Absolutely. Still, who knows what I babbled in delirium. Maybe that's why Matt offered to make the kill.

No more time to rationalize. A shout from behind us meant the dead sentry's discovery. More shouts, then gunfire. Three long-spaced shots. Code. It wasn't ours, because we didn't have one.

They'd summoned help.

"Fuck," snarled Matt, but the expression ghosting across his face wasn't anger.

The look I've seen before. Whatever he hides from me.

We picked up our pace but still left no trail. We're superb in the woods. The noisy people after us were terrible. For three miles we worked the stands of pines, the heavy brush, the green brambles and sagebrush, the outcroppings of rocks.

We're going to make it. Get away clean. My heart banged my ribs so hard they felt bruised.

First because I knew we were going to live.

Then because I knew we were going to die.

I heard it before I saw it.

Lu and Terror fixed their eyes on the sky ahead of us, froze, growled soft and nasty.

A deadly black helicopter popped up over the ridge, missiles and guns hanging from the frame. Black uniformed soldiers, wearing respirators, sat in the open sides. They held rifles and automatic weapons. Nose down, it flew over us, circled and flew back.

Matt yelled, "That's a Homeland Security bird." Then he squinted, laughed and waved. "Chrome, hey, it's me, Matt! Daro? Justin, is that you too?" He turned to me. "We're saved – I know three of those guys. Chrome's piloting."

They didn't wave back. Two of the soldiers fired shots before the helicopter jinked skyward like it was yanked by a rope.

Rock chunks peppered my face and arms. Expert forces missed? Not a chance.

"Brothers in arms – they couldn't kill me. Run," Matt screamed. "Break right and take cover."

Lu and I were already gone. Into the trees, into the rocks, head down, sliding from spot to spot, searching the sky for the chopper.

"Oh, shit," Matt said, ghosting in beside us. Terror skidded to a stop beside Lu.

"What, Matt?"

"They brought Strykers. Mean fuckers, damn fast too."

Two huge eight-wheeled combat vehicles raced across the skyline, headed our way. The helicopter circled once, then turned and streaked in the direction of the air force base. The nimble Strykers peeled off as well, wheels churning, throwing puffs of dust and ash as they followed the black chopper away from our hiding place.

"Matt? What just happened?"

"I'm not sure," he said. "But I doubt it's over. We still have to deal with the people following us." His head came up fast, turned. "Oh fuck."

They came over the ridge in a wave, fanned about eight feet apart, a group of well-armed soldiers between us and freedom. They wore camo and respirators. Too far away to know male from female, or see facial features. I counted six as they crested the hill. *Dad would say plan for ten. For every enemy you see, plan for at least one you don't.*

Behind us, crashing through the underbrush, I heard sounds of our pursuers from the farmhouse.

The new group of incoming spread wide. Moving into the trees, they worked their way toward us.

"Elude them? Let the two groups find each other?" the darkness suggested.

"Matt?" I spoke the way Dad taught me. Matthew should hear, but no one else.

"Right here," he suddenly crouched beside me. Terror's big brown eyes peered over Matt's shoulder.

"I made at least six – out in front."

"Yes, plan for ten."

I half-smiled. "Did they see us?"

A muscle knotted in Matthew's jaw. "Not yet. If they're working together, we have to assume the chopper told them. Those soldiers in the bird missed on purpose."

"Why are they after us?"

"My friends aren't. My assumption is – for people on the ground – the military is making sure every infected person dies. And maybe those who might become infected. And those who might live to tell what they saw. Collateral damage," he said. His mouth twisted. "Never thought I'd be on the target side."

"What do we do?" I asked. "Can we set them against each other?"

"We'll try," his smile bared teeth, vicious enough I recoiled inside. "We keep each other in sight, stay low. That group of rocks ahead and slightly to my right. See it?"

"Yes."

"Run, Katie. Wait for nothing. I'll take Terror. Ready?"

"Affirmative."

"Go now!"

They spotted us. I heard guns bark but they weren't prepared and we were fast. It was impossible for them to see where we went. Thanks to the trees, we weren't visible.

"Hey," yelled one. "We're looking for Za's group. You them?"

We didn't make a sound or a move.

Our concealment possessed three good points: a deep swale, neighboring hillsides wide with rocks, tumbleweeds and raspberry vines with wicked stickers. Beyond grew a stand of blue pines, the trunks of several thick enough to conceal Matt. The bad thing: the side, in the direction of the incoming group, lay wide open.

We'd be seen once they got closer. We couldn't avoid it. The area we occupied wasn't large enough to hide all of us. One person plus a large dog, maybe yes. Despite wanting to fight together – in order to live – we had to separate.

Matt caught my gaze, lifted a brow.

I nodded, whispered, "Left or right?"

"Your choice, Katie. Pick a spot where you don't have to shoot across your body."

Very smart. I took a lesson. "Leave our duffels and supplies hidden here?"

Matt's single nod. "For now."

His two word answer jump-started me. I unbuckled Lupine's pack, stashed mine beside it. Shrugging my weapons harness until it rode easy on my body, I locked eyes with my wolf, felt our intents synch. Low-profile, stealthy as phantoms, we crept through the trees in search of incoming hunters. I knew Matt and Terror did the same.

I worked a slow lateral line, making my way to the furthest armed man. *I'll kill him first. Then, with no one behind me, I can work my way in.*

Lupine crept beside me, silent as a ghost, belly near the ground. Death on four legs. Ears up, gleaming eyes fixed on our prey, she didn't growl. But her lips writhed and peeled away from her fangs.

Our prey stepped on a log. It collapsed beneath him, and he lurched forward, crashing through the underbrush. In his struggle to stay upright, he jammed his rifle muzzle in the dirt and leaned on it for balance.

"Oh fuck," he swore, then, "Sorry for the noise." He bent his knees, leaned forward.

No soldier – maybe weekend National Guard?

"If you take him before he straightens," observed my mindvoice. "It tilts the odds greatly in your favor. And makes you taller than he."

Unfair and unsporting, yes. I gave him no chance to recover. I'd learned from the first kill. Slashing and sawing across a neck was hard, messy work.

I'll try a different method. Two quick high steps put me behind him, Ka-Bar in my hand. Grabbing his face, I tilted it back and plunged the knife into the side of his neck.

Sever the arteries and windpipe, whispered the black part of me.

I shoved the blade forward, then yanked it out.

A crunch of bones split the air. The horrible sound told me Lupine gripped the man's gun hand in her massive jaws. Dying, in his half-crouched position, the pain made my victim attempt to roll up on his toes.

A hot-cold sear burned up my side. *The bastard sliced me.* My knees turned to butter. I couldn't gauge how bad. *I've got to finish this quick.* I slipped the blade under his ribs, shoved the point in and up, searching for his heart.

He wheezed, doubled up on the ground, drummed his heels.

"Help me drag him into the weeds," I whispered to Lu.

My head swam. I felt my side, found it warm and sticky.

"Hurry," said the darkness.

I sheathed my weapons, dropped into a crouch, grabbed his belt and his shirt collar. Lupine gripped the man's clothing and together we dragged his body against a pile of tumbleweeds. I shoved his corpse under the brush with my foot, squatted and pulled more weeds over him.

I stayed down, swallowing against rising bile. I pressed my fingertips against the burning slash on my side; checked the depth of the cut. *Not too bad.* I wrapped my bandanna around my ribs, tied it tight.

So where was my next target?

Lu rumbled, nearly noiseless, but the ground vibrated with it. She moved, silver blending with the gray-green weeds toward the beige rocks. My protector launched, an airborne missile, before I pushed to my feet.

"Urk," Lu's kill managed before she tore through his throat. It wasn't neat and tidy. Blood fountained and gouted and sprayed. My wolf in action – an absolutely awesome display of sheer power. We were two for two, undetected, without raising suspicion. And perhaps, if luck was with us, we were down to four enemies.

Nothing from Matt and Terror. God, are they okay?

"Your father trained them," said my mindvoice. "They're awesome. Matt's probably worrying about your silence."

Lupine's head whipped to her right, body rigid like a hunting dog in point. Trouble.

I didn't move … much. Just the slowest, most miniscule sideways movements until I reached the trunk of a big pine. Lu slid with me. Company coming, for sure. I needed to assess.

My pulse pounded in my temples like twin hammers. My injured side throbbed.

Two sets of footsteps climbed the hill. A white-tail doe and fawn leaped from the trees and bounded away.

I can wait until the people pass. Or I can be proactive.

"Been pretty quiet, Dave. Except for that idiot yelling. Do you think everything's okay with the others?" The low contralto of a woman's voice made my brain twitch. "Hold my gun a sec, while I tie my shoe." A grunted complaint, a scuffling noise, then knees popped. "Okay, give it back."

A woman. What if she's not a threat?

"No," said the voice in my head. "Think. She's got a gun."

"The people we're hunting won't make noise," said her companion. "We screw up, we're dead. So let's mind our business. Shut up."

"Best be careful," the woman said. "Piss me off and I might shoot you."

"Now, Dee," said the man. "Don't talk like that. I'm your friend."

"Yeah," the woman said. "I've had enough killing already. I hate these orders – shooting everyone – sick or not."

My stomach twisted. Confirmation the woman was an enemy thawed my body, unstuck my brain. No morality issue – not now. Beside me Lu pushed her nose against my leg. I laid a brief caress on her head. *I'll have to shoot them. So much for stealthy. Sorry, Matt.*

Their voices told me they approached the small hill directly in front of me. I knelt behind a rampant blackberry bramble, kept Lupine close. With the eye-searing morning sun bright at my back, they'd never see what killed them.

I slid the Sig from its holster and racked the slide. The large boxy weapon felt good in my hand. I pulled the Glock, repeated the drill.

"Dave, did you hear something just then? Kinda metallic?"

"God, woman, you're a pain in the ass. Just shut up and walk, willya?"

Laughter bubbled inside, and I kept it there. *Better and better.* These two were bound to provide an opportunity. I settled in to wait.

Two hats appeared above the crest of the hill. First, I spotted a white woven cowboy hat with a feather and silver band; then came the navy ballcap with Nampa Grange embroidered across the front. It threw me for a second – Dee topped Dave by a full head.

A band clamped my chest. *Now I'm rattled? Shooting instead of close knife work is safer.* Dad said always take the best target first …. *Shit, that's the woman.*

"So what?" asked the darkness. "Do it."

I aimed for Dee's chest, the biggest part of her. I'm good with guns, but a headshot with a handgun at a range greater than six feet is difficult. I squeezed the trigger, oh so gently. Two shots split the silence, but I only fired once.

My target and her partner jerked in the direction of the noise. My bullet took her in the meaty part of her upper arm, the one holding her weapon.

"Oh shit, oh shit, oh shit." My eyes roved, a hurried scanning, searching for a fatal spot on either target. I didn't worry about Matthew. Not then.

Dee and Dave spun like dust devils, spraying bullets in all directions. At least they didn't know where I hid. They stood, silhouetted against the robin's egg blue sky. Dee held one hand over her wound, her gun hung by her side. She released her grip on her arm, stared at her red palm and at the red blooming through her shirt sleeve.

Dave shuffled in a circle, his pistol held in a sideways grip, scanning the countryside.

I waited until his back squared in front of me – he had to die – no need to risk getting shot. I tightened my finger on the trigger and the Sig bucked in my hand. The back of Dave's blue plaid shirt exploded – guaranteed the front was a mess. He folded like a deflating balloon and dropped in a heap.

Dee sprang away, backed from his body. Spinning in my direction, she fired off three shots.

"You murdering fucker, whoever you are. I'm gonna kill you." Panting and wild-eyed, she fired again.

I felt a sharp stab in my shoulder, something else raked through my hair. *Goddamn.*

I sighted in on the gaudy necklace bouncing on her chest. I began my squeeze on the Sig's trigger, waited for her to turn. She was emptying the clip when the bright silver and turquoise spot came into focus. I blew the squash blossom pendant right into her body.

My forehead burned, I swiped it with a wrist. It came away covered with blood. I explored my shoulder with the other hand, found slick and red. *Bullet grazes or rock chips. They can wait.*

Gunfire from Matt's side grabbed my attention.

Icy claws of a bad premonition skittered up my spine.

"Oh shit, Lu. Matthew!" Keeping low, taking cover in the bushes, rocks and behind the trees, we stealthed our way toward the sounds of fighting. I felt wired and sick, but fear for Matt kept me steady, backtracking to the place I'd seen him last.

Lupine and I crept onto a flat rock slab, surrounded on three sides by basalt outcroppings. The open area provided a view into the tableau playing out below.

Matt and Terror sheltered in a cluster of trees, surrounded by boulders. Four men hid in a rough quadrant pattern, one per section. They used a steady pattern of single gunshots to keep my friends confined.

"Might as well come out, make it quick." I marked the speaker, a short muscular guy, built like a power lifter. Then I watched long enough to see their plan.

One man moved forward, toward Matt and T-dog, always in sight of his friends. They worked in a pattern – when one reached his target spot, the next closed in. Continuing in rotation, the men didn't know only their procedure kept them alive. Matt wouldn't shoot because he didn't know where I hid.

He will.

They thought they were going to rush a civilian. They'd likely have been successful – if that had been the case. But they dealt with Matt and T-dog. These men had never seen anything close to that pair.

My mind went white-hot; my thought processes fired like snapped electric wires. Red film covered my vision.

"Oh, Katie," whispered the evil dark in my soul. "I've helped you so far, but you've been provoked. If you ever wanted a chance to let me out to play, this is it."

"Yes," I whispered. "It certainly is." The tips of my ears sizzled. I calculated bullet trajectories, came up with the basics of a plan.

My smile felt unnatural. It only bared my teeth. Cold and fierce, it contained no humor. I focused on my resolve; then abandoned the remnants of my conscience and my soul.

I shouted, "Matthew! I'm at your three o'clock. Let's party!"

My reward: two dark fast-moving streaks, and the chatter of gunfire.

Chapter Thirty

I rested the 30.06 on a fallen tree branch. A great spot, really. The big stable limb had several protruding branches loaded with needles – they provided exceptional cover although I didn't need it. I stretched out on the ground, propped up on my elbows, took a relaxed grip on the gun. The scope put my target right in front of me, actually too close. Overkill.

If I miss from here, I should just go home. The feral smile creased my face again.

My target stopped moving, stood still while the next man in rotation began creeping toward Matt and Terror. His mouth ran, spewed a continual stream of taunts and threats. The loud bluster grated on my nerves and I changed my mind. *I'll put the first bullet where it will shut him the hell up.*

I shifted the rifle, moved the crosshairs from the man's torso to his throat.

"Hey," he yelled. "You there in the rocks. Might as well come out – if you do, we'll kill you fast. We have orders. Everybody dies."

I oh-so-gently squeezed the trigger.

The silenced bullet, sent simultaneously with the man's shouted words, nearly went unnoticed. The sudden quiet from the loudmouth did not.

"Gordy? Did you shoot?" yelled the tall thin man. "Something didn't sound quite right."

Gordy lay in a crumpled pile, twisted just enough I saw the gaping hole where his throat should be.

Ha.

"Gordy, goddammit, you okay?"

No, Gordy's not okay. Gordy will never be okay again. A mean little chuckle escaped me despite my efforts to hold it in. *Shoot at my friends, will you?* Adrenaline leached from my system, burning away my pre-shot tension, making my fingers tremble. I waited for the weightlifter's friend to speak again.

"Gordy? Answer me, you damn bastard."

His words covered the sound when I jacked another shell into the chamber.

"Great shot," cackled the dark inside. "Get ready. Move, move, move. You have at least three more to help eliminate – probably more like six – before they get lucky and start shooting back."

I want to, but I can't. Not even into the next quadrant because I'd told Matt where Lu and I hid. He was on the hunt. Lupine and I needed to stay out of his way – be ready to help from here.

Gordy's skinny friend continued to call, with increasing concern.

Lupine's nose twitched, her eyes glued on a spot in the brush. I saw puffs of dust, saw the sudden violent rustle of bushes. *Fighting! And I can't freaking see.*

I heard the deep cough of an angry *Bouvier*. I trained the scope on a space between the trees. Saw Matt's head whip back, watched blood spray, and then stream from his nose. He staggered; steadied his shoulder against a rock, snapped his head around and leaped aside. I saw a baseball bat whack a tree trunk, bark chunks sprayed.

I heard the scream of a male voice – Terror had to be in the mix. The bat whipped through the air, and I caught a glance of Matt dancing and dodging. Through the scope I spotted a big muscular woman pull her hand back for a strike, saw a huge blunt fist hammer her temple. She dropped like a sack of wet sand.

A third man leaped on Matt's back, took him down. I saw blue-jeaned legs and dark brown boots head skyward as Matt exploded off the ground. He gripped the man by his throat and belt buckle. I swear I heard things crack and snap as Matt smashed him against a boulder.

"Jesus H. Christ, Lu. He's damn good," I whispered. "But there are so many. One of them could get lucky." I moved the scope, hunting a way to even the odds. But I didn't dare shoot – Matt was everywhere. Spinning, kicking, striking. A crash, and an appalling scream reached me. It wasn't Matt's voice.

"He busted someone up good, for sure," cackled the darkness inside me, full of glee.

I saw Matt wind his camo shirt around one forearm; I saw the flash of his big knife. "Oh shit," I said. "Oh no." My heart shoved into my throat. I couldn't move. I just watched, waited, hoped for a chance to help.

I scanned with the scope, saw Matt slip beneath another blow. One long leg lashed out, and his boot smacked into something I couldn't see. I heard a grunt, and a howl. Another woman sneaked between the trees, ran across a patch of open ground, and disappeared into the sagebrush on the far side.

Too damn fast for me. I tracked her with my scope all the way but never got a shot.

Matt's blade hand flashed up, then sliced down. A shriek broke the silence. I heard deep growling, and furious *Bouvier* coughs.

Beside me, Lupine echoed Terror's rage. When the pitch of her growl changed, it clued me. I saw brush shaking, then a blood spattered man slipped from the circle of trees, ran through the bushes, and disappeared. I stuck my scope on him, followed the movement of the undergrowth. Waited, patient as a cat on a bird. The scarlet-smeared man emerged into an open area and ran right into my crosshairs.

I fired. His arm jerked skyward, but he didn't slow. I kept him in my sights, made an adjustment in my calculations. Led him just a tiny bit more with the gunbarrel; squeezed the trigger again. He dropped like a sack of potatoes. And stayed down.

I swung my scope back to Matt and Terror. A new soldier charged through the trees and boulders, into the center of the fight. *How many are in there trying to kill them?* I couldn't see who was winning. All I got were glimpses of fists, of hand strikes, of flying boots and roundhouse kicks. I saw sprays of blood. Heard heavy smacking sounds, the impacts of flesh on flesh. And screams.

I caught glimpses of Matt's spinning body, and lashing hands and feet. Knew it was him – he was a head taller than those he fought. I saw people fall. One after another, he destroyed his opponents. Terror's coughs were followed by shrieks as he picked off Matt's assailants one by one.

Matt's fast. Jesus, he's fast. Bigger and quicker than Dad. Terror is amazing.

Rifle in hand, I guerilla-crawled forward, but stayed in the no-fire area where Matt expected Lu and me to be. We crept through dirt, crawled over hardscrabble and weeds. Lupine's belly dragged softly on the ground; she vibrated with the need to fight. Perhaps she knew Terror needed her. But she stayed with me.

About thirty yards in, I found my sniper spot. And my next victim.

He stepped forward, out of a stand of blue pines, took a cursory glance around. He didn't see me, or my motionless silver-gray shadow. He headed for the fight in the trees.

"Gordy? Answer me. Goddammit, man." Where anger threaded his words before, now I heard fear. "Abort the fucking mission, the chopper pilot said?" he snarled. "Abort, my ass! They're killing my friends. Somebody's gonna pay."

You stupid bastard. You should have listened. You'll pay for this mistake with your life. You all will. Then what he'd said hit me. Matt got it right – his friends had saved us – or tried. They'd called for a mission abort. Some people just hadn't wanted to listen – some people would die.

I didn't permit the new information to distract me. Right here, right now – plenty of people were trying to kill us. The man I tracked entered my scope, stepped into my crosshairs. I squeezed the trigger. My shot echoed across the stillness.

His head exploded in a pink spray; his body dropped like puppet with cut strings. A hot jolt surged through me, releasing stress I didn't know I held. My head felt too light; it revolved like a merry-go-round.

A shot cracked.

"The bastard in those rocks winged me," a man screamed. I saw him wrap his hand around his arm and run into the woods. *Close to Matt.*

"Gordy, move in. Immediately!"

About now the dumb shit will be looking at his injury. Matt will finish him.

I centered him in my scope, confirmed he crouched at the base of a tree, his weapon on the ground beside him. He'd slit his bloody upper sleeve, but now he worked to unbutton his shirt.

"Like shooting fish in a barrel," giggled the voice in my head.

Watching through the scope, I saw his dirty fingers fumble with the third button.

Crack. Red bloomed bright, crimson mist blew into the air. His mouth stretched into an 'o' of pain and disbelief as he stared down at the bloody hole replacing his button and fingers.

Great shot, Matt.

The shout from quadrant three echoed, bounced off rocks and boulders.

"Raymond?"

"Yeah?"

"Can you see Gordy?"

"Not from here, Sam."

"Carl?"

Silence hung heavy, I swear I heard mental wheels grinding. "Gordy? Report in."

"Not in this lifetime," snarked the black kernel in my soul.

"Several down, more to go," I whispered to Lu as the sick boiling in the pit of my stomach settled. "Let's move a little closer."

A crashing in the underbrush signaled someone fighting his way through the brambles. From the direction of his voice, this must be Sam. He stumbled into the open, an easy chunky target, directly between me and Matt's battleground.

This close, I can't miss. I settled in for my shot.

"Careful, Katie," said my dark side. "He could trip and fall down."

If he did … I might shoot Matt or Terror. I relaxed my finger on the trigger.

Lupine slid away before I sussed her intent. I couldn't call her back, it would betray both her presence and my position.

"Trust her," said my mindvoice. "She's more than capable."

I trained my crosshairs on Sam, just in case, and prepared to watch a master hunter at work.

She took him from behind. A hundred eighty pounds of wolf landed between his shoulder blades, long powerful jaws scissored his neck. The heavy man, off balance in his rush through the woods, took three semi-leaping steps and went down. His weapon sailed end over end, far ahead of him.

Through the finite detail of the scope, I saw each bright red squirt where a fang ripped skin. I heard muffled shrieks. Then I watched those vicious jaws close and rend and chew. Lupine didn't growl, she shook him by the remains of his neck. Four times. Hard. Then, licking the crimson smears from her muzzle, she turned, grinned in my direction, and loped to my hiding place.

My stomach stuck like a sponge in my esophagus. *Will I ever get used to it?* Still, wrapping my arm around her neck, I gave her a tight squeeze. One deserving team member to another.

"One to go, Lu. I think," I whispered. "Not counting the runaways. At least far as we know. God love you, girl."

Lupine's massive chest rumbled, the only warning I received before she left my side like a silver rocket. Low profile on the hardscrabble, she raced for something only she saw. Or heard. Whatever she knew, it mattered.

I tracked her invisible passage, not by movement, but by the direction she'd gone. A flicker of gray, a hint of black, flash of silver, the flutter of a branch disturbed in her passing. Then the roar of an enraged T-dog.

Moving the scope, I found a charcoal shape charging across the open no-man's land. From my vantage point, I saw two bodies – one huge and silver and one massive and black – converge on a central point. Carl?

A bright flash from a gun barrel tilted skyward. A single shot fired before the man disappeared in a crush of fur and fury. *Did he hit one of my dogs?* I saw his arm lift, something glittered in his hand. *A knife. The bastard has a knife.* I clenched my teeth to hold back my screams, my curses. I stuffed the 30.06 in its place on my weapons rig, gripped my Sig and Glock; pushed to a crouch.

"What if he's not the last of them?" asked the darkness.

"Then I guess they'll try to shoot me," I snarled and surged into motion, pushing sideways through the brush. Everything morphed into slow motion as I watched the glittering blade descend. I heard a whine; then a roar. Saw T-dog's wide muzzle grip the man's wrist and crush.

Ululating screams, high and frantic, sliced like a stiletto through the summer air. Then, the noise choked in mid-shriek. The only sounds now were snarls, deep rumbling growls, and Terror's cough of wrath.

I skidded to a stop. Close enough to get a good visual on the three-party clusterfuck, I truly, honestly wished I hadn't. Terror and Lupine tore the man to pieces.

God. He hurt them. He had to – to push them past their training. I needed to know how bad they were injured – right now. And I had to wait.

My heart stopped. The remains of my tiny breakfast came up. Keeping a hand on my rifle, I leaned away, and vomited into a nearby bush.

"You better check on Matthew. He fought at least half a dozen in there. He might need medical attention," whispered the darkness in my father's voice.

"Oh, Christ. He's so damned good, I didn't think," I swiped my mouth on my sleeve. Guns in my hands, I stayed down, ran crouched and kept a watchful eye on the countryside as I raced toward the trees.

"Matthew?" *Talk to me.*

"Katie?" His voice sounded breathy; I didn't like that one bit.

"Yeah, Matt. I'm coming in. Please don't shoot."

"I promise I won't," he said and chuckled, deep and sexy.

It grabbed me right in the crotch.

"You better not," I said, working hard to keep my words casual and teasing. *Damn me, I'm sure I failed.*

I crossed the last fifty feet to Matt's fight arena so fast Dad would have been delighted – either with my speed or my stealth. Worry amped my run.

The growling and crunching off to my right told me my friends worked out their frustrations.

I won't look. I won't. I won't.

I did.

God.

The two were covered in burgundy and multi-colored body bits. Blots and clots and smears. The ground held an assortment of mangled once-human parts. A killing frenzy possessed my friends – prompted, I was sure – by their wounds.

Carl's death was his own fault. Entirely.

He cut them.

He pissed them off.

He died.

I hesitated, watched just a second too long. I saw Lu pull a chunk of flesh from the man's arm, flip her slender silver snout toward the sky, and swallow it.

Oh fuck. Gorge rose in the back of my throat. I needed to see about Matt. I refused to watch Lu and T-dog eat Carl.

"You should be delighted," whispered the cold part of me. "Saves their chow for another day."

"Incoming," I called, soft-voiced, put a hand on a waist-high rock and vaulted into Matt's hiding place in the clearing. First glance showed four dead bodies – one's head twisted at an unnatural angle, another's slashed throat gaped open to the vertebra. Another had a gunshot dead center in his chest and the huge dent in the woman's skull still oozed brains. My second look revealed another body in the trees, the handle of a knife protruding from his chest.

Matthew sat on the ground, covered in blood. I saw pink and gray matter on one big boot. I sucked audible air.

"Jesus H. Christ, Matthew. How bad are you?"

"Looks worse than it is," Matt said. "You know how head wounds bleed." Then one large hand, smeared with red, touched my cheek. "God damn it, you're hurt too."

"I'm fine. A scratch. You know how head wounds bleed." I cracked a grin, gave him an arch glance. I knelt beside him in the dirt, felt stones dent my knees, and didn't care. Gently pushing his chin to one side, I inspected the angry red crease running horizontally across his temple. An inch to the inside, hell, maybe less than that, and he'd have been dead.

My heart didn't like it. Not one bit. It took off like a racehorse, thumping, thundering along until I feared it would explode. Still, Matt was right. His wound wasn't dangerous, just messy.

"What else is damaged?" I wanted to put my hands on him. I feared to put my hands on him. "Tell me."

"I'm ashamed to admit that guy," Matt tilted his head at one of the bodies. "Had decent skills. I went several rounds with him. He beat on me pretty good. I think he broke a couple ribs, and nearly dislocated my shoulder – kicked my knee too." Matthew smiled, tiny lines crinkled the corners of his eyes. "Good news – he is no longer living and I am. Bad news – two got away. Maybe more."

"I watched through my scope."

"How many for you?" Matt asked. "I heard shots."

"Two, I guess. I think I finished one of yours. Lu killed one," I said. "Made it look easy."

"Terror ripped out a throat. Shit, that dog can fight."

"I'll go retrieve our packs, the med supplies are in them."

"You can't carry them all."

"I probably can. Or I'll make two trips. Better still, I'll wait a sec for the dogs to finish and …."

"Finish what?"

I don't know what showed on my face but Matthew stilled, motionless as the first time I saw him.

"They're eating." I retched behind my cupped palm. "Don't look."

"Oh," he said, and I watched all the emotions I'd felt play out in those deep sapphire eyes.

"I'll go grab the bag with the med kit."

"No," he said. "Too many people out there trying to kill us. You need the dogs with you."

I wanted to argue, but Matt had it right. "Okay."

"Smart man," said my dark side. "Listen to him."

I pushed to a crouch, then peeked over the boulders. I didn't worry about anyone sneaking up on us. Lupine and Terror were out there. Busy or not, they'd sound the alarm.

"Matt, if you can, I'd like to wait until they …um … finish and come to us."

"Sure, Katie. I'm not gonna die here. I've handled worse pain."

Well, yes, I figured so from his scars. The day across Succor Creek leaped to mind, when I saw him without his shirt. I leaned my back against the rock behind him, tucked my elbow against my seeping side, slid down to sit. And wait.

"We're going to need to hole up for a day or two, Katie. Got any ideas?"

"My cave. It's close. No one knows it but me. And you. Todd's dead, he won't be telling anyone."

"Perfect." Matt exhaled, his relief evident. "I'd forgotten it."

"We'll patch ourselves together," I said. "And move out when you're ready."

Terror and Lu poked their heads through the opening in the rocks. They'd licked their muzzles. Those were their only semi-clean spots. The stench of blood, bowel and offal, flowed from them in waves. The air in our little hiding place suddenly felt thick enough to tear in pieces.

I breathed through my mouth and checked them over. Surface slashes on both muzzles, a cut on one side of Terror's mouth and a divot above Lu's left eye looked like a deflected knife blade. Both their coats were missing hunks of fur, chopped in random spots, but I couldn't see any blood on their bodies.

"He slashed at them when they took him down. I don't see anything serious."

"We'll patch them up too," Matt said. "While you're gone, I'll salvage these guys' ammo."

A gust of wind blew past the dogs, blew their stench into our hiding spot.

"Christ on a motorcycle," said Matthew.

"Umhmm," I managed. Clapping my hand over my mouth, I pinched my nostrils together. "Going now, okay? Maybe I can run them through the creek." My words were muffled, but Matt nodded. "I couldn't stand them in the cave, stinking like they do."

"Great idea. Take all the time you need." Matt panted a little with his words. I figured his ribs were giving him fits. "If you can get them clean, I can wait." The long dimples deepened; his grin made my heart turn handsprings.

"You have enough ammo? Just in case?"

"Two full clips for my Uzi, plenty in my rig for my handguns." He gave me an openhanded gesture at the bodies. "Plus theirs. I'm good."

"Then I'll be right back."

Pushing to my feet, I moved from the safety of the rocks through the cover of the trees. A hand signal brought the dogs with me, another kept them at a distance. Far enough I almost couldn't smell them.

Chapter Thirty-One

We moved fast and stealthy through the forest.

A sudden realization turned my lungs to ice. I stopped, stared at Lu and Terror but I really didn't see them. I saw into my soul instead.

"Fuck," I whispered and leaped into a sprint. Hard, like demons pursued me, too fast to sustain. I couldn't stop myself.

The dogs paced me; gave me odd glances. Like perhaps I'd lost my mind.

Why am I running? No one chased me. Matt's injuries weren't serious.

"It's me," I whispered. "I'm running from me. I'm trying to escape the new Katie – the one who plots and fights and shoots and stabs other human beings."

"Stop it," said my darkness. "Stop it right now."

Doesn't matter how fast or far – I'll never escape what I've done. Things other people will judge reprehensible. Why don't I hate me?

"The gift or curse from your father," interjected the voice inside. "It allows you to do the necessary, keeps you sane."

"I killed," I said. My heartbeat pounded in my throat, my temples. I stopped, leaned against a tree.

"You had to," said my inner self. "Or be killed."

"I murdered," I said, and my eyes flooded.

"People planned to kill you, the dogs and Matt. It was necessary."

When we reached the creek, Lu and Terror waded and drank their fill. Although they found swimming enjoyable, it took some hard work to convince them to lie down and roll over. I gave the command and both heads swiveled my way.

Those eerie yellow eyes studied me. Almost like Lupine said *WTF?* Two mournful cocoa orbs pleaded with me. Both shook their heads no. *When did they learn that?*

"Listen, you two," I whispered. "You stink. No, you reek. Your fur is so thick, neither one of you will be wet to the skin. Get busy."

I snapped to near-military attention, locked my eyes with theirs, projected fierce command. Gave the signals again; this time my hand chopped hard.

Lupine stuck her nose in the air, whuffed in disgust, and did it. In the creek on her back, on the river rocks, she kicked, pawed the air and scrubbed the mess from her fur. Terror gave me one more pleading glance, then down he went, rolling and wiggling in the water.

They got their revenge. They came out of Succor Creek on the fly.

"No, oh no," I said and tried to run.

They flanked me, closed in a herding pattern, and pressed tight against my legs. Grinned. And shook.

"Shit." I checked my clothes for man-parts and blood. The only stains I found were my own, old ones from before. I was soaked to the skin, but not icky. "You terrible dogs," I said. "Let's go get our things."

We double-timed it through the woods. It seemed forever, probably because I couldn't get the killings out of my head. Those were major, major acts – for good or bad. *Yes, I had to. Yes, I did it with mercy. But shouldn't my conscience be bothering me? Who or what am I now? I'm not sure the old Katie would even know me. Am I afraid of what I might do in the future? Or am I relieved I lived up to Dad's expectations? Should I, perhaps, be proud of me?* Before I realized it, we were back at the rocks where Matt waited.

Matthew took one look at us, at me, held his sides and wheezed a laugh.

"Don't even ask," I snapped.

Matt allowed me to clean the crease on his head before he took my bandages and peroxide and oh-so-gently, wiped the blood from my face.

"Shit, Katie, you've got a slice on your sore cheek," he snarled. "Right across the goddamn scar." Soaking a new gauze pad, he passed it across my forehead. His black brows pulled together in a vee, and his lips pressed into a thin line. Dark blue eyes widened. "What's this? Blood on your side?"

"Shallow, Matt. No worries."

"Fuckers," he said, shot me a glance and turned red. "Ah, sorry."

"Matthew, I've heard the word before. I've actually used it. It's all good. I haven't checked …." I glanced at the dogs and Matt caught me.

"There's a rock chunk embedded in your forehead. I'd bet a flying chip sliced your cheek."

"But they …."

"Wait just a sec, okay? I'll remove the rock and bandage your side. Then you can see to Lu and T-dog."

"What about you?"

"I'll take care of me." He fished in his pack, came up with two bottles. "Here." He handed me two amoxicillin capsules, took two for himself. Opening the second, he shook three pills into his hand. "Painkillers. One for you, two for me." His wicked grin lit a fire in my pants. "Because I'm bigger."

"Can't argue with you there." I turned to Lu and T-dog. "The bastard cut at them with a boning knife," I said. "Right before they tore him to shreds."

Patting them down, I fished in my pack, found the sunscreen, then the peroxide. I swabbed the dog's shallow slashes; searched them for more cuts. No other damage. They'd be fine. I rubbed my face with SPF 30, turned to offer it to Matt.

I found him stripped to the waist. *God. Libido in overload.* My pulse took off like a runaway horse. *The man's trying to wrap broken ribs and all I want to do is jump him.*

"Here, let me," I said and tried for a totally neutral tone. Tried for a bored expression that said *I see naked men every day. You're nothing special.*

It spoke to how badly he hurt, how easily he handed me the elastic bandage.

"Should you be standing? Before I wrap the ribs, I mean?" I said, breathing through my nose, slow, deliberate. God help me, I couldn't remember what Dad said. "I hate to make you move …."

"I'll have to get up sooner or later." Matt's small half-smile flashed.

It lit a Fourth-of-July sparkler in my heart.

When he put both hands on the ground to lever to his feet, I extended mine. "Would you rather I pull you?"

"Nah, just let me get my feet under me and my legs will do the work." His face twisted at the motion. "Oh hell. The son of a bitch really nailed my knee." But despite the comment, Matt came off the ground smooth and strong. Never gave a clue to his injuries.

He's tough. Really, really tough. A true Don Davis grad.

His skin, the smooth part unmarked by awful scars, looked soft. I tried to ignore my imagination of how it would be beneath my hands. I tried to slow my galloping heart, tried to hide my lungs pumping like bellows.

Instead, I concentrated on Dad's lessons, and wrapped his ribs. When I finished, I bent, grabbed his shirt and helped him slip it back on. And mourned the loss of the sight of his gorgeous torso.

"Nice job, Katie. Feels great."

I offered him the sunscreen; he slathered his face and handed it back. I stowed the tube in my leg pocket. "We ready to travel?"

"We're banged up, yes. We'll have to watch our wounds – can't risk anything going toxic. Right now, though, we have to go."

It's not what he said ... about having to go ... it's how he said it. A chill frisson crawled my spine. *Shit. A premonition – a bad one.*

I reloaded Lupine and Terror with their packs. Thought a second about Matt's ribs and bad knee. I removed all the heavy items from Matthew's duffle and split them between the dogs' packs and mine.

"C'mon, Katie. I hate to push, but we need to move."

He sounds nervous. We killed them all. Why such a rush? It's like he just remembered something? I strapped my pack around my waist, shrugged my weapons rig until it rested easy. A warm fuzzy rush slid through my veins, a wonderful sense of well being, of happiness. *Ah. The pain killers are beginning to work.*

"Can you take the lead?" Matt's voice held urgency. "I know the direction to the cave, but you know the countryside. Let's not walk any further than we have to."

"Right." My small hand motion moved Lupine to my right, and a pace ahead. I knew, although I couldn't hear him, Matt ghosted three or four steps behind. Terror followed, protecting our backtrail.

We hiked slow, taking our time, careful not to stress our injuries. I constantly checked our surroundings, and each time I looked back, I saw Matt doing the same.

We worked at never cresting a rise, careful never to present four outlines silhouetted against the skyline, backlit by the sun. Instead, we picked our way across the basalt rocks, through piles of tumbleweeds, wove through stands of pines.

About halfway to the cave, Matt started limping.

"Wait right there a sec, would you?" I asked, then left the trail and canvassed the countryside. On the ground by a small stand of junipers, I found an aged chunk of wood. Maybe a branch, maybe a sapling trunk? Whatever its origin, it just might make a decent walking stick.

"Can you use this?" I said and found myself drowning in his sapphire eyes.

"I can," he said, and broke our gaze. "Thanks, Katie."

Desire heated, licked at my inner thighs. I turned before he saw, and led the way east. We descended the ravine, the place where I first spotted Matt, crossed Succor Creek, topped off our canteens. Topped off our pain pills.

"We need to hurry," Matt said. "Right now, hurting or not. Plus, in a bit the meds will work and we'll be moving easy again."

Matt's antsy – wish I knew why. We're home free. "The stones in the riverbed can be slick, Matt. But you already know that." I stepped into the creek, Lupine splashing beside me. Behind us, Matt and Terror sloshed through the burbling fast-flowing water.

Once across, I sent Lu first, then led the way through the boulders, up the sagebrush covered incline, into the red-brown stone of the canyon's far side.

"Early settlers named this part of the high plains desert the Honeycombs," I whispered back over my shoulder. *Matt's got ears like Dad. He'll hear, but no one within six feet of us could.*

"I can see why," he murmured. "This is lava flow, right? All these holes. I'd say they got it right."

"I usually love to climb them – love the challenge. With the different sizes of pockets, it's easy to find finger and toe holds." I motioned Lupine ahead, moved to follow, trusting her to find a path with minimal vertical movement. *Right now, I'd kill for a simple hiking trail.*

"We're fine, Katie. Don't beat yourself up because you don't know every inch of this terrain."

Still, I caught Matt's unease. I worried and caught myself holding my breath. I wondered if Matt did the same. I didn't want to fight any more – ever – but especially not today. My head sang with tension from my kills; my scraped-raw nerves were hair-triggered and on edge, still prepared for anything.

I must have whimpered a cry of relief when we reached my little cairn of stones. I'd built the trail marker five years ago.

"You okay, Katie?" Matt's voice floated up to me.

"Umhmm, Matt. We're just over a half mile out." The climb made me puff, and I worried for Matt's ribs and knee. Yet there'd been no grunt, no complaint. Except for short comments, there had been complete silence behind me.

Warm well-being still flooded my body. Time to take advantage of it, make better time. Yet with the meds, Matt might not realize he did more damage to his knee. He'd keep up, no matter what. *We can afford some extra time.* I slowed my pace a little, not enough to make him suspicious, but just enough in case he needed a break.

We've made it. We're safe. Three tall rock columns stood upright, all alone in an open field. Wildflowers, red-orange globemallow, sagebrush and rough grasses covered the fertile dirt. Clumps of rocks dotted the wide, shallow swale.

"We here, Katie?" Matthew's low voice sounded easy. He didn't hurt right now either.

"Yes," I said over my shoulder. "See the lava spires? They're called Three Fingers. We go around behind because, years and years ago, two more columns fell – they slid and angled together. The entrance to my safe place is hidden between them."

"I recognize it now," he said. "You took the idiot in there from the other side."

"We can relax." I sucked a deep breath, did a whirly spin with airplane arms. My pulse hammered hard in my throat. A happy smile, giddy – more accurately loony – spread across my face, and I took a quick step toward our goal.

Before me, Lupine froze. Hackles stiff, a warning rumbled deep in her chest.

Terror made a funny huffing noise.

"No. Not now, goddammit." Despair twisted like a stiletto in my heart.

"Problem, Katie?"

"Something – the dogs are warning …." My hand gripped steel, and to my surprise, without conscious decision, I already held my Sig in my hand.

Then I heard the sound. So unlike anything else, so unmistakable. I stopped breathing.

"Oh fuck," I whispered.

"If you'd been paying attention," said the little voice inside. "You'd have heard it for yourself."

The area shaded by the big rocks in front of my safe haven held a pile of sleeping rattlesnakes. Agitated, upset, the serpents woke. The interwoven snakeball writhed and separated and coiled.

Whoa, shit. I froze, tried to stand motionless but the tableau thrashing before me made my insides roil and shudder. I breathed, twitched the tiniest bit, and about two dozen lidless eyes tracked my minute motion. *Oooo, God.*

"Katie, do I hear what I think?"

"Yeah, Matthew, you sure do. Aw, hell," I whispered, tried for humor. "Them's some really big snakes."

He didn't laugh. He was supposed to. *Dammit!* I needed him to.

"They in striking distance of you or Lu?" Matt's words held frustration.

"I stopped the second you did, but I'm two steps below you. I can't see the ground."

"I think we're too far away. I think we're okay."

"You planning to shoot them?" A hint of laughter lay beneath the words.

"No." So now he made jokes? I thought of jamming the SigSauer back in its holster, decided I wouldn't move. Not just yet. "It's silenced. Will it still make too much noise?"

"I'd rather not …" he said and the same odd something colored his words. "What do you locals do?"

I fought the wave of hysterical laughter bubbling inside. "This local has never done shit with snakes, Matthew." I watched their flickering tongues, hypnotic weaving of the flat spade-shaped heads. Felt like weaving with them. "I just never run into any."

"Don't look at them, Katie. You're wobbling."

"Jeez, Matt. With your ribs, your bow's out of the question. Be a rare feat anyway, I think. Snake vs. crossbow. I'm no help, I've never used one." I studied the rattlers, counted them. Nine of the damn things, every one coiled, ready to strike, buzzing like crazy. Warning us away.

I sipped air, did my best to remain motionless.

"Shit, Mr. Special Forces Man," I said. "You're the bloody expert. What do we do?"

He laughed. *I'm busy standing still so I don't spook the snakes, and he's laughing?*

"What is so freaking funny?"

"I'm not laughing at you – it's me. There's only one thing scares me irrational."

"Ah … and that would be …?"

"Yup. Snakes. Were you planning to sleep in the cave? Last thing I want is to wake up with one in my bed."

"Well, hell, Matthew. What do we do? Stand around here with our thumbs up our asses until they decide to move on? What can we do to make them crawl away, into the rocks, away from my cave?"

"They don't like fire, right? We could light something and toss it in there."

"A flare would scatter them. But it would signal our position. And it's summer," I said. "We can't risk a stray spark." A small humming sound, a few words of a song behind me. *He's singing? WTF? Maybe it's like whistling in a graveyard.*

"I'm going to toss my rope over your head, right into the center of them,"

Matt said. "With luck, they'll crawl away."

I heard movement behind me, a muffled grunt of pain.

"So far, so good," I said. "Now what?"

"Now when I say 'Move', you back up. Fast. Bring Lu with you. Okay?"

"Okay," I breathed. And saw bright crystal sparkles on a black background. *Dizzy, can't faint.*

"Unlock your goddamn knees, Katie," said the darkness in my father's voice, using my father's expression. "Else you will pass out colder'n a mackrel."

What does that mean? Shit, who cares?

"Move!"

Overhead, the rope sailed, loops coming apart, spreading, covering an ever widening area.

I flicked my hand at Lupine and leaped. I crashed into Matt, heard him groan. My wolf landed right beside me. Terror whined. Then we four backed and backed and backed.

The line landed on and among the reptiles. They hissed and bit. I inspected the ground, looking for splashes of venom. I didn't see anything weird. *Did they bite each other? If so, would they die?* Snakes slithered away from Matthew's rope, away from the cave entrance. They scattered, headed for higher ground, between the rocks and boulders and tumbleweeds. Away from us.

Matt's knee gave, one foot came up, caught me on the shin hard enough to knock me against him. I tripped, grabbed for his flailing arm to keep him from falling. Instead I missed, fetched him a lick in his bad ribs.

He moaned and went down.

I turned my ankle on a loose stone and fell on him.

"They're gone," I said. "Dear God, Matthew. Are you okay? I smashed you pretty hard."

"Fine," he managed, but it sounded a lot like a lie. "But maybe … uh … you could get off me now?" Heat surged through my body – every vein, every capillary on fire. My ears were going to combust any second now, no question.

I scrambled, hurrying to move. Put a knee wrong. Heard him groan much louder. "Oh shit, Matthew. Oh dear. I'm so sorry."

"Katie," he said, and I think he spoke through clenched teeth. "No more apologies. Just could you please move?"

"Sure, oh yeah." I leaped to my feet, stiffened my marshmallow knees, backed up and turned away to give him lots of room. And some privacy. "I'll just go check the cave interior. Although I doubt there's a thing in there."

"Sure," he said. "Great."

I heard his breath whistle with his efforts. He moved, wheezed, made quite a bit of noise. *Bless me, what did I do to the poor man?*

"What about the snakes and later?" Behind me, Matt took a step. Then a second, coming in my direction.

"It's a fifty-fifty split." I started for the cave, directing my feet to move – one before the other. Nothing happened. The thought of nine big snakes made my guts quiver, ripple. In an instant, every muscle in my body went loose and jiggly.

"Now the pressure's off, you're going to fall down?" snarked my darkness.

"You shut up," I snapped. But secretly, I appreciated the damn voice's help. *I'm a lot more brave when I'm pissed.*

Lu wagged her tail and stuck her head in the cave mouth. Terror passed me and disappeared inside the dark opening.

"What's a fifty-fifty split?" Matt asked.

"Opinion – whether snakes will cross a rope or not. Cowboys swear by it. They make a circle around their bedrolls and they say the snakes stay outside the loop."

"Can't hurt." Matt's voice shook, just the tiniest bit. "I'm all for it. Meanwhile …."

Terror barked, his deep voice sharp with a look-what-I-found alarm.

Lu went airborne, sailed through the opening into the dim interior.

Matt shot me a questioning glance and I shrugged.

"Not dangerous, not an emergency," I said. "But it means something to him."

We took off our packs, climbed through the hole in the rock wall, dragged in our gear. Terror met me, holding a piece of cloth in his mouth. A camo scarf, with an insignia I now recognized. Then I saw the dark blotch in the center and the paper pinned to it.

The world did a slow spin around me and I reached a hand for something, anything, to keep me on my feet. A big warm hand gripped mine, another held my shoulder until my world stood still. "Matthew," I whispered. "The fabric – it has to be Dad's." *Please tell me it is.*

T-dog wouldn't let Matt have it, but he finally gave it to me. He whined when I handed it to Matthew to carry to the sunlight.

"It's Don's, Katie, and it's addressed to you," he said.

"Dad's been here. H-how long ago?"

"No date on it, no way to tell for sure. Blood's dry. But it has to be since we were here last. Terror wouldn't have missed it. No matter what."

A glad song danced in my heart, pounded in my throat. "He's still alive, Matt. Dad's alive." My hands shook. "Dammit. How could we miss him? And why didn't he come home?"

"I wish I knew," Matt murmured. "God knows, I wish I knew. What does he say?"

"Dear Katie," my father wrote. "I made it back and I saw the group in our house. I recognized Za. Avoid her at all costs – she's responsible for your mother's breakdown, she's hunting me, and she'll kill you on sight – just because you resemble me. I'm searching for you and your mother. I pray you're alive and safe and that you find this note. I'm headed back to Boise, then perhaps on to Mountain Home. I'll keep searching until I find you. If you get this letter, and it's possible, bring your Mom to Boise and find me. Love, Dad."

I'd wanted to sit, take a nap, get a bite to eat. Those could all wait. I wanted to find my father more.

"And what will he say when you show up alone?" asked the dark kernel in my soul. "How will you explain her death?"

"Don't know," I whispered. "All I know is I want my Dad."

I shrugged into my pack, motioned to Lupine and stepped to the cave opening. "C'mon, Matt. Let's get going, fast. We gotta catch him."

Chapter Thirty-Two

"Whoa, Katie," Matt's deep voice said. "Not right now. We need some time to recover."

"The hell," I snarled. "If you won't come, then screw you. I'll go alone."

I took one step toward the opening, felt my pack straps cut into my waist. *Matthew? How dare he grab it?*

I didn't intend to, really. But the *mad* came up so hard, so fast, I kicked back, connected with his knee. I pulled free, spun and aimed a strike at his head.

Matt grunted but he slipped my punch and captured my wrist.

I hooked my other hand into claws, went for his face. Found my wrist gripped tight.

"Jesus H. Christ," he said. "Would you fucking calm down?"

I snarled.

Lupine growled and Terror whined.

"Katie," Matt said. "Goddamn it, listen to me. I'm going to hold you until you do. And if you think to sneak away, I'll tie you up."

"If I were you," snarked the dark voice in my head. "I'd calm down. See what he has to say. And comfort the wolf."

The thick red haze in front of my eyes slowly dissolved, and I stared up at the huge man holding me without effort. I twisted, felt the skin on my wrists heat, but I couldn't free myself.

"Better," he said. "We need to talk about this. To plan. If I let you go, will you be reasonable?"

"Might as well," said the mindvoice. "Since you can't do anything else."

I considered biting Matt, felt him prepare for another attack and knew the idea for futility.

"It's all good, Lupine," I said; saw her body relax. The low rumbling signaling imminent death ceased too. "You too, T-dog."

They sat but never took their eyes from Matt and me.

"What in hell is there to talk about? Dad's alive, he's been here. He's headed for Boise and we can catch him. I thought you wanted to find him too?" I heard the mixture of whine, need and anxiety in my voice.

"I do, Katie. More than anything. But we can't go tonight. Why would we?"

"Before he gets further away!" My shout echoed in the cave.

Matthew flinched, moved to the opening and scanned outside. "Katie, we don't know when he left, or which direction he went. And none of us are in any condition to go on – much less fight."

"We probably killed all the bad guys already," I snapped.

"No guarantees of it." He shook his head. "We have to recover. Think like your father would."

Well, shit. That tears it. Dad would skin me for haring off into the dark without preparation. Or Matt.

"Talk," I growled, shot a glance at the dogs and said, "Go investigate, okay?"

They whuffed and lolled pink tongues at me like they understood. They did.

"Can I let you loose? Will you wait. Just listen a minute?" Matt's voice sent a wave of heat into the join of my legs. "I'd really rather not have to chase you with a sore knee."

Damn. I don't want to hurt him. I don't want to go without him. "Yes," I said. "At least for now."

My *mad* didn't want to go back into calm, quiet mode. I thought about the things I yelled at Matt and the warmth of shame crawled my chest, neck and face.

"I'm sorry, Matthew," I said.

"It's fine. Let's make sure there are no nasty things lurking inside?"

We joined T and Lu in scouring the cave. No predators, no danger. Just my warm, empty safe place with no sign of bear or big cat. All good.

Matt laid his rope in a double loop around the outside of the cave mouth and rolled his eyes. In embarrassment? Maybe in frustration? We settled in close to the opening to talk and tend our hurts in the remaining daylight.

"You've got a hell of a kick, Katie," he said.

Oh God, did I get his injured knee? I don't know what crossed my face, but his voice went soft. "You connected with the thigh on my good leg. I'll have a bruise, but you didn't damage anything."

Embarrassment made my skin flush. *I injured Matt twice – first I fell on him outside, I kicked his knee, too.* Little electric sparks danced in my fingertips. "Matt, I have to apologize for hurting you out there. Um … and just now."

Twin black brows arced toward his hairline. "What?"

"Well, outside I fell all over you and I ...." Speech failed me.

"Uh, Katie, maybe you took a whack on the head. I knocked you down out there – not the other way around."

"I ... ah ... are you sure?" *Lie. He's making me feel better.* A rush of affection swamped me; unshed tears stung my eyes.

"Absolutely sure. How's about we each take our antibiotics and redo our bandages? Then plan?" Matt sat in the cave entrance, scanning the countryside. He turned, evaluated me with those dark sapphire eyes and smiled, a lopsided thing that hit me square in the heart. "And no more bullshit about apologies and blame?"

"Very okay by me," I said and liked him even more.

By the time dusk arrived, we were coated in antiseptic, bandaged and comfortable.

Matt slid a sideways glance at me, cleared his throat.

"What?" I said. *I'm getting to know his signals.*

"I was thinking ... out there, then on the hike here ... you are a member of the group now. You should have a nickname like the rest of us."

"Oh ... okay." The thought simmered, boiled, and settled into a happy stew of emotions. "Sure. Did you have one in mind?"

"Well," he said. "Watching you fight, watching you move through the terrain. You kinda aren't even there sometimes, like a ghost."

"So you wanna call me ghost?" I snorted. "Not terribly flattering, is it?" I thought again. "Or, given what you do ... maybe it is?"

"Not ghost, Katie. I thought of Wraith. Suits you. What do you think."

I rolled the word around in my mind, then tried it out on my tongue. "Wraith. Yes, it's good. I like it. Wraith, it is."

"Done," he said and laughed. "Wait until Don finds I've named his daughter. Only fair after what he hung on me."

"Fingers," I snickered, then laughed out loud. "Not the most flattering. I think I prefer Nitro."

"I do too, Katie," he said. "I do too."

"How long, Matthew? Until you think we can leave?"

"Let's see how we are in the morning. We've got to be able to run and fight. Don't forget Terror and Lupine are banged up too. We have to think of them. If they're forced to defend us, they could be killed."

"And you didn't think of them, not at all, did you?" sniped the dark little voice in my head.

No, I thought back at it. *I didn't. For shame.* Red crept the back of my neck, crawled across my face.

"Matt, you hungry?" I rummaged in my pack to hide my blush. "We have hiker's meals, MRE's, and some dried and canned stuff."

"What's the canned – it's heaviest to carry."

"Spam, Pork and Beans and a few other things."

"Be still my heart," Matt's laugh made me warm all the way through. "You pick, I'll eat."

I pulled out a can of Spam and popped the top. Wrinkled my nose.

"Matthew, do you want this? I don't think I can."

He quirked one dark brow, and tilted his head across the cave. "Maybe, there's a better use for it."

My eyes followed his line of sight – I felt a grin tug at the corner of my mouth.

Two heads zeroed on me, unswerving attention. Two pair of ears perked, two noses twitched.

I laughed and split the can between Lu and T-dog. Too little food for either one of them, but then they'd dined on Carl earlier today.

"Gack," I said and told my mind to go somewhere else. Fast. And stay there. Then, I opened two cans of chili and a can of peaches. I ate half my chili, passed the rest to Matt. We shared the peaches, passing the can back and forth in companionable silence.

Matt produced two packs of lemon cookies from his duffle, handed one to me. He gave half of his to Terror, and I did the same with my wolf.

"Katie?"

"Hmmm?"

"You never told me how you got Lu." Matthew leaned back against the cave wall, shifted his bad knee. "Gotta be a good story."

"Last year, she staggered in from the woods. Her ribs stood out like carved wood under her fur. Matthew, she might have been two – maybe four months old. She locked eyes with me, showed all her teeth, but I knew she wasn't a threat – just scared and starving. She knew what she wanted and so did I. I ran in the house and grabbed Mom's leftover pork chops."

"I'm surprised your Dad didn't shoot her."

"He tried," I said. "He yelled she was either a wolf or a hybrid. Likely rabid. He ordered me to stay away from her. He grabbed his rifle."

Matt regarded Lu. "Her devotion to you is remarkable. So then what?"

"I screamed at Dad – first time ever. Told him she was only a baby, and if he killed her, I'd hate him forever."

Matthew studied my face, searched my eyes for a very long time. Nodded. "I believe you. Did Don?"

"I'm not sure, exactly."

"What happened?"

"A terrible rage – so bad I couldn't see – took me over," I said, careful not to mention my *mad*. Matt didn't need to know about it. "I knew I couldn't, I wouldn't allow him to hurt her. When I heard him chamber a round, I stepped in his line of fire. My face to Lupine, my back to Dad."

Matthew sucked air. "Christ, Katie. He'd probably already begun his trigger squeeze."

"Yes, I'm sure he had. Dad doesn't waste time." At a snort from Matt, I smiled.

"Yes, Katie," he said. "I know him too. That's what made it funny. Please go on."

"I defied him, Matt – for the first time in my life." I glanced at Lupine, got a wave of her silver plumed tail. "Yes, girl, I'm talking about you."

"I knew, Matthew, sure as the sun comes up in the east, Lupine wasn't rabid, just starving."

"God. What did Don do?"

"Nothing. He just sat down on the porch step, really hard. Laid the gun down beside him, put his head in his hands. Then he shook – all over." I sneaked a glance at Matt, then another at Lupine. "I'm sorry I scared him, I am. But I'm not sorry about anything else."

"I'd have never believed it, Katie. Honest. If I hadn't seen her with you. She's yours, no question. What's Don think of Lu now?"

"He's glad I have her, Matt. Real glad. He must have apologized to her at least a hundred times."

My watch said eight. My body clock said maybe twelve hours longer. Exhaustion, both mental and physical, steamrollered me. I think I dozed.

Even though Matt pitched his voice low, I jumped when he spoke. I started awake, my heart hammering like a locomotive. My mind touched the events of the fight, then caromed like a banked pool ball shot.

"Sorry, Katie. I didn't mean to scare you. Didn't realize you were sleeping."

"It's okay." I laughed, and it felt nice. "I didn't know I was sleeping either. What did you say?"

"I'm just going out on reconnaissance."

"No need." I said. "We're safe here."

"Just the same …."

There's something not quite right about his voice? Silly Katie. Everything's fine.

"All good," he said when he returned.

We sat in the dark, the dogs snoozing between us. An occasional paw twitch, a muffled whimper said they dreamed.

"Want a small fire?" Matt asked.

"Nah. It's a warm night, plus the light might draw attention."

"Agreed. You comfortable, Katie? Need meds?"

"No, but I have some pain stuff too, just so you know."

"Should we sleep in shifts?"

"Not necessary, Matt, unless it makes you feel better. The dogs are the only alarm we need."

The sleeping bag smoothed the worst of the lumps on the cave floor but when I stretched out, a monster boulder stabbed my lower back. I rolled off the bag, pulled it to one side, swept the ground with my hand. *This?* How could a tiny embedded rock produce such irritation?

I pried it free and hucked it out the cave opening. Resmoothing my bag, I lay down and sighed in contentment. Or maybe just fatigue.

Lupine gave a little groan, stretched full length beside me. All hundred eighty pounds of soft fur, solid security between me and the outside world.

I relaxed against her length, let my body go. I swear my sigh came from my bootsoles; I tried an exploratory stretch. My muscles charleyhorsed, pulled into hard knots in my feet, calves and back. I swallowed a scream, dashed the sudden wet from my face.

I'm not crying from the pain, I'm not. I can't spook Matt.

I concentrated on lying still; tried not to pant. I willed my body to relax. After an eternity, the knots loosened. I moved very carefully, every motion a slow deliberate testing.

Are they gone? Yes, it appeared they were. I kept my guard up while I bunched the top of the down bag into a comfy wad. I wiggled, found a spot on my side, moved my head until it felt right. Too excited about Dad, too scared of the cramps returning, I knew I wouldn't sleep.

The warm furry mass shifted against my back.

I opened my eyes to see dawn filling the cave opening with diffused light. Dust motes lifted, and danced. I still lay with my head on the lump of smashed down bag, in the exact same place. *I don't believe I moved all night*

– not once. An uncomfortable, bloated feeling, an urgency in my lower body brought me completely awake. *Oh God, I really need to pee.*

I made my first mistake of the day. I shifted position, thought to sit up and slip outside without disturbing Matt.

Tears squirted from my eyes. A sound like "Ahmmm" escaped before I pinched my lips together to hold in the howl. Every inch of me either ached or shrieked from bruises, strains, skinned areas. I felt like I'd been pounded with a crowbar.

"Sore?" The deep voice made my nether parts twitch and swell.

How can I hurt so bad, have to pee and still think about sex?

"Shit, Matt. I'm killed." I fished in my duffle, found the pain pills and my water. *Milk would be better but it's not available.* I swallowed one of the heavy duty ones, realized my hand trembled just from holding the canteen. I frowned at the traitorous thing; then remembered my manners. "How about you?"

"Same. But I've been awake for nearly an hour so I've worked out most of my kinks." His cheerful voice made me want to smack him.

"He's likely taken something too, Katie," suggested the mindvoice. "And it's already working."

I decided to hate him – at least for now – because he appeared and sounded comfy. My mind and my bladder fought a war inside my body. *Which one wins?*

My mind wanted – honestly, truly, wanted – to wait for the pill to work before I twitched another muscle. But the fullness in my abdomen fast approached painful. It held the power to force me up and out of the cave before I wanted to go.

My bladder won. Wait any longer and I wouldn't make it outside. *I refuse to wet my pants.* I sat up. Damaged muscles and irritated angry nerve endings screeched. I sucked air.

Behind me, Lupine rumbled, twitched and hauled to her feet. Her little whine told me she hurt too. She started a shake, thought better of it, and headed for the cave opening.

A stab of pain skewered my bladder. So sharp, so unexpected I nearly lost control. The pressure to pee ratcheted up to unbearable. *With or without my permission, it's gonna release.* Rolling to all fours, I whooshed out the breath, whimpered worse than Lu, and shoved to my feet.

"Katie? You okay?" Matt's words were threaded with concern.

I felt his eyes on me, reading my body language.

Then he said. "Oh."

"Umhmm," I mumbled, eyes fixed on the cave opening. Moving fast as my stiff body allowed, knees pressed together – *please God, don't let him notice* – I headed outside like my life depended on it. For sure my dignity did.

Stretched out on my sleeping bag, I studied my traveling companion. The angle of Matt's body favored his injured ribs. He lay propped against the cave wall, close to the opening. In the daylight, he lay relaxed, comfortable.

I don't believe it. How can he be okay with just hanging out?

We needed to be on our way. *Can't he see?* I watched him, but he never moved. His eyes were closed and his breathing came slow. *He's asleep?* Military training, yes. Dad said always sleep and eat. And relieve yourself. Every chance you get because you never know when opportunity might come again.

Okay, fine. But still, I fretted. I wanted to head out right now to find Dad. *And Matt's taking a nap?*

"Look again," snarked the blackness in my mind.

I checked him over a little more – and smiled. Matt seemed unprepared, but his hand rested near the butt of his H & K. And there, leaned against a rock, in easy reach, sat his sniper rifle.

"Matthew?" I whispered. Just in case he slept. His answer came fast, voice unfuzzed by slumber's cobwebs.

"No, Katie. Not yet."

"But …."

"Katie, we have no idea which way to go or how long he's been gone from here. I'm sorry – I want to find him too." Matt's voice deepened, discouraged. "It's better we take another day – maybe two – to mend and make sure nothing gets infected. Broken bones and open wounds can't be ignored. You were right when you said this is the best place."

The deep rumble of his voice jolted a response in my body. Thanks to kisses from Todd and Matt, my awakened desire rumbled constantly like the low idle of a Ferrari. Matthew's presence just cranked it up.

"It's going to get worse," said the logical mindvoice. "Trapped in a snug cave with him."

"How did you know? I mean that I wanted to leave now?" I tried to keep my breathing steady, make my words sound calm.

"If it's possible for a person to pace while lying on a sleeping bag, then you were." A hint of laughter laced his teasing words.

"What …? Oh." I felt the warmth creep across my face. I yanked my mind out of desire and into the conversation.

He saw – probably deliberately misunderstood. "No need to be embarrassed," he said. "I'd rather be moving too. But not today."

"Voice of good sense," whispered my alter-self. "Smart man. Pay attention."

"What we can do," Matt said, "is listen for emergency broadcasts and recheck our maps."

What we should do is make love. But he won't. So I guess I'll do what he wants.

I sat in the cave entrance, the sun warming my face. On the other side of the opening, Matthew half-leaned against a boulder. His close proximity made it hard to breathe, hard to think. He made my body heat, ache with longing.

"Dad said when the sickness struck, panicked people headed south and west."

"Which means the towns between here and Boise may have all been cannibalized for supplies?" A vee furrowed between Matt's brows.

I wanted to smooth it away, convince him otherwise. Ease his worries. *Ah hell, be honest. All you want to do is touch him – any excuse is fine.* I wrenched my mind away from beds, and skin on skin and said, "Probably, but there are small convenience stores, the Mom and Pop kind, on the side roads. We're going cross-country; we might get lucky and find some untouched."

"Where? Show me on the map, if you remember."

"I don't really know for sure. Dad kept Mom and me at the farmhouse – we never left. But I think the intersections, or close to them, should be where they'll be." I shuffled the pages we'd torn from the Thompson Guide – pointed between where we hid and Boise. "Likely here, here. And here."

"Farmhouses too," Matt said. "Those might be best. Especially if the owners died from The Great Awful."

"True," I said. "People wouldn't go inside for fear of catching it – but we don't have to worry."

"Okay, good,"Matt's eyes glowed gemstone blue in the sunlight, the corners of his eyes crinkling with that wonderful smile. "None of these take us much out of our way. It costs us nothing but a few minutes to check."

I answered his grin with a big smile of my own. *I'm finally doing it – going out there. After all these years.*

"You said first snowfall usually comes in November? Right?" Matt asked. "If Boise or Mountain Home doesn't work out, we'll still have plenty of time to get back to your house? We could winter safe there. Right?"

"Yeah, but when the snow starts, it dumps. And it stays. We don't want to be caught out somewhere between."

The expression of consternation on Matt's face made little fingers of ice grip my lungs.

"What?" I demanded. "What did you just think?"

"What if all the explosions, the earthquakes, the shifted tectonic plates ... what if it changes the weather? Oh fuck, Katie! What if?"

All the air whooshed from my body, like somebody sucker-punched me in the gut. "Oh, shit, Matthew. I never even considered that. I just don't know."

Chapter Thirty-Three

We sat, both lost in thought. I don't know how much time passed. I didn't know what Matt thought about, but I worried about the weather.

When I couldn't stand the silence any longer, I dug out the chunk of Cougar Gold cheese and a couple of apples. Matt added his box of Wheat Thins. He pulled a short blade from his leg pouch and sliced.

Two heads, two pair of eyes lifted from sleep. Two dogs grunted to their feet, stiff, sore, but willing to suffer to join us for lunch. They made us laugh, if only for a moment.

Lu growled.

Matt turned into the opening, so fast his motion blurred.

"You bastard," he said and reached for the long branch he'd dragged inside.

"What?" Then I knew. "The snakes back? Wanting their shade?"

"Affirmative, but they can't have it. Take that, you creepy thing." A stab with the stick, a vigorous sweeping across the ground. "Yeah, I didn't think you'd like it," Matt snarled. Self-satisfaction oozed from his words. "Thanks, Lu, for the alert."

"They won't bother us," I said. "Now they know we're here. Dad says they're non-confrontational." I tried to sound confident, but my eyes were busy checking every crack and crevice in the cave.

"Sure, whatever. I hope he's right. They still make my skin crawl." Matthew propped his branch in the opening, eased back into his semi-reclining posture. In the sunlight, I saw sweat beaded on his forehead, knew the movement hurt him although he never made a sound.

"They spook me too," I said. "I'm glad we've got Lu and Terror."

"You know, Katie," Matt said when his breathing returned to normal. "When I watched you fight yesterday? Even if I didn't know who your father was, I'd have guessed. You're smaller, obviously, but otherwise I thought I watched Don. You're good, real good. I didn't realize."

"Thanks," I managed. "I tagged Dad once in practice. I don't think he let me." And somehow found my throat swollen, full to bursting, as my eyes flooded. *What? Matt pays you a compliment and you go to pieces? WTF, Katie Davis?*

"Because you're afraid your father's gone forever," said the dark thing in me. "It wasn't the compliment."

I can't argue with that.

Matt didn't seem to notice my distress. "What I did wonder was why you wouldn't let me take the first guy down. I've killed before – it wouldn't have bothered me."

"Did it seem to bother me? Aside from the fact my hands shook afterward?" A cold little smile wanted to twist the corner of my mouth. I let it.

Matt's blue eyes turned cobalt, his jaw bunched. "You don't need extra baggage, Katie. Or guilt. Why did you insist?"

"You know why," I said. "Think about it. I'm an unknown, a girl. You needed to see it before you'd truly believe I can pull my weight. I'm Dad's daughter – I won't flinch from what must be done." I turned and stared hard at Matt. "You have to believe I'll hold up my end – whatever it takes. Otherwise, I'm afraid you'd risk yourself unnecessarily, get hurt or killed, trying to do for the both of us. We are a team."

His gaze roved the valley below us.

I saw through new eyes what Matt did: the rolling desert hills, the body of Lake Owyhee with its shimmering azure. The multi-hued palette of lava and basalt formations, now scarred by earthquake damage.

"How did one so young get such insight?" he mused.

I watched Matt's face, saw his eyes cloud and for a moment he went far away. Then he nodded, just once. "You're right. So tell me – how is it, at sixteen, you can kill a man and not react?"

"Oh, I threw up with the first one, Matt. Make no mistake. Dad held my head while I did."

"The first one …? Shit, Katie."

"Perhaps I should tell you what happened before you came along," I said. *About Mom.*

"Perhaps you shouldn't, Missy Katie," whispered the hard dark kernel lodged in my soul. "Perhaps you should keep your lips zipped. And also about a certain BB gun too."

Perhaps you're right, I thought. "Maybe later, Matt. Okay?"

"Sure," he said. "Whenever or never. Fine by me."

"I'll go up top," I said. "Look around."

"Okay," Matt's dark lashes lifted exposing eyes the blue of sapphires.

Good I'm leaving. Just the sound of his voice set desire churning deep inside me.

I stood and Lu lunged to her feet. She always went with me. Smart wolf – while I kept watch my very first shift, she dug a hole in the dirt in the shady spot below Three Fingers. She guarded, and kept cool, while I scanned the countryside from atop my favorite rock spire.

I hooked fingers and boots in now familiar depressions. I climbed to my spy spot, removed the binoculars lens caps, adjusted focus, and swept the area.

The close-in view yielded no movement, not even wild turkeys. I raised my glasses higher, expanded the area of surveillance. And caught an odd glint.

What? The sun reflected off something glittery. Something so familiar, so ugly the hair prickled on the back of my neck. I blinked, took another glance. My body coated in frigid sweat … even in the broiling heat of the summer sun.

My hands trembled.

I zoomed the binocs to maximum.

A woman wearing a big flashing necklace moved into a clearing below.

"No," I whispered. "Matt said she died." *It can't be.*

"It is," said my inner voice. "And she's got help."

Two tall men, both heavily armed, followed the woman. Grouped together, the resemblances of their facial features were unmistakable. Even though Za's hair shone brassy blonde; the men's a thin muddy brown, these three were family.

Pain filled my fingers where they cramped and spasmed on the binoculars. I kept my eyes fixed on Za, let go of the glasses one hand at a time, and flexed. The agony in my fingers eased, but the iron band wrapped around my ribs wound tighter. I perched on my rock never taking my gaze from the group. *Only three.* I watched them hike into the woods, disappearing in a ravine two canyons over.

My heart stuttered.

"I gotta talk to Matt." Rushing down the spire, before my weight-bearing foot was set, I released my handhold.

"Oh shit," I got out right before I went airborne.

When the black fuzz cleared, I discovered I lay flat on my back in the dirt. Looming above me, lit by the bright sunshine, were three dark shapes.

My heart hammered, tried to pound out of my chest.

When my brain straightened a bit more, I saw two canines and one human. Lupine and Terror whined and nudged me with cold noses. Matthew's language was truly awesome in its vulgarity. His hands were all over me, checking for damage.

"What the fuck?" he snarled. "Okay, nothing broken – that I can see." He carefully palpitated my ribs and I considered playing unconscious a bit longer, just for the sheer pleasure of his touch. "Goddam you, Katie," he swore. "If you don't wake up and tell me you're okay, I'm gonna kill you myself."

Time to let him know I'm fine.

Memory struck.

I sat bolt upright, bashing dog noses and clipping Matt's forehead with mine.

"Matthew." The shakes took me, and I struggled to get out my words. "M-M-Matthew! God, Matthew, I just … I can't believe …." My voice failed when fear closed my throat.

"Christ, Katie. Have you concussed yourself?" His military cursing dialed back to speech acceptable in mixed company. "Tell me where you hurt? How did you fall?" Matt's deep voice went lower still, became demanding. "Dammit, girl. Answer me. Tell me where you hurt."

"N-no. I mean, not serious, I don't think. But … Matthew … I just saw … God, I saw Za and two men."

Matt's eyes widened, then narrowed; their cobalt darkened past indigo. Something crossed his face. But before I was sure I saw it, Matt shuttered his expression. Like he'd pulled down a shade. He didn't like the news, but he wasn't shocked.

"You knew." I heard the hatchet edge of rage in my voice. "Didn't you? And you never said a word." The tops of my ears began to tingle as my *mad* roared awake. I grabbed a breath, fixed him with a hard stare. "Why the hell not? I thought we were partners – 50-50 ones? Or are you still into the big-manly-protect-the-little-woman thing?" My voice shook, I sucked air and the edges of my vision turned gray.

"You're hyperventilating," said the voice in my head. "Calm down and breathe."

I tried, I really did, but the words burst from me anyway. "People keeping stuff secret causes problems. If Dad had trusted me, given me more information, I might have kept some of the trouble from us. Or at least been nicer to Mom."

Matt's mouth fell open, then closed with a snap. "Katie, I wasn't … I didn't …"

"Oh, no. No excuses. You either tell me the truth now, or I'll leave and find Dad on my own. I won't partner with a liar." I found my Sig in my hand, pointed at Matt's forehead.

"What else haven't you told me?" I shouted. "Federal troops wouldn't be hunting and killing radiation survivors. That makes no sense." I paused for a breath, felt the darkness surge inside, seeking a target. One sat right in front of me.

"No," I said, "there's something else. Something big enough for national security to hunt and slaughter its own citizens. What is it, Matt? What?"

Two furry heads with bared teeth poked over my shoulders, their breathing harsh, their growling deep and serious. "Tell me the truth, or by God, we'll kill you. Right here, right now."

"I didn't know a lot of things for sure, Katie. Only guesses. When I heard rumors of this "collateral damage cleansing plan", I deserted. I came looking for Don, because I knew if he'd heard the same thing, he'd have no part of it.

After the federal prison building was destroyed, and two witnesses saw Za, her brothers and several prisoners escape, your father and I, and the rest of our unit, vowed to find and kill them. None of us knew – I think I'm the only one who suspected – Don had a family hidden away. I figured he'd go home and protect you, if you existed. That's the reason I was headed your way."

"You haven't told me why they're killing citizens." I kept the gun trained on his face. It didn't tremble.

"I don't know for sure."

"Tell me rumor, then. Tell me conjecture. But you better tell me something," I snapped and heard hysteria and fury mix in my words.

"The meteor," he said. "The one they put the containment tent around. I think it caused the plague. I think something alien came off the rock – the new part that got shoved above ground by the earthquake, I mean. I heard one scientist mention a *vicrobe* – the word they made up for the totally new life form – the germ or virus that came off the rock. The first people in contact with it died, but passed it on before they did. And it snowballed."

"So they kept it quiet, didn't warn anybody. They lied, and now they're killing everyone within four states to cover this up? And they could have caught and killed Dad because he was there. Even though he's immune? Like you? And me?"

Matt didn't say a thing. "I didn't lie to you. What should I have said, Katie?" His deep blue eyes searched mine. "Since I don't know anything for sure."

"Well, we're pretty damn sure now, aren't we?" I lifted half my upper lip in dersion. "Okay, you didn't lie. But you sure manipulated and stretched the hell out of the truth." My chin quivered and it made me mad. The lack of trust hurt like crazy. "You played fast and loose with me – didn't you trust me to handle things?" *I won't cry, I won't.*

"We still don't know everything," Matt said, and he ducked his head. "Like why the people in the chopper didn't kill us. They had opportunity."

"The chopper went sideways," I said. "Threw off their aim." Matt raised his head and I looked him in the eye. "You said you recognized some of them?"

"The pilot. Two of the soldiers in the open door." He shook his head. "I think Chrome jinked the helicopter to make them miss. Daro and Justin didn't even fire." Twin furrows appeared between his brows. "And then they just left. Makes no sense."

Blood suffused Matt's face, his full mouth thinned, lips pressed to a flat line. His words came low, controlled, steady. But more than a little clipped. "Let's get you back into the cave, wash off the dust and grit and see what's damaged."

Lupine rumbled, a near-growl and Terror whuffed. Both dogs watched us, heads moving from speaker to speaker, tracking the conversation, reading emotions, evaluating threat levels.

I opened my mouth, set to argue. I considered all he'd said.

Matthew's narrowed eyes, and the clench of his jaw gave me pause.

I shut my mouth. Holstered my gun.

"Good," he said. "At least you're rational. I worried you might have brain damage. While we tend your injuries, estimate when you'll be okay to travel, I'll tell you what I know. Deal?"

"Okay," I said, more to reassure the dogs than anything else because my anger seethed. "Deal."

It was funless. The second step, my ankle buckled.

Matt grabbed me, threw me over his shoulder in a fireman's carry. Grunted and muttered "…fucking solid muscle," mumbled something else followed by "weighs a ton" and finished the short walk around the Three Fingers and into the cave. He slid a big arm around my waist for support, propped me upright against the opening while he moved my sleeping bag into the good light at the cave mouth. Then he helped me lie down.

Lupine sat between me and the outside. Terror surveyed the area, laid down and rested his muzzle on two huge front paws near my head.

"From what I saw," Matthew said, stripping off my right hiking boot and sock. "This ankle is sprained – bad. Gonna be a bitch to walk on. Right?" He prodded and squeezed and I gasped and nodded.

"Okay, then, what else?"

"Matt, I want to know …." My words were rising, getting higher in pitch and volume before he laid one big hand across my mouth.

"Why don't you announce to the world where we are?" Sarcasm laced his words.

Oh shit. I closed my mouth, nodded and he took his hand away.

"First," Matt said, and I figured he had no idea how scary he appeared, "you will tell me everywhere you hurt. Then, while I fix what I can, I will tell you what I know." His sapphire eyes narrowed. "Otherwise, I tell you nothing. *Capisce?*"

I narrowed my eyes right back, considered my options. I didn't have any.

"Fine," I said and tried hard not to snarl. "My left shoulder hurts like a son of a bitch, so does my left elbow. The right ankle, you know about. I have sharp rib pain – left side again. Maybe cracked, hurts to breathe. I musta bounced off something on the way down. Any scrapes, cuts, bruises you can see as well as I can. Okay? Now talk."

"I'll wrap the ribs first," Matt said and looked me in the eye. His frozen gaze reminded me of a Great White shark when he added, "One more thing, Katie. I never lie."

I fought to hide my shudder. *Who is this other Matt? Oh, Katie, have you fucked up again?*

"No," said the dark voice in my head. "Check the dogs."

Although T-dog and Lu watched us with unwavering attention, their bodies were relaxed, unthreatening.

I gave up on my arguments and realized the after-effects of my fall were really starting to hurt. I just closed my eyes for a minute and nodded.

"Here," said Matt's normal voice. "Can you sit up while I bind your ribs?" I opened my eyes, found him holding out two pills and an open canteen.

"Sure," I said. "Thanks, Matt. Really."

"Your shirt, Katie?"

"Yes," I said. "Just give me a minute." *So glad I'm in a sports bra. I'd die from shame and lust if I had to strip all the way down.*

"But, he took care of you when you were sick?" said the mindvoice.

Different, I thought back at it. *Now both of us would be embarrassed because of everything that's gone on.*

Matt worked – wrapped my ribs and gave me back my shirt. Then he bandaged my ankle. He cleaned, disinfected and bandaged scrapes and rips; tweezered grit from abrasions.

I grunted and groaned and tried to be tough. I almost made it.

"Here's what I know about Za, Katie. I'm not proud of my part in it – I hoped she died. She should have."

"What?"

"Remember when I left you in the woods? I went to the farmhouse to clear bodies and burn them. Disinfect it before I brought you inside. Za and her brothers were in your parents' bedroom. They were very sick – all infected with The Great Awful."

"Yes. And you said she was dead."

"Well, I was certain she would be. Za taunted me, Katie. She said she knew my Dad and had a story to tell me. Good thing I stayed in the hall because after she got done talking, she took a shot at me."

"Matthew, how in hell could Za know who you were?"

"The woman may be a serial killer but she's smart. She saw the insignia on my weapons harness, and the resemblance I have to my father. 'You're Cipher's son', she said." Matthew's face went a sickly green beneath his tan. "Right before she tried to kill me, Za ripped her shirt open – she's got our insignia tattooed on her chest. So she'd never forget, she said. A constant reminder. Her husband led the terrorist group Za and her four brothers joined. Our fathers killed her husband and two of her brothers on a mission. She vowed revenge. She found my father, made him fall in love with her. He introduced her to the entire group, took her to parties and barbeques."

"But I don't see … oh … your father … Cipher … oh, God." I said, and then the door, that up until now only cracked the tiniest bit, blew wide open. Memories flooded, I could see and smell the blood like it happened minutes ago. Ten years of suppressed terror and rage tore from my throat in a single unending scream.

Matt's gentle hand covered my mouth, his other arm held me tight without regard for my arm or ribs. Somehow he knew exactly what I needed. The world revolved in lazy slow spins and my vision went black.

I woke, screaming, the small helpless child in the abandoned house with my mother shrieking in the next room.

"Hush, hush, baby," a soft voice said. "You're safe now. I've got you."

The fog cleared. *I'm sixteen, not six, hidden in a safe spot with one of the two men in the entire universe I trust.* Tears poured from my eyes, soaked my tee shirt and Matt wiped them away, held me tight, and let me cry.

Lupine and Terror crowded tight, getting close as possible. I put a hand on each big head. "It's okay, guys," I said. "Honest."

"Katie," Matt whispered. "If you can bear to tell it, it might help. But if you never do, it's also completely okay with me."

Thank you, God, for this man. The sobs subsided into hiccups, and then into shudders. Bits and pieces kept falling into place. *My left hand holding the dripping knife, the sheath in my right. Matt's dad – Cipher – carrying me to the SUV. The awful man losing his head. Dad giving me medicine to make me forget. And I almost did. Mom ... God, Mom spent time in the same facility where the military put Za, her brothers and their friends. Did the bitch get to Mom? Torment her in that awful place? Not only am I leaving here to find Dad, I am going to kill Za and her brothers. Twice. But before I do, I'm making her tell me if she hurt my mother. If she did, she will pay.*

I must have been silent too long because Matt's chin gently tapped the top of my head. "Katie? You still with me?"

"Matt, can you go on talking – just for a bit? Telling me what else happened, I mean?" I twisted, locked eyes with him, got a half-smile. "I thought – when I was in my right mind back at the house – you were hiding something. You always looked so tired. I just didn't know why."

"Sure." Matt's chest heaved once, he cleared his throat. "The bodies in the yard were easy. I piled them like cordwood to burn – prevent disease. When I started carrying the dead from the house I started to worry."

Matt must have realized he still held me very tight. The pressure of his arms eased. I appreciated it, it had hurt some, but I found I missed the feeling of security.

"So when I finished clearing the house, I went back to your folk's bedroom. Found it empty. No bodies, no clothing, no packs, no guns. Then I got scared." Matt's voice caught, then he went on. "It looked like they'd actually dragged each other out. I wanted them to die, at the same time hoping you'd live." Matt gave me a half-smile. "Lyn worked with your Dad, then with me. She knew your father was immune, she told me so. That's why I hoped you'd make it."

"And I did, thanks to you."

"So, I put Lupine at the front door and Terror at the back. I knew no one could get to us without them sounding the alarm. When I got you set in your room, I gave you enough sedative to keep you in bed when I couldn't be with you. Then I went hunting bodies. Praying I'd find them."

"But you never did."

"No, but I hoped they'd just gone farther away than I'd yet searched – and died. So I didn't tell you – I didn't have an answer. And I didn't want you to worry, just get well."

"And you kept hunting them – the whole time we were there?"

"Yes."

"So what else did Za tell you?"

"She bragged about being so smart, how she suckered my Dad. How he told her all the squad secrets, how he thought she'd marry him. I don't know what happened then, but Za told me The Great Awful wouldn't kill her, and when she got better she and her brothers would find and kill me too." Matt's hands fisted against me, then relaxed. "She said she'd get the rest of us. Said she hadn't found Snake or his family again but she would."

"She found us once, Matthew. Oh yes, she sure did. Well, at least some of her people did. She set our kidnapping up – I remember hearing one of them say." I felt the deep breath Matt took, but he didn't speak, he just waited. "But she hadn't found Mom and me the second time. Now I know why Dad hid us like he did. If The Great Awful hadn't happened, if the power grid hadn't gone down, she'd still be locked up in the asylum, and my mother would still be alive."

"I am so sorry, Katie. I wish to God I'd killed her." Matt's voice trembled with anger.

"And now she's after us." I clapped a hand over my mouth, then took it away slow. "Matt, I sort of remember screaming. Oh God, did I?"

"Well, yes – but, no. I mean, I muffled you. But now we need to think – how far away did you see them? What direction were they going?"

"Can you get me on my feet?" I blinked, felt like an owl. *No ... more like a wounded bird.* Battered and bruised, inside and out.

"Sure can," Matt said and rose in one smooth motion bringing me with him.

Holy shit, the strength in those legs, and he's got one injured knee. I staggered to the opening and pointed across the two ridge peaks. "They went in that canyon. See the tallest tree?" At Matt's nod, I went on. "They were walking south, so maybe – well, hell, Matthew, I have no idea how long ago."

"I do, Katie. I'll go up top and spy. If I don't come down for a while don't worry. See if you can sleep." Matt turned those deep blue eyes on me and I felt the pull of attraction, strong as the very first time.

I shoved it away. *I talked awful to him. Shame, Katie.* "Matthew?"

"Yeah?"

"I'm so sorry – what I said to you, earlier, I mean. You didn't deserve it."

"Yes, Katie. I think I did. I should have told you. But we're good, right?"

I nodded. "We're good."

Matt's smile made my knees turn to water. "I'll wait until dark if I need to," he said. "They might build a campfire. If they're high enough on a ridge, I'll spot them for sure."

Chapter Thirty-Four

"Gotta be all clear," Matt said, stepping inside the cave. "I've watched for three hours, and seen nothing." He moved easy, hardly favoring his knee. He took a look at my face and lifted a brow. "What's up?" he asked, then sat on his sleeping bag, cocked his head, and waited.

"There's another reason I have to find my father," I said. "Something I haven't told you – well, lots, really – but this is about my mother. Dad put me in charge. I failed. And he has to know." Tears sprang unbidden, surprising me. A huge racking sob, followed by another. And another.

Lupine whined; T-dog butted me with his massive head.

"God, I don't mean to be a baby," I got out. "I never cry. Only when I get mad." My nose filled, swelled, the back of my throat went hot. My chest awash, my tee shirt wet and stuck to me.

He moved fast, even with broken ribs, his hard muscled arm around my shoulders. "I wondered – about your Mom, I mean."

"I figured. I appreciated your not asking. It's awful, what I let happen." I sniffed, coughed and continued. "We lived out here because we hid. I didn't know we were in danger. Or why."

"Za," Matt said.

"Yes." I leaned into his comfort, snatched a deep breath. "After Dad got us here, Mom went into a hospital for a while. But her mind – well – when she came home she was different. She changed, became so very fragile. Matthew, she just wasn't ever right again."

"None of this is your fault. You couldn't fix her mental problems."

"She tried, she really did. But we got low on Mom's meds and Dad needed to go scrounge. He never came back. She ran out; she couldn't hold it together. Remember the trail along the cliff, the one about a mile out from here?"

"Yes?"

"Dad set me to watch her, keep her safe. She got away. It's where she jumped."

"Jesus H. Christ, Katie. This isn't your fault."

"Then whose would it be?" I heard my voice, high, thin, shrill. My chest compressed, my lungs shrank to tiny bits of ice. I couldn't breathe.

"You're losing it, girl," said the voice in my head. "You're out of control."

I took a deep breath, coughed a sob. "I couldn't even go get her – to bury her. A plague victim – crazy as a shithouse rat – fished her body out of the water. I heard him down below talking to her. He thought Mom was his wife." Hysteria rose inside, my heart hammered, blood pounded in my temples. "For God's sake. Matthew, he propped her up beside the creek and fixed her dead body a cup of tea. The damn dogs wouldn't mind me. They wouldn't let me go down there. They shoved and pushed me back to the house."

"Smart of them."

"Lupine left four big fucking toothmarks in my ass. And I forgave her. Can you believe that?"

"I beg your pardon …?" Matt's startlement evident – his body went rigid, the steel band of his arm tightened around me.

I must have whimpered because he muttered something and instantly eased his pressure. My body ached for it to come back.

"Yes. I leaped for my mother, tried to catch her. I almost did. But Lu chomped into the seat of my jeans, dug in. Matt, she hauled me back from the edge. I'd have gone over without Lu."

"Christ, Katie!" A hard ridged stomach vibrated with suppressed laughter. "I saw the four punctures when I took care of you – when I wasn't looking, of course." He tried to muffle his snort, but it got away. "I couldn't for the life of me figure how you got them." His entire body shook, then a laugh escaped.

My heart lurched, then soared because Matt didn't blame me for Mom's death. *Will Dad?* I couldn't guess. *Do I blame me? Perhaps now – not so much.*

Matthew's snicker startled me into a giggle of my own. A pitiful little thing, true, but still, a laugh.

"I'll go," he said. "Do a visual, have a listen."

I dozed, woke when he stepped into the cave. "Katie," he said. "I finally heard something. A broadcast about a sanctuary city forming in Boise. They're forming a community;they want people to help."

"Sounds like the one Mom and Dad and I heard when this all first started."

Excitement fizzed through me. Then I thought of Za

"Matt, it's exactly the trick someone like Za would use. A phony broadcast to pull in new victims."

His dark brows pulled together. "Do you think so, Katie? I know there were some good people at Mountain Home when I left."

"Do you still want to try Boise, Matt? Can we trust this information?"

"We can't trust anyone but ourselves," he said. "But we can watch from a distance. We'll know. If it's true, perhaps we can make a life there. At least for now. And if Don's not there, perhaps someone will have news about him."

"One broadcast said the plague spread through the rest of the country." I shivered, goosebumps crawled my arms. "Do you think everything's gone?"

"I'm more afraid of it than I want to admit."

"How long until we travel?"

"We need five good days, Katie. Before we can move fast and fight."

I saw his eyes fix on the cave wall, but I knew he didn't see it. Matthew's mind assessed, evaluated, and reached a decision.

"With Za out there," he said. "We better leave day after tomorrow."

I slept fitfully, my injuries, aches and pains lobbied for a bed, instead of my sleeping bag on the cave floor. And every movement from Matt's side of the cave woke me, found me tense, alert. *God, why won't he come over here and hold me?* Every rustle he made, every breath he took, whether awake or slowed in sleep, made my pulse go thready and beat too fast.

Daylight proved worse. Glancing at him, watching his beautiful mouth, dreaming of it on mine. Wondering what lay behind the emotions I saw play across his face. Trying to control my panting when he moved his hard capable hands. *I want them on me, no matter how bruised and sore I am.* I wanted to be held to quench my desire, yes. But also to lose myself in his arms so I didn't keep remembering the terrible day when Mom and I were prisoners of those awful people. *If I sleep, will I dream it? Relive it all again?* And Za hiked the neighboring hills, hunting Matt. And so, because we were partners, she also hunted me.

"If she ever sees you," whispered the dark little voice, "she'll know you're Don's kid. She'll never stop hunting."

Not until I'm dead, dead, dead.

I shuddered. I tried to distract myself with Lu and Terror, rubbing heads and scratching bellies. I took my comb and worked through their thick fur until they grumbled, got up, and laid down outside arm's reach. Still, in the cave, with nothing to do, all I could do was worry or think of Matt. *He's the better choice.*

So I let my imagination roam. Thought of what I wished he'd do to me. With me. *Whatever.*

"Sell your soul for a distraction? Maybe a deck of cards?" snarked my darkness. "Or a chessboard?"

I almost believe I would. My face heated, my heart beat hard between my legs. Desire flooded, pounded through every vein in my body. *How in God's name will I manage to live with this?*

The evening of our last day, we sat on opposite sides of the cave on our sleeping bags. No fire, no lights, no problems except my single one.

I've waited long enough. I'm so tired of wanting, aching, desiring to be held. I can't think straight because of the throbbing in my body. I'll endanger us – I can't see anything but him. I'm the reason we got so hurt, I didn't watch our surroundings. I know – well, not quite – exactly what I want. But I'm very sure Matt can fix it. I don't want to die without ....

"Matthew?" My voice startled me, low and throaty.

"Oh shit, Katie. Whatever the question, with that tone of voice, the answer's no."

"Matthew, we need to talk about things."

"No. Not if you mean what I think you do."

"I'm tired of being crazy from this. It's dangerous for both of us. I want to be held. Damn it, Matthew, I don't want to die a virgin."

"Katie, I can't." Matt got off his sleeping bag, moved back into the cave, leaned against the wall. "You're too young for me. You're Don's daughter."

"Things have changed. It doesn't matter any more."

"No. God, Katie, stop this. I can't. I won't."

"We're both immune to The Great Awful." I stretched supplicating hands. "Don't you see? Things are different now."

"Not in a community with civilized people." Matt's arms were crossed over his chest. Protecting himself? From me?

"I'm nearly seventeen. It should be good enough."

"When's your birthday?"

"Next week." A thought struck. "Matt, if the birth certificate we found is mine, I'm almost eighteen. What about that?"

I heard Matt's sigh, so deep, so loud, all the way from the back of the cave. "Fifty three weeks," he said. "Then we'll discuss it again. Believe me, I'm suffering too. But Katie, I can't ... I won't. Your Dad is my godfather, my superior officer, my instructor." I heard the horror in his voice, near hysteria in his next words. "We're practically brother and sister. God, no."

"Then we need to find him and get his consent. Maybe he's in Boise. But Matthew, I'm berserk from this. I can't think, I can't sleep. I know you're not either."

"Shit, you're killing me here." Matt shifted, leaned on one leg, the other foot behind him propped against the rock cave side.

"You have company in your misery." *More than you can imagine.* Fear filled my throat with dry cotton balls. *I gotta ask.* "Do you like me a little, Matt?"

"Katie, I like you a lot. Maybe more than that. But this is wrong. Wrong, wrong, wrong."

"If we find my father, or if we find someone who's a judge or minister?"

"Ummm …."

Then it all came out in a warm hot rush. I froze in horror as I heard myself say, "If we had someone to make it legal, would you marry me?" The tops of my ears, lit like bonfires. "I mean, oh shit, Matthew, I take it back." My insides went cold, shriveled. "I apologize."

"Good job," snickered the little black part inside.

"That got away – I didn't mean to blurt it out." My lungs, heaved, my fists clenched. "Matthew, I'm sorry."

The chuckle, low and sensual, hit me right in my lower abdomen. A flame lit, licked down the insides of my legs. I bit my lip, hoping the pain would stop my panting. No such luck.

Matt took a deep breath and I braced for the worst thing a sixteen-year old girl could imagine. Rejection.

Rejection's so much worse than death. I dropped my head in my hands so I didn't have to see his face. *I will not cry, I will not cry, no matter what he says.*

"Katie Davis, if we get through, when you are either old enough, or legal enough, would you marry me?"

What? Then the words, the meaning came right.

"Oh, God, Matthew. Yes. Oh yes." I launched across the cave, knocked him to the floor, piled on and got an unromantic response.

"Oooof."

I stoppered him with a kiss. Big hard arms came around me and he kissed me back. One very sweet chaste kiss. I hung on. The kiss changed, deepened.

Matt's tongue danced across my lips. His hands wrapped my back, slid down to cup my behind.

I explored his lips, the shape of his teeth with my tongue. My body strained and writhed against him, and I pressed my hips against his.

He groaned, gave up to our kiss, and plundered my mouth with the quiet desperation of a starving man.

I think after all our near brushes with death, this coming together affirmed for both of us we still lived. *Yes, oh God, yes. Give me what I need.*

Then Matt shook his head, gasped and grabbed my shoulders in huge hands. Broken ribs and all, he lifted me bodily up and away from him.

No, no, no. My body screamed. *Empty, needy, alone.*

"Now," he said. "You have to leave me be, Katie. I'm having a hard enough time as it is. Here's the deal. I will only marry you, honorably and with pride, if you let me get through this the best I can. I will not touch you until then."

"Goddammit, Matt," I snarled. I didn't recognize my voice, low and hoarse.

Lu raised her head from the cave floor. A little rumble echoed through the cave's quiet.

"Deal, Katie? Peace now, marriage later?"

"Shit, hell, damn." Then I nodded. A good man, a great warrior, and honorable too. Much to my dismay. But it also brought a smile. *Dad's gonna be happy to consent.*

"Okay, Matt, but there's just one last thing," I said just to hear him groan.

"Katie … please."

I opened my pack, pulled out Mom's favorite Thunder Egg and cradled it between my palms so it caught the moonlight.

"What is that?" Matt leaned over me; gazed down into the intricate colors and shapes of the crystals. "My God, it's gorgeous. Like something from a fantasy painting."

"This was my Mom's favorite, I found it for her. Here." I laid the egg in Matt's big hands, wrapped mine around his. "Now we'll make our promise on my mother's keepsake."

"I swear," Matthew said. "I solemnly do swear, Katie Davis, to marry you – soon as possible."

"I also swear to be your wife," I said. My eyes went hot and blurry. I looked up at Matthew, found his eyes suspiciously shiny too.

The Thunder Egg emitted a sound, the bong of a huge brass bell reverberated in the cave, echoed around us. Matthew's hands, beneath mine gripped the geode. His pupils dilated until they nearly eclipsed his sapphire irises. I stared at him; stared at the dun colored hull clasped in our joined hands. Stared at the sparkling crystals clustered inside it. Each shimmered and flickered, facets lit from within by an unearthly power. The multi-colored lights streamed between our fingers and played across the interior of the cave.

"This can't be happening. This is a goddamn rock, Katie. What the hell?"

"It is just a rock. I don't understand this ... I mean. God, what's it doing?" I took my fingers away and saw Matt's hands trembling as he held the Thunder Egg.

"Take this thing, Katie. Please."

I did. Gently placed it on the wrapping lying on the cave floor and watched it go quiescent. I backed away, slow and careful, like it was a live grenade.

"It's just ...," I said. "In the past – I thought I saw some odd things but wrote them off to my imagination."

Matt studied my face, studied me. I realized I was wringing my hands. I quit; then scrubbed my sweaty palms on my pant legs. Tucked loose damp tendrils of my hair behind my ears.

"It's just a mudball. See?" I picked it up again, turned it over, exposing the rough brown exterior. Handed it back to Matt.

He didn't want it, acted like it might ignite. I knew I wouldn't ever look at the thing the same way again. He turned the rock back, crystal side up, cradled it in both hands. Its crystalline quartz and agate interior sparkled in vivid shades of dark plum to pale lavender.

"Wasn't this thing blue before?" Matt's brows pulled together above his nose, two vertical furrows told me he worried.

"Yes," I nodded. "What do you see? In the crystals, I mean."

"I thought a sailing ship. A mast, the ship hull. And the waves." Matt's voice trailed away. "But then when I look again, I see something more – like a space ship from a movie. There!" He pointed. "Did you see that?" Worried sapphire eyes caught mine. "Please say you did."

"I saw something move in there, Matthew." My words came out in a whisper. "If that's what you're asking."

"Take this damn thing back for good." Matt's deep voice cracked on the last word. Where his hands brushed mine, they were cold and clammy. "It gives me the creeps." He took another look at me, a hard one this time. "Okay," he said. "You've had a good joke at my expense. Fine. You set this damn thing up to make that chime noise, and now you've got it rigged with a battery or something to make it ... yeah, do that." He pointed one big finger at the Thunder Egg's interior.

Now, that I held it, the interior glowed all blues – from cobalt it surged to sapphire, then morphed to palest azure like the sky.

"I didn't … it's not a joke. It never acted … well, I mean not before …." I floundered to a stop.

"What do you mean?"

"After the volcano, after everything went all to hell."

Whatever Matthew saw both reassured him and scared him. He nodded slowly, made a gesture toward the back of the cave. "Let's go sit for a minute. I want you to tell me about these things, and don't leave anything out. If you didn't prank me, then something just happened here. Something for which there is no rational explanation. I don't like that. Katie, I really don't."

"God, Matt!" I thought it was going to come out in a shout, but I whispered the words. "I don't understand either. It scares me, bad as anything ever did. I'm not ashamed to admit it." My legs wanted to fold, my knees wobbled like jello.

Lupine shoved under my hand, gave me her broad back for support and I made the half-dozen steps into the heart of the cave and sank onto the dirt. Lu wagged her tail, and so did Terror.

"Look at them, Matt. They're fine with whatever is going on with this stupid geode. It must be okay, no matter how weird it's acting. Don't you think?"

Matt dropped beside me. "Okay," he said, his face white beneath his tan. "Where did you get this one? And then tell me where these things come from." He stared at the geode, lying in beautiful crystal splendor by the mouth of the cave. "And tell me what you thought you imagined. I have never in my life believed in …," his throat worked, and he couldn't get the words out.

"You don't believe in the woo-woo stuff?" I couldn't help myself. I grinned, but then I shook my head. "Me either, and yet, what we just saw?"

"So, we agree on both counts. We don't believe in magic, or superpowers," Matt said and I nodded agreement. "But we just heard and saw something we can't explain."

I nodded again. "I never asked Dad because Mom was crazy enough. I didn't want him to worry about me too. Now I wish I had."

"There has to be an explanation," he said, and the rough blade of his voice held desperation. "Something logical." He shook himself like a dog shedding water, fixed his deep blue eyes on mine and said, "Explain. Please."

"Mom says … said." The heart strike of pain stopped my voice; the cave's interior shimmered silver.

A big hand enveloped mine, pressed gently. Gave strength and understanding without words.

I swallowed my sob, cleared my throat and started again. "Geologists believe the eggs formed in gas pockets – in the rhyolite lava flows of the Endocene Age – like round porous molds. Inside the pockets, water carried minerals, silica, agate or chalcedony. Piled up layers. When the Cascade Mountains pushed up, the eggs rolled all over. There are Thunder Egg areas and meteor strikes all over the world."

"I wonder," Matt murmured. "I wonder if all those other areas had volcanic activity, and a *vicrobe* outbreak. Quakes, explosions. Wouldn't that be a big coincidence?"

"I don't believe in them," I said. "Coincidences, that is. Cut off as we are, how can we find out?"

"Questions for later," he said. "Why name them Thunder Eggs?"

"Native American lore holds that Gods dwelled on Mount Jefferson and Mount Hood. Their legends tell of thunderstorms which were caused by the gods fighting. Throwing rock eggs – Thunder Spirits – at one another."

"Okay, that worked for them. But we know there is a rational explanation. Hopefully we can find it. You said you imagined something before?"

"I thought the damn things changed colors, sometimes, when I went close to them," I said. "And sometimes I thought I heard humming. Once I had chills, and fever. Goosebumps and kinda like heart palpitations. But I never was sure it was them." I searched Matt's eyes, found them so blue they were almost black. He nodded.

"Go on."

"Well, I only noticed this stuff after the volcano erupted and the *vicrobes* attacked. I was short on sleep, half crazy or maybe more worrying about Mom. Figured I didn't see what I thought, and forgot it. Until now."

It hit me then. Maybe I'd been suspicious all along but there's always truth threaded in any legend. Maybe the Indians saw something all right. And believed they saw warring Gods.

"Matthew? The darkness. You have it and you hear and see the crystals. I do too. Maybe Dad did and he just hid it from me?" I tried to breathe, but it came ragged and hard, like I'd been running for an hour. I snarled at the thing living inside me. "You. My dark side?"

Matt flinched, but kept silent.

"You talk. The last time I asked you, you brushed me aside. Have these Thunder Eggs got something to do with The Great Awful? With the meteor rising? With the volcano, and all the other trouble?"

"Yes," it said.

I don't know what showed on my face, but Matt shifted, just away from me a little.

"Tell me," I snapped.

"Nothing I know – right now – can help. Don't ask," it said.

"Ask your darkness, Matt. Does it know anything about this?"

His eyes glazed, and he went away for a moment. When he shook his head slightly, and refocused on me, he nodded.

"So did you get an answer?"

"I did," he said. "But it was yes … and no."

"So was mine," I said. "So somehow this all fits together. But we aren't allowed to know?"

"Evidently not," he said. "At least not now."

"Well, that's less than no help at all," I felt tears of fury burning. Realized I'd fisted my hands.

Matthew spoke, his quiet words calming. "What do we do, Katie? Way I see it, at least that rock thinks our relationship is good. So how about you wrap it up, put it away, and we go on like we planned." A flash of the old Nitro emerged. Matt gave me the smile that made me weak in the knees. "Let's pretend it never happened. Maybe we'll never hear from it again?"

"Sounds perfect. We have a plan," I said and felt love and desire flood my heart and my body.

I rewrapped the geode and put it in the bottom of my pack. Then Matt walked me to my side of the cave and pointed at my bedroll.

I grinned, nodded and lay down. *If you can't trust a man who swears on a zillion year old rock, who can you trust?*

Lupine stretched beside me. I wanted Matthew.

"Dammit!" I snarled, but under my breath. I heard a low chuckle from the darkness and the rustle of Matt's sleeping bag as he settled in. Heard Terror grunt as he took his post beside Matthew, lying between him and the opening.

Waves of longing, heat and desire washed through my body. *Yeah, sure, just try to sleep after all that.* To my surprise, the dawn woke me.

"Morning, Katie." The deep voice held a smile, a lilt, a promise.

"Morning, Matt." I searched his deep blue eyes, found warmth, found my future. *I want to tell you I love you, hear you tell me the same. But this is so strange. We're a couple, but yet we're not. And something totally weird has been added to the stew.*

My heart pounded in my chest, and then echoed further south. But I could bear it now because we'd settled things. *Matthew and I are together, planning a future. For his honor and mine, I can wait.*

"You're a liar," whispered the evil voice in my head. "You can't be trusted. You want him too bad."

You shut up, and leave me alone, I thought back at the dark. *I'm good with this.*

"Here's your breakfast." The granola bar appeared tiny in Matt's huge hand.

"Where are the furry ones?"

"Hunting, maybe. I didn't feed them this morning. Ready to travel?"

"I've been ready for days." I heard him rumble something and raised a forestalling hand. "Yes, Matthew. I admit, you were right about the healing and preparing."

"Well, I'll be damned," he said and laughed. "You're starting this relationship out right. You just might convince me to marry you."

"You're stuck, buster." A pulse beat in the vee of my jeans. *Just at his laugh? God, I'm pitiful.* "I'll sic my Dad on you, Matthew Scavelli, if you try to weasel out of it."

"Not fair, Katie." His low voice caressed me like a length of silk and I bit my lip to stop a whimper. "You're a bad girl."

"Not yet, but I have hopes." I gave him a long seductive glance from beneath my lashes and heard his breath hitch in his throat. Then I chuckled at his muttered swearing.

"Fair's fair, Matt. You tease me, I tease back."

"Damn, I can see you're gonna be a handful."

"You're a piece of work yourself." I sneaked another peek, just to admire his big hard body. "But don't you dare change."

I loaded my duffle, rolled my sleeping bag and tied it to my pack. Spun fast, and caught him looking at my ass.

He ducked his head, shook it in dismay, came and kissed me.

I tried to make it into something more, wrapped my arms around his neck, pressed my body close, chest to knees. Every part of me vibrated with need.

He knew. He disengaged. Gently, he held me at arm's length. "We've got to have a few rules."

"Matthew …."

"No, we have to agree. I want to touch you, kiss you, and a whole lot more, but we have to have a boundary. We can't ever, out there, be distracted. Yes?"

I nodded. Slow, reluctant, but in total agreement.

"Za's out there hunting me," Matt said.

"Yeah, and me too," I nodded. *I want Matthew bad. To get him, we've got to make Boise, or Mountain Home – and find Dad.* "Agreed," I said. "You're a hard man, Matthew Scavelli. But you're right."

I filled the dog's backpacks, checked my guns, my ammunition. Beside me, Matt loaded his gear, settled his things. Shrugging into his weapons harness, he turned to me.

"Let's go up on the bluff top for a final reconnaissance before we head out."

"Okay. Where are those damn …? Oh, there you guys are."

Two huge furry canines loped into the cave, red smears coated their muzzles. I swear they grinned at me, then T-dog belched.

"Appears we can save the chow for later, just like you thought." I picked up Lu's pack, placed it on her back, and strapped it solid. She didn't complain, just wagged her tail, high and excited.

Across the cave, Matt did the same for Terror. His stub tail rotated madly.

They are ready too. We all want to be outside, moving, in the fresh air. How did I ever think we could winter in here? Except … if we had to, we'd survive.

Settling my harness comfortably on my torso, I assessed my situation. Leaving my home with Matt never entered my wildest dreams. How could it? I didn't know he existed.

This isn't even close to my life plan, but it's the right thing for me. I know it is. And we have the common goal of finding Dad. I know he's still alive – I have that feeling. The nay-saying mindvoice can go straight to hell. I haven't had any bad premonitions lately. But Za's hunting us.

I followed the broad back of my husband-to-be up the almost-trail between rocks to the top of the plateau and into a small spot between two boulders. My breath came in quick little pants while I coveted his body, his grace of movement. I watched him fish the emergency radio from T-dog's pack, set it up and crank.

I used the binocs and scanned the ground below. I didn't see a thing.

We crouched, waited and listened.

Matt lifted a brow in question.

"Yes," I said. "Let's go. We can check every time we stop?"

"Fair enough," he said and the flash of white teeth and long deep dimples in his tan face made my body tingle.

"We'd better leave, Matt," I whispered, and heard the breathy wanting in my voice.

He heard it too because he mumbled, "Shit. God help me. I'm in so much trouble here."

"Don't blame me," I said and laughed, low and quiet. "It's your fault. I go into heat every time I look at you."

Matt emitted a choked sound, and I laughed again. Then I gave Lupine a signal and she slid into her usual place beside me.

"You leading?" I asked.

"Yes," Matt turned, gave me a basilisk stare. "Although, perhaps you should. I don't know if I trust having you behind me."

"Coward?" I quirked one brow.

"I think you know better," he said, and chuckled. The low, sensual one which always hit me right in the gut.

"Damn you, Matthew," I said.

"Fair's fair, Katie. You taught me well."

He turned and worked his silent way back between the rocks. Just like Dad, Matt always took a route below the skyline.

"No give-aways," I said.

"Right, Katie. Ready?"

"I sure am."

At a gesture from Matt, Terror took forward scout. My husband-to-be moved out next. I followed him, and Lu roved as rear guard.

I refuse to be distracted by those wide shoulders, narrow waist, high tight ass. I will pay attention to my business. I will. I will.

"You better," said the dark kernel in my soul. "If you want to live to enjoy them."

Excellent advice, I told alter-me. Then I settled my guns in their holsters, ready for anything. I adjusted my pace, dropping into a ground-covering stride to match those of the big warrior ahead of me.

The Great Awful has come and done its worst. Yes, Za and her brothers are out there but I won't let her ruin today, or my future. I'm still here, and I have a wonderful man and the whole of my life stretching before me.

I lifted my head, inhaled the breeze, smelled the heat and scents of the high plains desert. My wide smile of anticipation nearly split my face. Surrounded by three loyal friends, being loved and loving in return, I hurried, with joy and hope, to meet my future.

Kaylan has been an avid reader and writer all her life, especially action thrillers. Then a co-worker loaned her Dune. Hooked by the first three pages, science fiction remains her favorite genre.

Her lifelong goal – writing a novel – became a reality with the science fiction release of Survivors' Dreams (2011). A fast-paced action thriller set in a far futuristic galaxy, filled with danger, tension, romance and conflict. Kra'aken survivors battle for their lives on a hostile planet ruled by a vicious alien species, bound by vows to obliterate the Kra'aken race.

Growing up in the rough and exotic terrain of Eastern Oregon, Kaylan loved the geodes – called Thunder Eggs – found in the regions rock formations. The elusive and strange beauty of the crystal formations inside the geodes, inspired her Young Adult dystopian fiction – The Great Awful (2014).

Kaylan lives in the Pacific Northwest with her extraordinary husband and quirky Pixiebob cats. Surrounded by all the glory of the area – from breathtaking mountains, rain forests, lakes and ocean – the beauty of nature inspires her muse to create strange, fascinating and dangerous environments.

Kaylan enjoys reading, writing, weight lifting, needlework, and collecting vintage jewelry. The acquisition of an exceptional Juliana parure, provided the inspiration for her Urban Fantasy, Bijoux Majik, which will be released during the summer of 2014.

To learn more about Kaylan Doyle visit her website at
KaylanDoyle.com

Interact with Kaylan on her Facebook Fanpage at
Author Kaylan Doyle

CPSIA information can be obtained
at www.ICGtesting.com
Printed in the USA
FFOW02n1650170218
45060041-45451FF